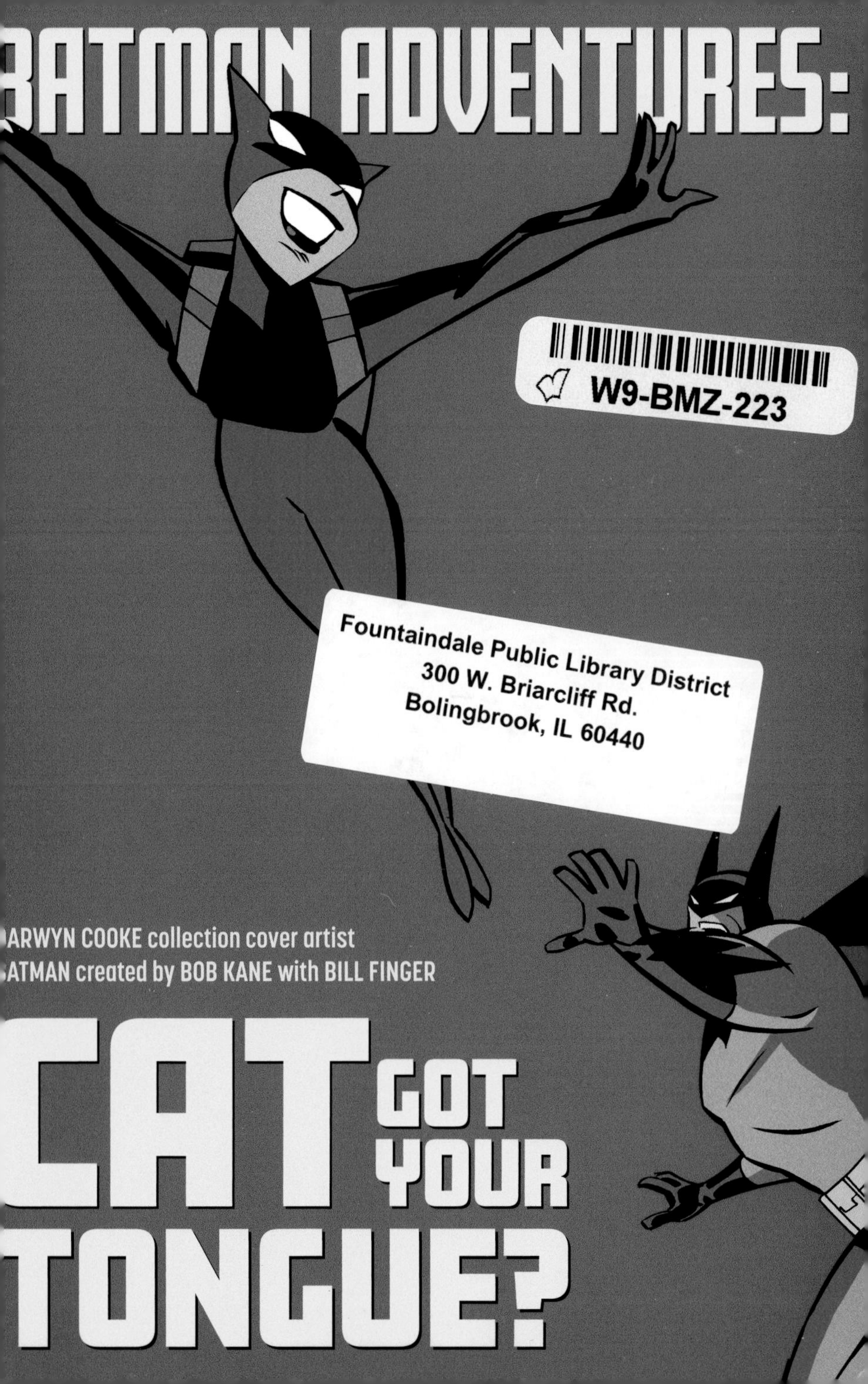
BATMAN ADVENTURES:
ARWYN COOKE collection cover artist
ATMAN created by BOB KANE with BILL FINGER
CAT GOT YOUR TONGUE?

K.C. CARLSON
DARREN VINCENZO
KEVIN DOOLEY
JOAN HILTY
Editors - Original Series

FRANK BERRIOS
CHUCK KIM
HARVEY RICHARDS
Assistant Editors - Original Series

REZA LOKMAN
Editor - Collected Edition

STEVE COOK
Design Director - Books

AMIE BROCKWAY-METCALF
Publication Design

CHRISTY SAWYER
Publication Production

MARIE JAVINS
Editor-in-Chief, DC Comics

DANIEL CHERRY III
Senior VP - General Manager

JIM LEE
Publisher & Chief Creative Officer

JOEN CHOE
VP - Global Brand & Creative Services

DON FALLETTI
VP - Manufacturing Operations & Workflow Management

LAWRENCE GANEM
VP - Talent Services

ALISON GILL
Senior VP - Manufacturing & Operations

NICK J. NAPOLITANO
VP - Manufacturing Administration & Design

NANCY SPEARS
VP - Revenue

BATMAN ADVENTURES: CAT GOT YOUR TONGUE?

DC Comics, 2900 West Alameda Ave., Burbank, CA 91505
Printed by LSC Communications, Crawfordsville, IN, USA. 7/23/21. First Printing.
ISBN: 978-1-77951-080-8

Library of Congress Cataloging-in-Publication Data is available.

PEFC Certified

This product is from
sustainably managed
forests and controlled
sources

PEFC/29-31-337   www.pefc.org

CONTENTS

hapter 1:
atch as Cat Can 5

hapter 2:
laws 15

hapter 3:
he Truth About Cats and Gods! 39

hapter 4:
issed Connections 63

hapter 5:
econd Timers 87

hapter 6:
ne Step Ahead 111

hapter 7:
ninvited Guest 131

review:
lash Facts 136

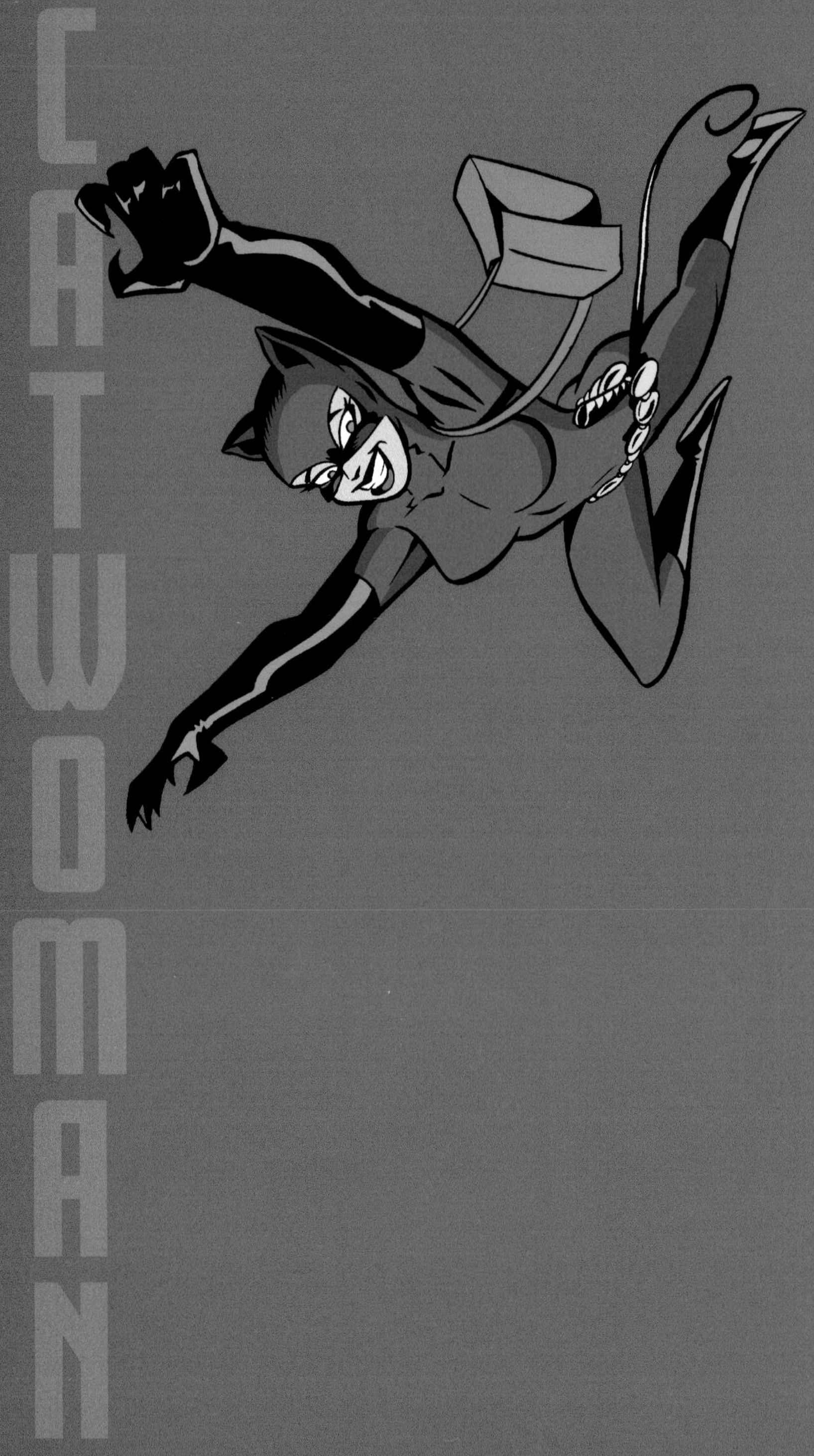
CATWOMAN

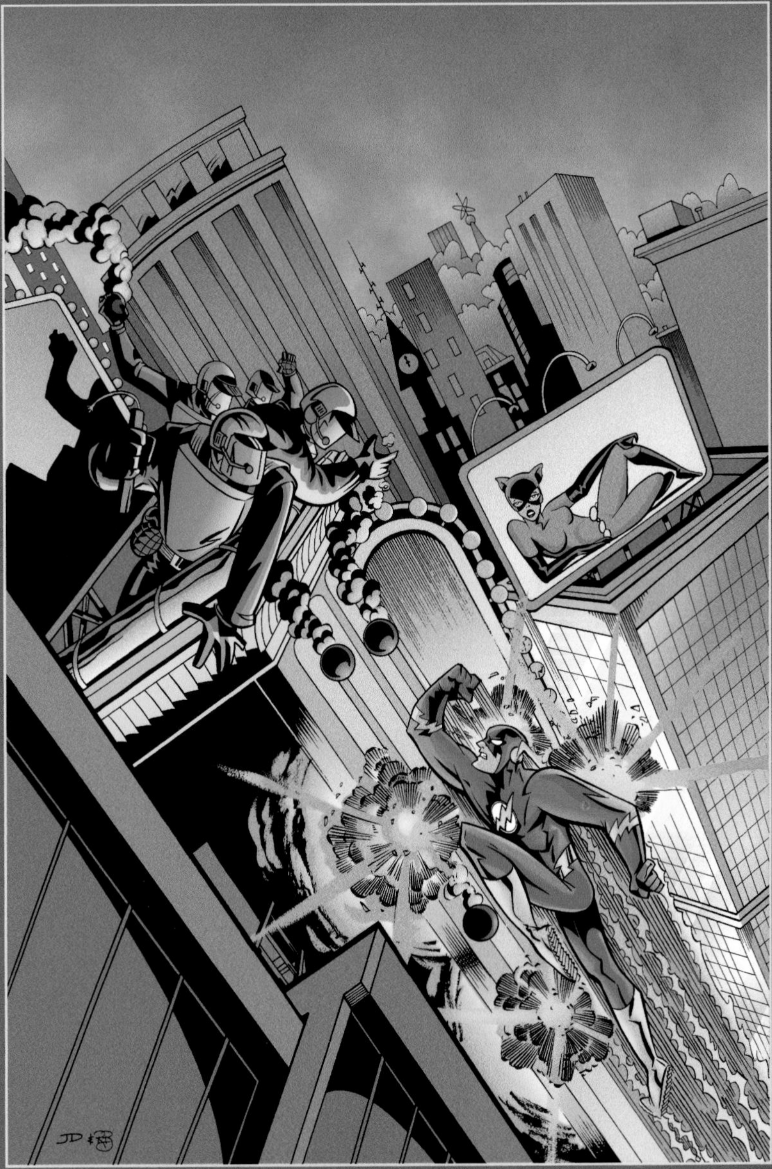

CHAPTER 1: CATCH AS CAT CAN

CATWOMAN

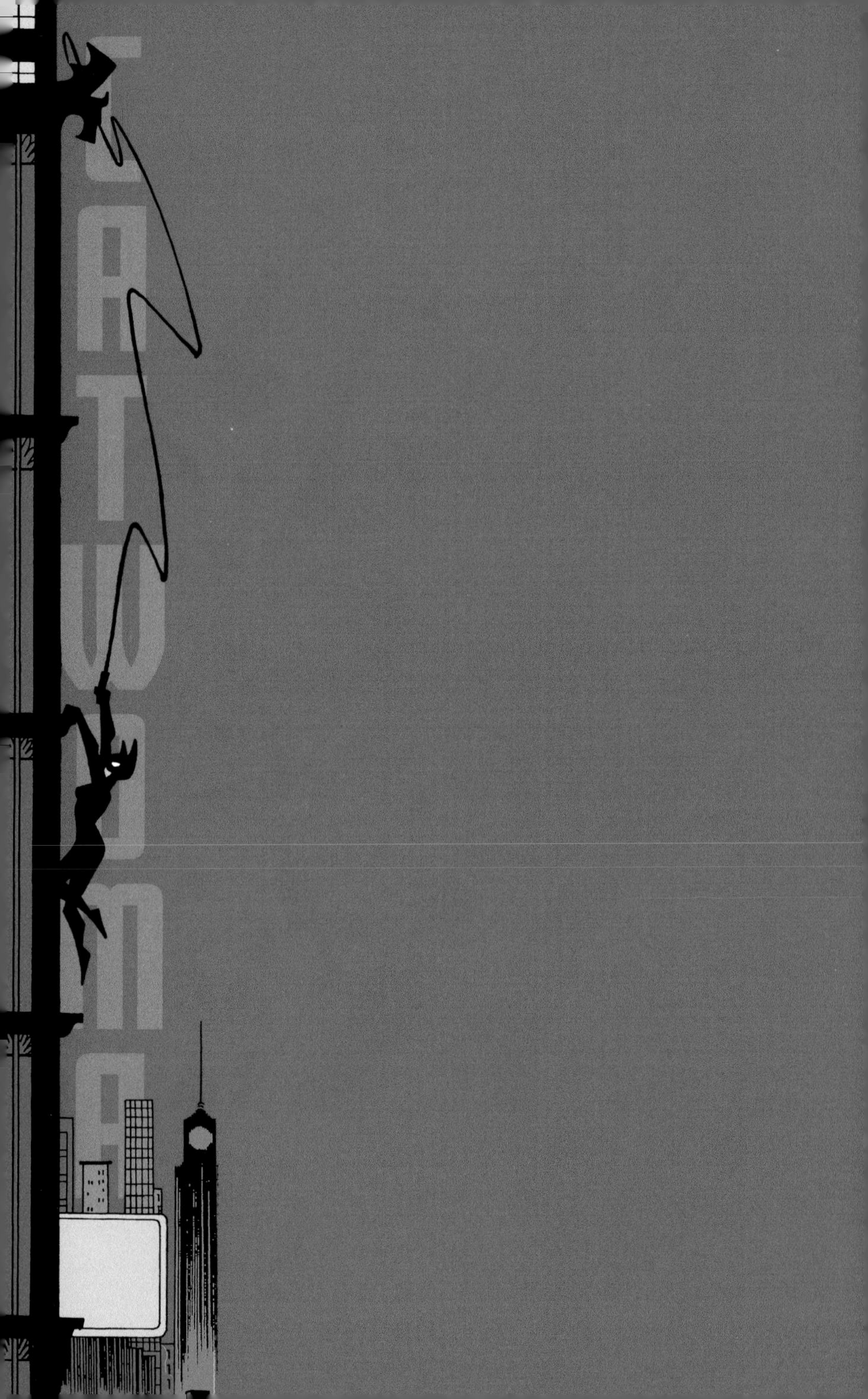

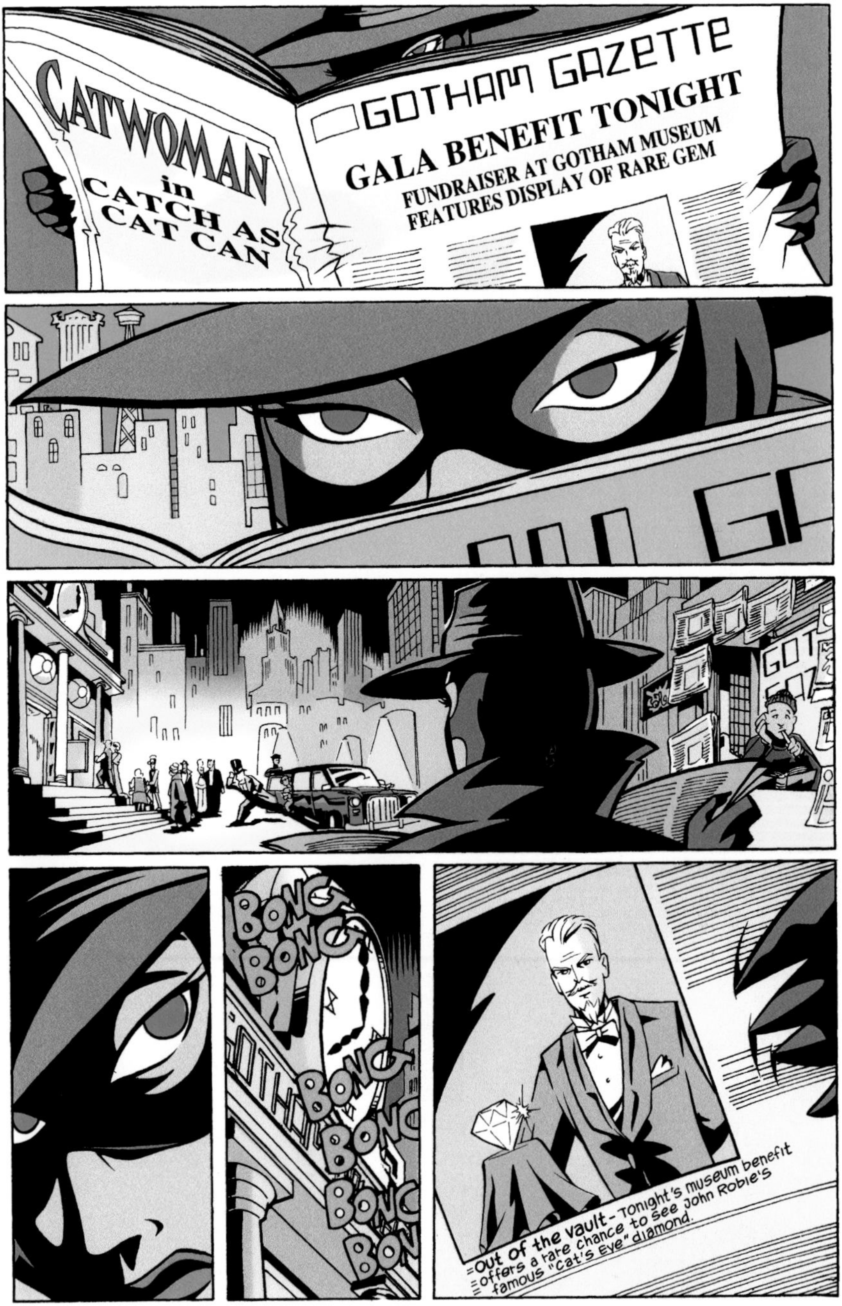
CATWOMAN in CATCH AS CAT CAN
GOTHAM GAZETTE
GALA BENEFIT TONIGHT
FUNDRAISER AT GOTHAM MUSEUM FEATURES DISPLAY OF RARE GEM
BONG BONG
BONG BONG BONG BON
Out of the vault - Tonight's museum benefit offers a rare chance to see John Robie's famous "Cat's Eye" diamond.

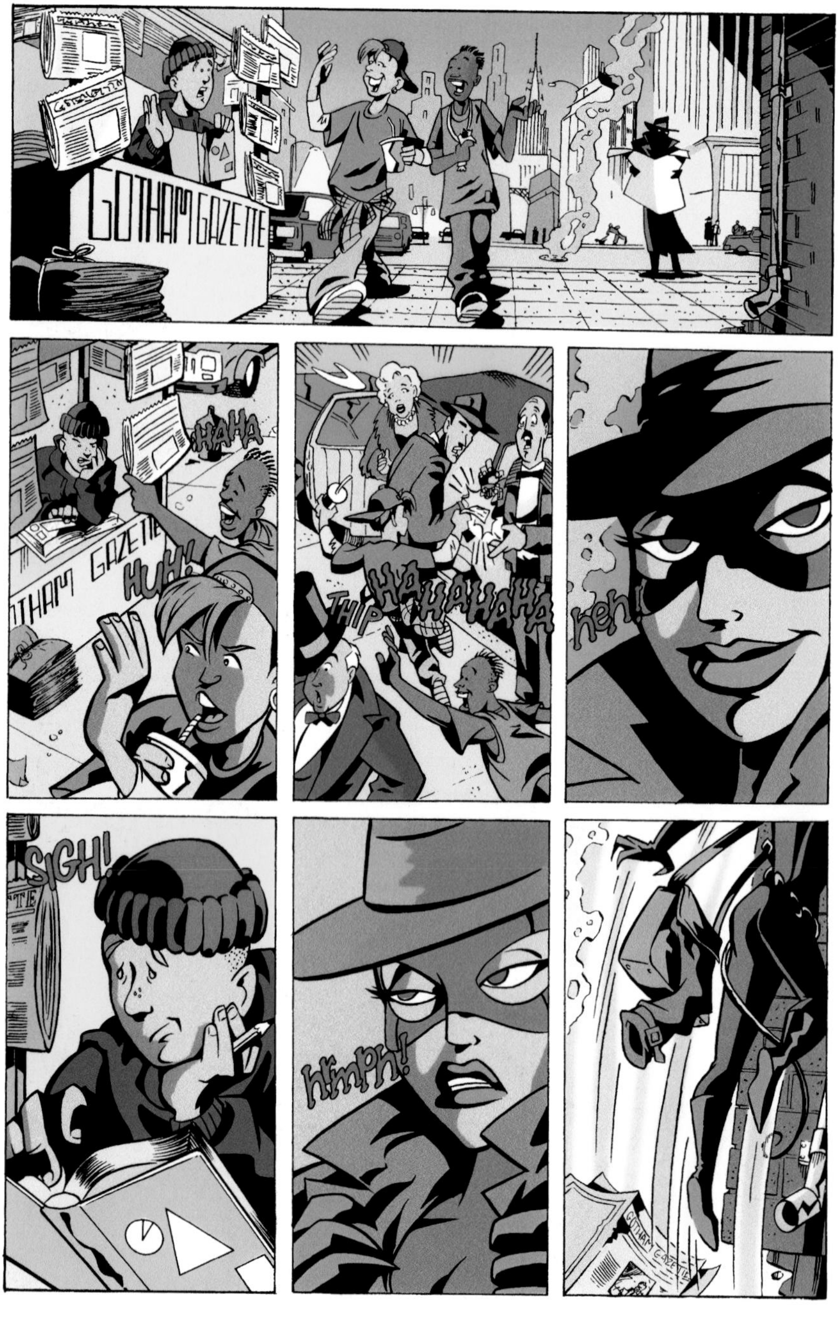
GOTHAM GAZETTE
HAHA
HUH!
THIP
HAHAHAHAHA
heh!
SIGH!
hmph!
GOTHAM GAZETTE

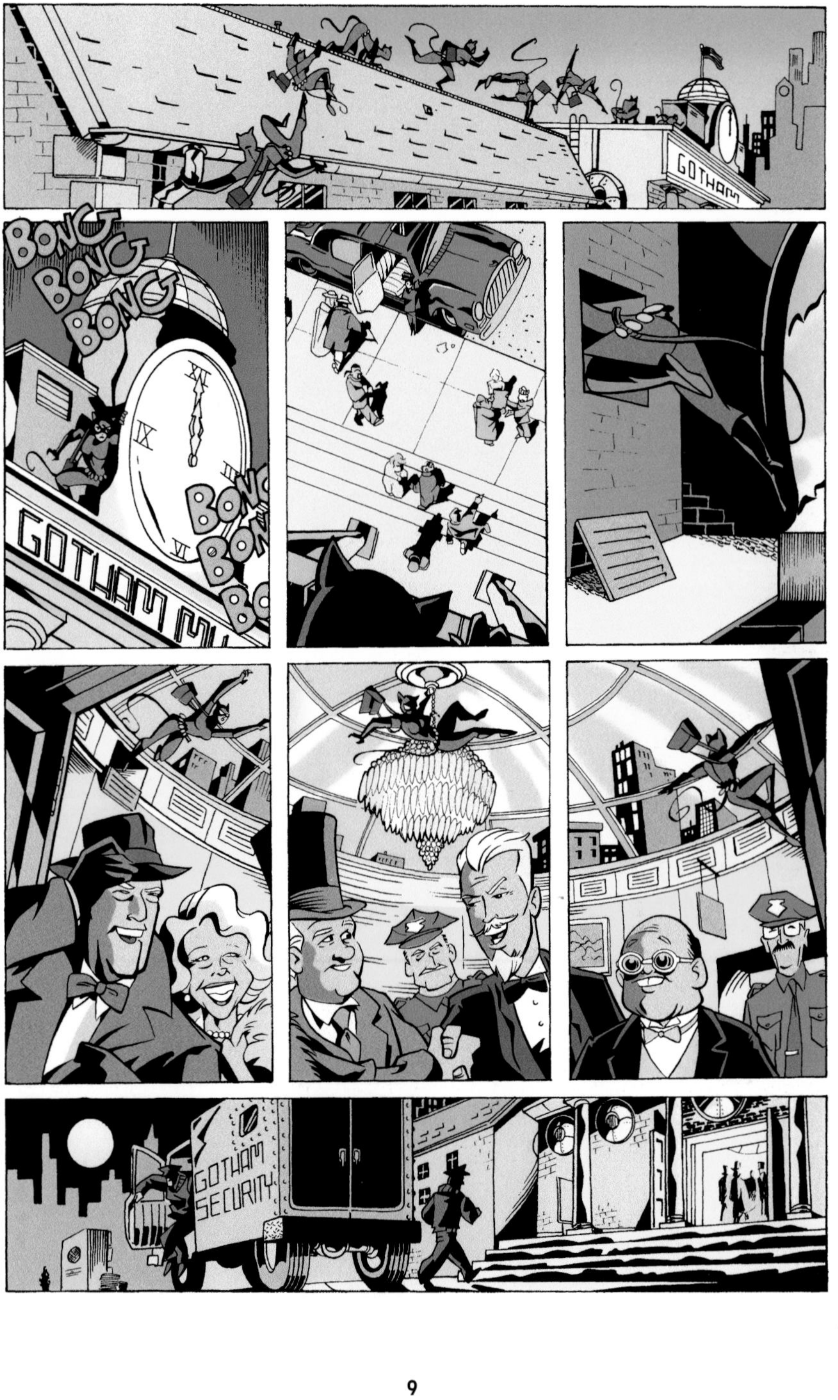
GOTHAM
BONG
BONG
BONG
GOTHAM
GOTHAM
SECURITY

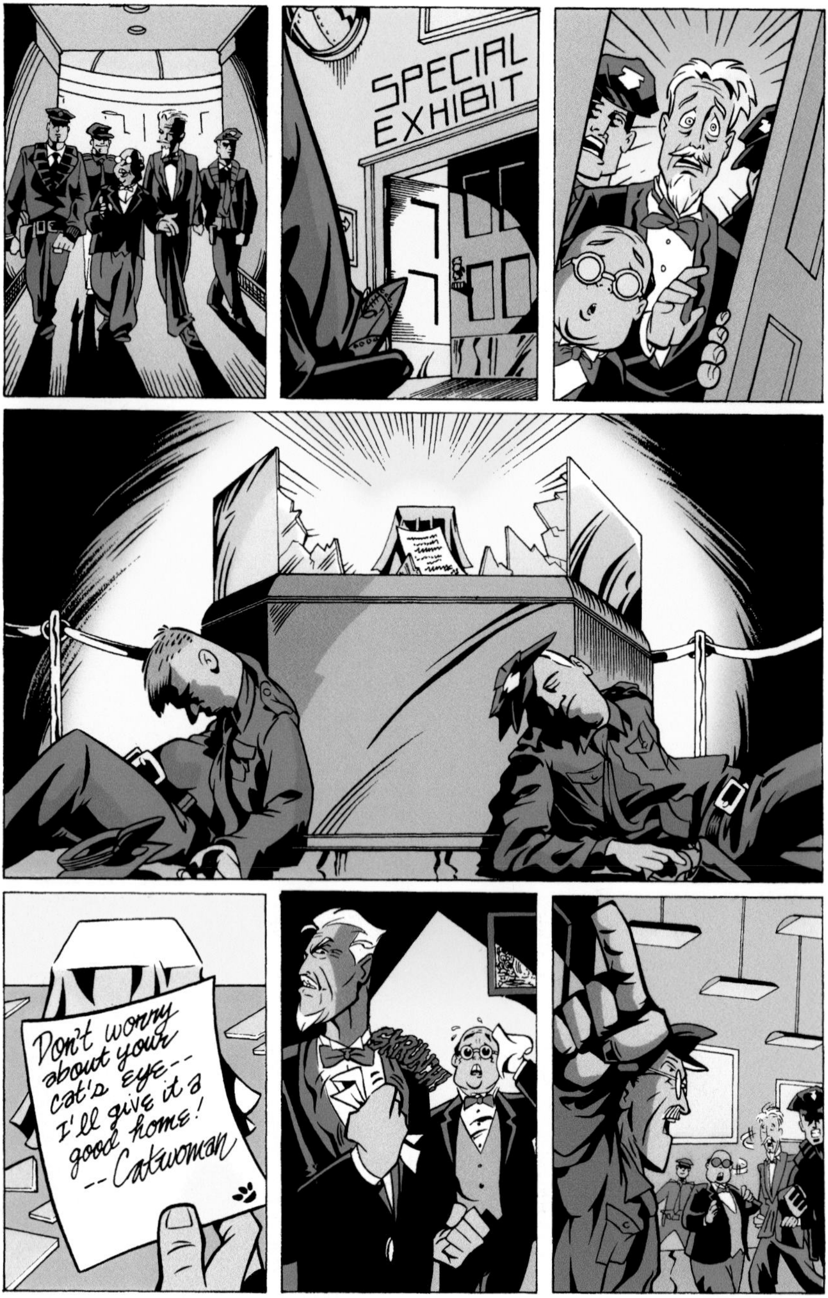
SPECIAL EXHIBIT
Don't worry about your cat's eye-- I'll give it a good home! --Catwoman
SKRUNCH

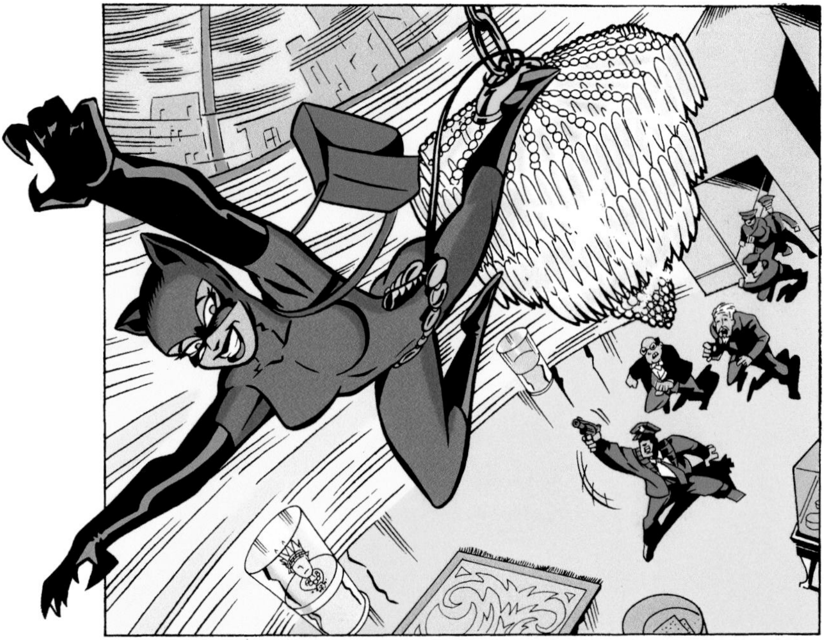

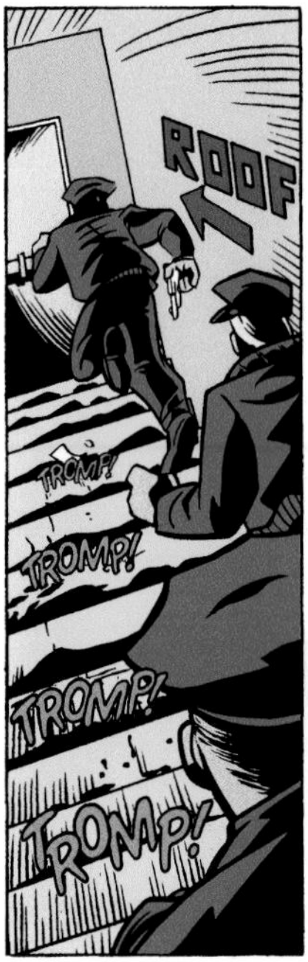

ROOF
TROMP!
TROMP!
TROMP!
TROMP!

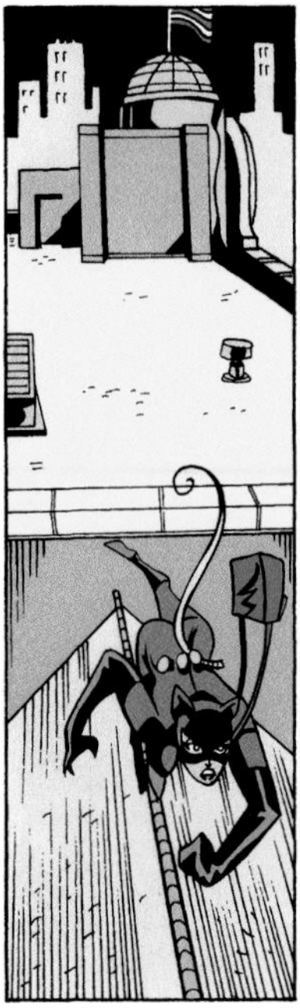

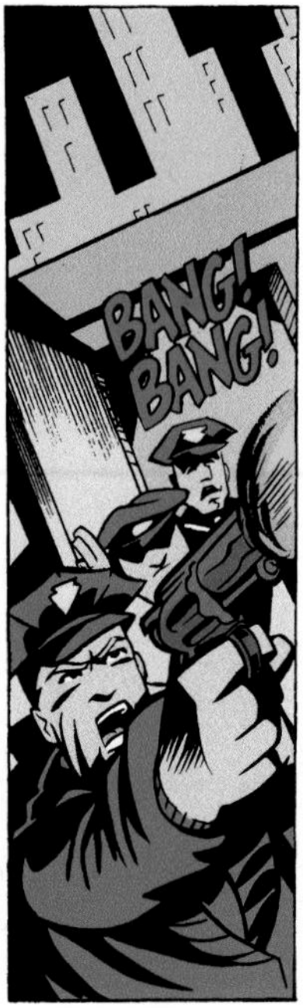

BANG!
BANG!

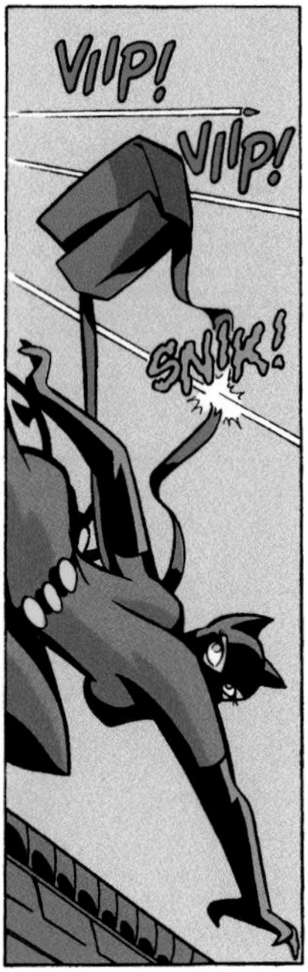

VIIP!
VIIP!
SNIK!

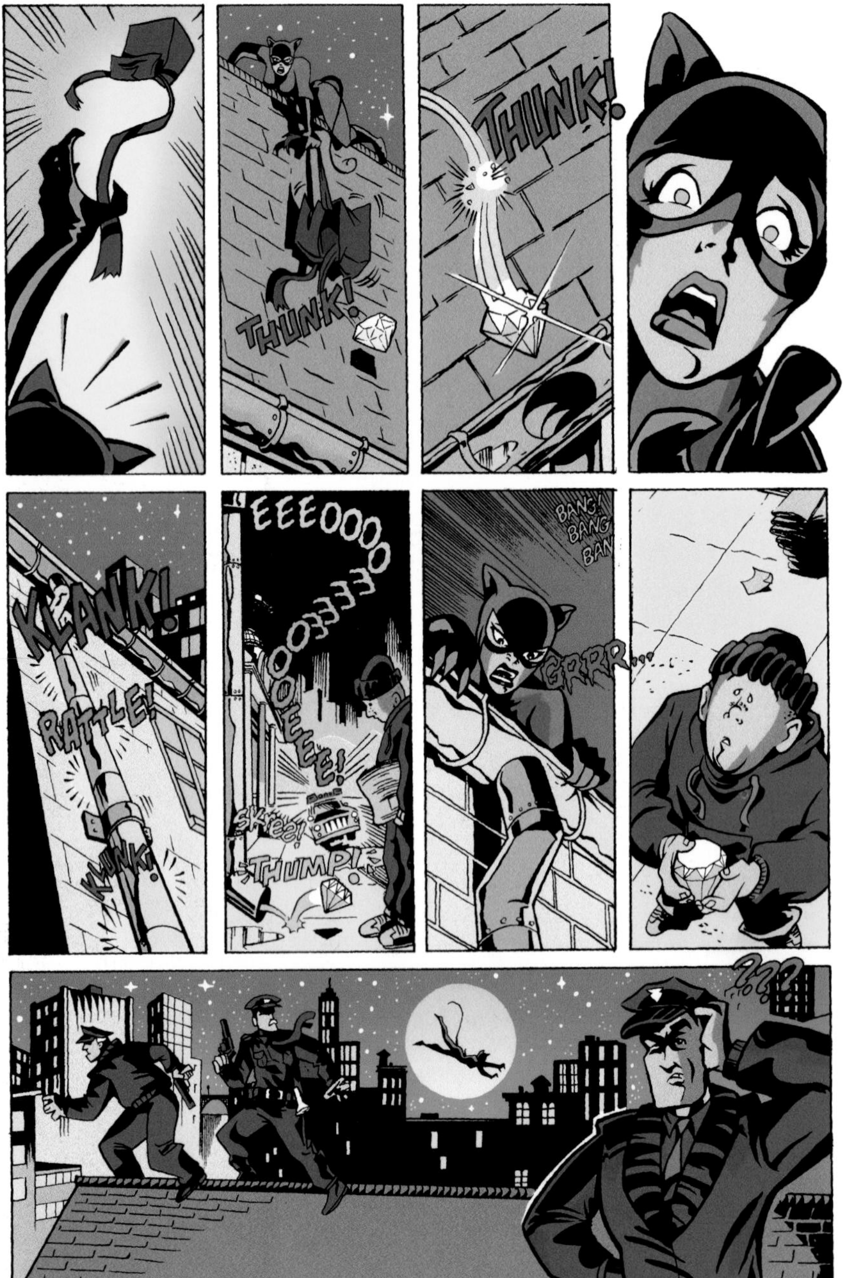
THUNK!
THUNK!
THUNK!
KLANK!
RATTLE!
KLUNK!
EEEOOOOEEEEOOOOEEEE!
SKREE!
THUMP!
BANG!
BANG!
BANG!
GRRR...
???

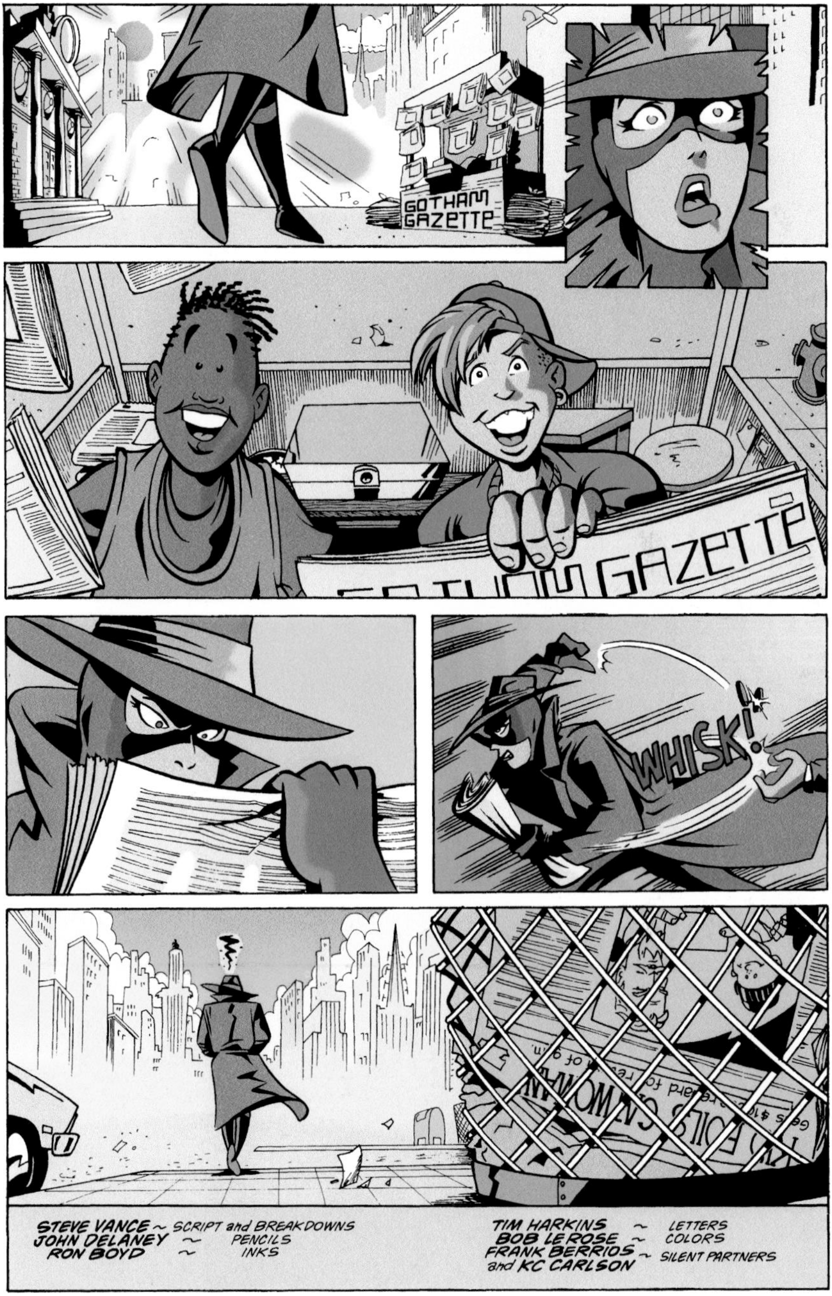
GOTHAM GAZETTE
GAZETTE
WHISK!

STEVE VANCE ~ SCRIPT and BREAKDOWNS
JOHN DELANEY ~ PENCILS
RON BOYD ~ INKS
TIM HARKINS ~ LETTERS
BOB LE ROSE ~ COLORS
FRANK BERRIOS and KC CARLSON ~ SILENT PARTNERS

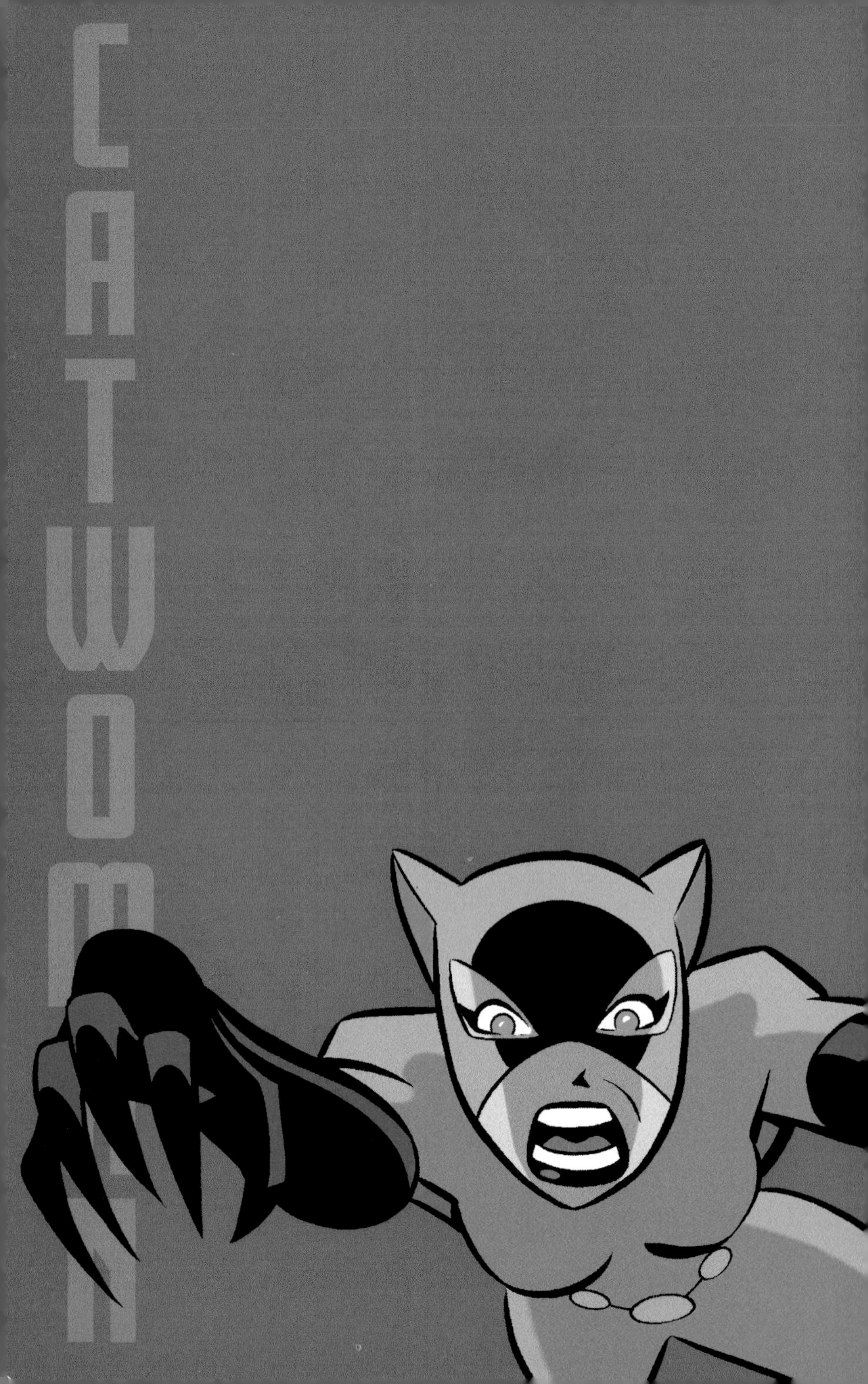
CATWOMAN

CHAPTER 2: CLAWS

CATWOMAN

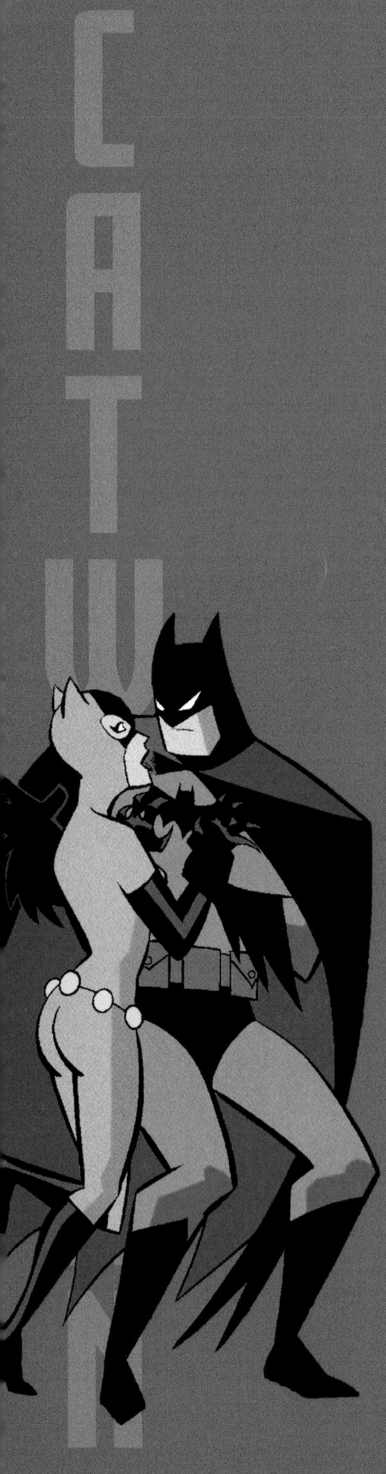
CATW

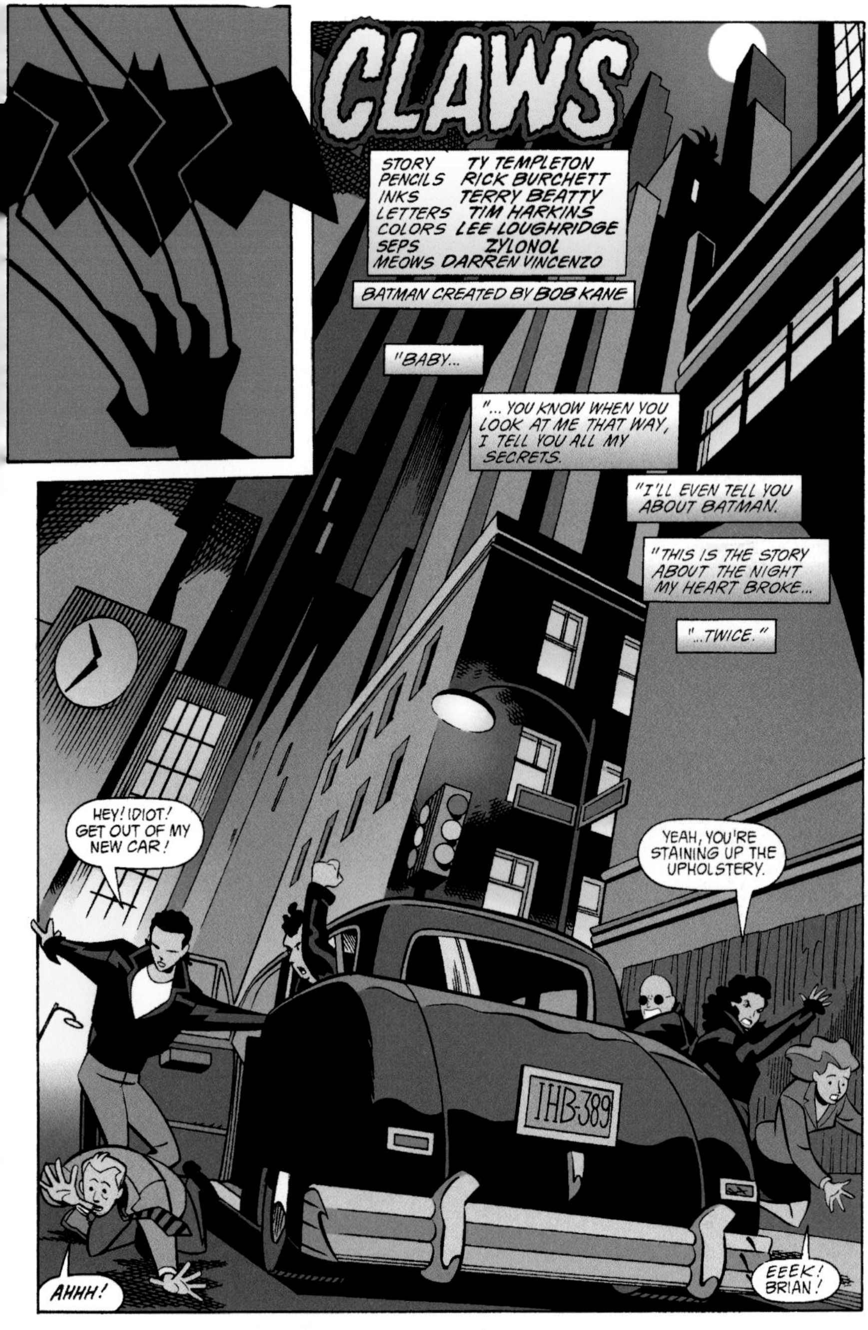
CLAWS
STORY TY TEMPLETON
PENCILS RICK BURCHETT
INKS TERRY BEATTY
LETTERS TIM HARKINS
COLORS LEE LOUGHRIDGE
SEPS ZYLONOL
MEOWS DARREN VINCENZO
BATMAN CREATED BY BOB KANE
"BABY...
"... YOU KNOW WHEN YOU LOOK AT ME THAT WAY, I TELL YOU ALL MY SECRETS.
"I'LL EVEN TELL YOU ABOUT BATMAN.
"THIS IS THE STORY ABOUT THE NIGHT MY HEART BROKE...
"...TWICE."
HEY! IDIOT! GET OUT OF MY NEW CAR!
YEAH, YOU'RE STAINING UP THE UPHOLSTERY.
IHB-389
AHHH!
EEEK! BRIAN!

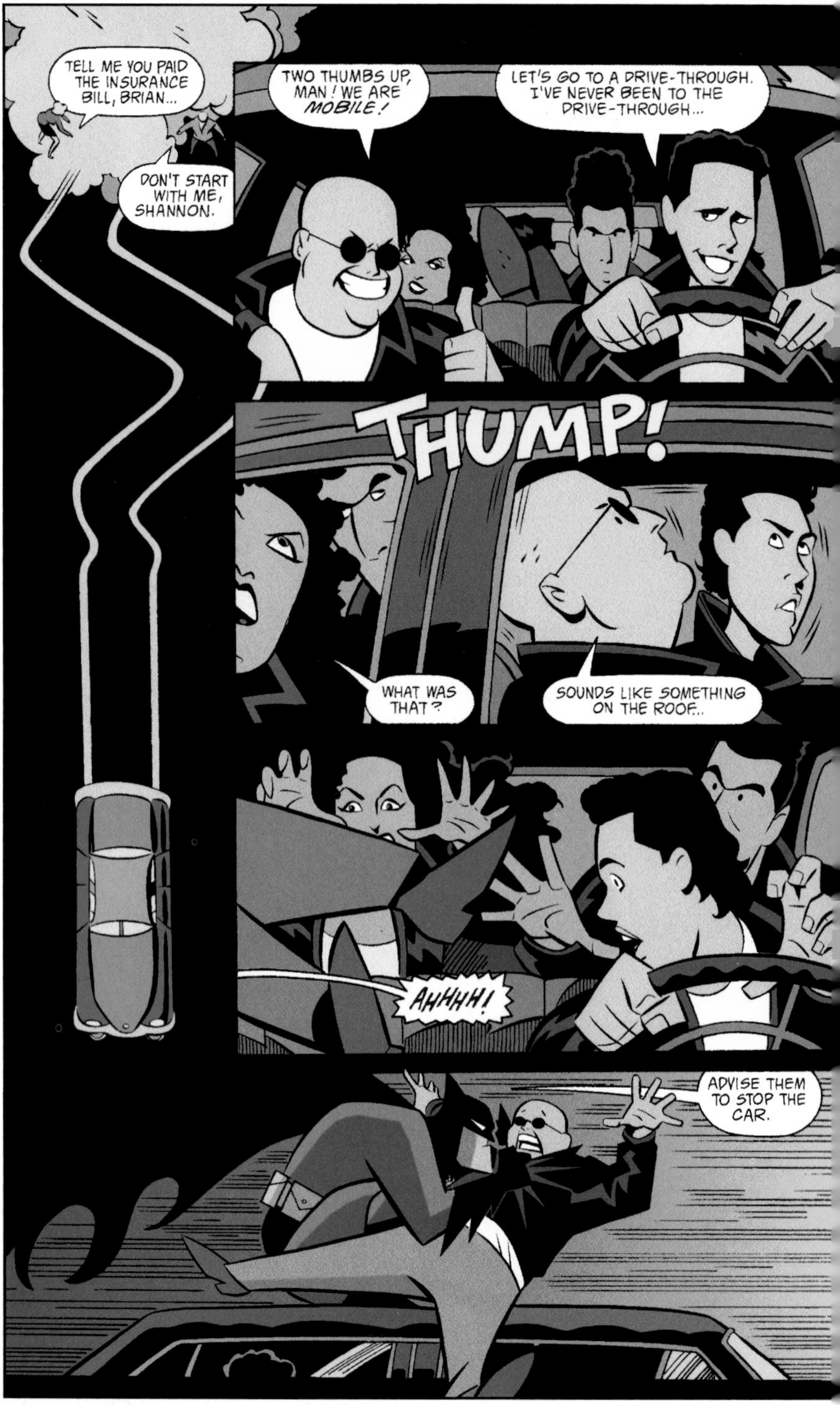
TELL ME YOU PAID THE INSURANCE BILL, BRIAN...
DON'T START WITH ME, SHANNON.
TWO THUMBS UP, MAN! WE ARE MOBILE!
LET'S GO TO A DRIVE-THROUGH. I'VE NEVER BEEN TO THE DRIVE-THROUGH...
THUMP!
WHAT WAS THAT?
SOUNDS LIKE SOMETHING ON THE ROOF..
AHHHH!
ADVISE THEM TO STOP THE CAR.

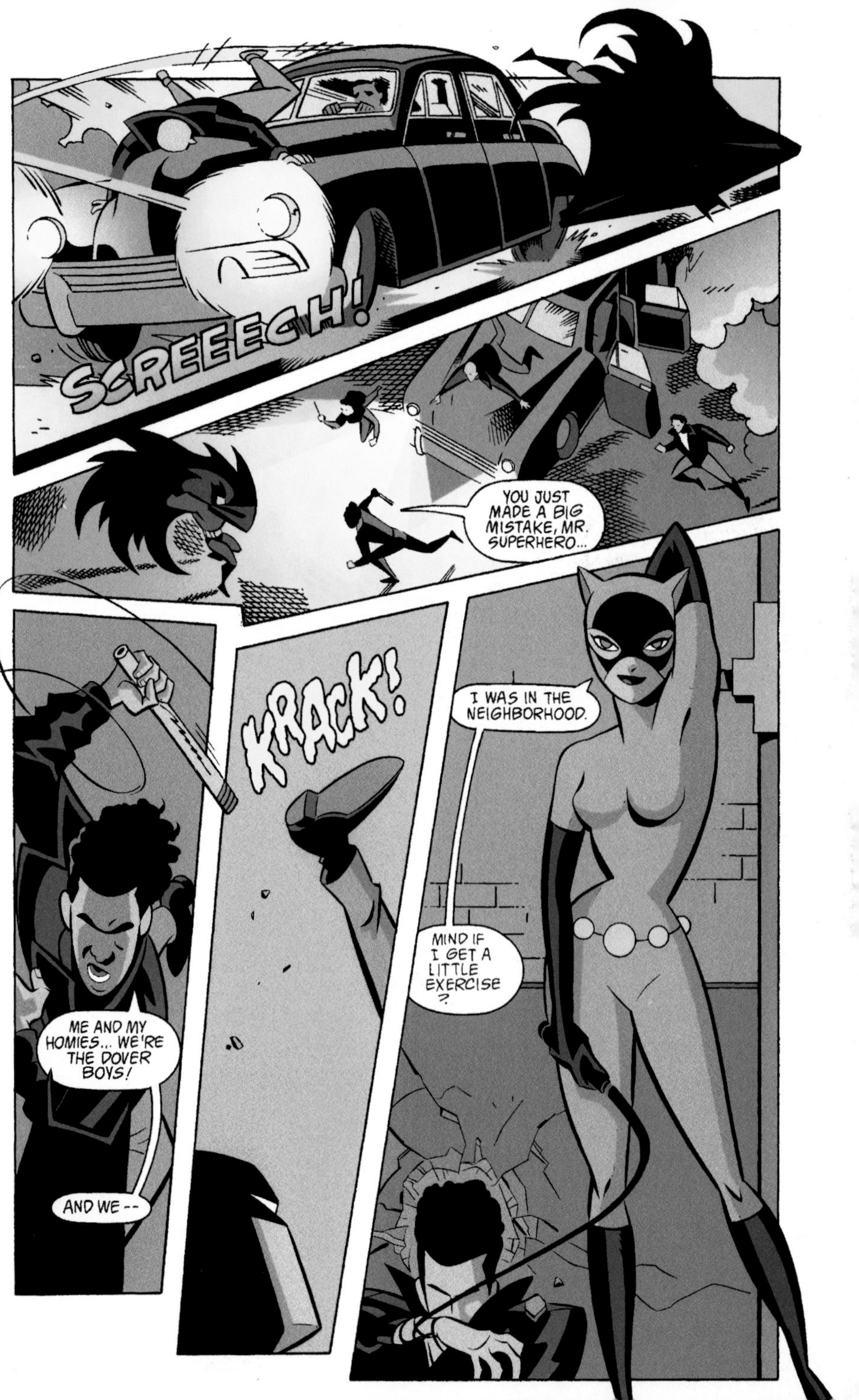
SCREEECH!
YOU JUST MADE A BIG MISTAKE, MR. SUPERHERO...
ME AND MY HOMIES... WE'RE THE DOVER BOYS!
AND WE --
KRACK!
I WAS IN THE NEIGHBORHOOD.
MIND IF I GET A LITTLE EXERCISE?

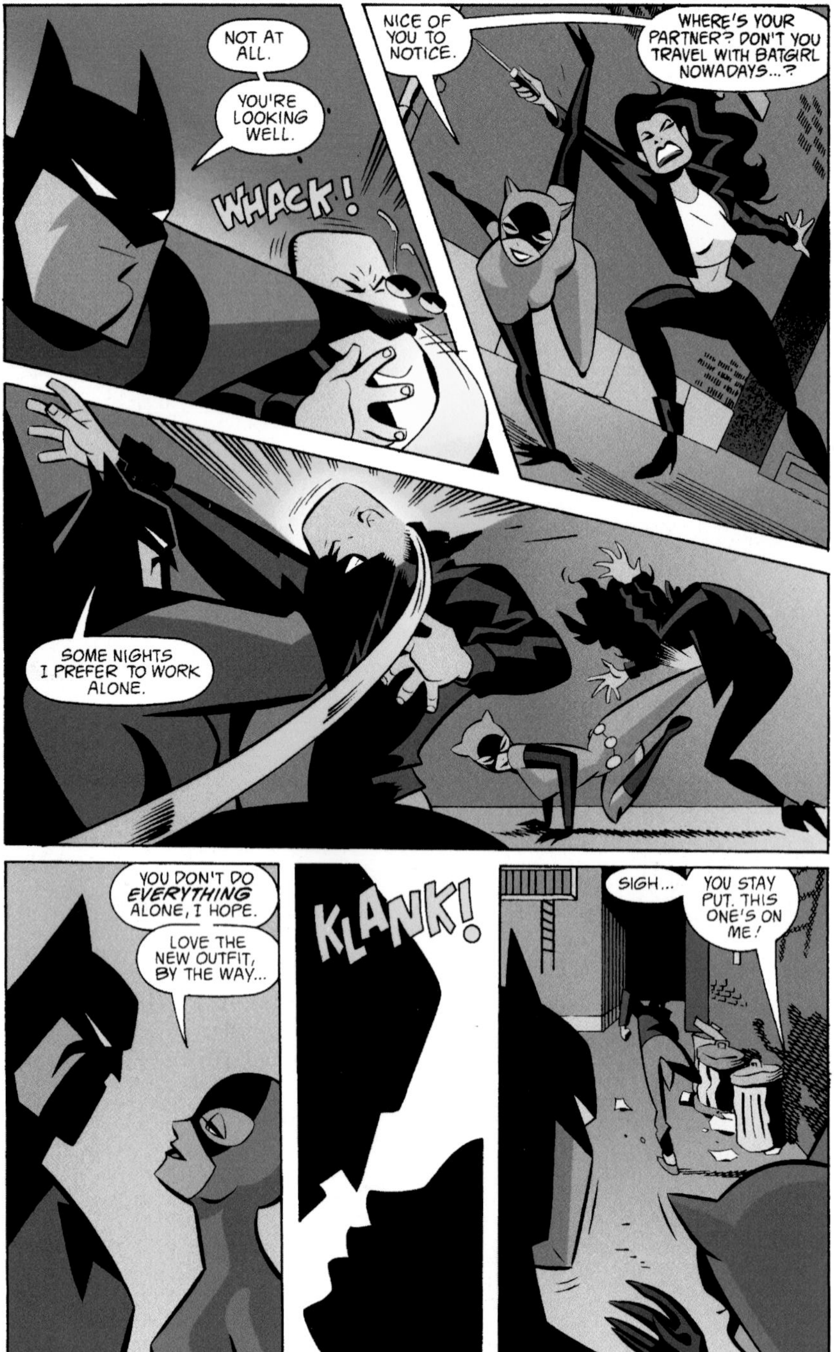
NOT AT ALL.
YOU'RE LOOKING WELL.
WHACK!
NICE OF YOU TO NOTICE.
WHERE'S YOUR PARTNER? DON'T YOU TRAVEL WITH BATGIRL NOWADAYS...?
SOME NIGHTS I PREFER TO WORK ALONE.
YOU DON'T DO *EVERYTHING* ALONE, I HOPE.
LOVE THE NEW OUTFIT, BY THE WAY...
KLANK!
SIGH...
YOU STAY PUT. THIS ONE'S ON ME!

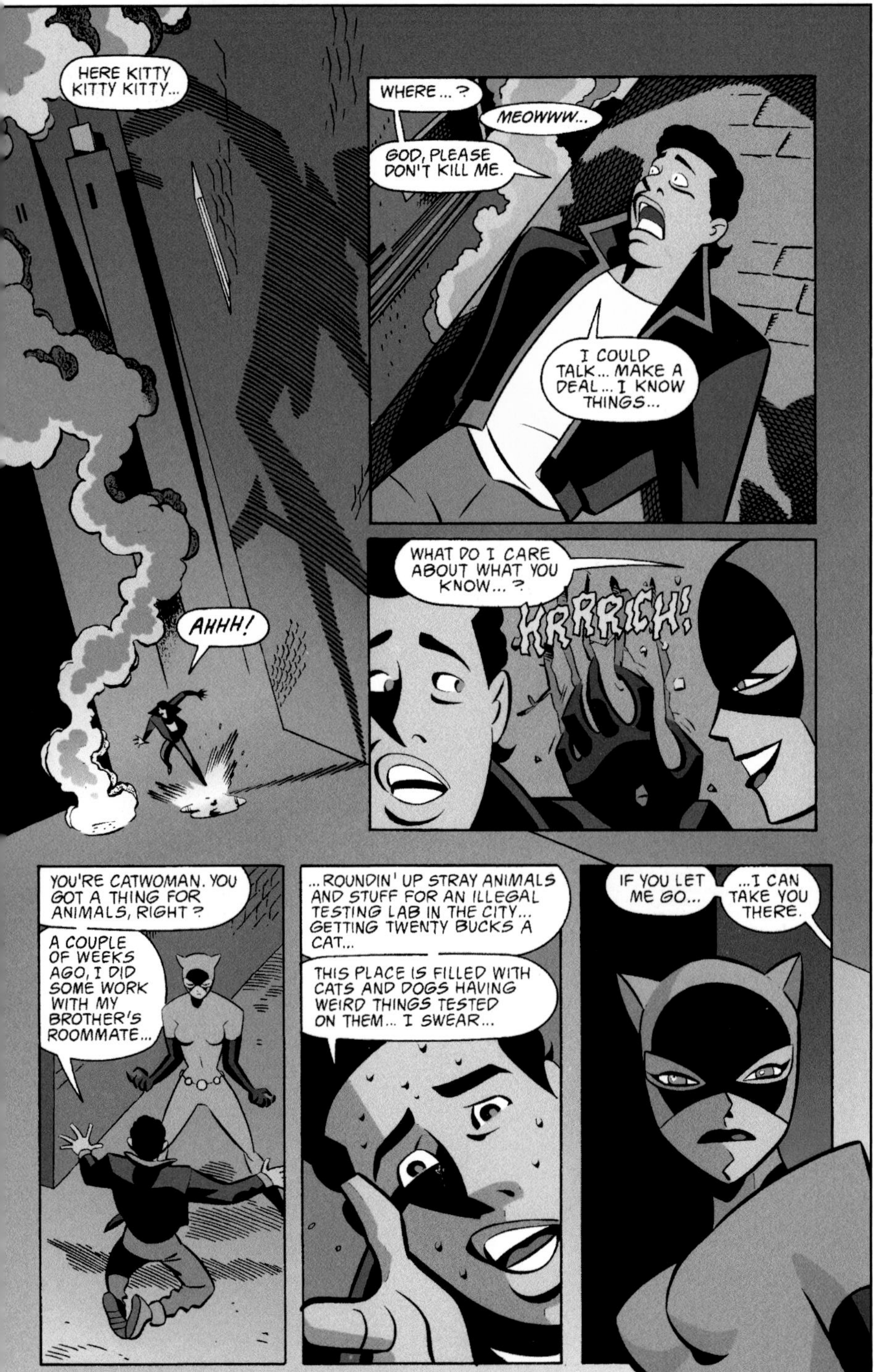
HERE KITTY KITTY KITTY...
AHHH!
WHERE...?
MEOWWW...
GOD, PLEASE DON'T KILL ME.
I COULD TALK... MAKE A DEAL... I KNOW THINGS...
WHAT DO I CARE ABOUT WHAT YOU KNOW...?
KRRRICH!
YOU'RE CATWOMAN. YOU GOT A THING FOR ANIMALS, RIGHT?
A COUPLE OF WEEKS AGO, I DID SOME WORK WITH MY BROTHER'S ROOMMATE...
...ROUNDIN' UP STRAY ANIMALS AND STUFF FOR AN ILLEGAL TESTING LAB IN THE CITY... GETTING TWENTY BUCKS A CAT...
THIS PLACE IS FILLED WITH CATS AND DOGS HAVING WEIRD THINGS TESTED ON THEM... I SWEAR...
IF YOU LET ME GO...
...I CAN TAKE YOU THERE.

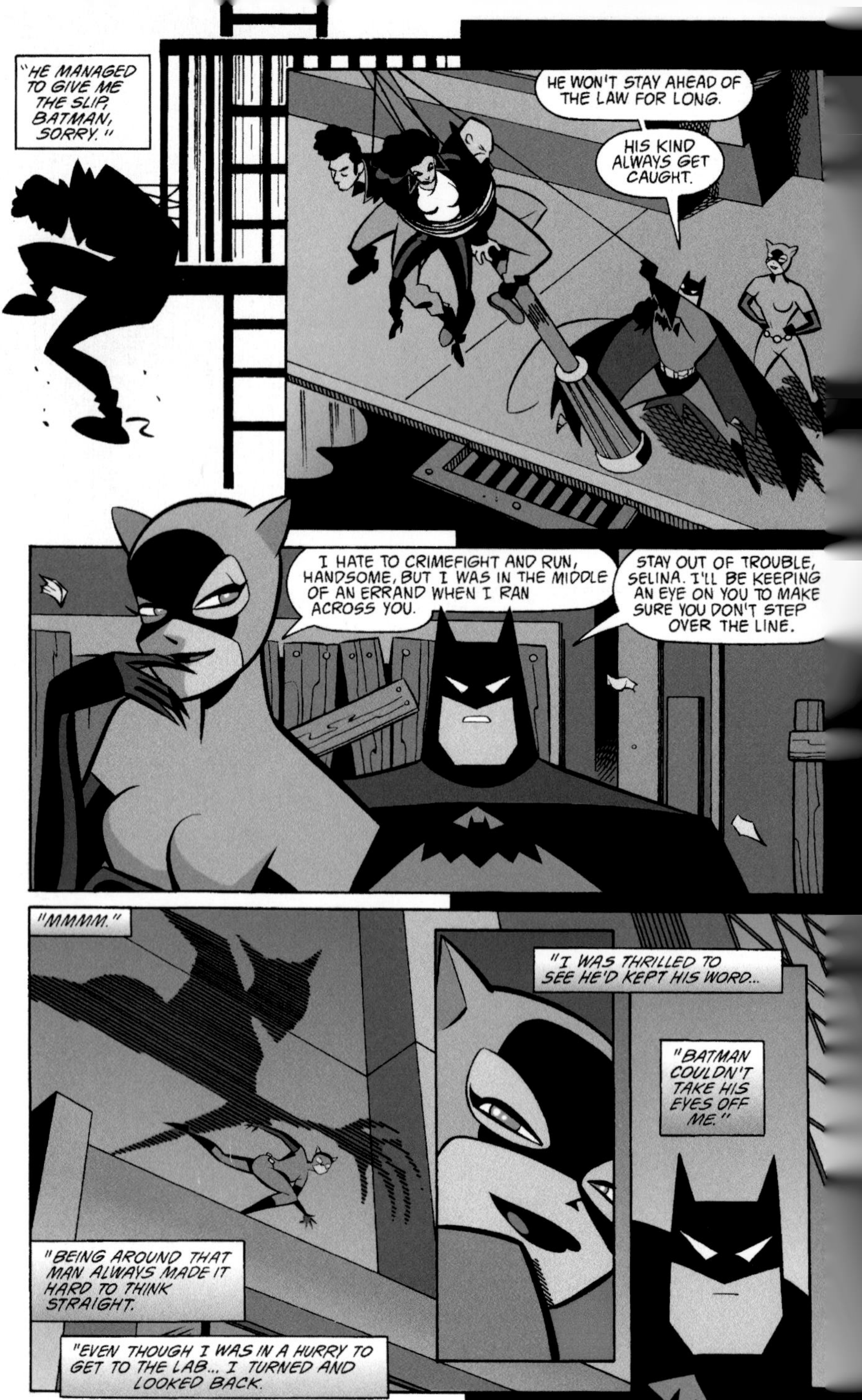
"HE MANAGED TO GIVE ME THE SLIP, BATMAN, SORRY."
HE WON'T STAY AHEAD OF THE LAW FOR LONG.
HIS KIND ALWAYS GET CAUGHT.
I HATE TO CRIMEFIGHT AND RUN, HANDSOME, BUT I WAS IN THE MIDDLE OF AN ERRAND WHEN I RAN ACROSS YOU.
STAY OUT OF TROUBLE, SELINA. I'LL BE KEEPING AN EYE ON YOU TO MAKE SURE YOU DON'T STEP OVER THE LINE.
"MMMM."
"BEING AROUND THAT MAN ALWAYS MADE IT HARD TO THINK STRAIGHT.
"EVEN THOUGH I WAS IN A HURRY TO GET TO THE LAB... I TURNED AND LOOKED BACK.
"I WAS THRILLED TO SEE HE'D KEPT HIS WORD...
"BATMAN COULDN'T TAKE HIS EYES OFF ME."

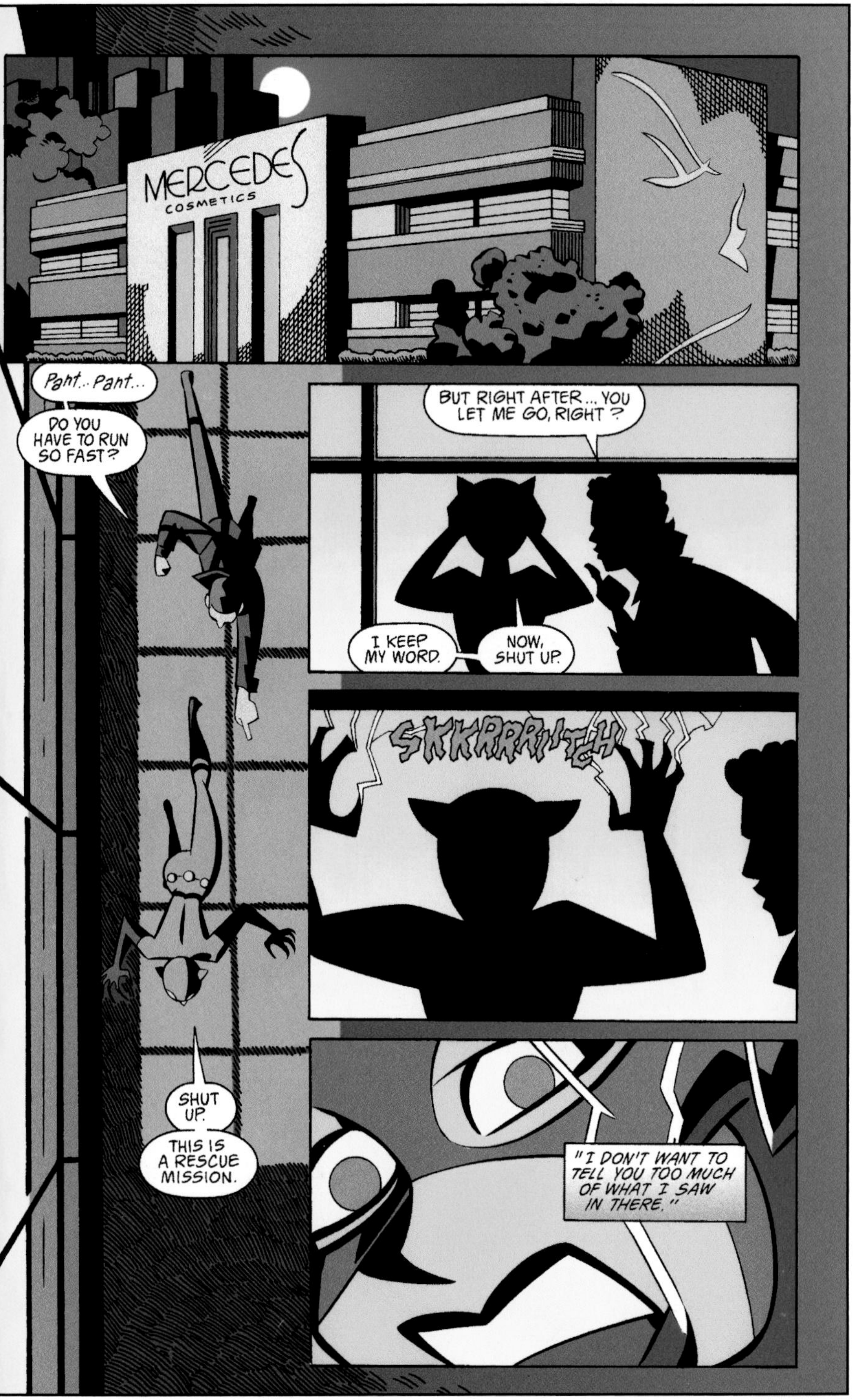
MERCEDES
COSMETICS
Pant... Pant...
DO YOU HAVE TO RUN SO FAST?
BUT RIGHT AFTER... YOU LET ME GO, RIGHT?
I KEEP MY WORD.
NOW, SHUT UP.
SKKRRRITCH
SHUT UP.
THIS IS A RESCUE MISSION.
"I DON'T WANT TO TELL YOU TOO MUCH OF WHAT I SAW IN THERE."

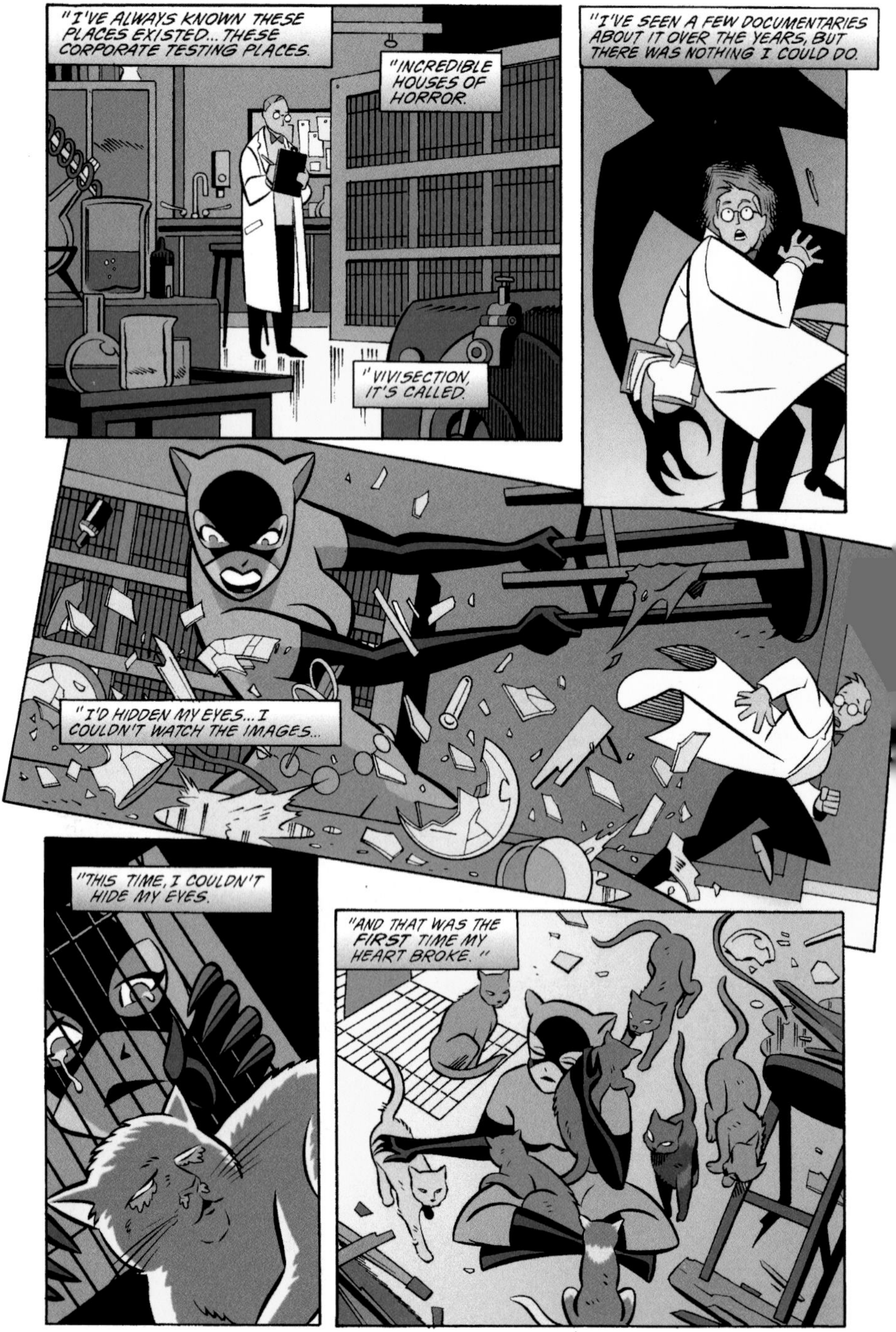
"I'VE ALWAYS KNOWN THESE PLACES EXISTED... THESE CORPORATE TESTING PLACES.
"INCREDIBLE HOUSES OF HORROR.
"VIVISECTION, IT'S CALLED.
"I'VE SEEN A FEW DOCUMENTARIES ABOUT IT OVER THE YEARS, BUT THERE WAS NOTHING I COULD DO.
"I'D HIDDEN MY EYES... I COULDN'T WATCH THE IMAGES...
"THIS TIME, I COULDN'T HIDE MY EYES.
"AND THAT WAS THE FIRST TIME MY HEART BROKE."

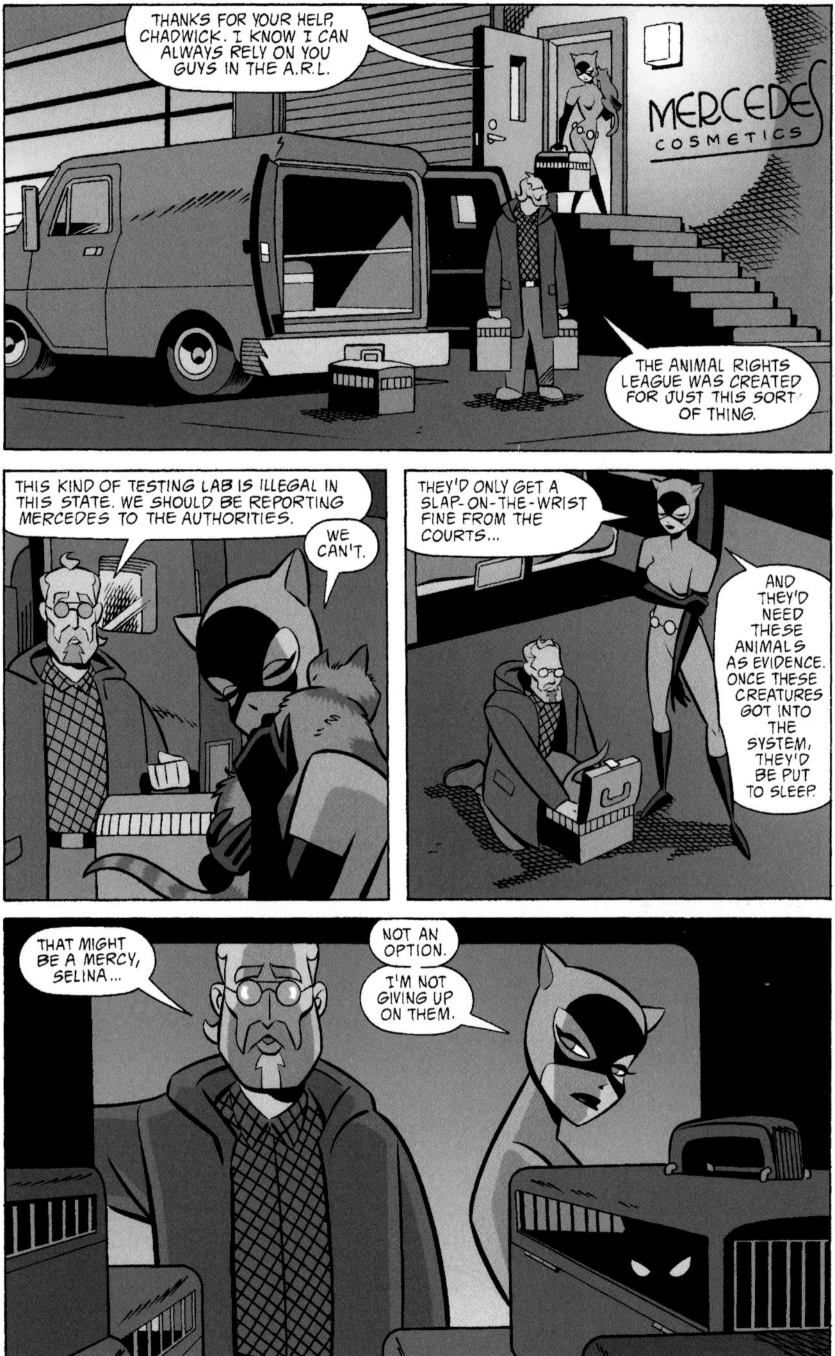
THANKS FOR YOUR HELP, CHADWICK. I KNOW I CAN ALWAYS RELY ON YOU GUYS IN THE A.R.L.
MERCEDES COSMETICS
THE ANIMAL RIGHTS LEAGUE WAS CREATED FOR JUST THIS SORT OF THING.
THIS KIND OF TESTING LAB IS ILLEGAL IN THIS STATE. WE SHOULD BE REPORTING MERCEDES TO THE AUTHORITIES.
WE CAN'T.
THEY'D ONLY GET A SLAP-ON-THE-WRIST FINE FROM THE COURTS...
AND THEY'D NEED THESE ANIMALS AS EVIDENCE. ONCE THESE CREATURES GOT INTO THE SYSTEM, THEY'D BE PUT TO SLEEP.
THAT MIGHT BE A MERCY, SELINA...
NOT AN OPTION.
I'M NOT GIVING UP ON THEM.

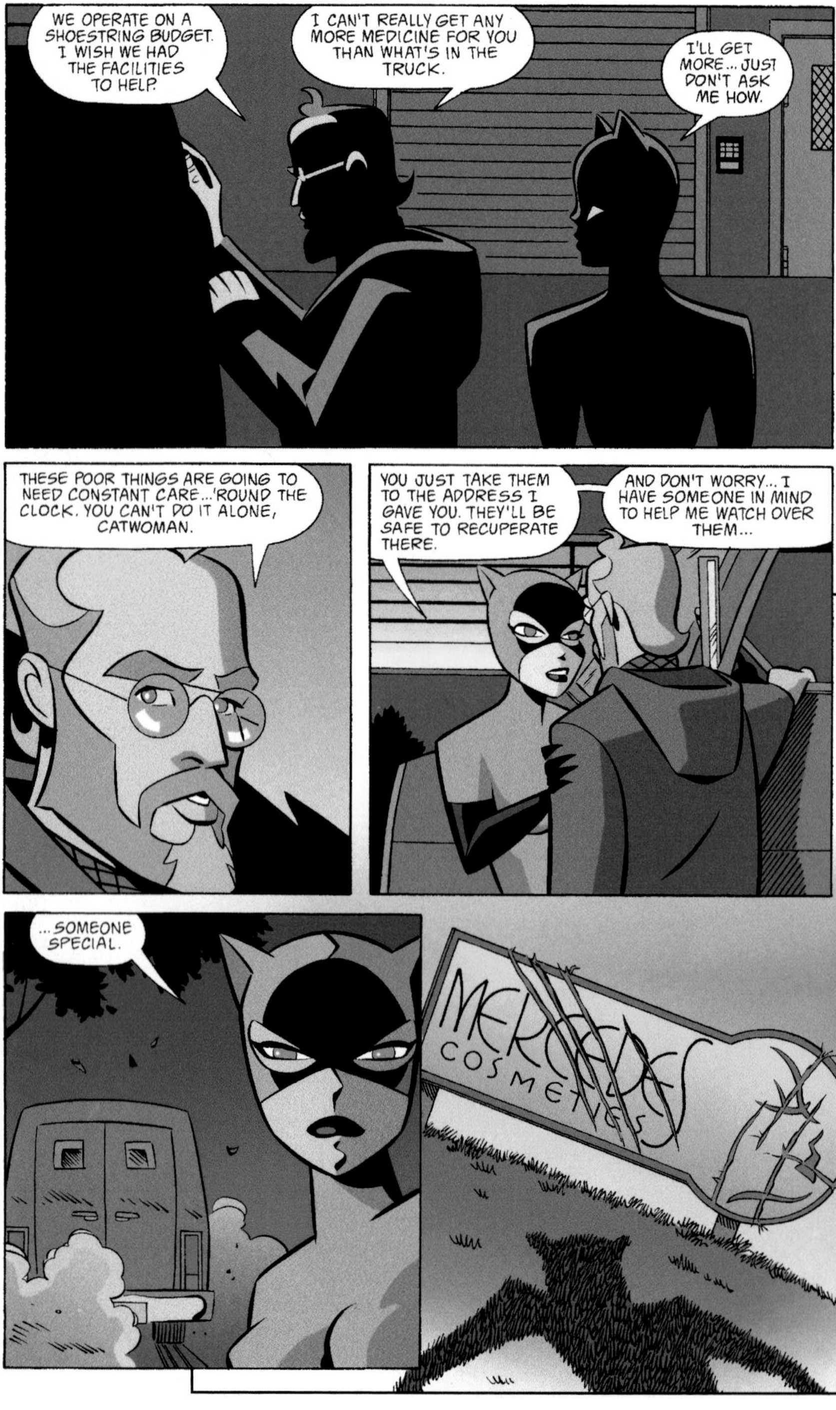
WE OPERATE ON A SHOESTRING BUDGET. I WISH WE HAD THE FACILITIES TO HELP.
I CAN'T REALLY GET ANY MORE MEDICINE FOR YOU THAN WHAT'S IN THE TRUCK.
I'LL GET MORE... JUST DON'T ASK ME HOW.
THESE POOR THINGS ARE GOING TO NEED CONSTANT CARE...'ROUND THE CLOCK. YOU CAN'T DO IT ALONE, CATWOMAN.
YOU JUST TAKE THEM TO THE ADDRESS I GAVE YOU. THEY'LL BE SAFE TO RECUPERATE THERE.
AND DON'T WORRY... I HAVE SOMEONE IN MIND TO HELP ME WATCH OVER THEM...
...SOMEONE SPECIAL.
MERCEDES COSMETICS

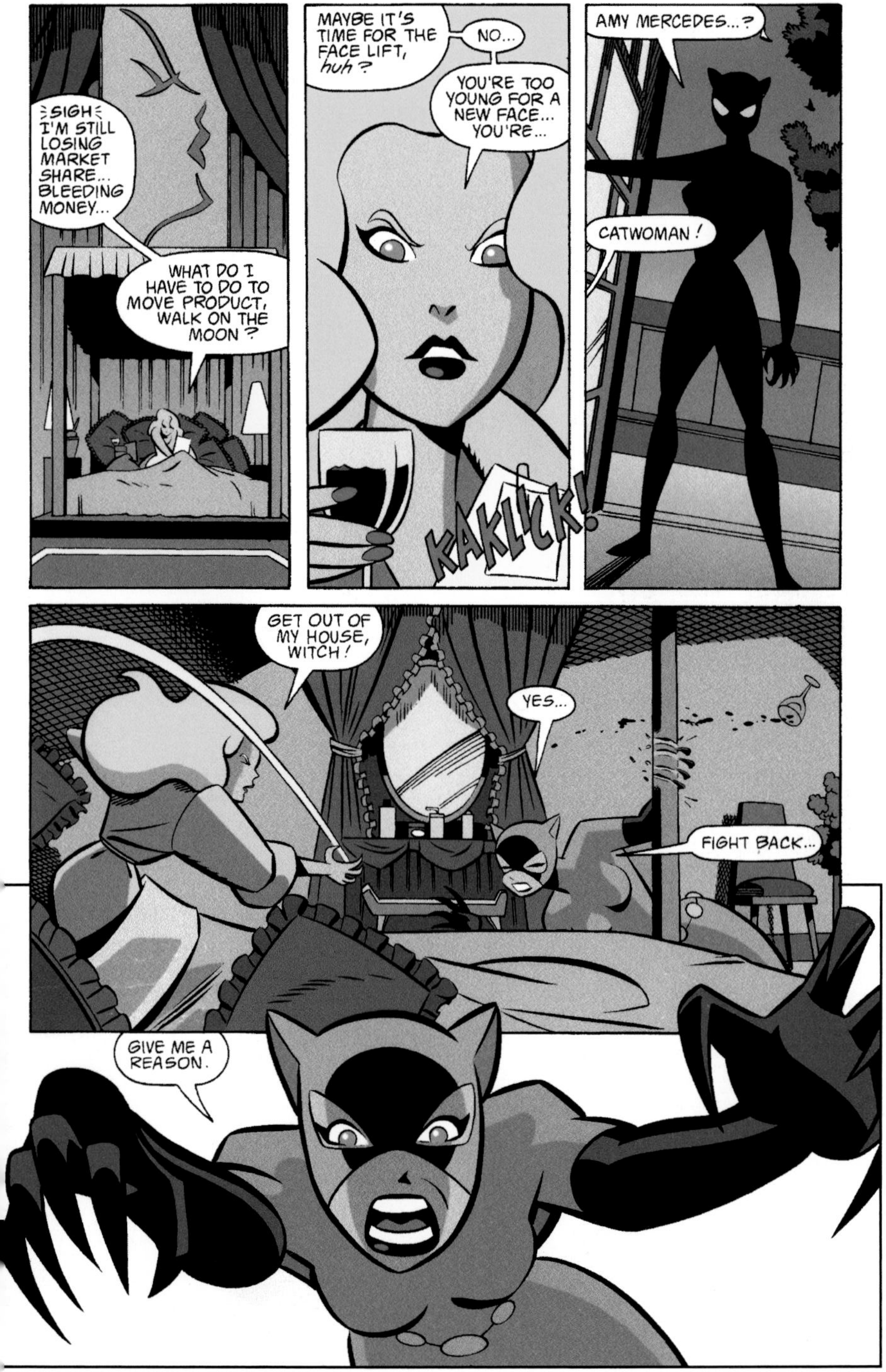

≷SIGH≶ I'M STILL LOSING MARKET SHARE... BLEEDING MONEY...
WHAT DO I HAVE TO DO TO MOVE PRODUCT, WALK ON THE MOON?
MAYBE IT'S TIME FOR THE FACE LIFT, *huh*?
NO...
YOU'RE TOO YOUNG FOR A NEW FACE... YOU'RE...
KAKLICK!
AMY MERCEDES...?
CATWOMAN!
GET OUT OF MY HOUSE, WITCH!
YES...
FIGHT BACK...
GIVE ME A REASON.

YOU'RE DEAD, CATWOMAN.

YOU ARE *SO* DEAD...

AND YOU ARE FAMOUS FOR BEING A *"HANDS-ON"* COMPANY PRESIDENT, MS. MERCEDES...

SO I WON'T BELIEVE YOU DON'T KNOW ANYTHING ABOUT YOUR COSMETICS TESTING FACILITIES...

...AND WHAT BUTCHERY WENT ON THERE.

THIS IS ABOUT *THAT*?

YES, THAT.

I HAVE TWENTY-FOUR SICK CATS ON MY HANDS THAT NEED CARE AND ATTENTION TO GET WELL...

THAT'S GOING TO BE YOUR JOB.

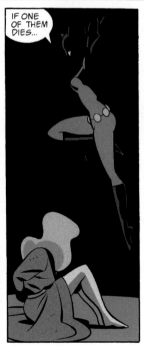

IF ONE OF THEM DIES...

...YOU'RE NEXT!

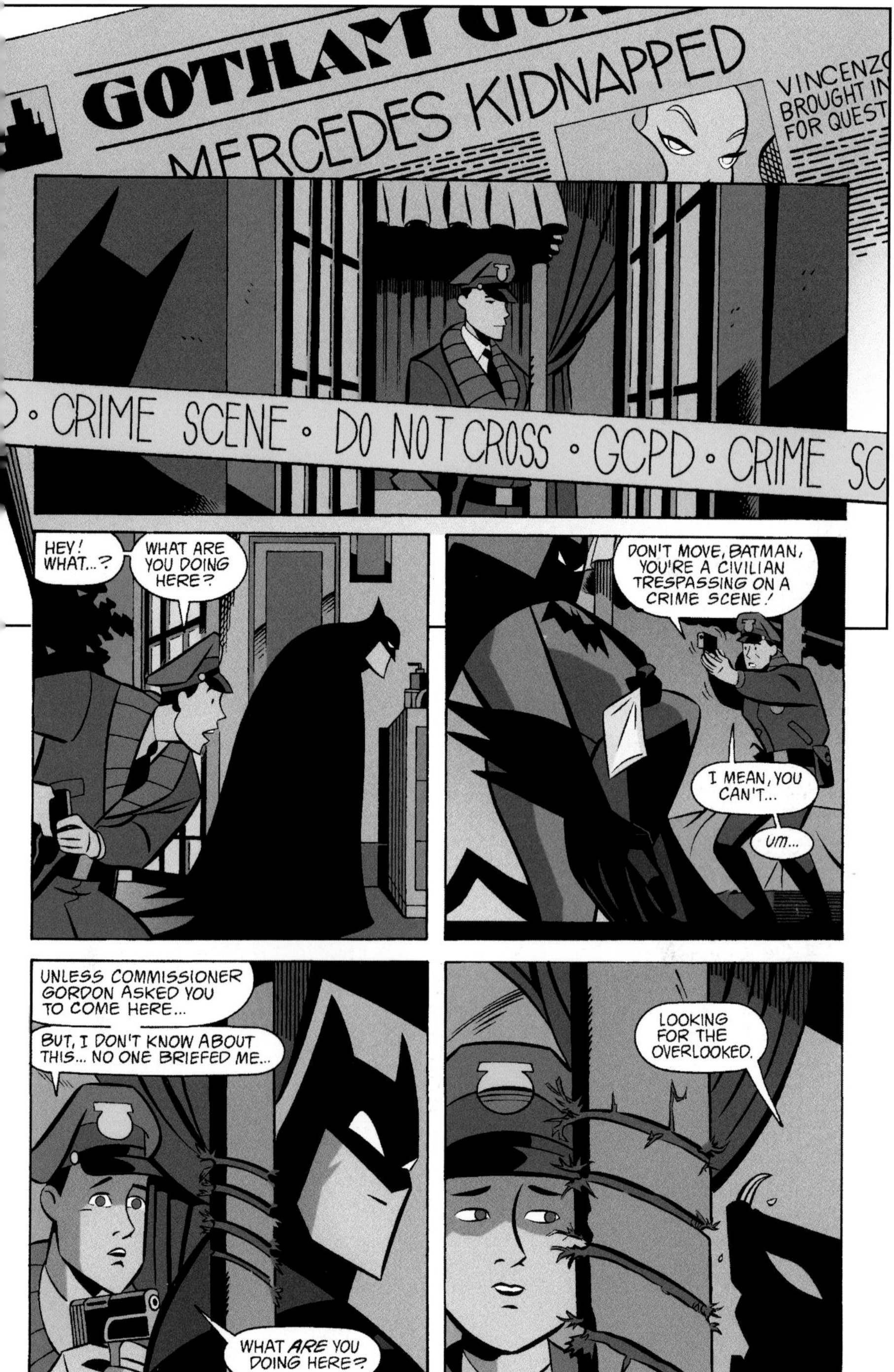
GOTHAM
MERCEDES KIDNAPPED
VINCENZO BROUGHT IN FOR QUEST
CRIME SCENE • DO NOT CROSS • GCPD • CRIME SC
HEY! WHAT...?
WHAT ARE YOU DOING HERE?
DON'T MOVE, BATMAN, YOU'RE A CIVILIAN TRESPASSING ON A CRIME SCENE!
I MEAN, YOU CAN'T...
UM...
UNLESS COMMISSIONER GORDON ASKED YOU TO COME HERE...
BUT, I DON'T KNOW ABOUT THIS... NO ONE BRIEFED ME...
WHAT ARE YOU DOING HERE?
LOOKING FOR THE OVERLOOKED.

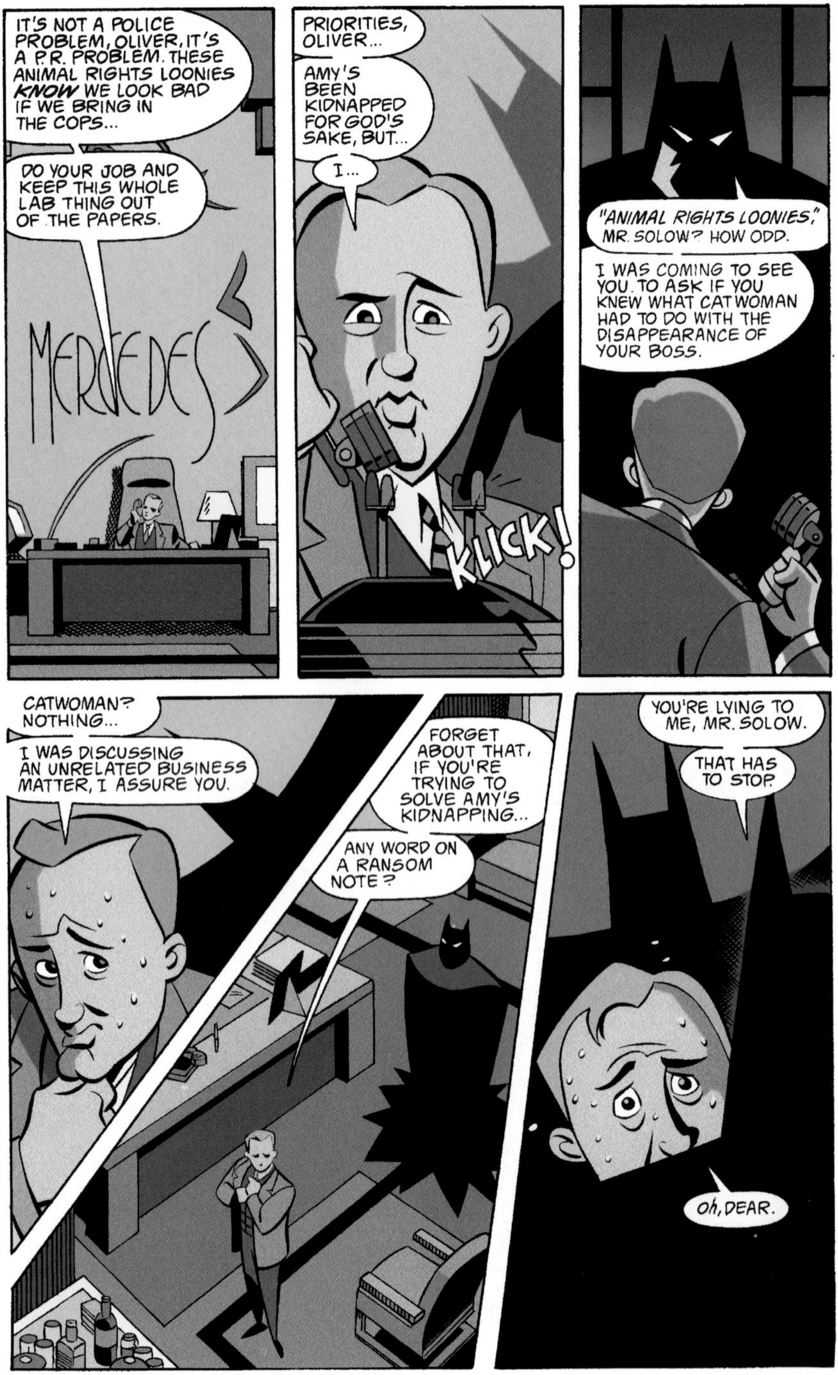
IT'S NOT A POLICE PROBLEM, OLIVER, IT'S A P.R. PROBLEM. THESE ANIMAL RIGHTS LOONIES *KNOW* WE LOOK BAD IF WE BRING IN THE COPS...
DO YOUR JOB AND KEEP THIS WHOLE LAB THING OUT OF THE PAPERS.
MERCEDES
PRIORITIES, OLIVER...
AMY'S BEEN KIDNAPPED FOR GOD'S SAKE, BUT...
I...
KLICK!
"ANIMAL RIGHTS LOONIES," MR. SOLOW? HOW ODD.
I WAS COMING TO SEE YOU. TO ASK IF YOU KNEW WHAT CATWOMAN HAD TO DO WITH THE DISAPPEARANCE OF YOUR BOSS.
CATWOMAN? NOTHING...
I WAS DISCUSSING AN UNRELATED BUSINESS MATTER, I ASSURE YOU.
FORGET ABOUT THAT. IF YOU'RE TRYING TO SOLVE AMY'S KIDNAPPING...
ANY WORD ON A RANSOM NOTE?
YOU'RE LYING TO ME, MR. SOLOW.
THAT HAS TO STOP.
Oh, DEAR.

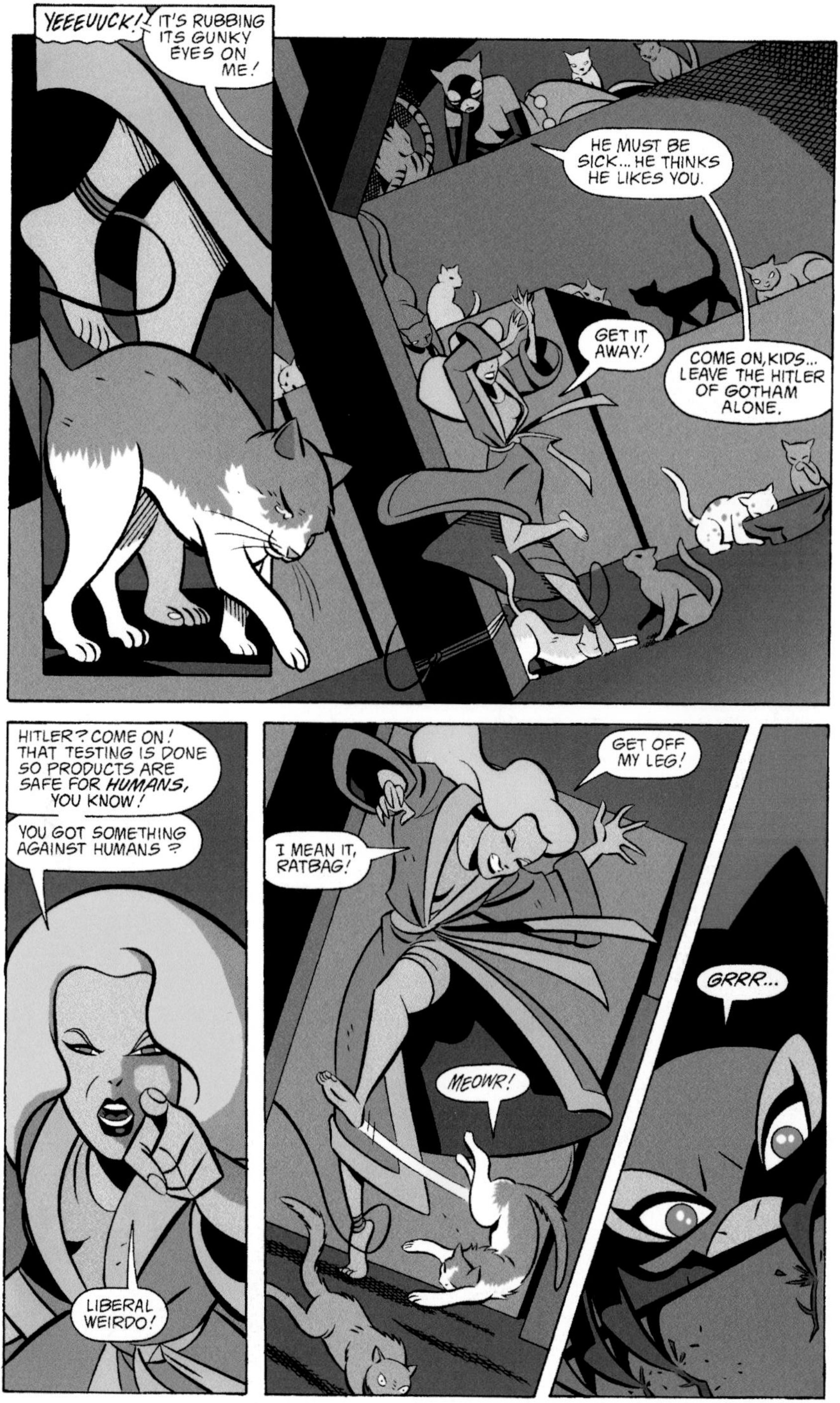
YEEEUUCK!
IT'S RUBBING ITS GUNKY EYES ON ME!
HE MUST BE SICK... HE THINKS HE LIKES YOU.
GET IT AWAY!
COME ON, KIDS... LEAVE THE HITLER OF GOTHAM ALONE.
HITLER? COME ON! THAT TESTING IS DONE SO PRODUCTS ARE SAFE FOR HUMANS, YOU KNOW!
YOU GOT SOMETHING AGAINST HUMANS?
LIBERAL WEIRDO!
GET OFF MY LEG!
I MEAN IT, RATBAG!
MEOWR!
GRRR...

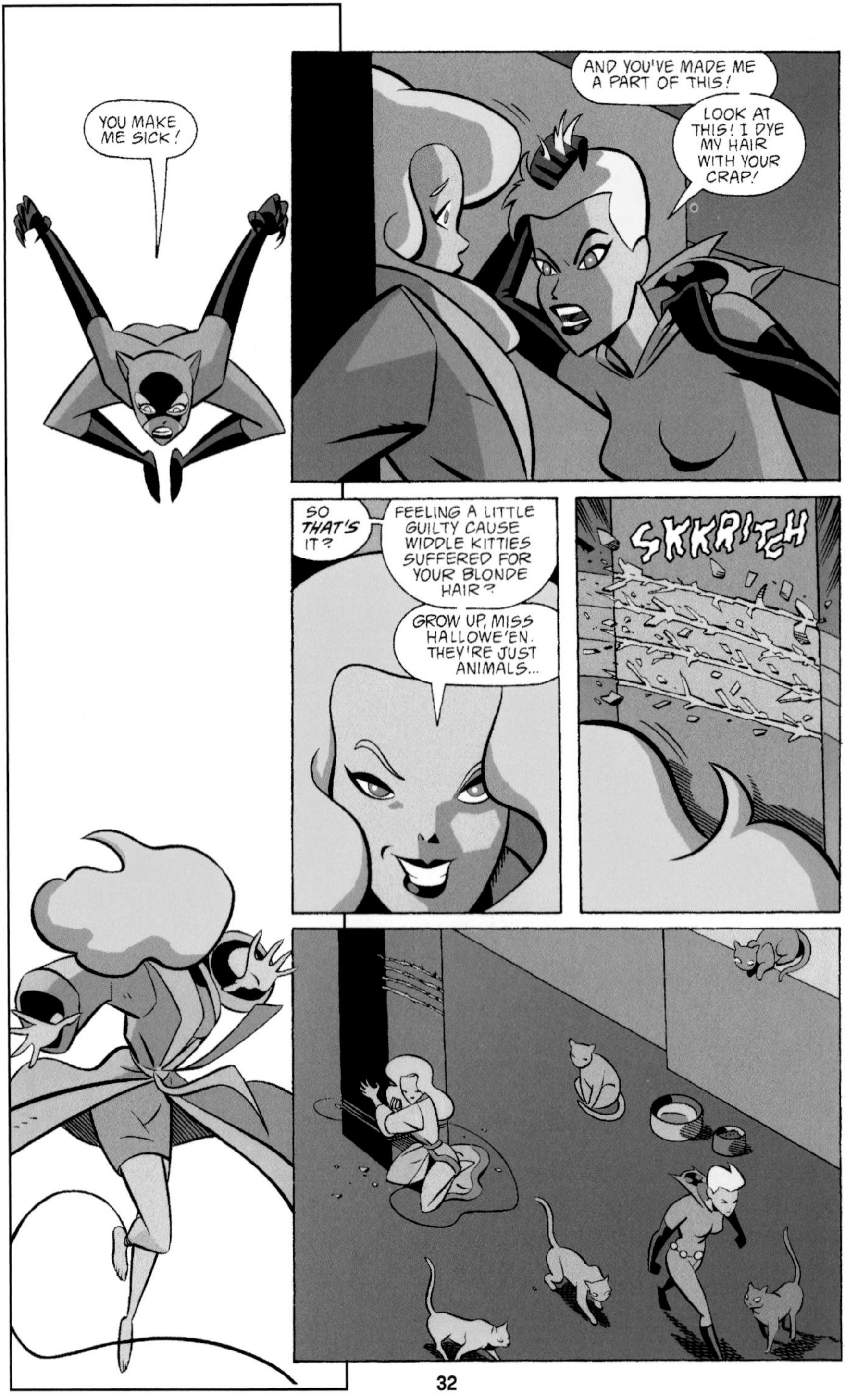

YOU MAKE ME SICK!
AND YOU'VE MADE ME A PART OF THIS!
LOOK AT THIS! I DYE MY HAIR WITH YOUR CRAP!
SO THAT'S IT?
FEELING A LITTLE GUILTY CAUSE WIDDLE KITTIES SUFFERED FOR YOUR BLONDE HAIR?
GROW UP, MISS HALLOWE'EN. THEY'RE JUST ANIMALS...
SKKRITCH

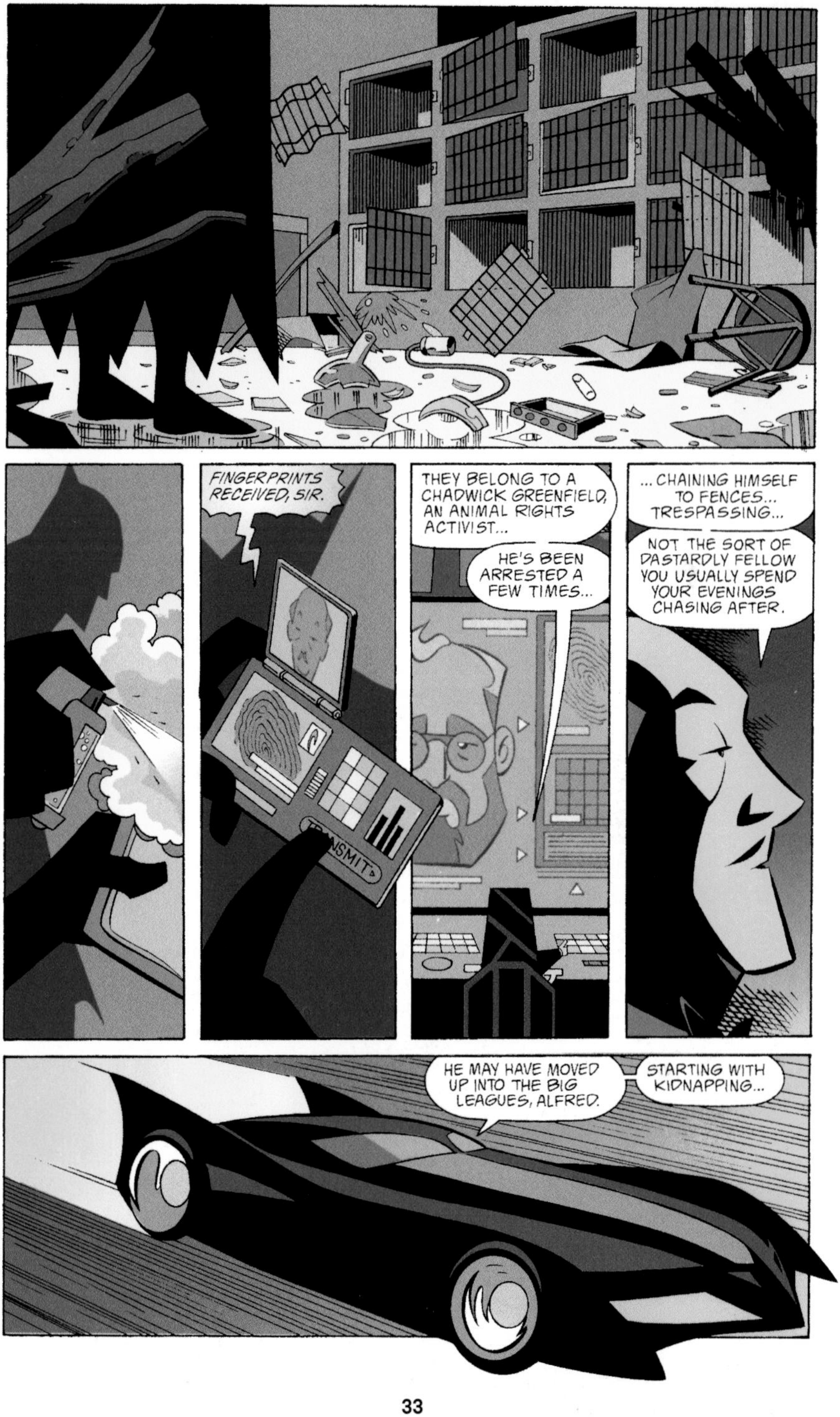
FINGERPRINTS RECEIVED, SIR.
TRANSMIT
THEY BELONG TO A CHADWICK GREENFIELD, AN ANIMAL RIGHTS ACTIVIST...
HE'S BEEN ARRESTED A FEW TIMES...
...CHAINING HIMSELF TO FENCES... TRESPASSING...
NOT THE SORT OF DASTARDLY FELLOW YOU USUALLY SPEND YOUR EVENINGS CHASING AFTER.
HE MAY HAVE MOVED UP INTO THE BIG LEAGUES, ALFRED.
STARTING WITH KIDNAPPING...

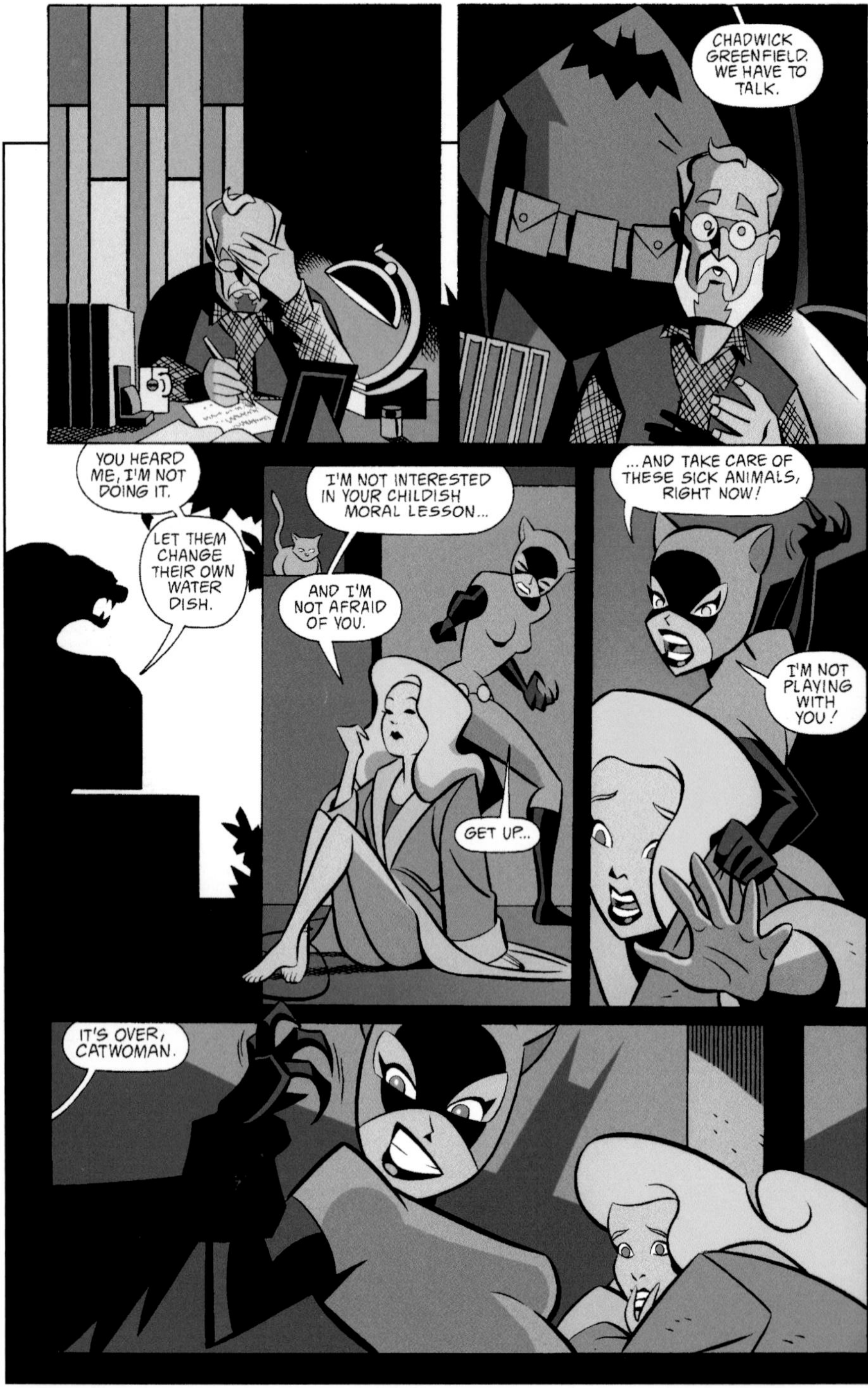
CHADWICK GREENFIELD. WE HAVE TO TALK.
YOU HEARD ME, I'M NOT DOING IT.
LET THEM CHANGE THEIR OWN WATER DISH.
I'M NOT INTERESTED IN YOUR CHILDISH MORAL LESSON...
AND I'M NOT AFRAID OF YOU.
GET UP...
...AND TAKE CARE OF THESE SICK ANIMALS, RIGHT NOW!
I'M NOT PLAYING WITH YOU!
IT'S OVER, CATWOMAN.

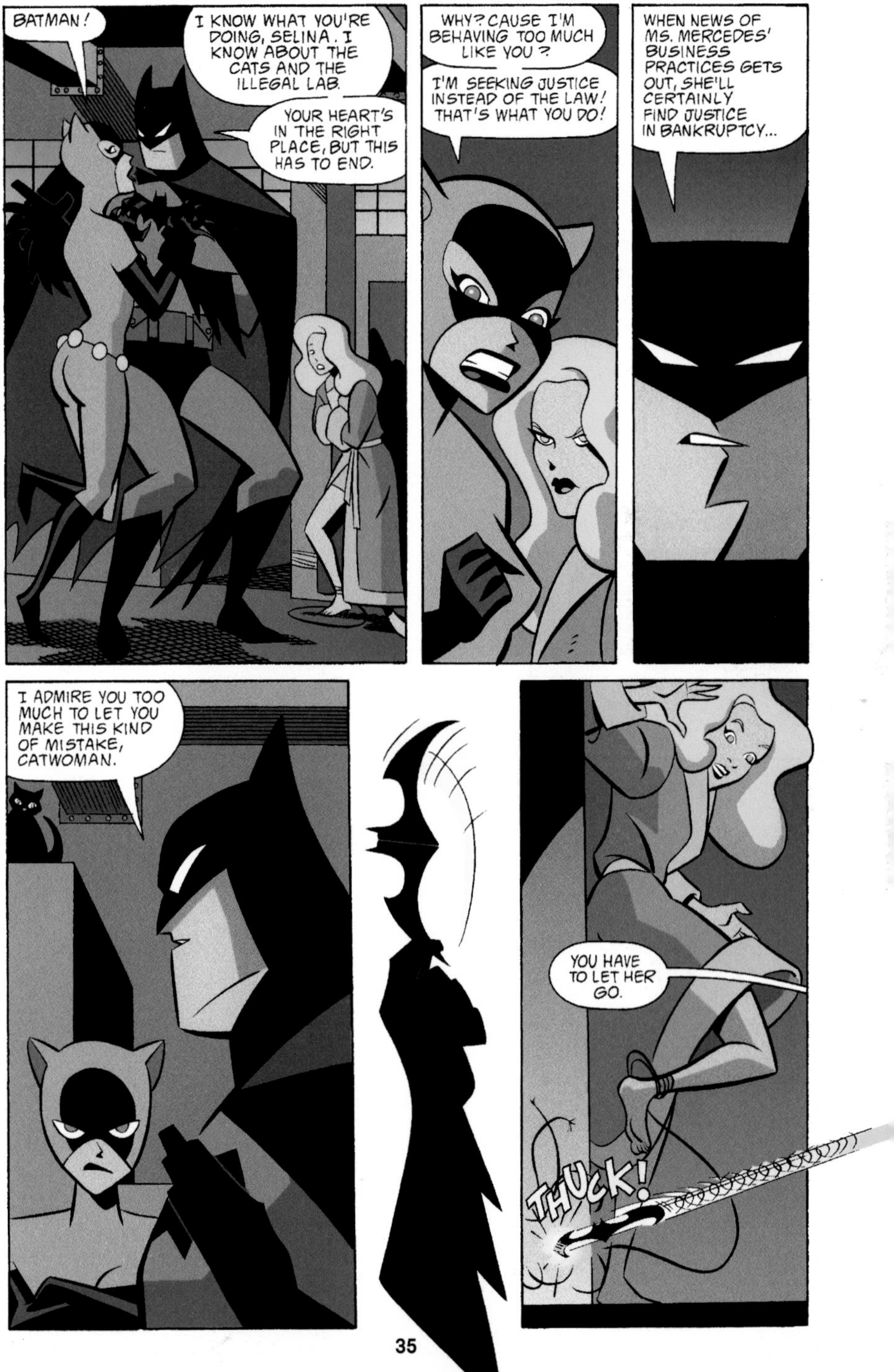
BATMAN!
I KNOW WHAT YOU'RE DOING, SELINA. I KNOW ABOUT THE CATS AND THE ILLEGAL LAB.
YOUR HEART'S IN THE RIGHT PLACE, BUT THIS HAS TO END.
WHY? CAUSE I'M BEHAVING TOO MUCH LIKE YOU?
I'M SEEKING JUSTICE INSTEAD OF THE LAW! THAT'S WHAT YOU DO!
WHEN NEWS OF MS. MERCEDES' BUSINESS PRACTICES GETS OUT, SHE'LL CERTAINLY FIND JUSTICE IN BANKRUPTCY...
I ADMIRE YOU TOO MUCH TO LET YOU MAKE THIS KIND OF MISTAKE, CATWOMAN.
YOU HAVE TO LET HER GO.
THUCK!

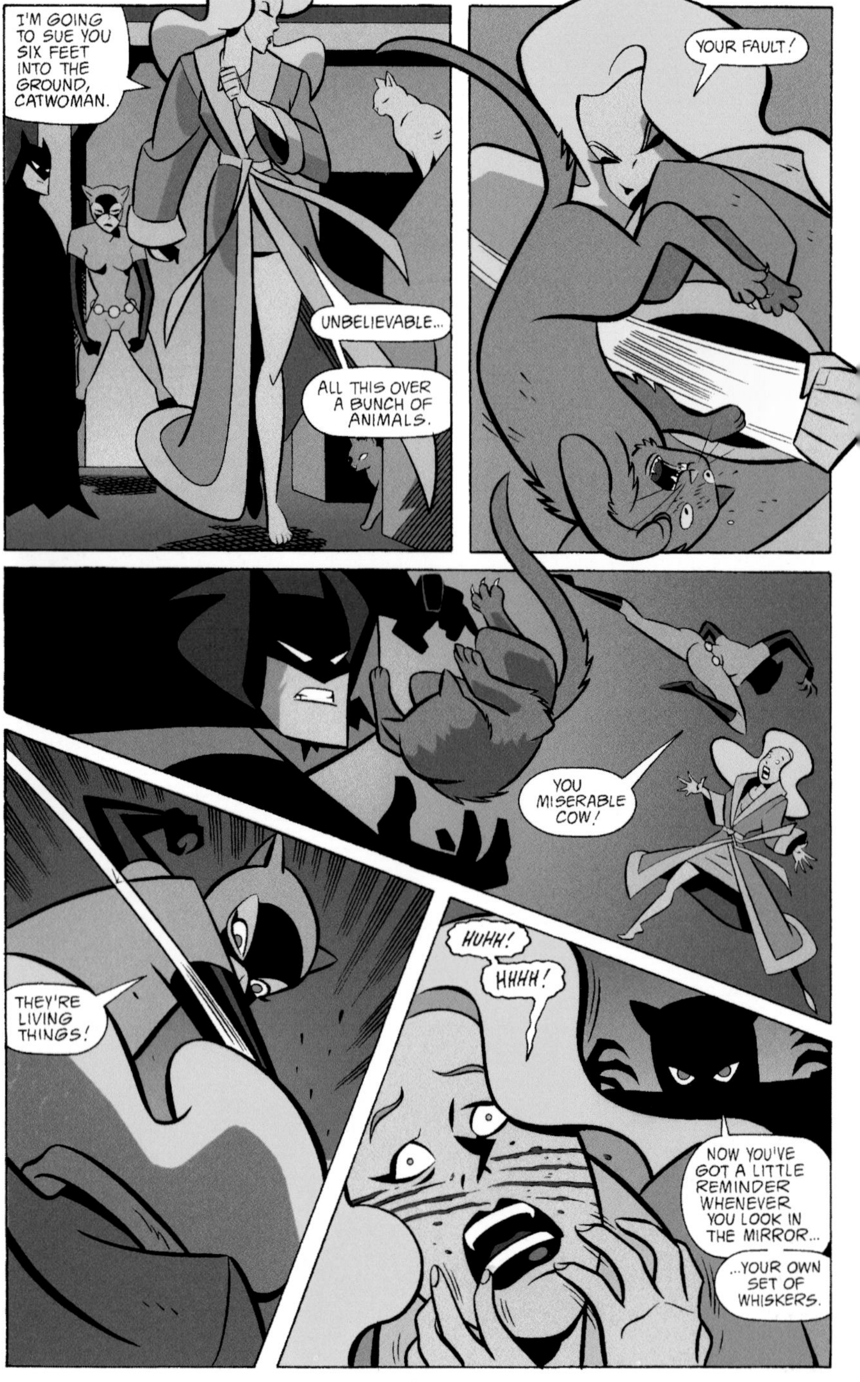
I'M GOING TO SUE YOU SIX FEET INTO THE GROUND, CATWOMAN.
UNBELIEVABLE...
ALL THIS OVER A BUNCH OF ANIMALS.
YOUR FAULT!
YOU MISERABLE COW!
THEY'RE LIVING THINGS!
HUHH!
HHHH!
NOW YOU'VE GOT A LITTLE REMINDER WHENEVER YOU LOOK IN THE MIRROR...
...YOUR OWN SET OF WHISKERS.

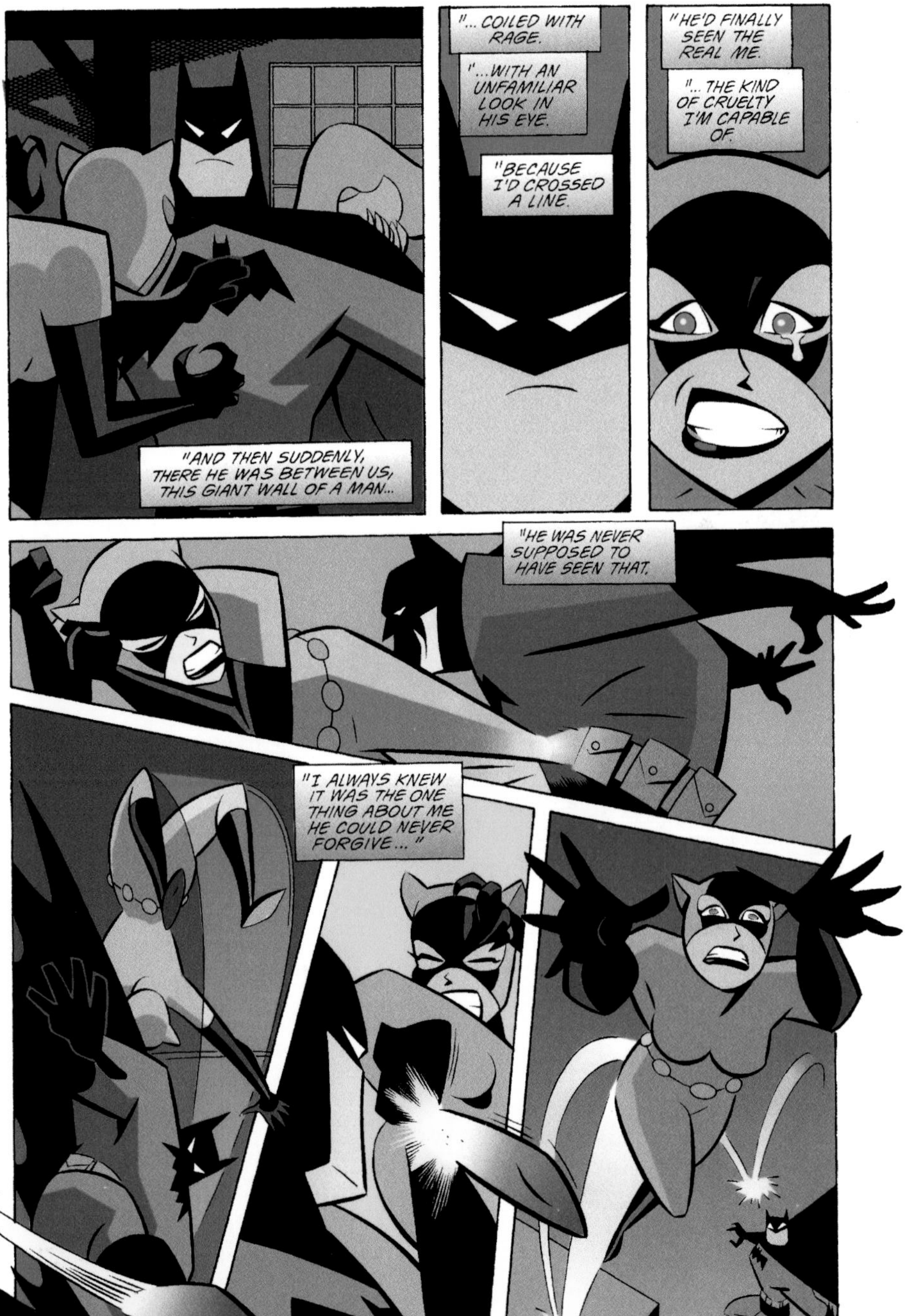
"AND THEN SUDDENLY, THERE HE WAS BETWEEN US, THIS GIANT WALL OF A MAN...
"... COILED WITH RAGE.
"...WITH AN UNFAMILIAR LOOK IN HIS EYE.
"BECAUSE I'D CROSSED A LINE.
"HE'D FINALLY SEEN THE REAL ME.
"... THE KIND OF CRUELTY I'M CAPABLE OF.
"HE WAS NEVER SUPPOSED TO HAVE SEEN THAT.
"I ALWAYS KNEW IT WAS THE ONE THING ABOUT ME HE COULD NEVER FORGIVE ..."

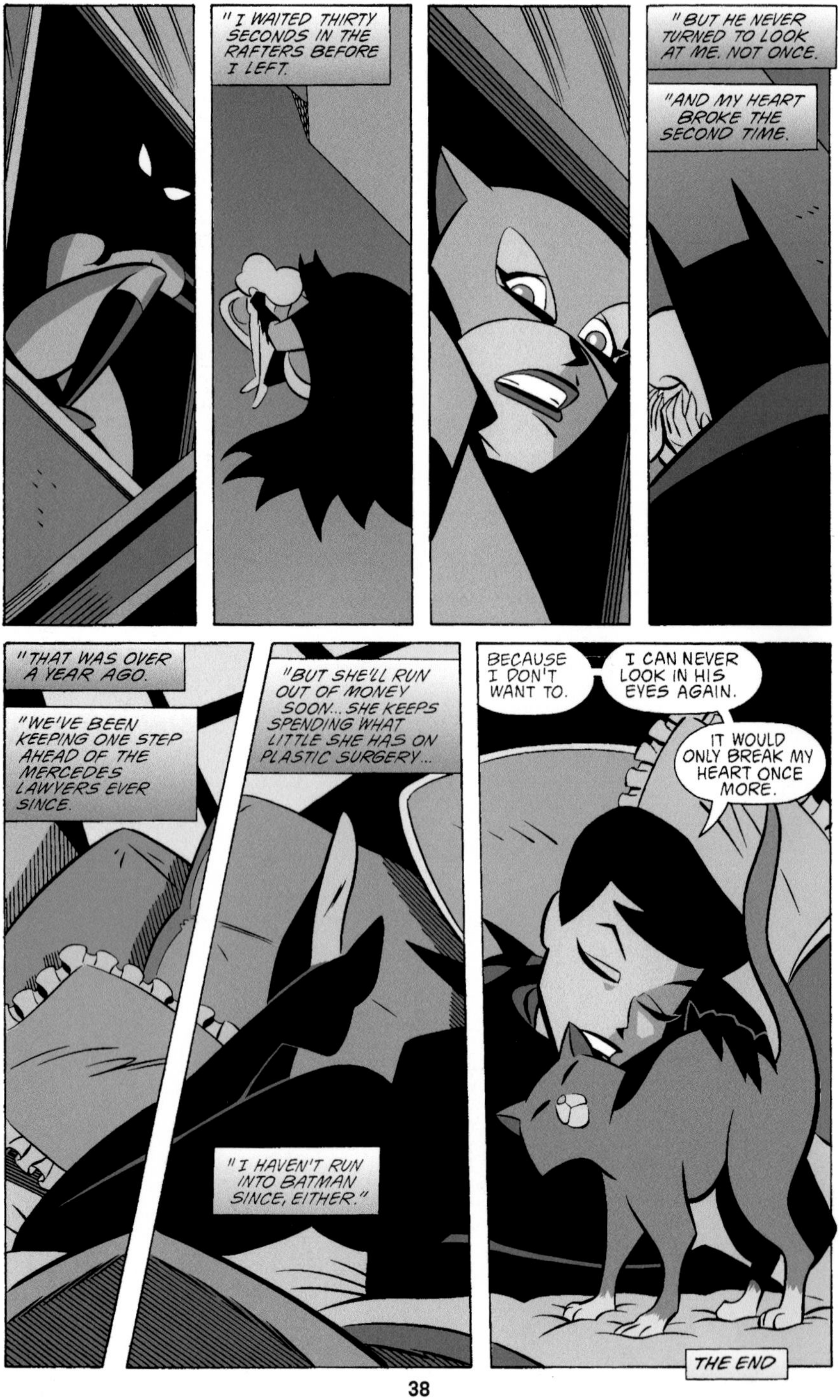
"I WAITED THIRTY SECONDS IN THE RAFTERS BEFORE I LEFT.
"BUT HE NEVER TURNED TO LOOK AT ME. NOT ONCE.
"AND MY HEART BROKE THE SECOND TIME.
"THAT WAS OVER A YEAR AGO.
"WE'VE BEEN KEEPING ONE STEP AHEAD OF THE MERCEDES LAWYERS EVER SINCE.
"BUT SHE'LL RUN OUT OF MONEY SOON... SHE KEEPS SPENDING WHAT LITTLE SHE HAS ON PLASTIC SURGERY...
"I HAVEN'T RUN INTO BATMAN SINCE, EITHER."
BECAUSE I DON'T WANT TO.
I CAN NEVER LOOK IN HIS EYES AGAIN.
IT WOULD ONLY BREAK MY HEART ONCE MORE.
THE END

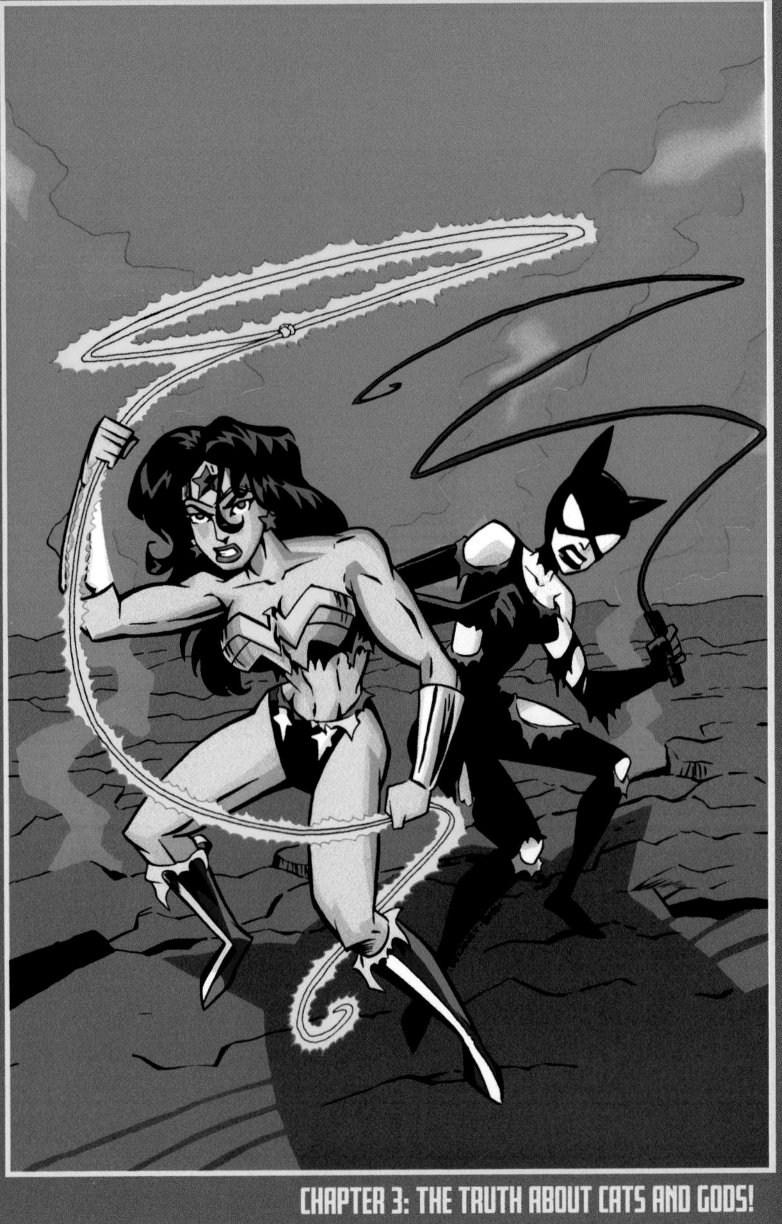

CHAPTER 3: THE TRUTH ABOUT CATS AND GODS!

CATWOMAN

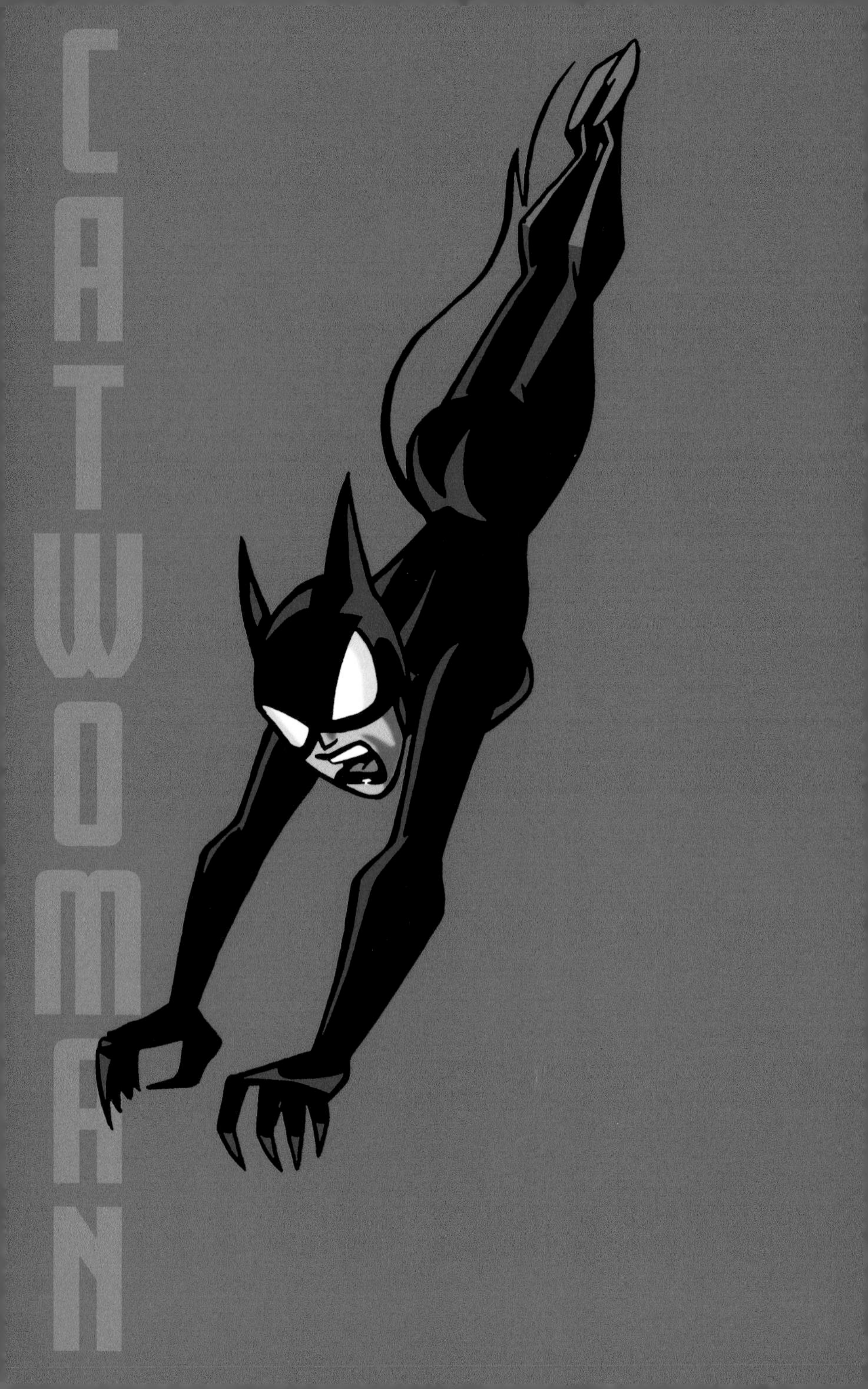
CATWOMAN

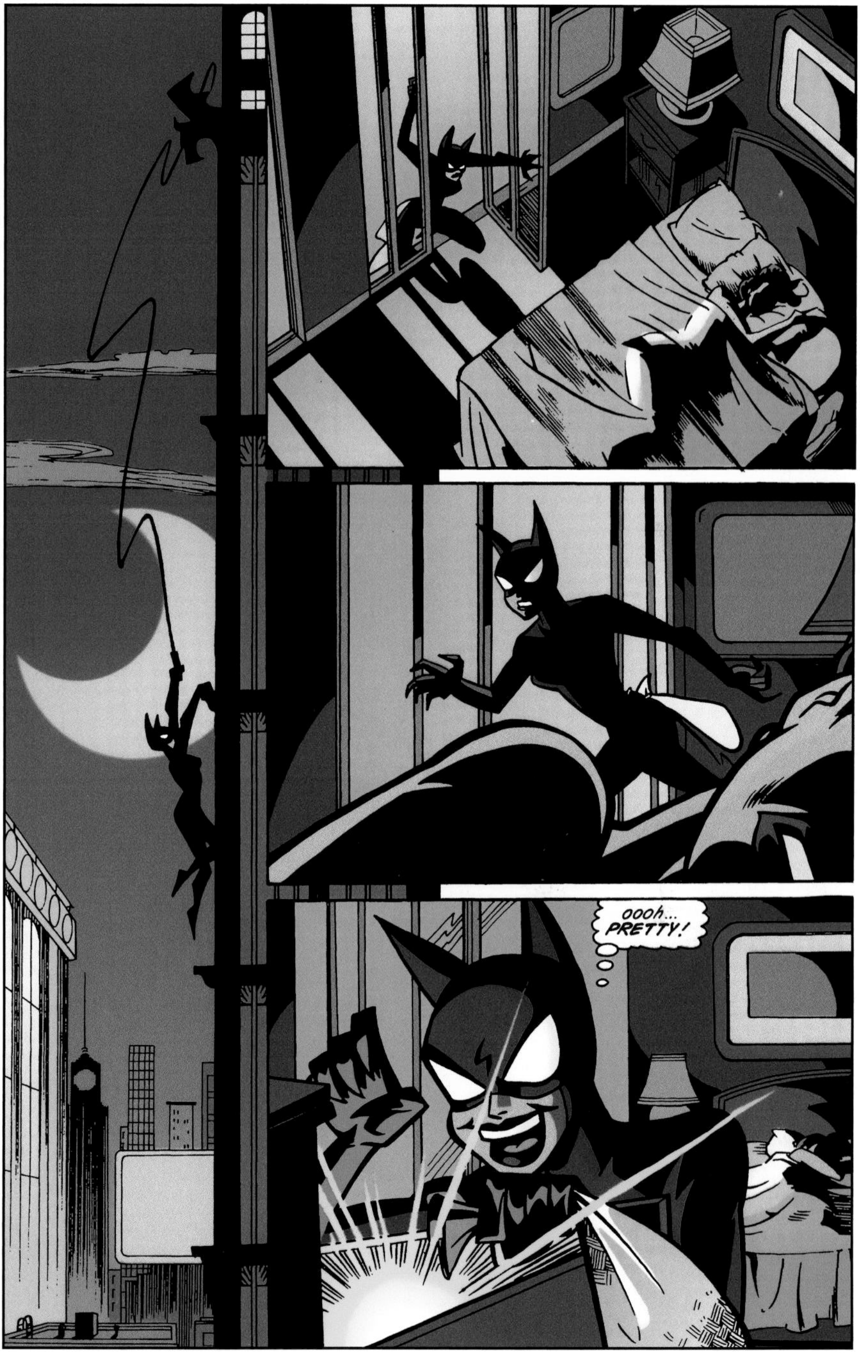
oooh...
PRETTY!

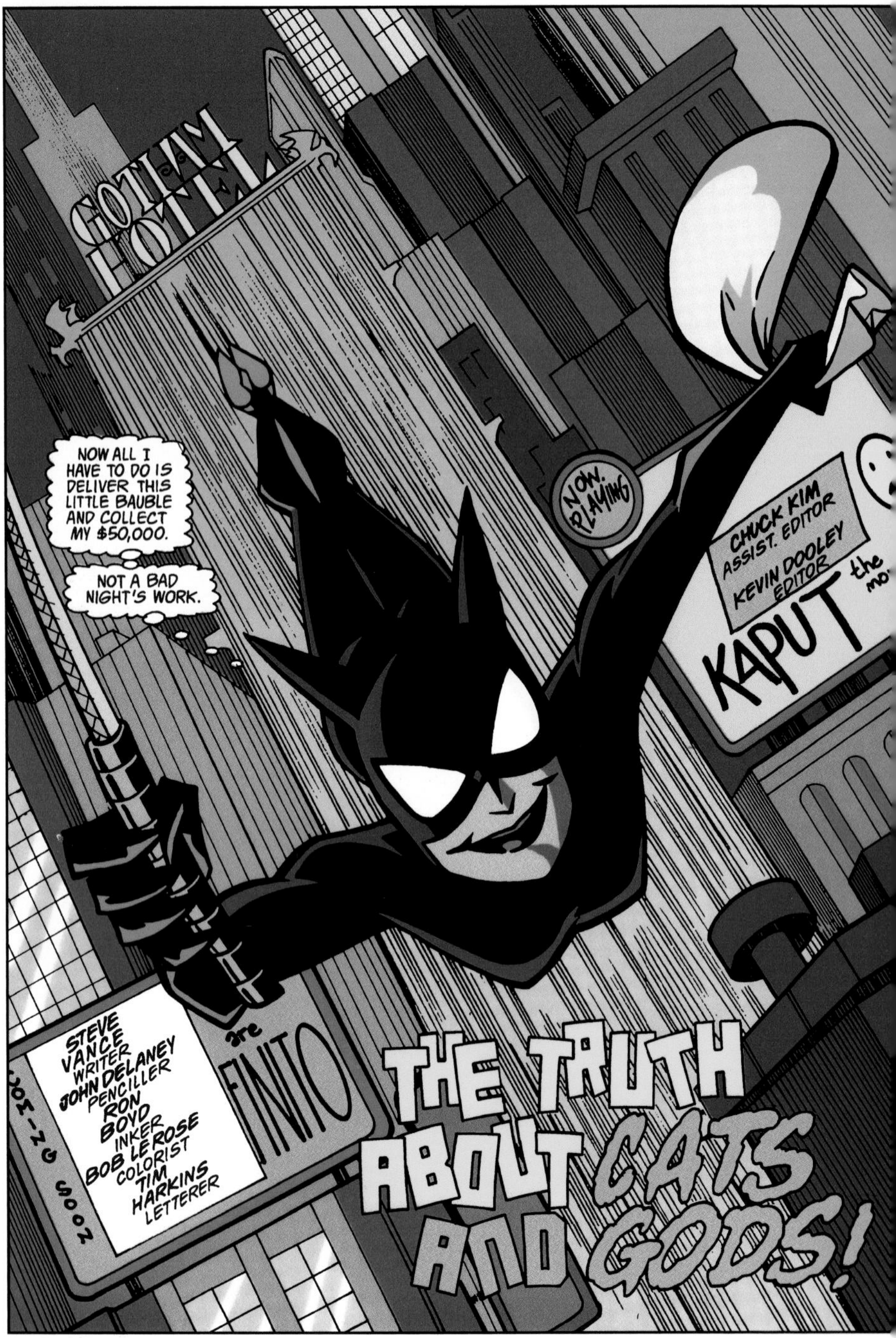
GOTHAM HOTEL
NOW ALL I HAVE TO DO IS DELIVER THIS LITTLE BAUBLE AND COLLECT MY $50,000.
NOT A BAD NIGHT'S WORK.
NOW PLAYING
CHUCK KIM ASSIST. EDITOR
KEVIN DOOLEY EDITOR
KAPUT the
STEVE VANCE WRITER
JOHN DELANEY PENCILLER
RON BOYD INKER
BOB LEROSE COLORIST
TIM HARKINS LETTERER
are FINITO
THE TRUTH ABOUT CATS AND GODS!

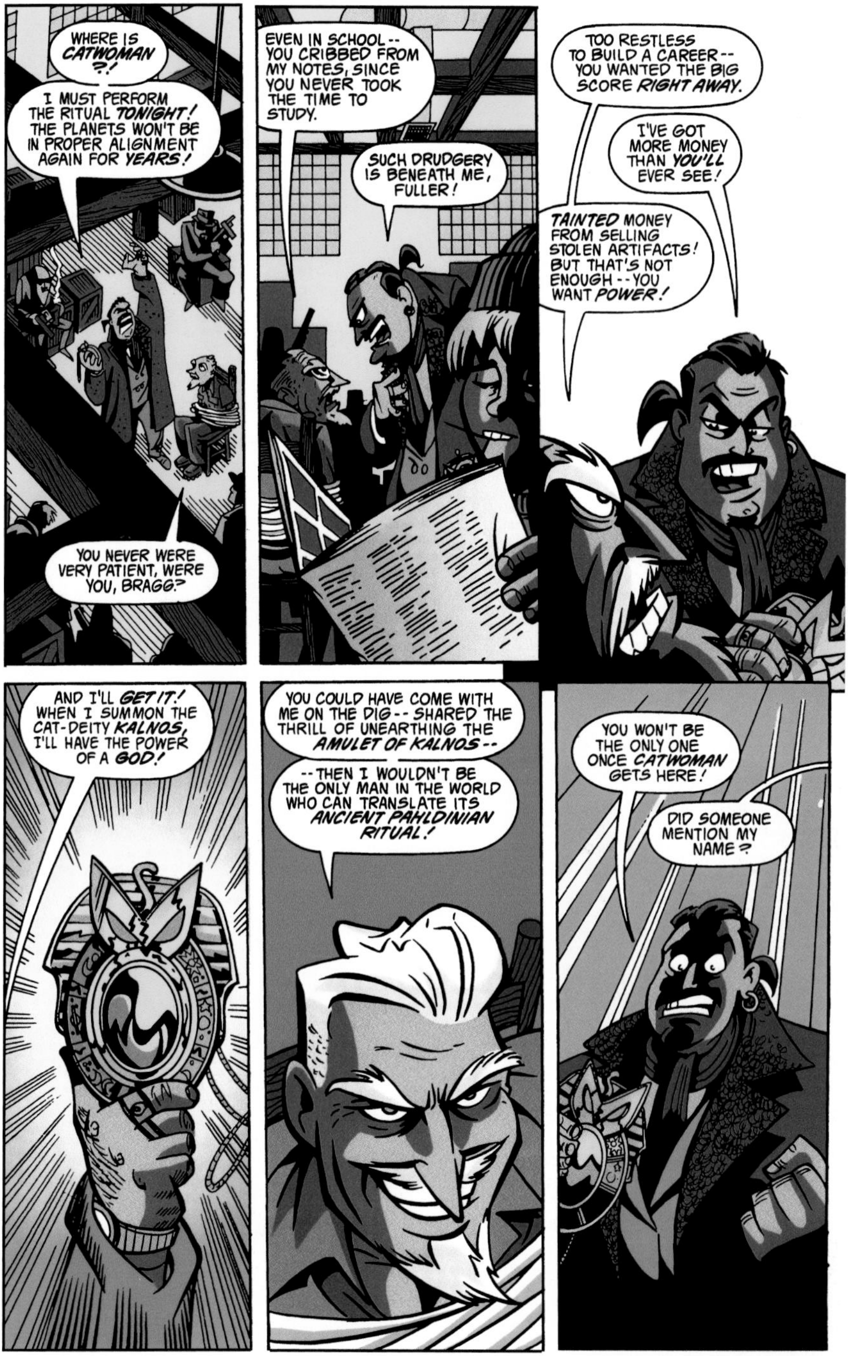
WHERE IS CATWOMAN ?!
I MUST PERFORM THE RITUAL TONIGHT! THE PLANETS WON'T BE IN PROPER ALIGNMENT AGAIN FOR YEARS!
YOU NEVER WERE VERY PATIENT, WERE YOU, BRAGG?
EVEN IN SCHOOL -- YOU CRIBBED FROM MY NOTES, SINCE YOU NEVER TOOK THE TIME TO STUDY.
SUCH DRUDGERY IS BENEATH ME, FULLER!
TOO RESTLESS TO BUILD A CAREER -- YOU WANTED THE BIG SCORE RIGHT AWAY.
I'VE GOT MORE MONEY THAN YOU'LL EVER SEE!
TAINTED MONEY FROM SELLING STOLEN ARTIFACTS! BUT THAT'S NOT ENOUGH -- YOU WANT POWER!
AND I'LL GET IT! WHEN I SUMMON THE CAT-DEITY KALNOS, I'LL HAVE THE POWER OF A GOD!
YOU COULD HAVE COME WITH ME ON THE DIG -- SHARED THE THRILL OF UNEARTHING THE AMULET OF KALNOS --
-- THEN I WOULDN'T BE THE ONLY MAN IN THE WORLD WHO CAN TRANSLATE ITS ANCIENT PAHLDINIAN RITUAL!
YOU WON'T BE THE ONLY ONE ONCE CATWOMAN GETS HERE!
DID SOMEONE MENTION MY NAME?

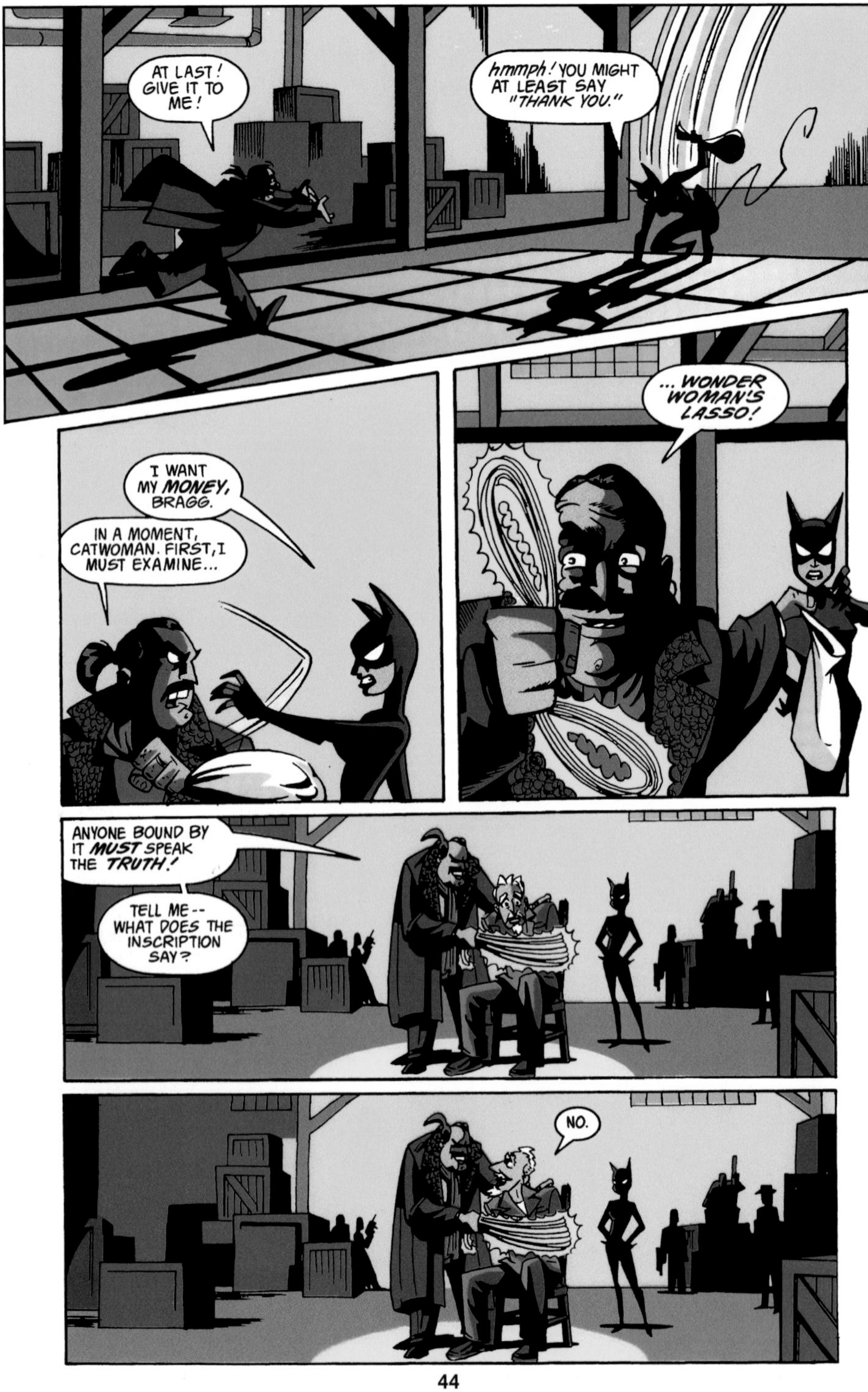
AT LAST! GIVE IT TO ME!
hmmph! YOU MIGHT AT LEAST SAY "THANK YOU."
I WANT MY MONEY, BRAGG.
IN A MOMENT, CATWOMAN. FIRST, I MUST EXAMINE...
...WONDER WOMAN'S LASSO!
ANYONE BOUND BY IT MUST SPEAK THE TRUTH!
TELL ME -- WHAT DOES THE INSCRIPTION SAY?
NO.

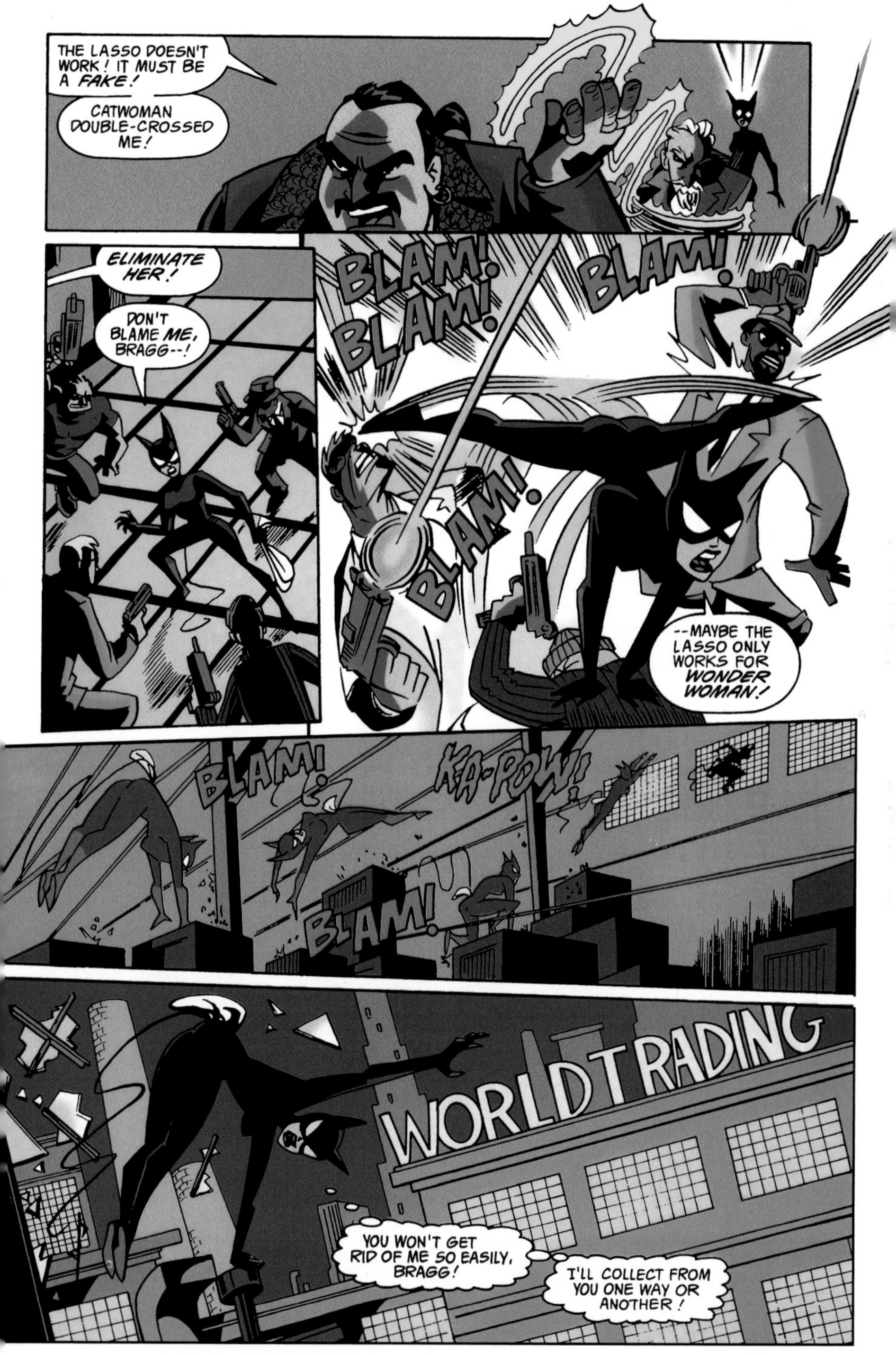
THE LASSO DOESN'T WORK! IT MUST BE A FAKE!
CATWOMAN DOUBLE-CROSSED ME!
ELIMINATE HER!
DON'T BLAME ME, BRAGG--!
BLAM! BLAM! BLAM!
BLAM!
BLAM!
--MAYBE THE LASSO ONLY WORKS FOR WONDER WOMAN!
BLAM!
KA-POW!
BLAM!
WORLD TRADING
YOU WON'T GET RID OF ME SO EASILY, BRAGG!
I'LL COLLECT FROM YOU ONE WAY OR ANOTHER!

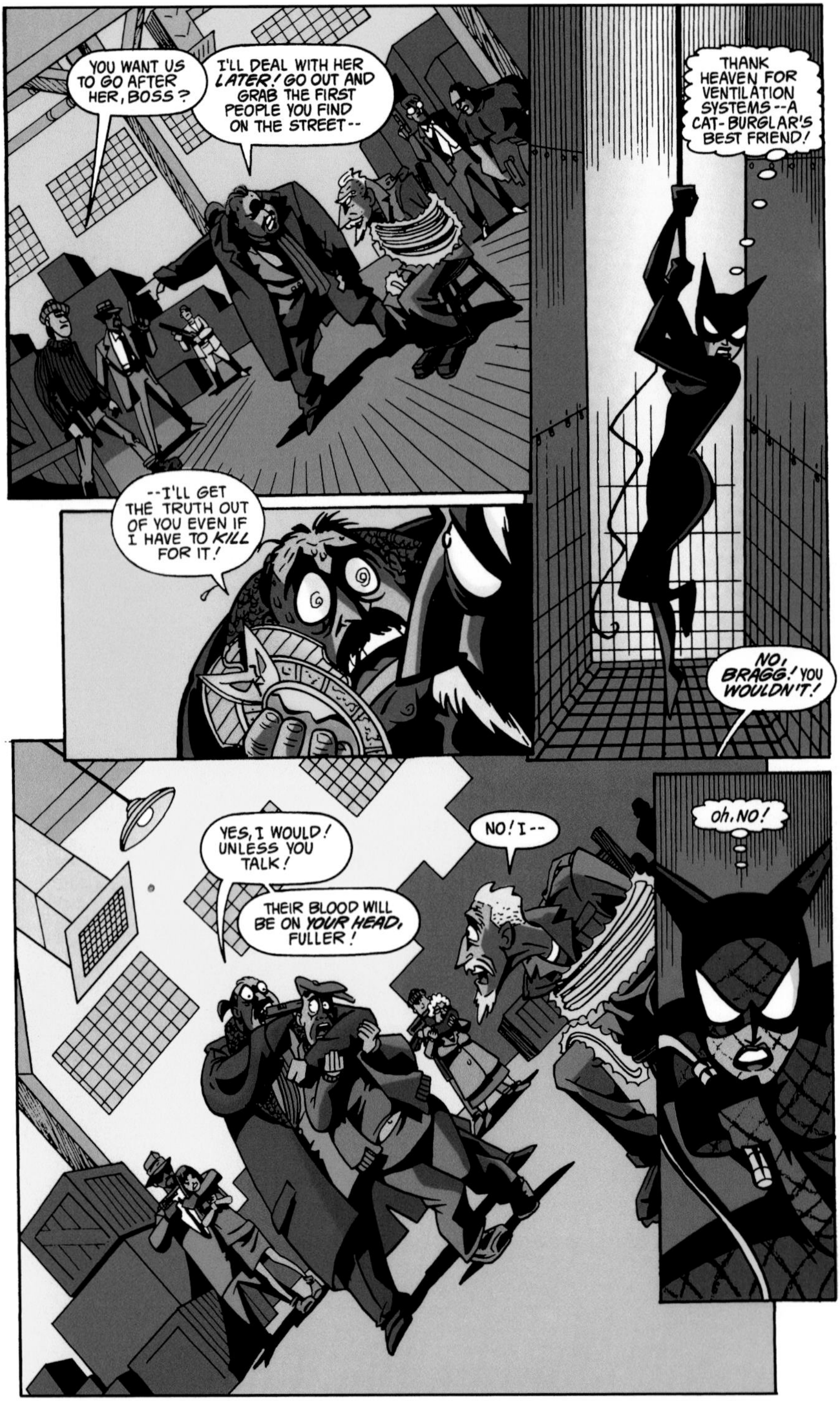
YOU WANT US TO GO AFTER HER, BOSS?
I'LL DEAL WITH HER LATER! GO OUT AND GRAB THE FIRST PEOPLE YOU FIND ON THE STREET--
THANK HEAVEN FOR VENTILATION SYSTEMS--A CAT-BURGLAR'S BEST FRIEND!
--I'LL GET THE TRUTH OUT OF YOU EVEN IF I HAVE TO KILL FOR IT!
NO, BRAGG! YOU WOULDN'T!
YES, I WOULD! UNLESS YOU TALK!
THEIR BLOOD WILL BE ON YOUR HEAD, FULLER!
NO! I--
oh, NO!

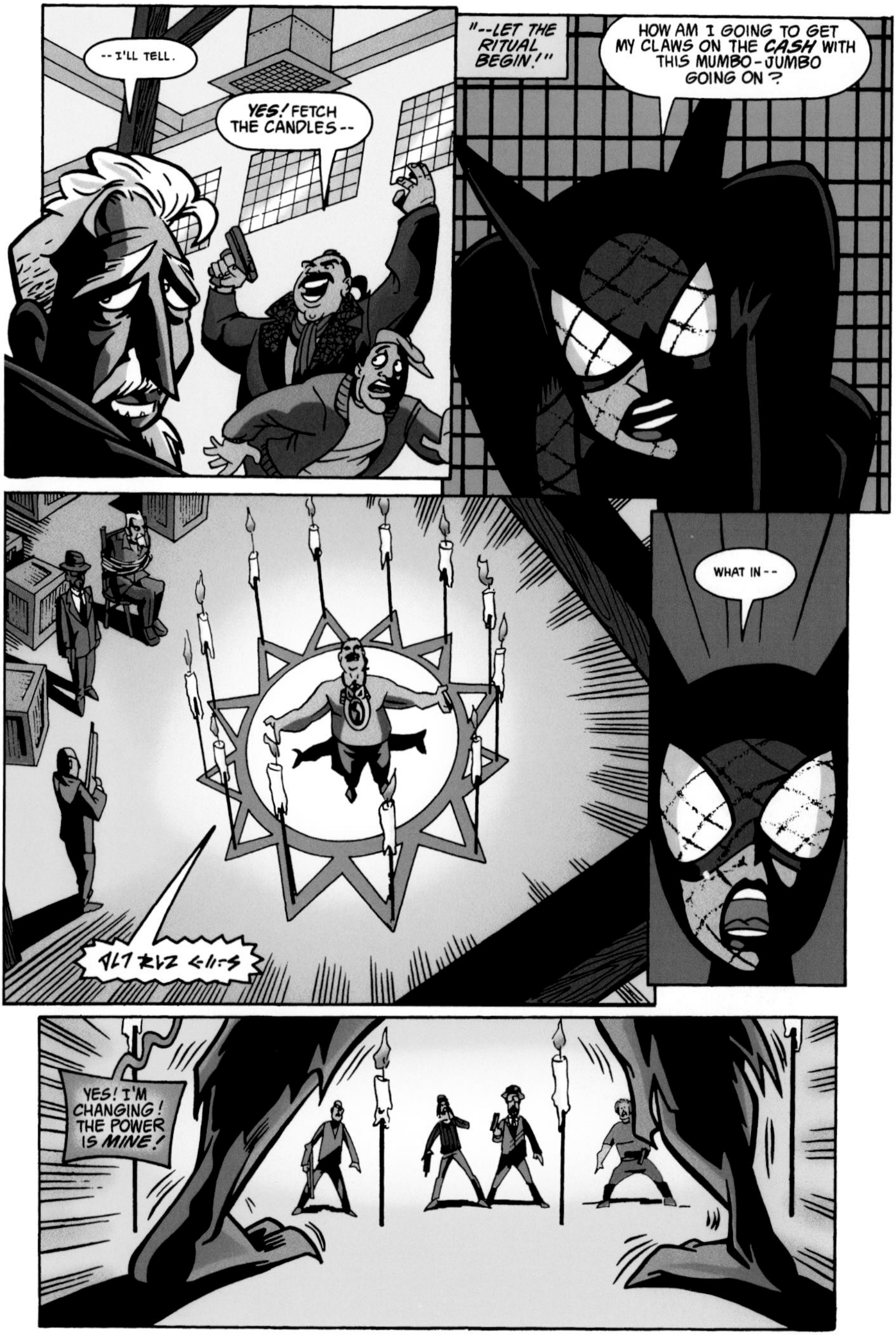
-- I'LL TELL.
YES! FETCH THE CANDLES --
"--LET THE RITUAL BEGIN!"
HOW AM I GOING TO GET MY CLAWS ON THE CASH WITH THIS MUMBO-JUMBO GOING ON?
WHAT IN --
YES! I'M CHANGING! THE POWER IS MINE!

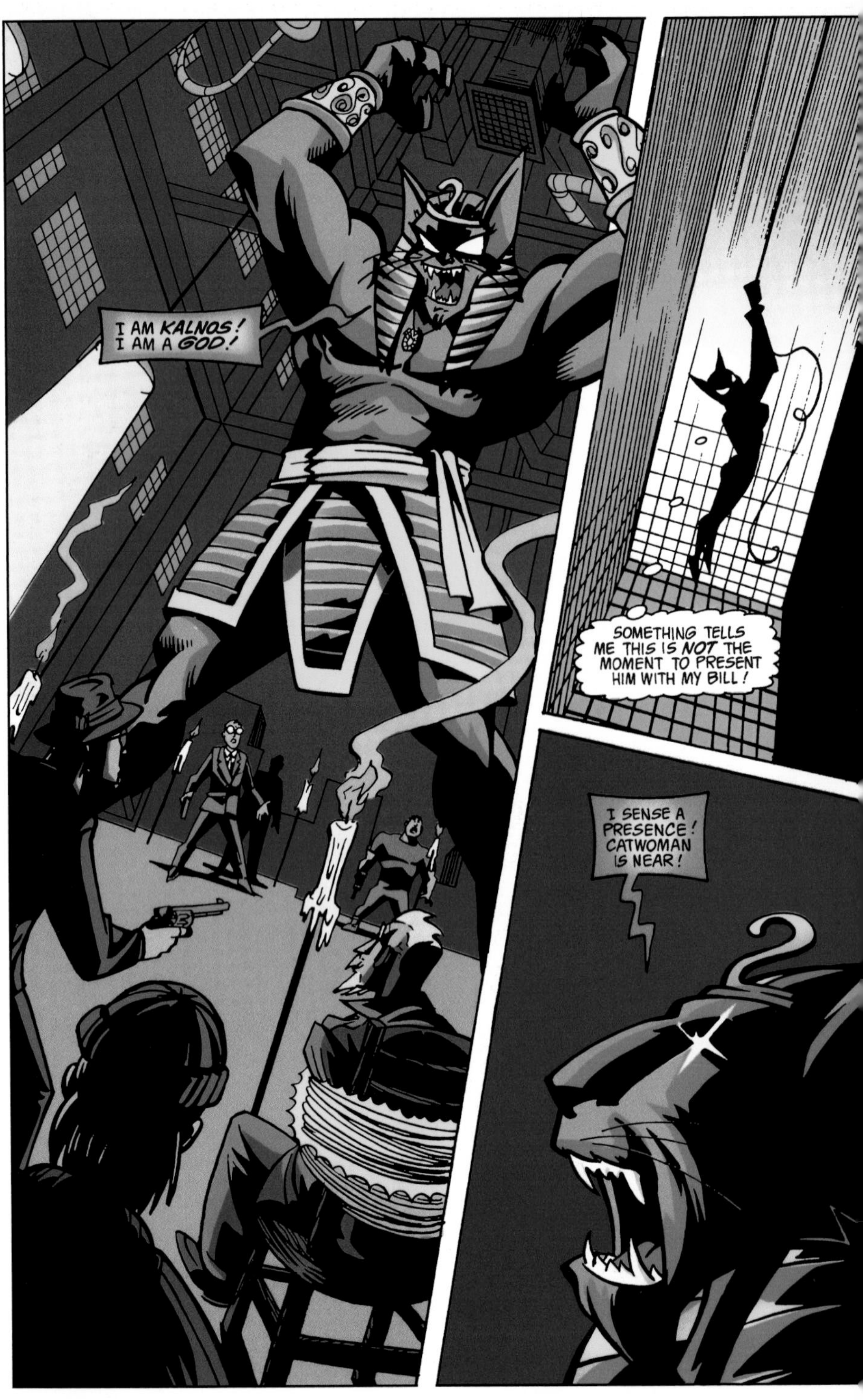
I AM KALNOS! I AM A GOD!
SOMETHING TELLS ME THIS IS NOT THE MOMENT TO PRESENT HIM WITH MY BILL!
I SENSE A PRESENCE! CATWOMAN IS NEAR!

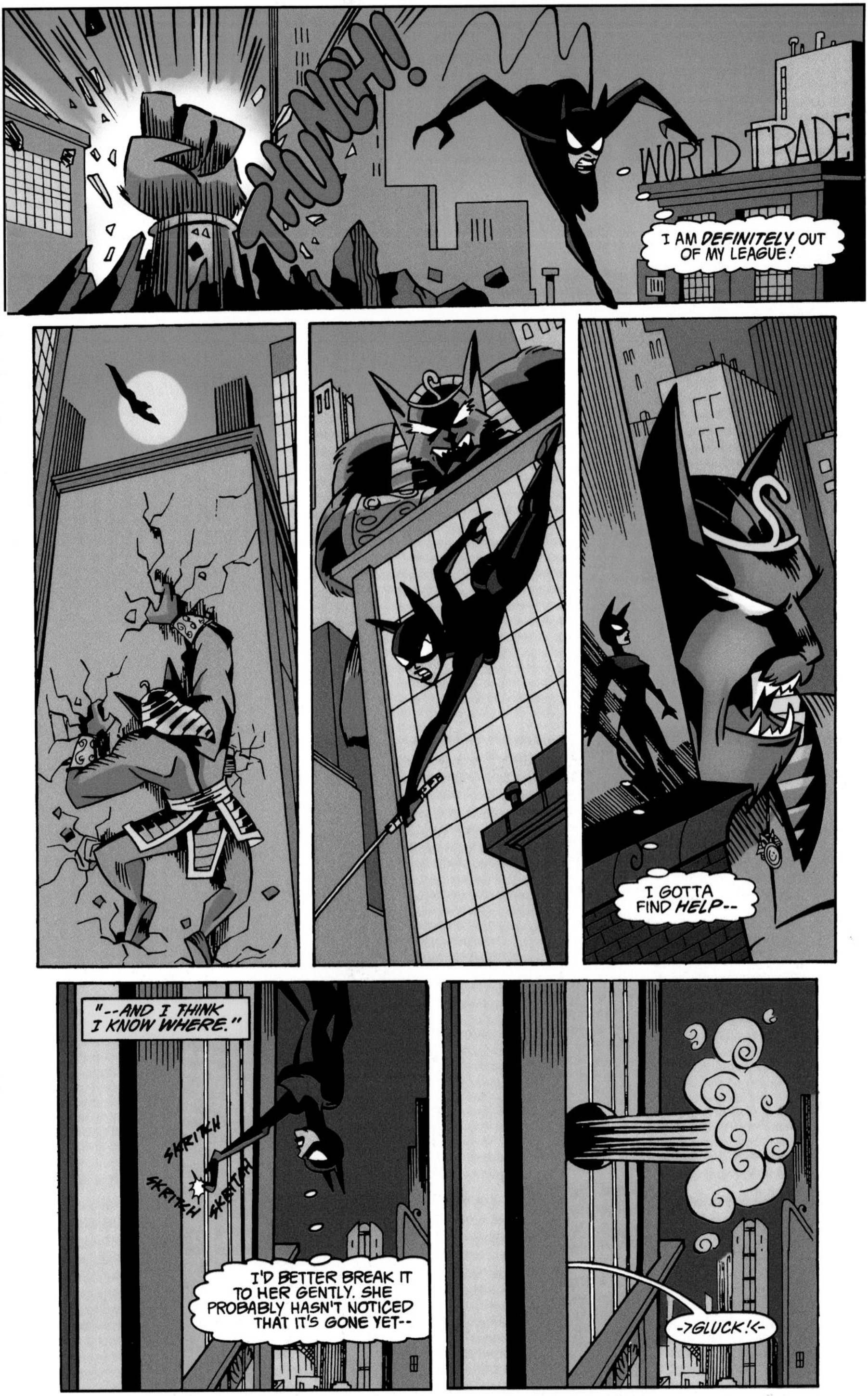
THUNCH!
WORLD TRADE
I AM DEFINITELY OUT OF MY LEAGUE!
I GOTTA FIND HELP--
"--AND I THINK I KNOW WHERE."
SKRITCH
SKRITCH
SKRITCH
I'D BETTER BREAK IT TO HER GENTLY. SHE PROBABLY HASN'T NOTICED THAT IT'S GONE YET--
->GLUCK!<-

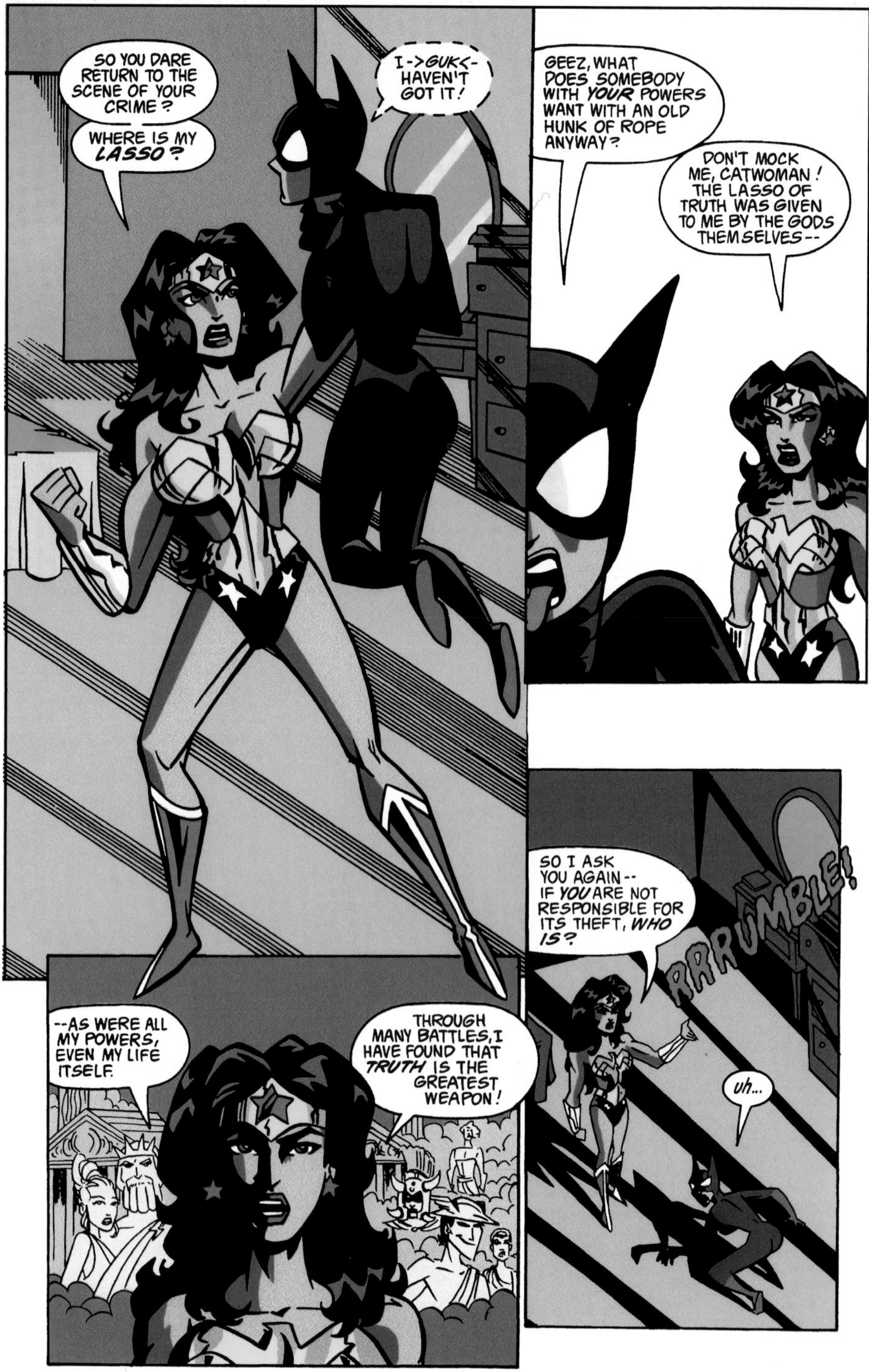
SO YOU DARE RETURN TO THE SCENE OF YOUR CRIME?
WHERE IS MY LASSO?
I->GUK<- HAVEN'T GOT IT!
GEEZ, WHAT DOES SOMEBODY WITH YOUR POWERS WANT WITH AN OLD HUNK OF ROPE ANYWAY?
DON'T MOCK ME, CATWOMAN! THE LASSO OF TRUTH WAS GIVEN TO ME BY THE GODS THEMSELVES--
--AS WERE ALL MY POWERS, EVEN MY LIFE ITSELF.
THROUGH MANY BATTLES, I HAVE FOUND THAT TRUTH IS THE GREATEST WEAPON!
SO I ASK YOU AGAIN-- IF YOU ARE NOT RESPONSIBLE FOR ITS THEFT, WHO IS?
RRRUMBLE!
uh...

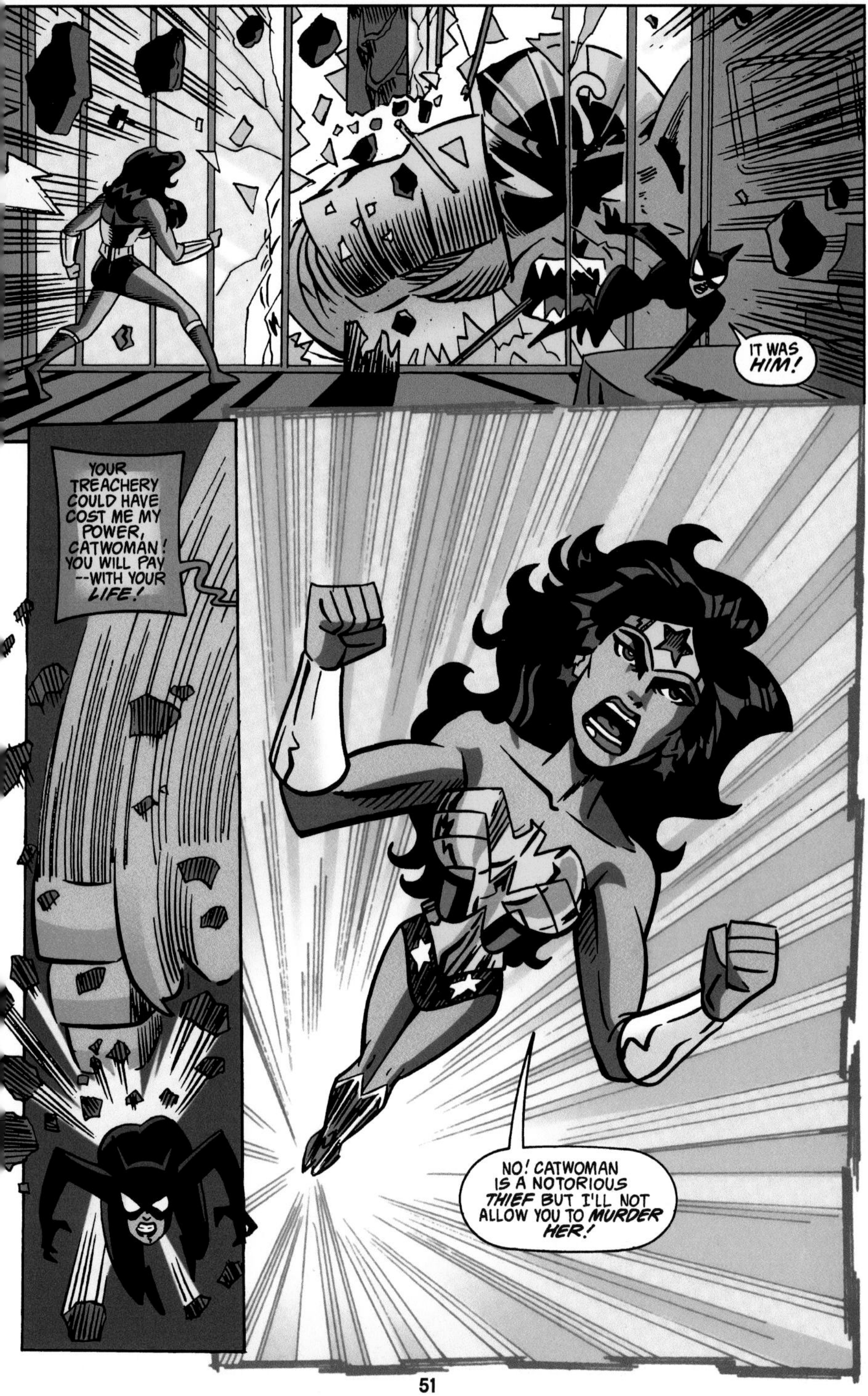
IT WAS HIM!
YOUR TREACHERY COULD HAVE COST ME MY POWER, CATWOMAN! YOU WILL PAY --WITH YOUR LIFE!
NO! CATWOMAN IS A NOTORIOUS THIEF BUT I'LL NOT ALLOW YOU TO MURDER HER!

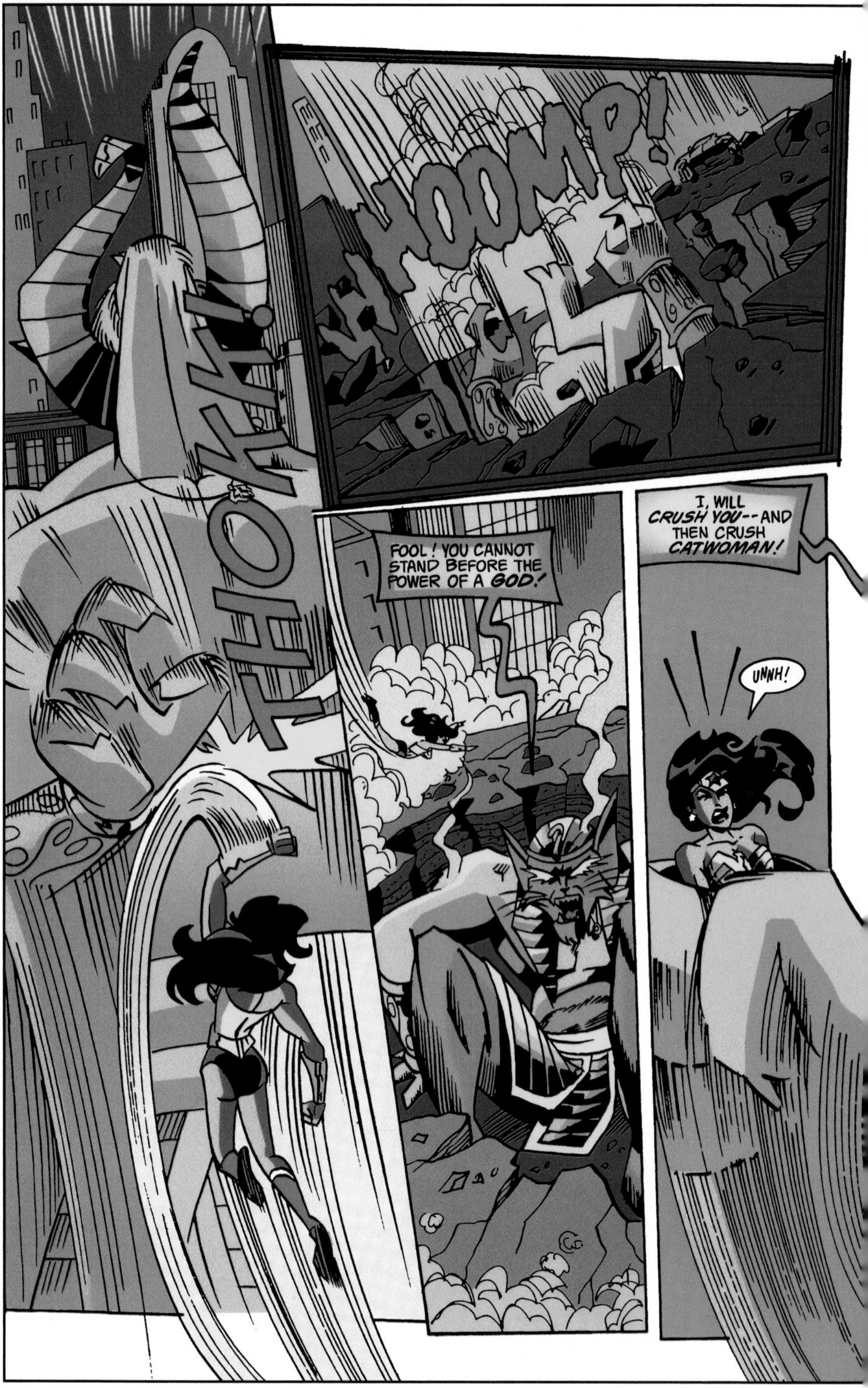
WHOOMP!
THOOM!
FOOL! YOU CANNOT STAND BEFORE THE POWER OF A GOD!
I, WILL CRUSH YOU--AND THEN CRUSH CATWOMAN!
UNNH!

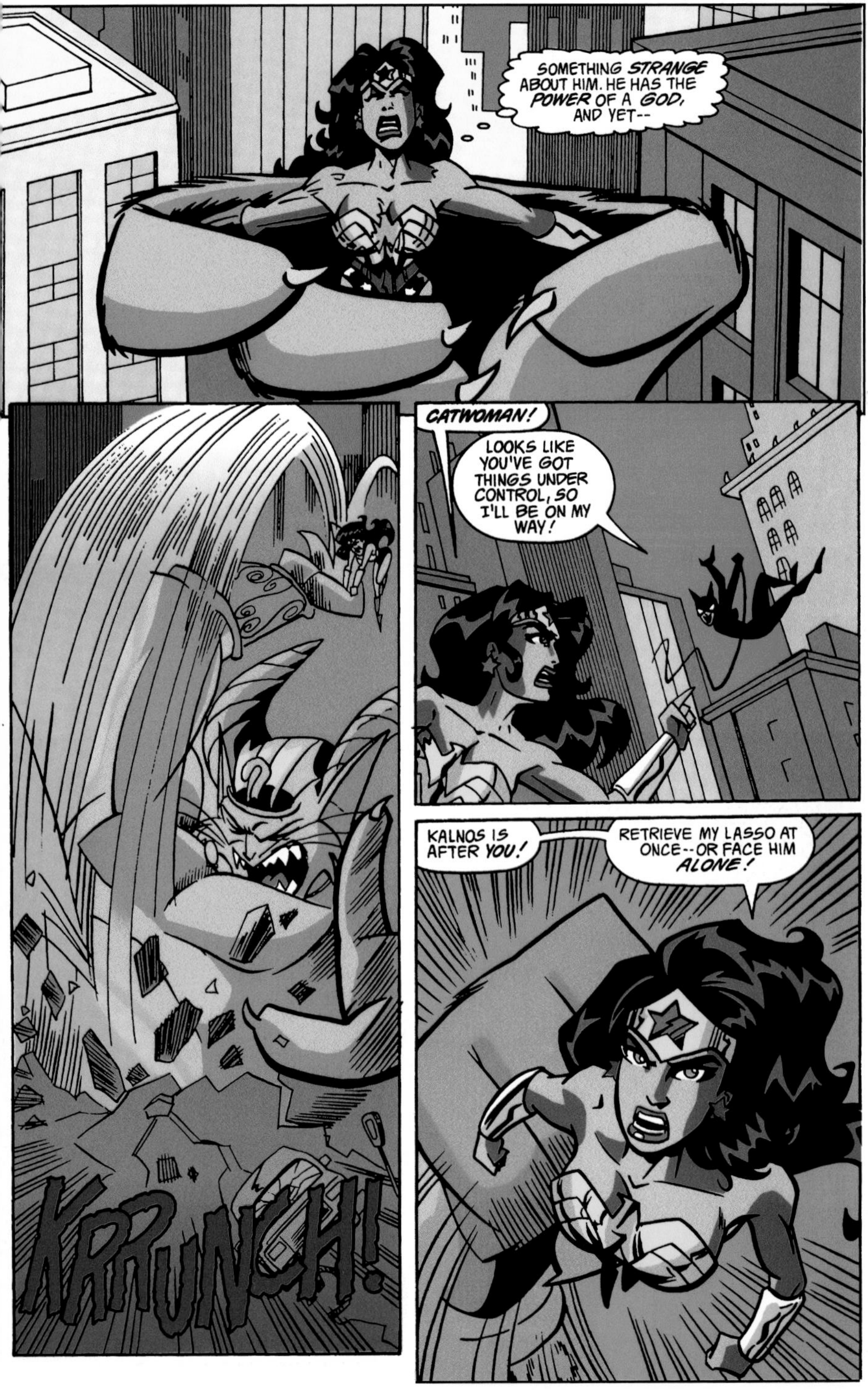
SOMETHING STRANGE ABOUT HIM. HE HAS THE POWER OF A GOD, AND YET--
KRRUNCH!
CATWOMAN!
LOOKS LIKE YOU'VE GOT THINGS UNDER CONTROL, SO I'LL BE ON MY WAY!
KALNOS IS AFTER YOU!
RETRIEVE MY LASSO AT ONCE--OR FACE HIM ALONE!

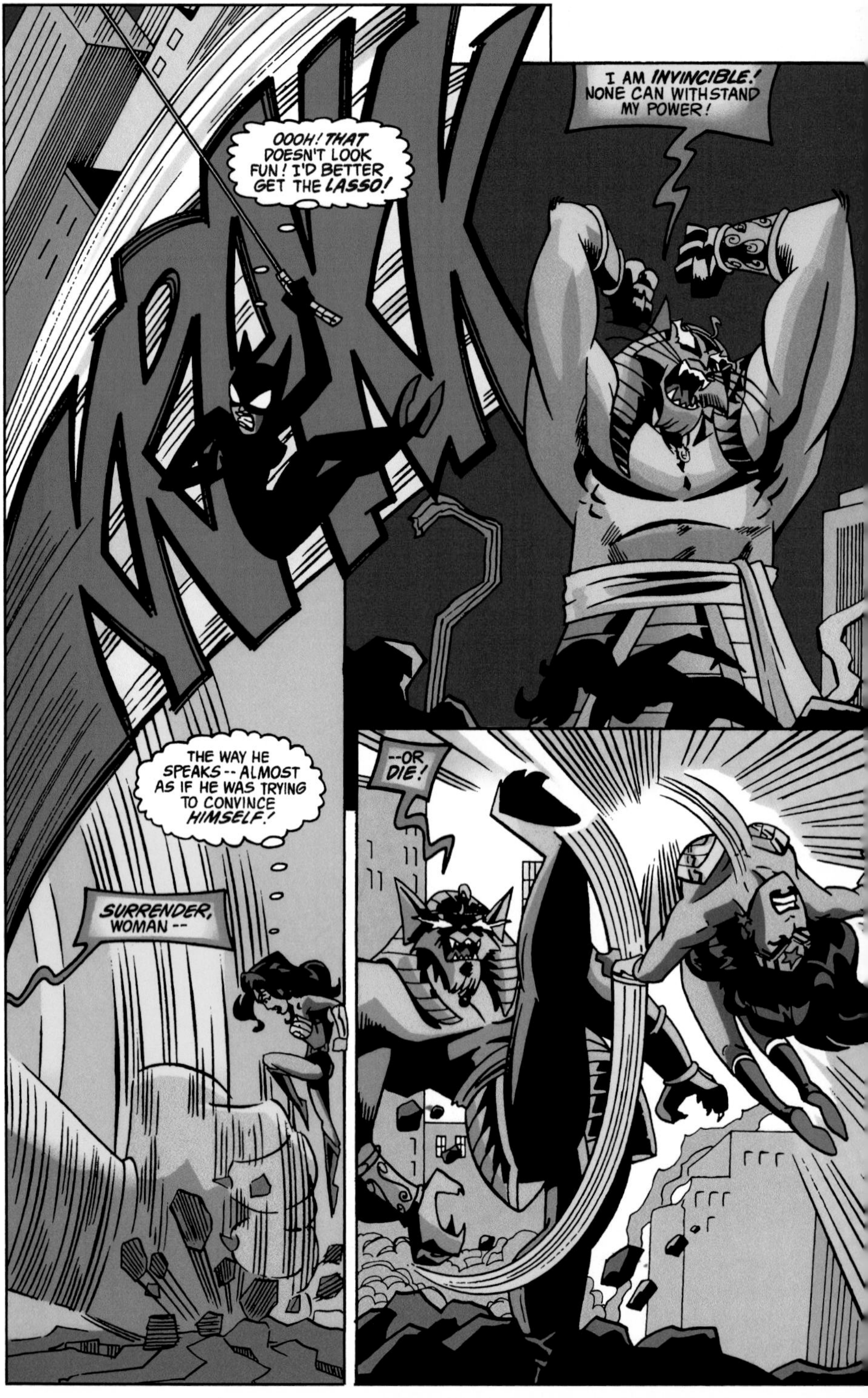
OOOH! THAT DOESN'T LOOK FUN! I'D BETTER GET THE LASSO!
I AM INVINCIBLE! NONE CAN WITHSTAND MY POWER!
THE WAY HE SPEAKS -- ALMOST AS IF HE WAS TRYING TO CONVINCE HIMSELF!
SURRENDER, WOMAN --
--OR DIE!

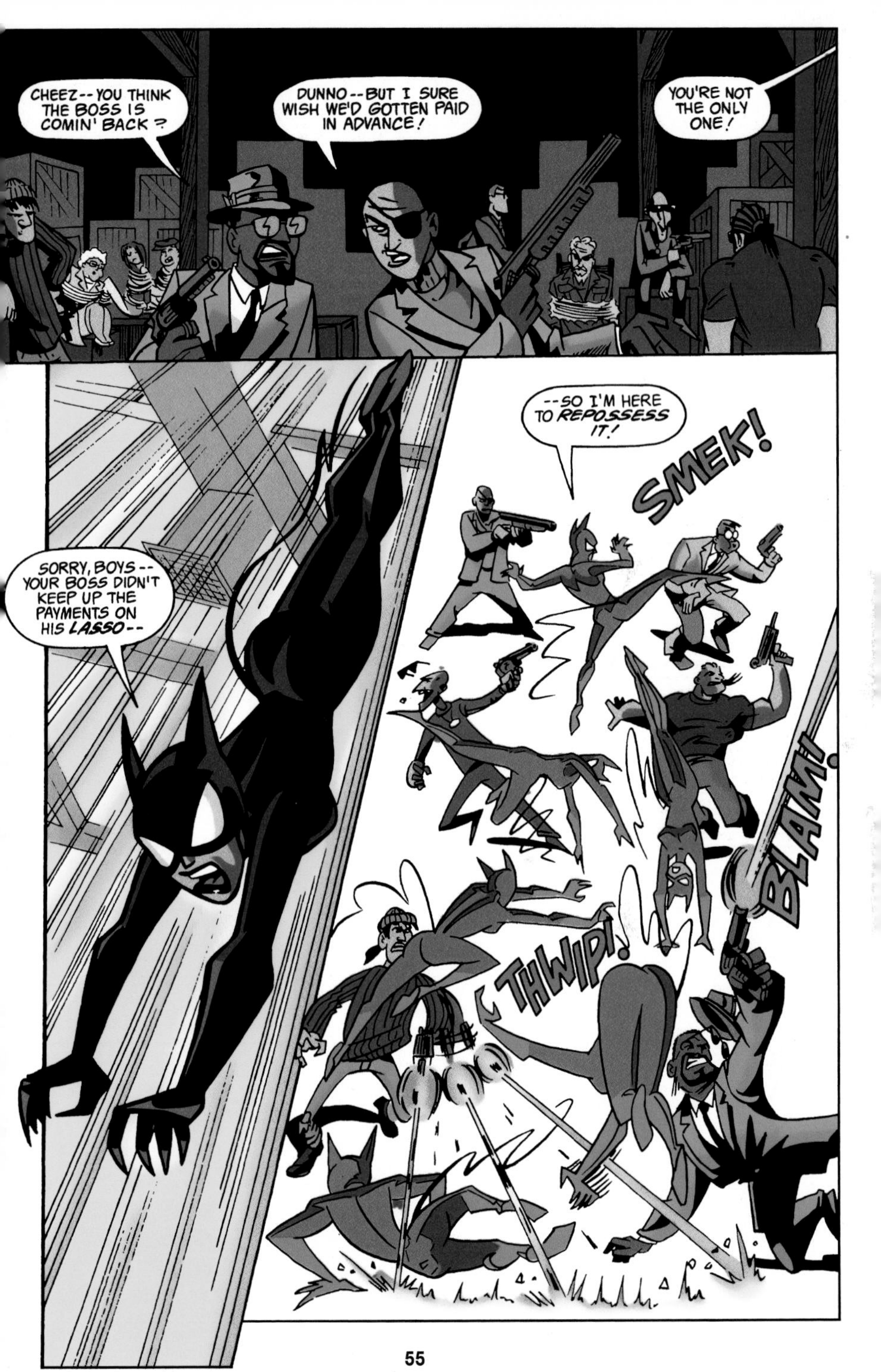
CHEEZ--YOU THINK THE BOSS IS COMIN' BACK?
DUNNO--BUT I SURE WISH WE'D GOTTEN PAID IN ADVANCE!
YOU'RE NOT THE ONLY ONE!
SORRY, BOYS--YOUR BOSS DIDN'T KEEP UP THE PAYMENTS ON HIS LASSO--
--SO I'M HERE TO REPOSSESS IT!
SMEK!
BLAM!
THWIP!

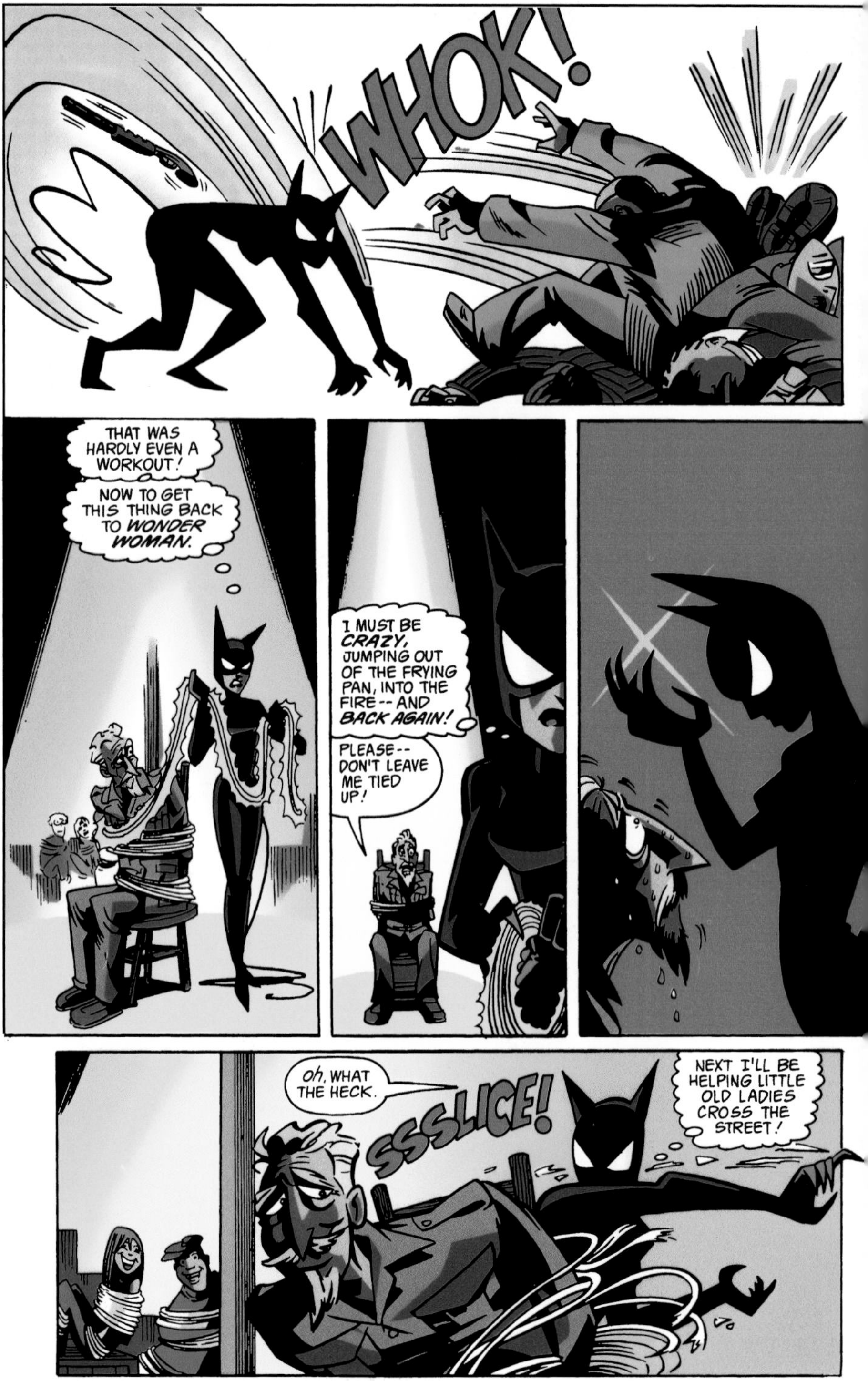
WHOK!
THAT WAS HARDLY EVEN A WORKOUT!
NOW TO GET THIS THING BACK TO WONDER WOMAN.
I MUST BE CRAZY, JUMPING OUT OF THE FRYING PAN, INTO THE FIRE-- AND BACK AGAIN!
PLEASE-- DON'T LEAVE ME TIED UP!
Oh, WHAT THE HECK.
SSSLICE!
NEXT I'LL BE HELPING LITTLE OLD LADIES CROSS THE STREET!

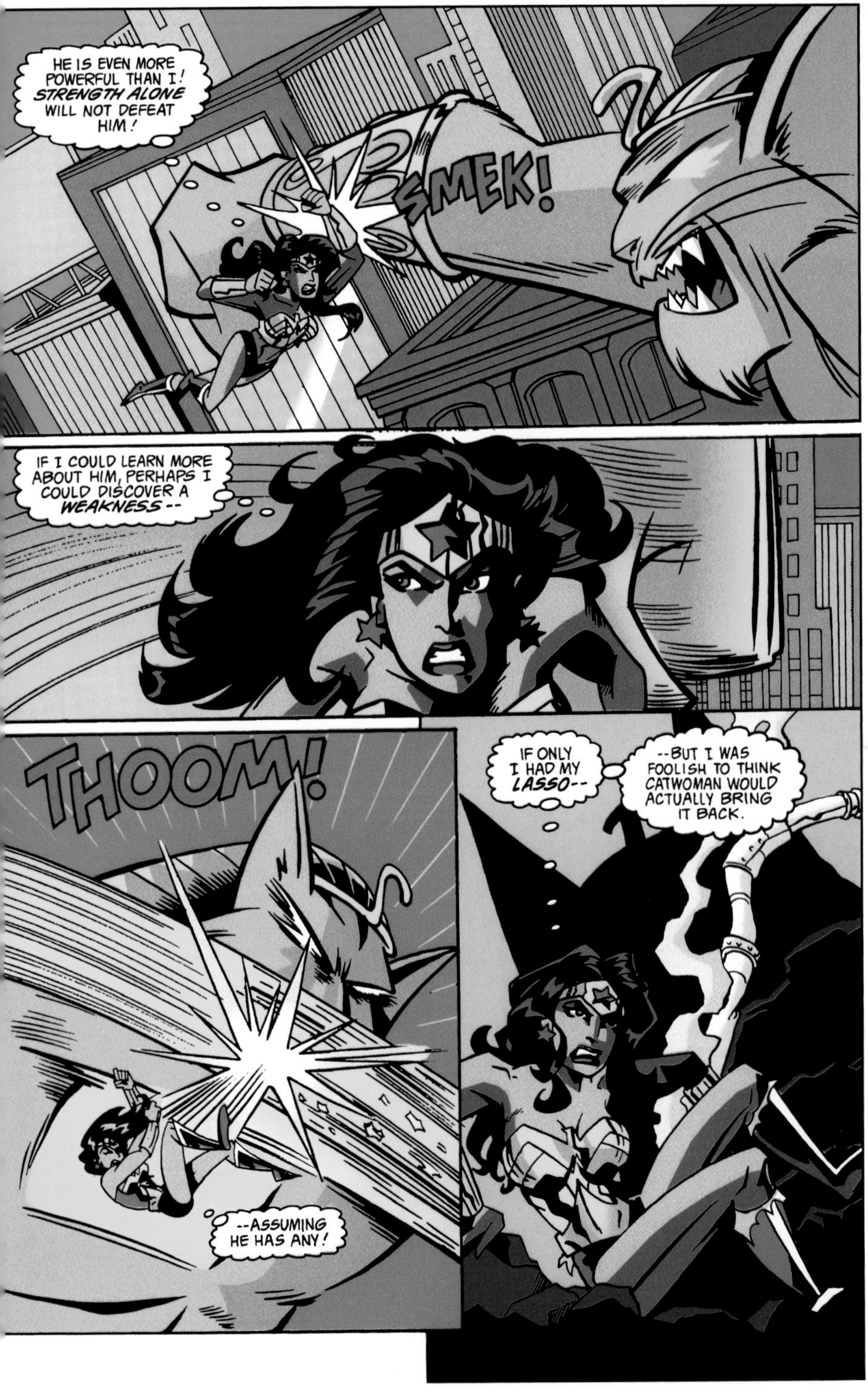
HE IS EVEN MORE POWERFUL THAN I! STRENGTH ALONE WILL NOT DEFEAT HIM!
SMEK!
IF I COULD LEARN MORE ABOUT HIM, PERHAPS I COULD DISCOVER A WEAKNESS--
THOOM!
--ASSUMING HE HAS ANY!
IF ONLY I HAD MY LASSO--
--BUT I WAS FOOLISH TO THINK CATWOMAN WOULD ACTUALLY BRING IT BACK.

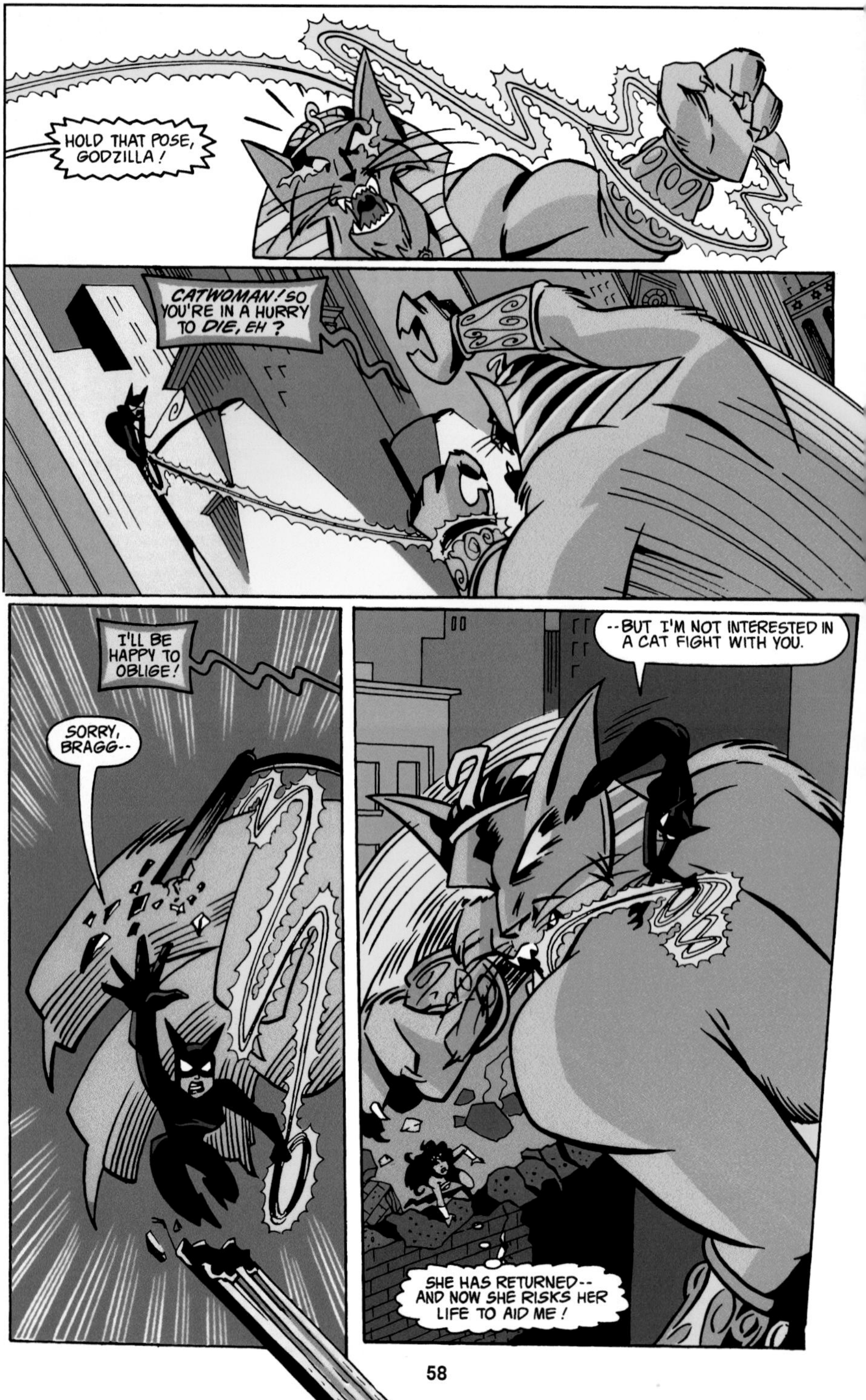
HOLD THAT POSE, GODZILLA!
CATWOMAN! SO YOU'RE IN A HURRY TO DIE, EH?
I'LL BE HAPPY TO OBLIGE!
SORRY, BRAGG--
--BUT I'M NOT INTERESTED IN A CAT FIGHT WITH YOU.
SHE HAS RETURNED-- AND NOW SHE RISKS HER LIFE TO AID ME!

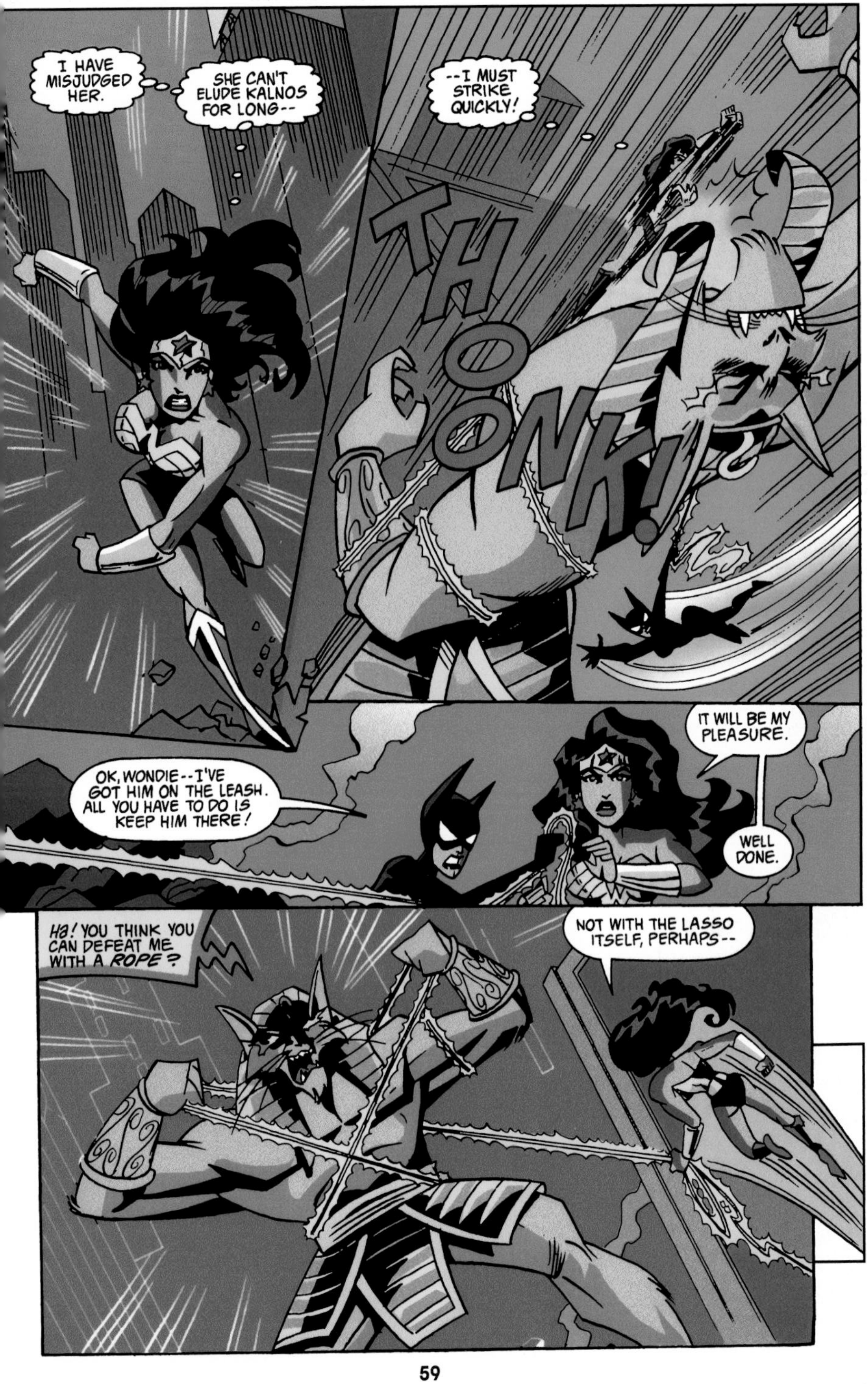
I HAVE MISJUDGED HER.
SHE CAN'T ELUDE KALNOS FOR LONG--
--I MUST STRIKE QUICKLY!
THOONK!
OK, WONDIE--I'VE GOT HIM ON THE LEASH. ALL YOU HAVE TO DO IS KEEP HIM THERE!
IT WILL BE MY PLEASURE.
WELL DONE.
HA! YOU THINK YOU CAN DEFEAT ME WITH A ROPE?
NOT WITH THE LASSO ITSELF, PERHAPS--

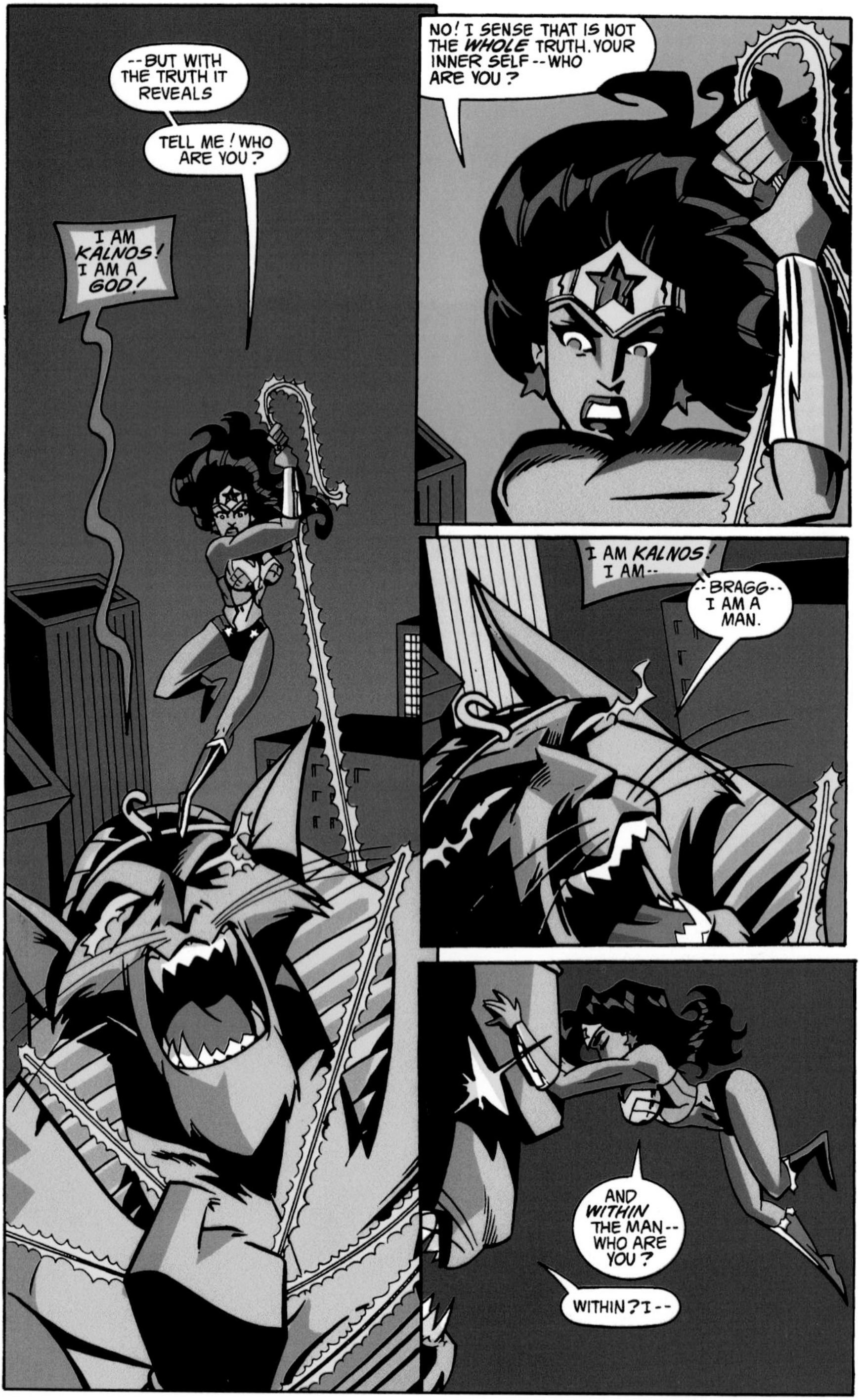
--BUT WITH THE TRUTH IT REVEALS
TELL ME! WHO ARE YOU?
I AM KALNOS! I AM A GOD!
NO! I SENSE THAT IS NOT THE WHOLE TRUTH. YOUR INNER SELF--WHO ARE YOU?
I AM KALNOS! I AM--
--BRAGG--I AM A MAN.
AND WITHIN THE MAN--WHO ARE YOU?
WITHIN? I--

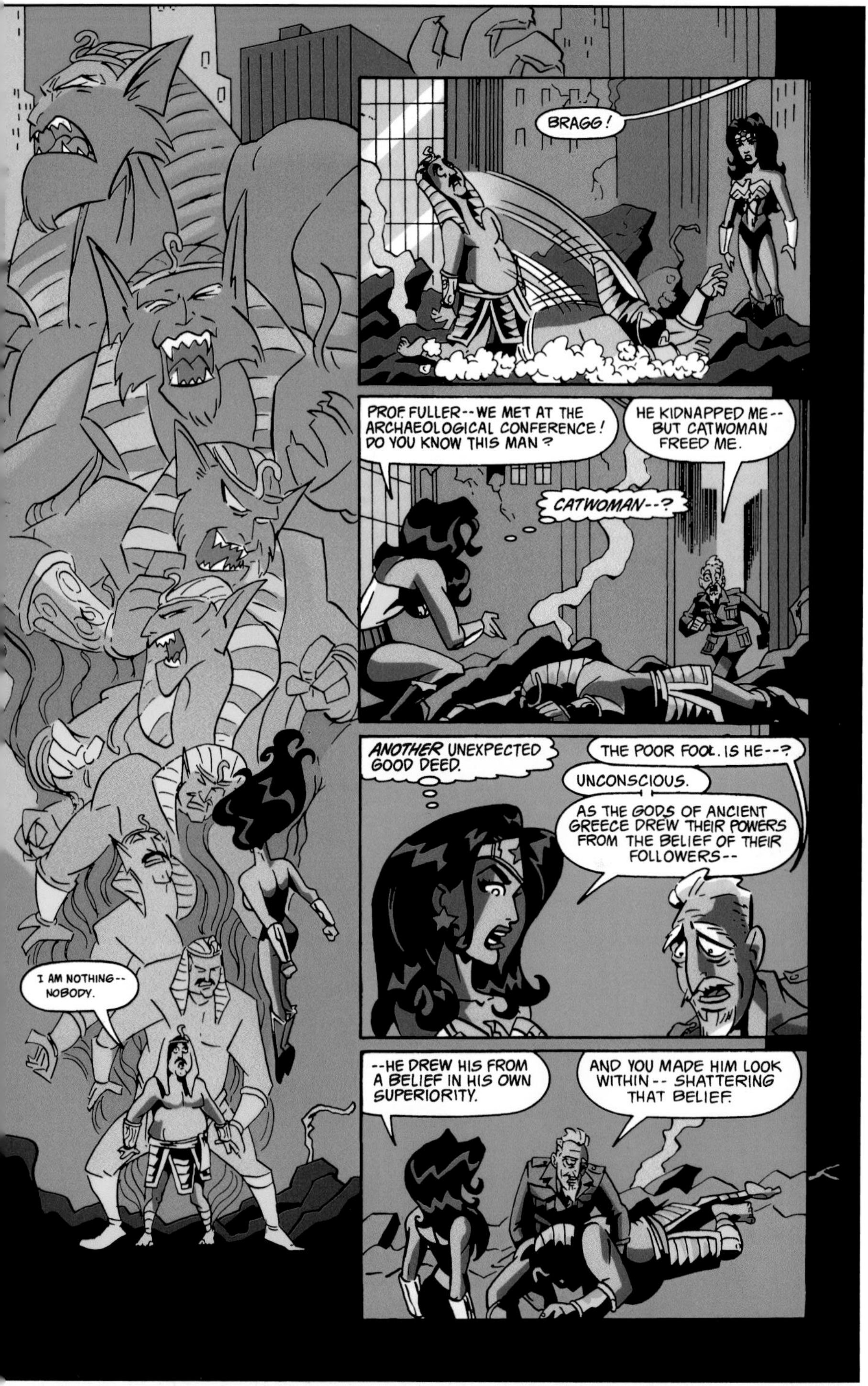
BRAGG!
PROF. FULLER--WE MET AT THE ARCHAEOLOGICAL CONFERENCE! DO YOU KNOW THIS MAN?
HE KIDNAPPED ME--BUT CATWOMAN FREED ME.
CATWOMAN--?
ANOTHER UNEXPECTED GOOD DEED.
THE POOR FOOL. IS HE--?
UNCONSCIOUS.
AS THE GODS OF ANCIENT GREECE DREW THEIR POWERS FROM THE BELIEF OF THEIR FOLLOWERS--
I AM NOTHING--NOBODY.
--HE DREW HIS FROM A BELIEF IN HIS OWN SUPERIORITY.
AND YOU MADE HIM LOOK WITHIN-- SHATTERING THAT BELIEF.

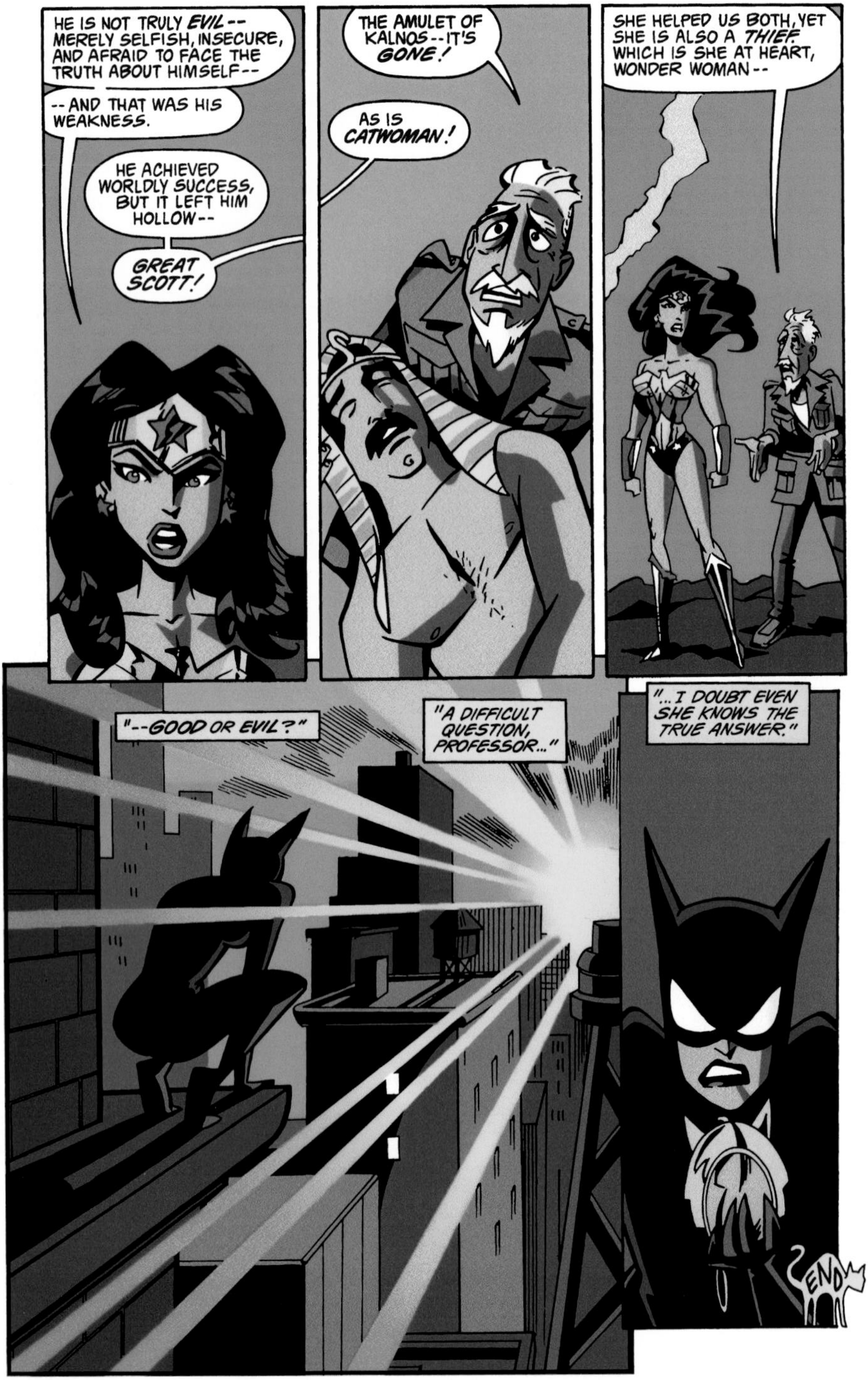
HE IS NOT TRULY EVIL-- MERELY SELFISH, INSECURE, AND AFRAID TO FACE THE TRUTH ABOUT HIMSELF--
--AND THAT WAS HIS WEAKNESS.
HE ACHIEVED WORLDLY SUCCESS, BUT IT LEFT HIM HOLLOW--
GREAT SCOTT!
THE AMULET OF KALNOS--IT'S GONE!
AS IS CATWOMAN!
SHE HELPED US BOTH, YET SHE IS ALSO A THIEF. WHICH IS SHE AT HEART, WONDER WOMAN--
"--GOOD OR EVIL?"
"A DIFFICULT QUESTION, PROFESSOR..."
"...I DOUBT EVEN SHE KNOWS THE TRUE ANSWER."
END

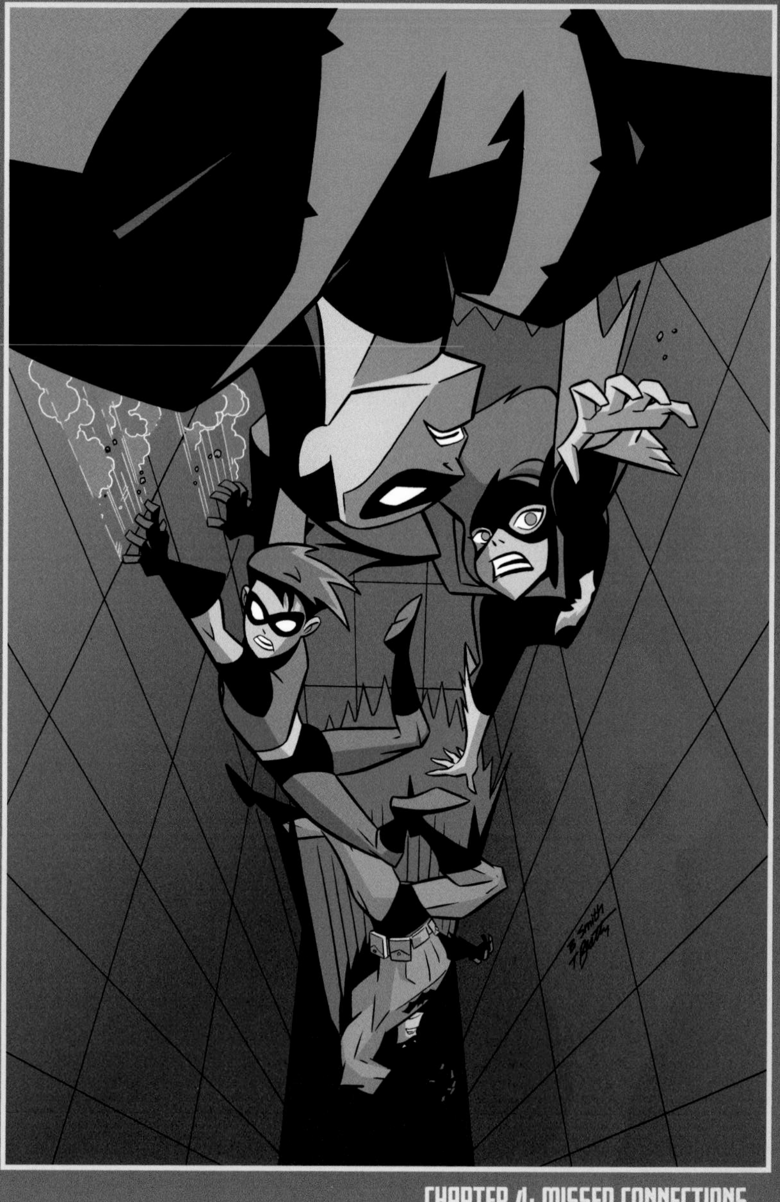

CHAPTER 4: MISSED CONNECTIONS

CATWOMAN

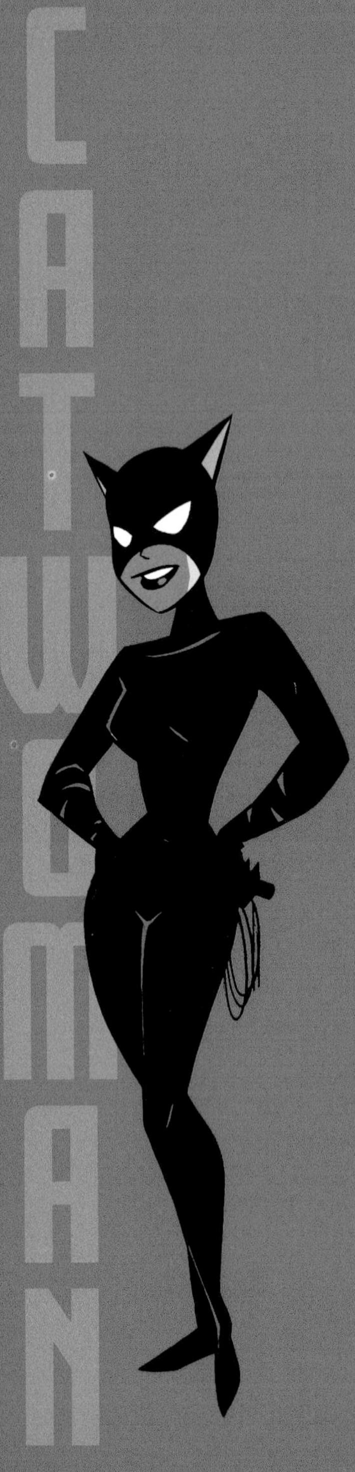
CATWOMAN

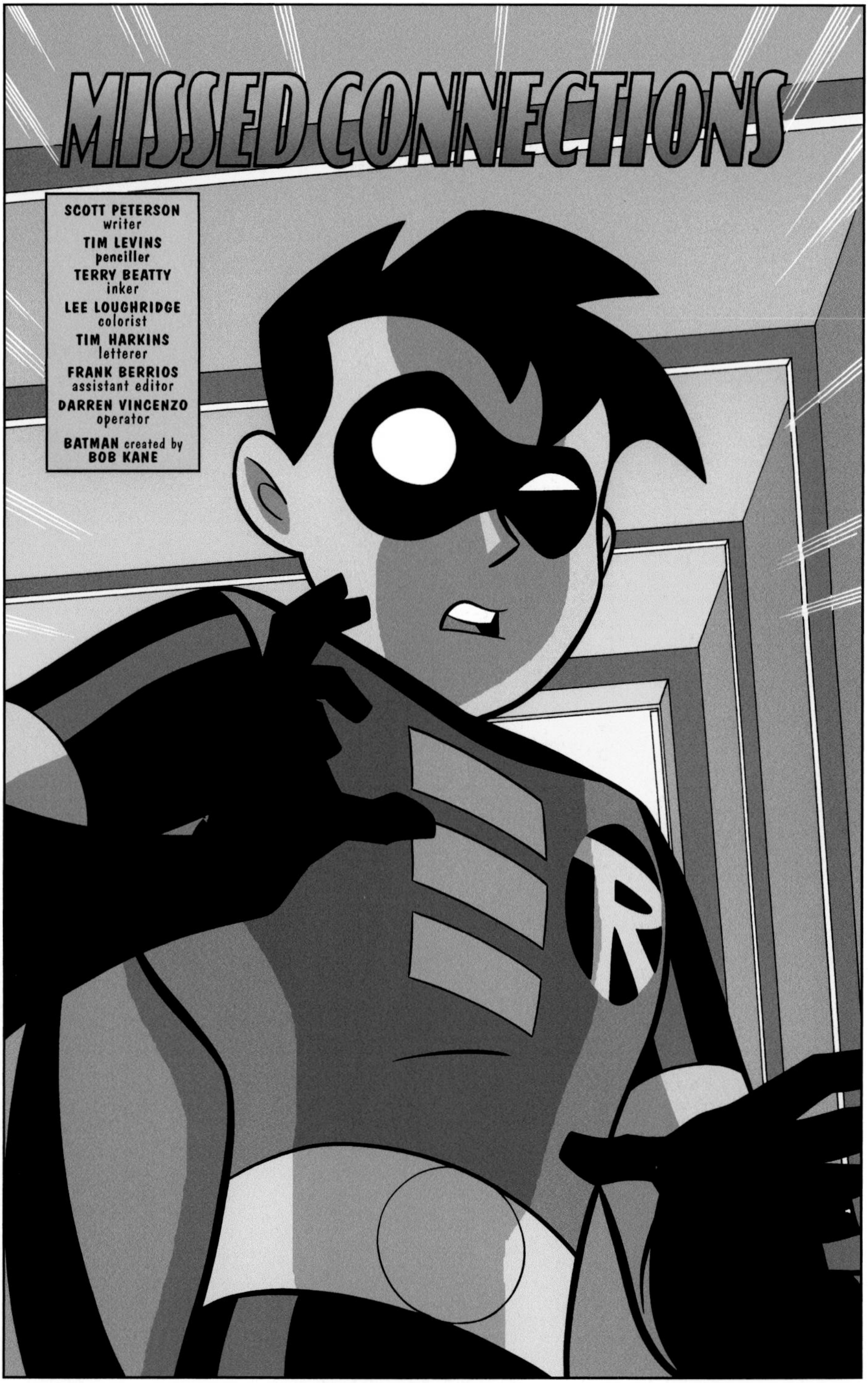

MISSED CONNECTIONS
SCOTT PETERSON writer
TIM LEVINS penciller
TERRY BEATTY inker
LEE LOUGHRIDGE colorist
TIM HARKINS letterer
FRANK BERRIOS assistant editor
DARREN VINCENZO operator
BATMAN created by BOB KANE

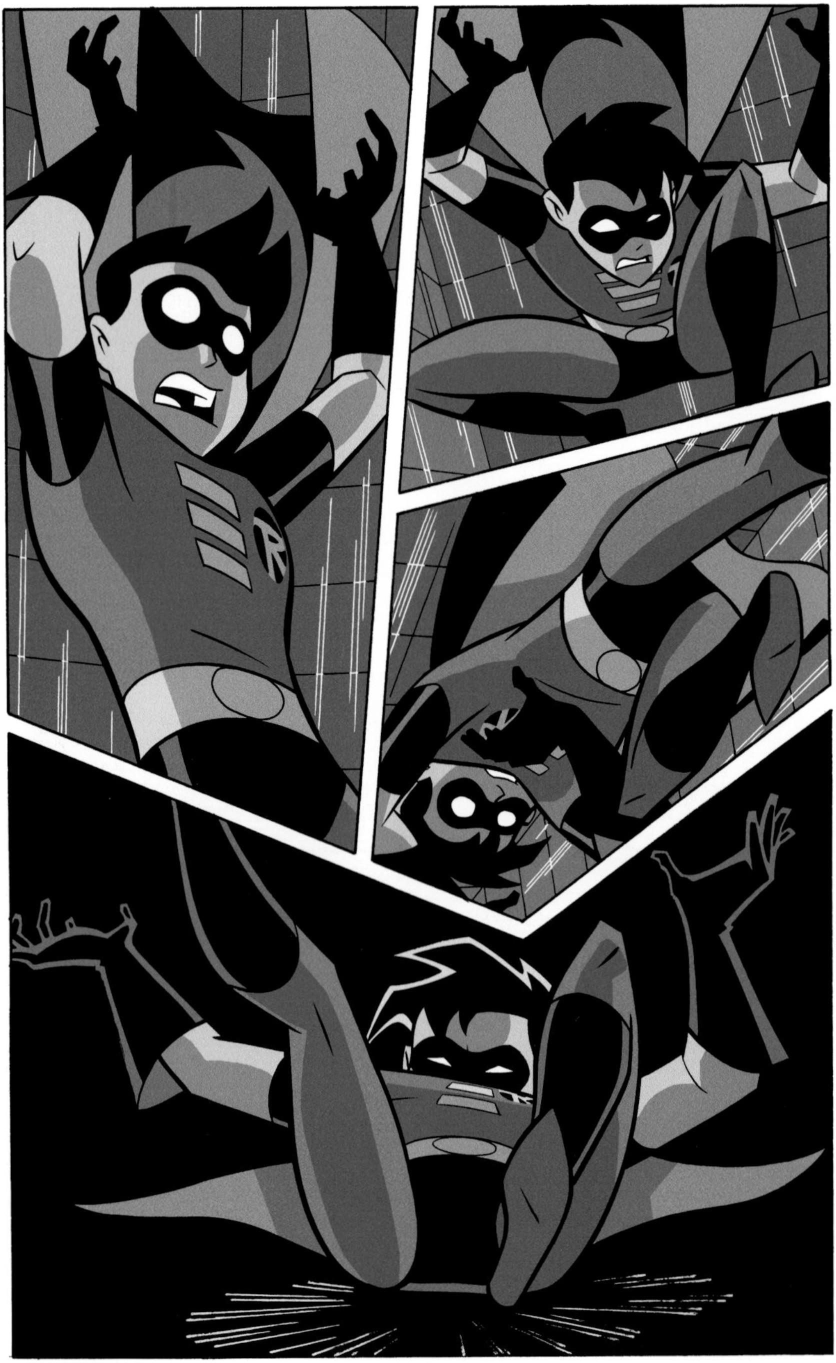

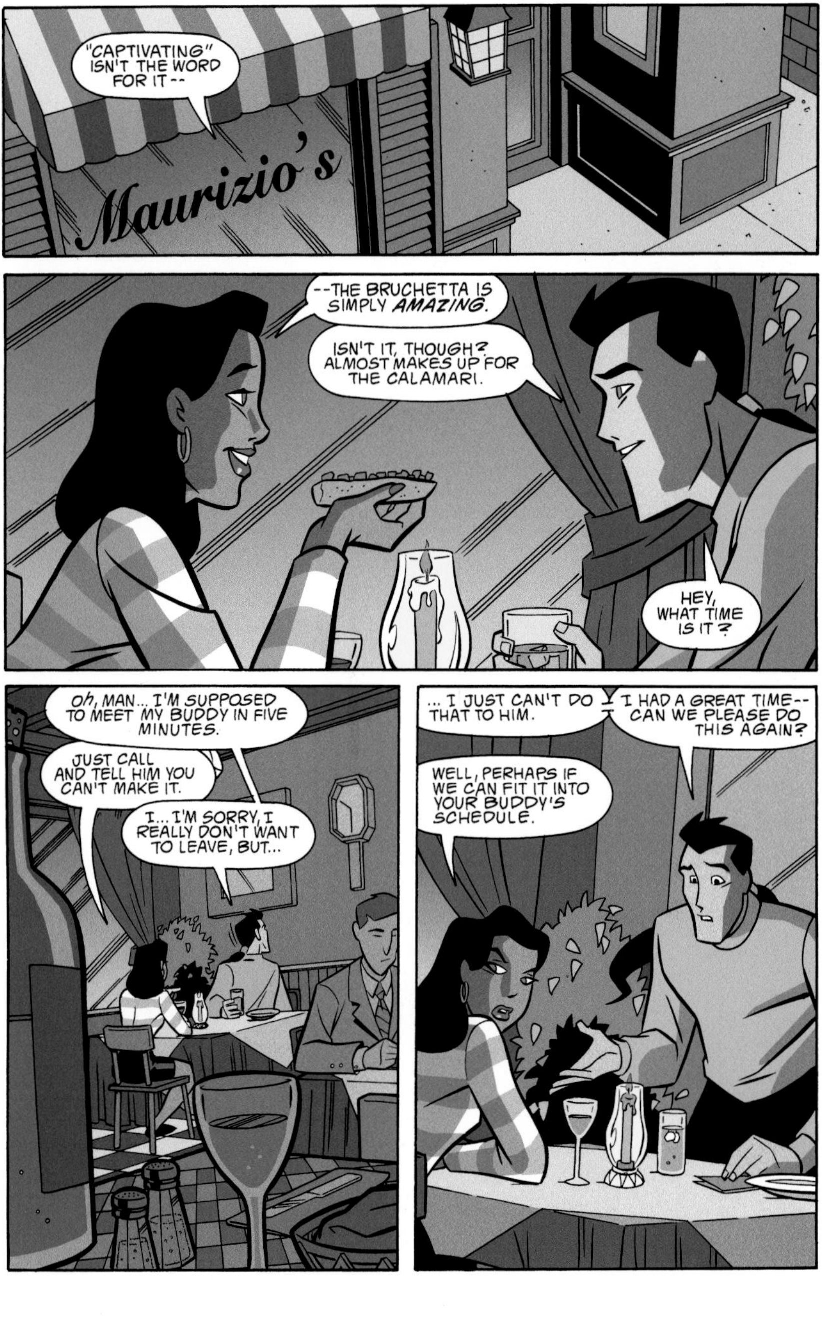

"CAPTIVATING" ISN'T THE WORD FOR IT--
Maurizio's
--THE BRUCHETTA IS SIMPLY AMAZING.
ISN'T IT, THOUGH? ALMOST MAKES UP FOR THE CALAMARI.
HEY, WHAT TIME IS IT?
Oh, MAN... I'M SUPPOSED TO MEET MY BUDDY IN FIVE MINUTES.
JUST CALL AND TELL HIM YOU CAN'T MAKE IT.
I... I'M SORRY, I REALLY DON'T WANT TO LEAVE, BUT...
... I JUST CAN'T DO THAT TO HIM.
I HAD A GREAT TIME-- CAN WE PLEASE DO THIS AGAIN?
WELL, PERHAPS IF WE CAN FIT IT INTO YOUR BUDDY'S SCHEDULE.

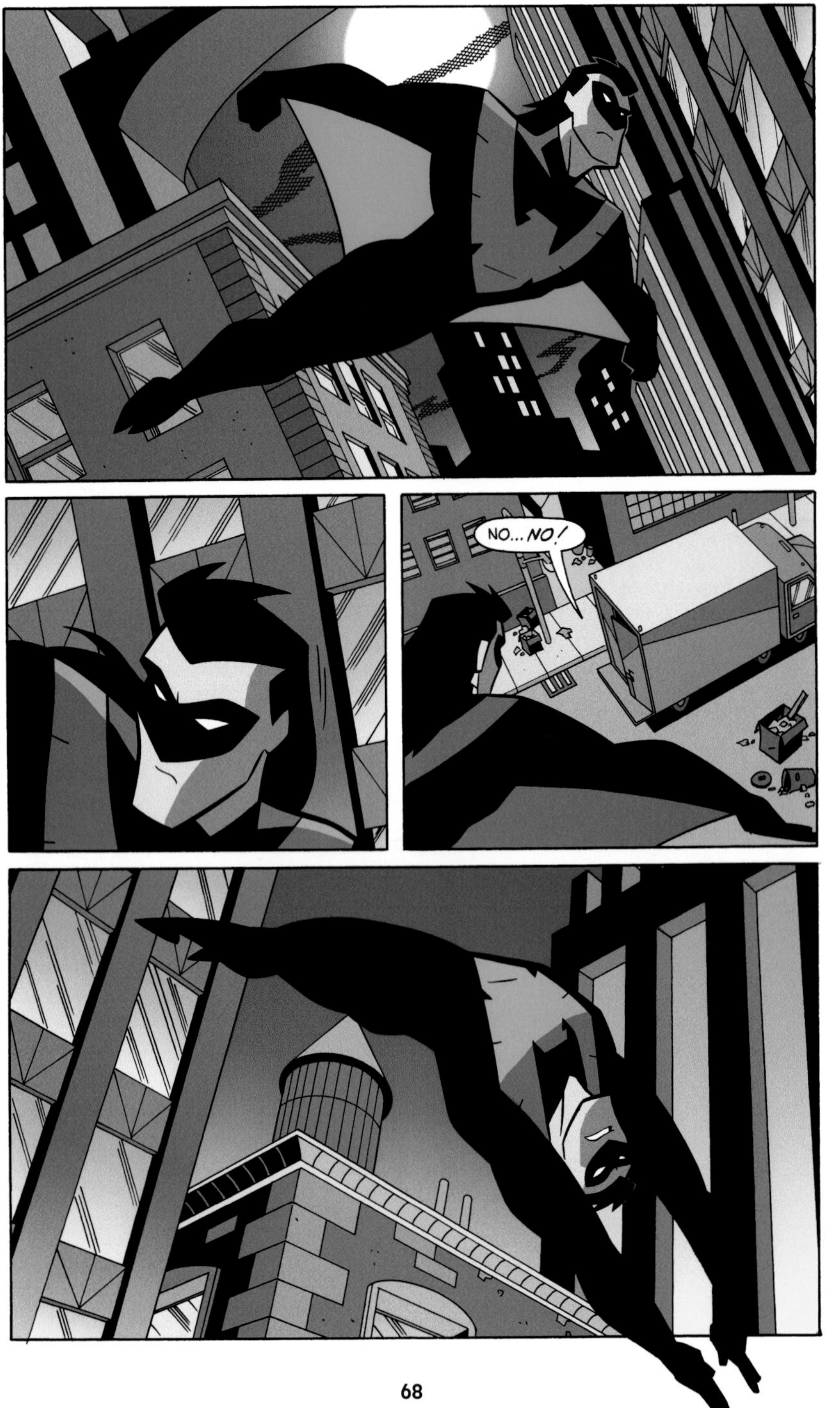
NO... NO!

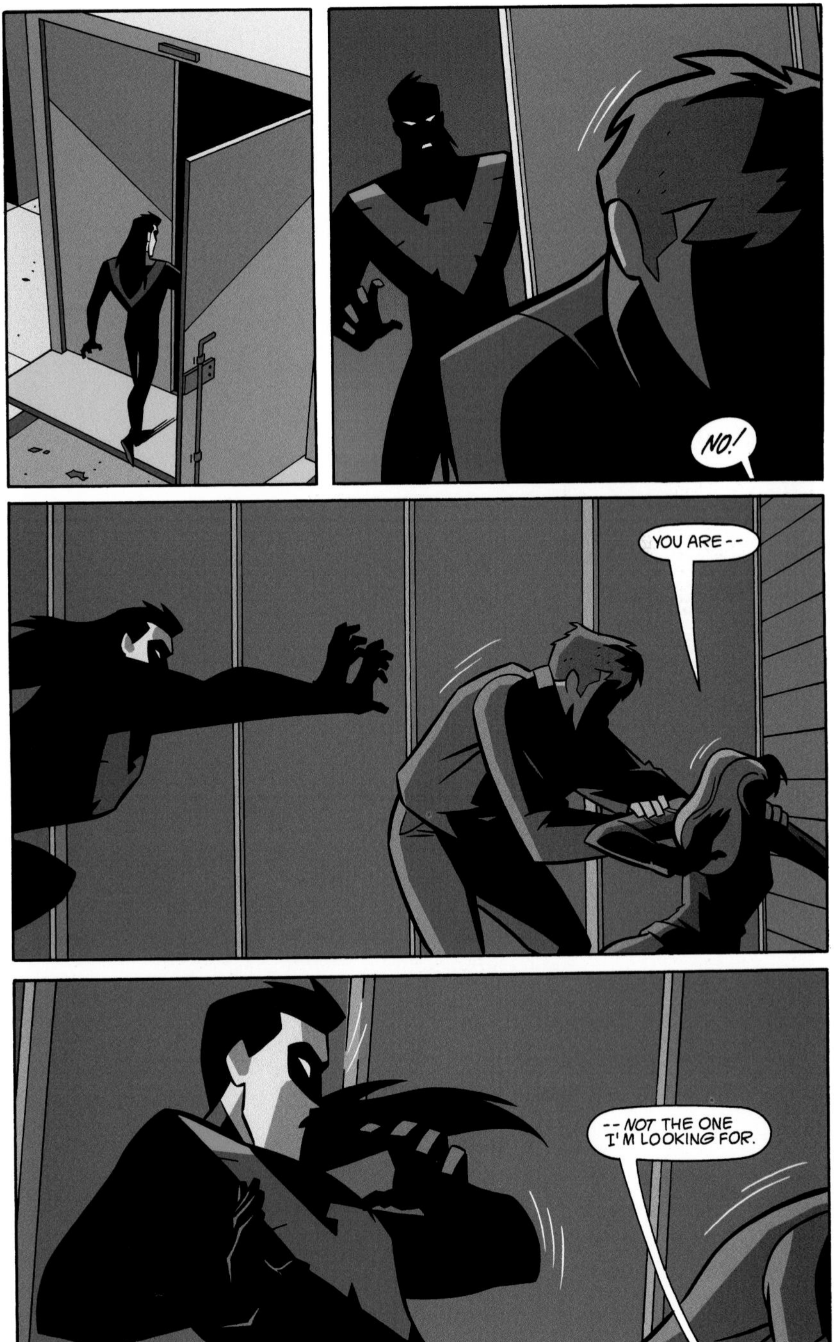
NO!
YOU ARE--
--NOT THE ONE I'M LOOKING FOR.

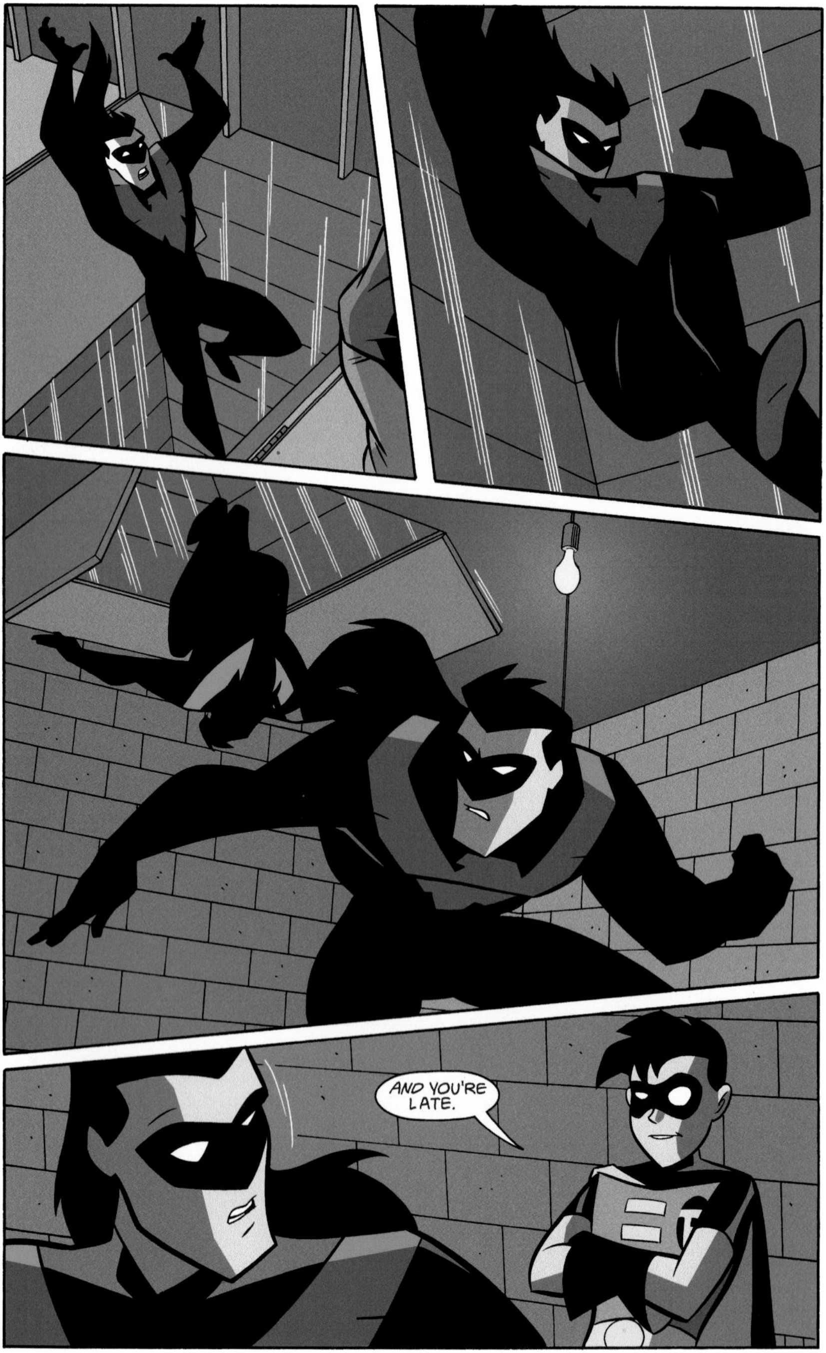
AND YOU'RE LATE.

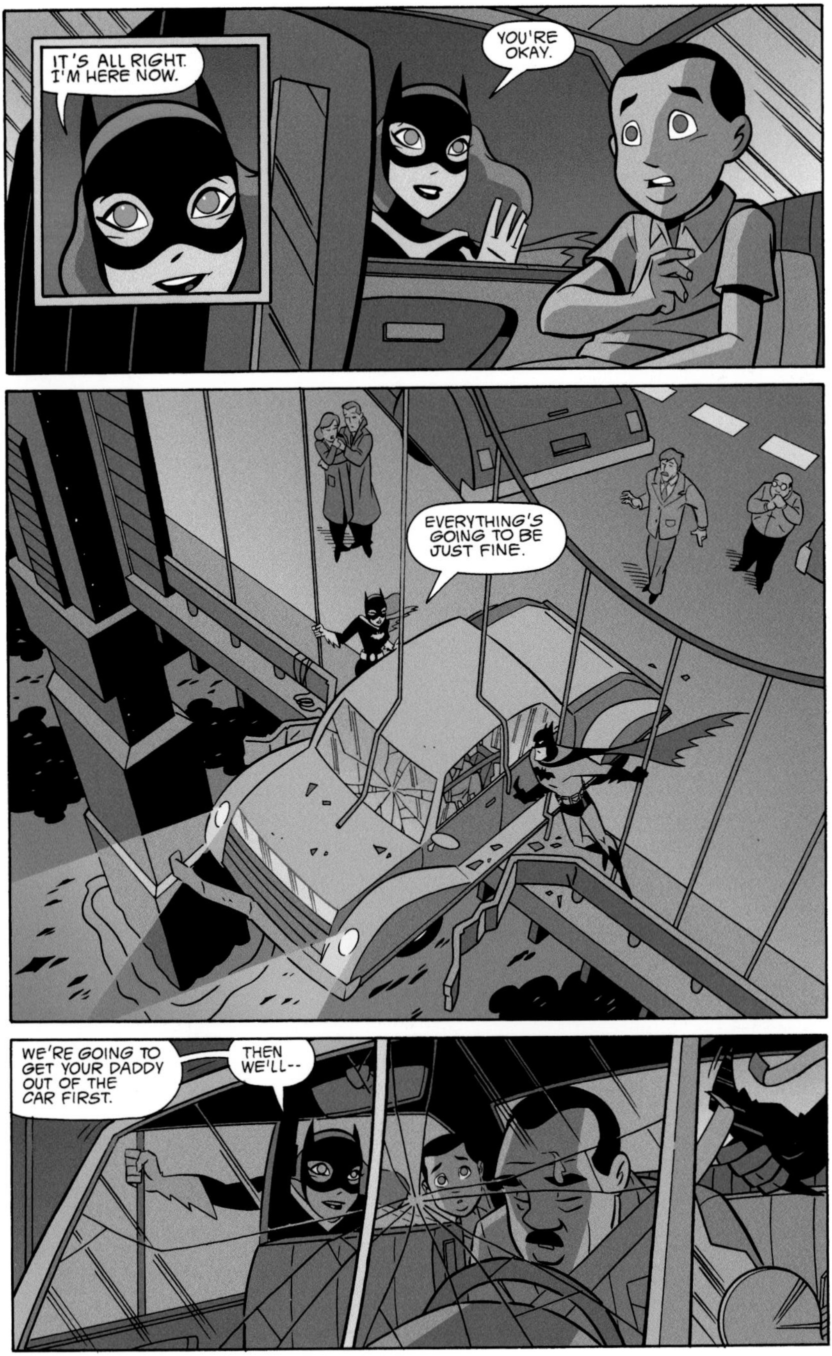
IT'S ALL RIGHT. I'M HERE NOW.
YOU'RE OKAY.
EVERYTHING'S GOING TO BE JUST FINE.
WE'RE GOING TO GET YOUR DADDY OUT OF THE CAR FIRST.
THEN WE'LL--

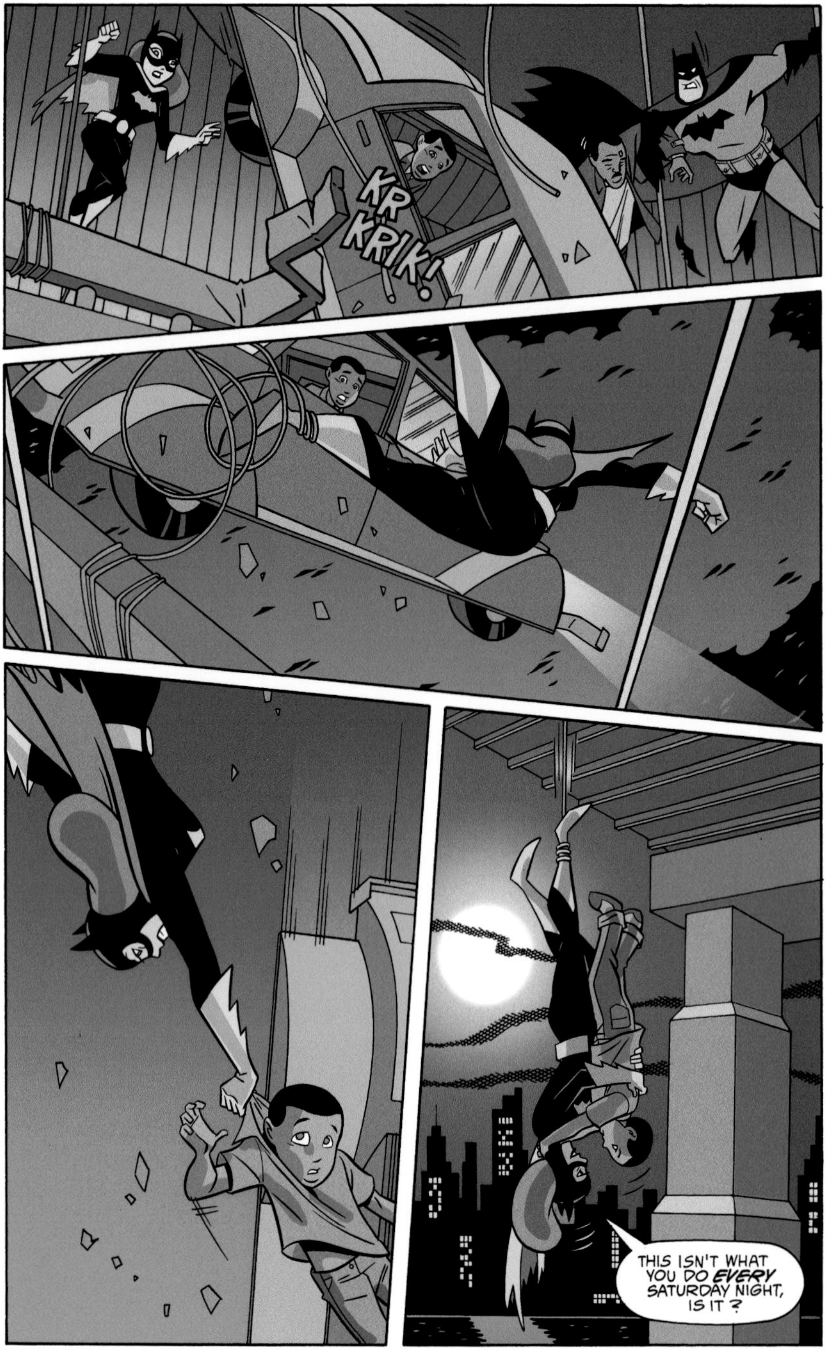
KR KRIK!
THIS ISN'T WHAT YOU DO EVERY SATURDAY NIGHT, IS IT ?

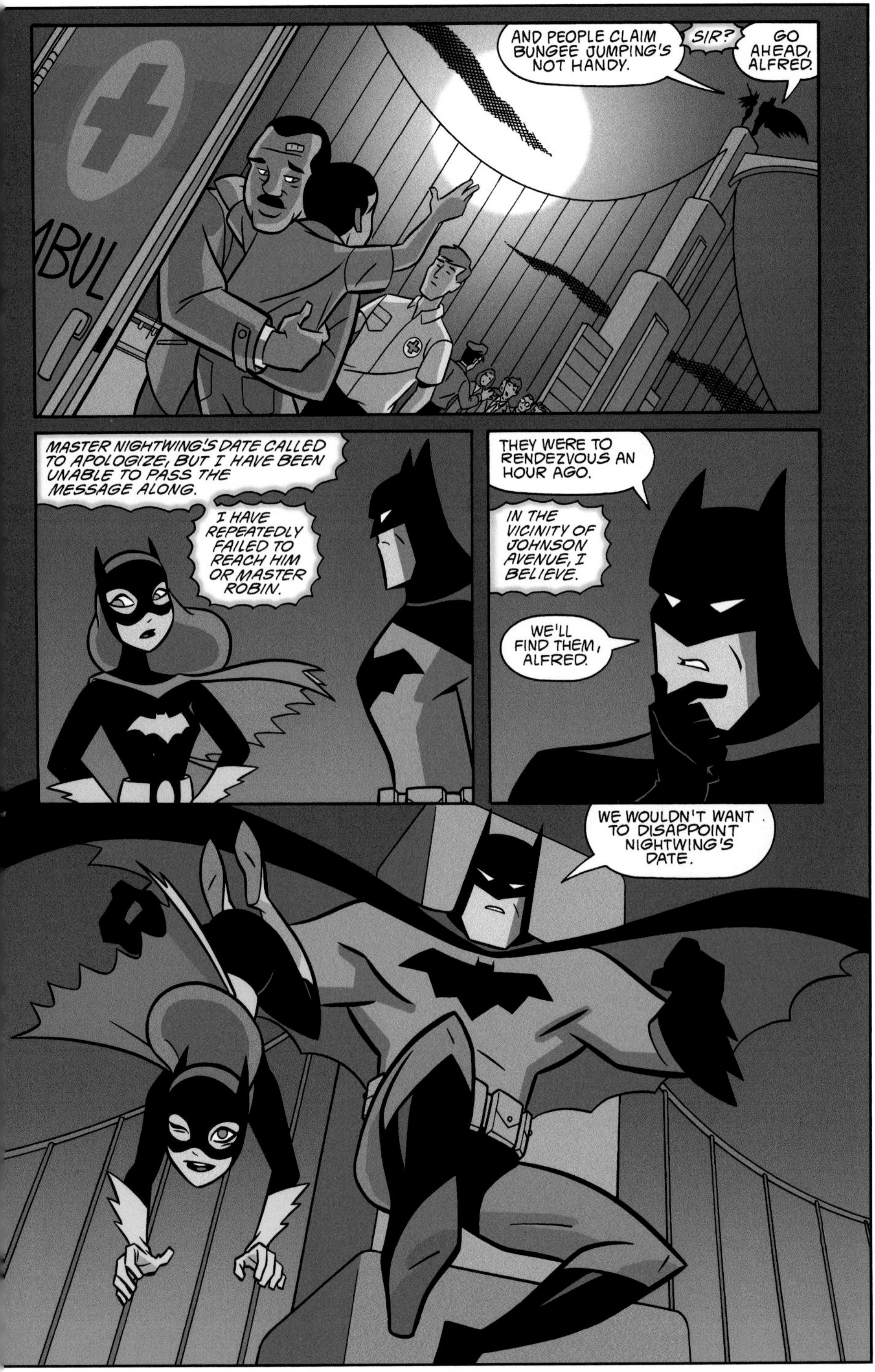
AND PEOPLE CLAIM BUNGEE JUMPING'S NOT HANDY.
SIR?
GO AHEAD, ALFRED.
MASTER NIGHTWING'S DATE CALLED TO APOLOGIZE, BUT I HAVE BEEN UNABLE TO PASS THE MESSAGE ALONG.
I HAVE REPEATEDLY FAILED TO REACH HIM OR MASTER ROBIN.
THEY WERE TO RENDEZVOUS AN HOUR AGO.
IN THE VICINITY OF JOHNSON AVENUE, I BELIEVE.
WE'LL FIND THEM, ALFRED.
WE WOULDN'T WANT TO DISAPPOINT NIGHTWING'S DATE.

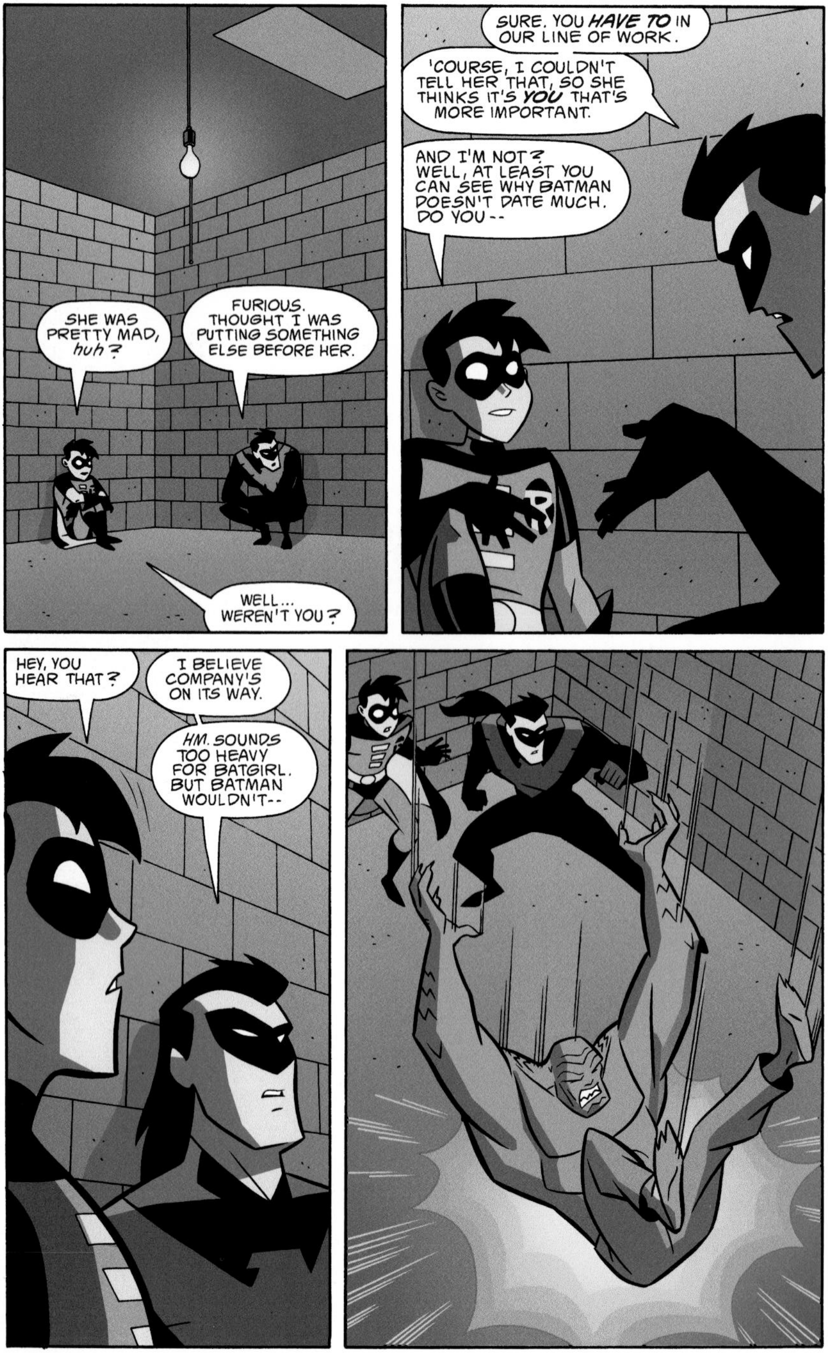
SHE WAS PRETTY MAD, huh?
FURIOUS. THOUGHT I WAS PUTTING SOMETHING ELSE BEFORE HER.
WELL... WEREN'T YOU?
SURE. YOU HAVE TO IN OUR LINE OF WORK.
'COURSE, I COULDN'T TELL HER THAT, SO SHE THINKS IT'S YOU THAT'S MORE IMPORTANT.
AND I'M NOT? WELL, AT LEAST YOU CAN SEE WHY BATMAN DOESN'T DATE MUCH. DO YOU--
HEY, YOU HEAR THAT?
I BELIEVE COMPANY'S ON ITS WAY.
HM. SOUNDS TOO HEAVY FOR BATGIRL. BUT BATMAN WOULDN'T--

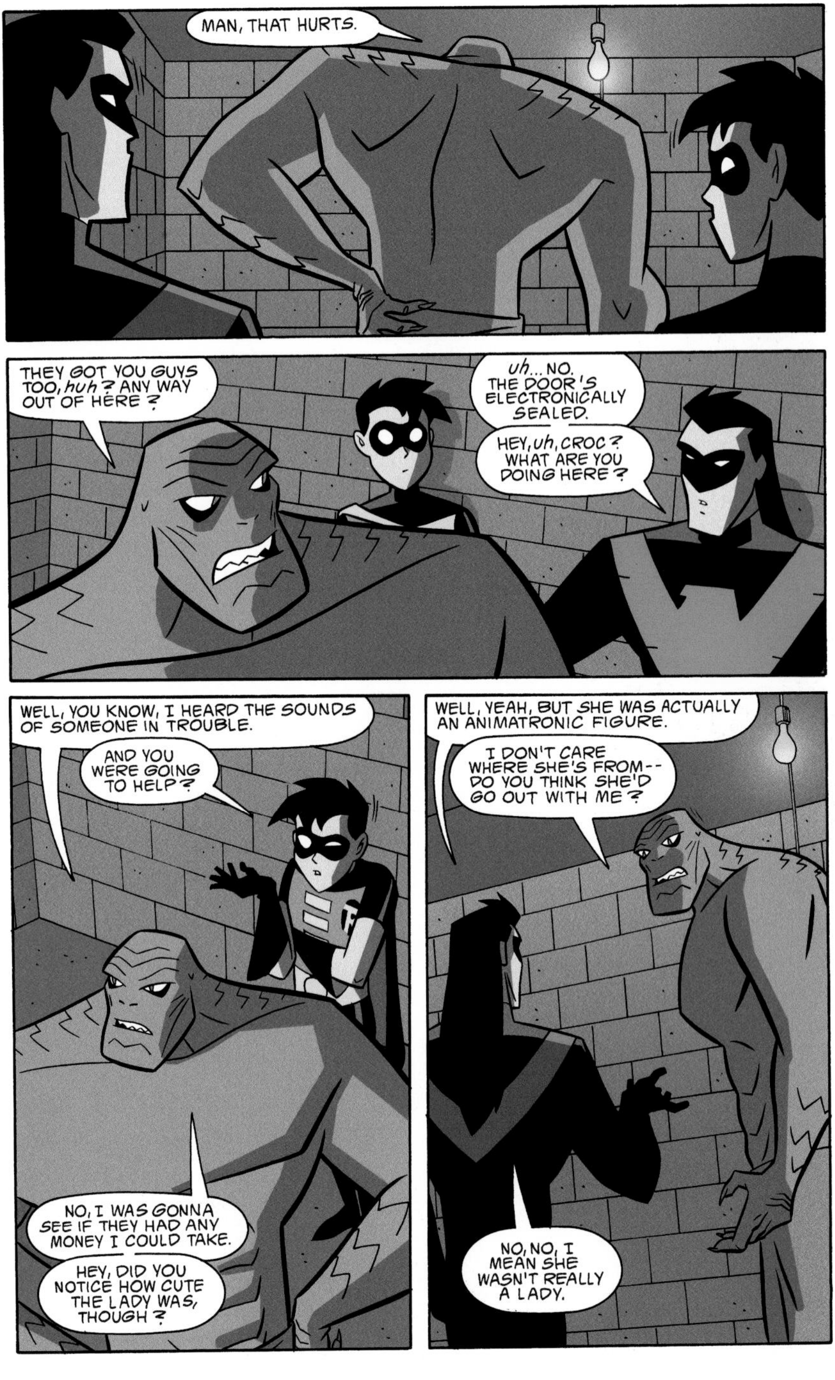

MAN, THAT HURTS.
THEY GOT YOU GUYS TOO, *huh*? ANY WAY OUT OF HERE?
uh... NO. THE DOOR'S ELECTRONICALLY SEALED.
HEY, *uh*, CROC? WHAT ARE YOU DOING HERE?
WELL, YOU KNOW, I HEARD THE SOUNDS OF SOMEONE IN TROUBLE.
AND YOU WERE GOING TO HELP?
NO, I WAS GONNA SEE IF THEY HAD ANY MONEY I COULD TAKE.
HEY, DID YOU NOTICE HOW CUTE THE LADY WAS, THOUGH?
WELL, YEAH, BUT SHE WAS ACTUALLY AN ANIMATRONIC FIGURE.
I DON'T CARE WHERE SHE'S FROM-- DO YOU THINK SHE'D GO OUT WITH ME?
NO, NO, I MEAN SHE WASN'T REALLY A LADY.

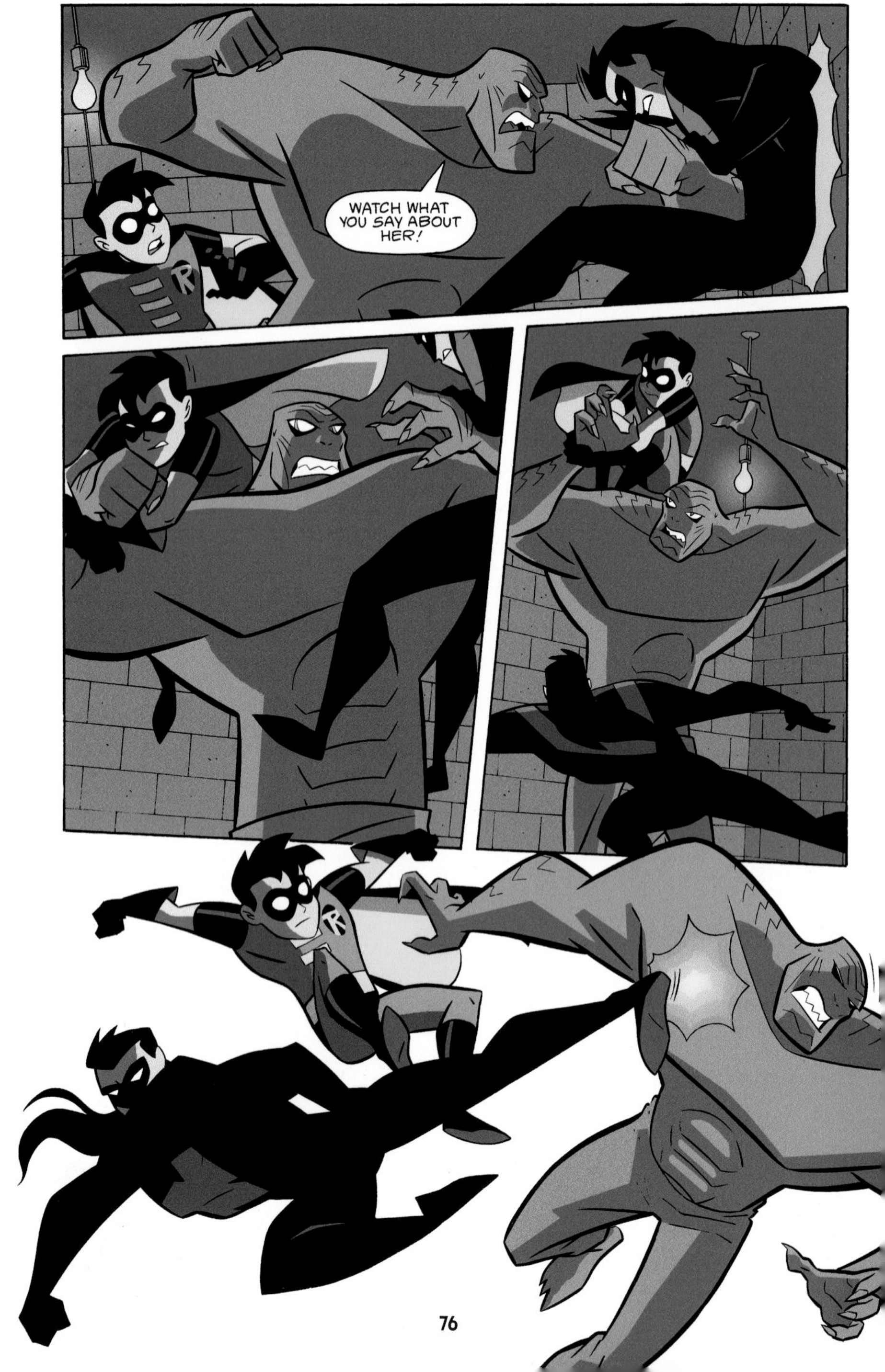
WATCH WHAT YOU SAY ABOUT HER!

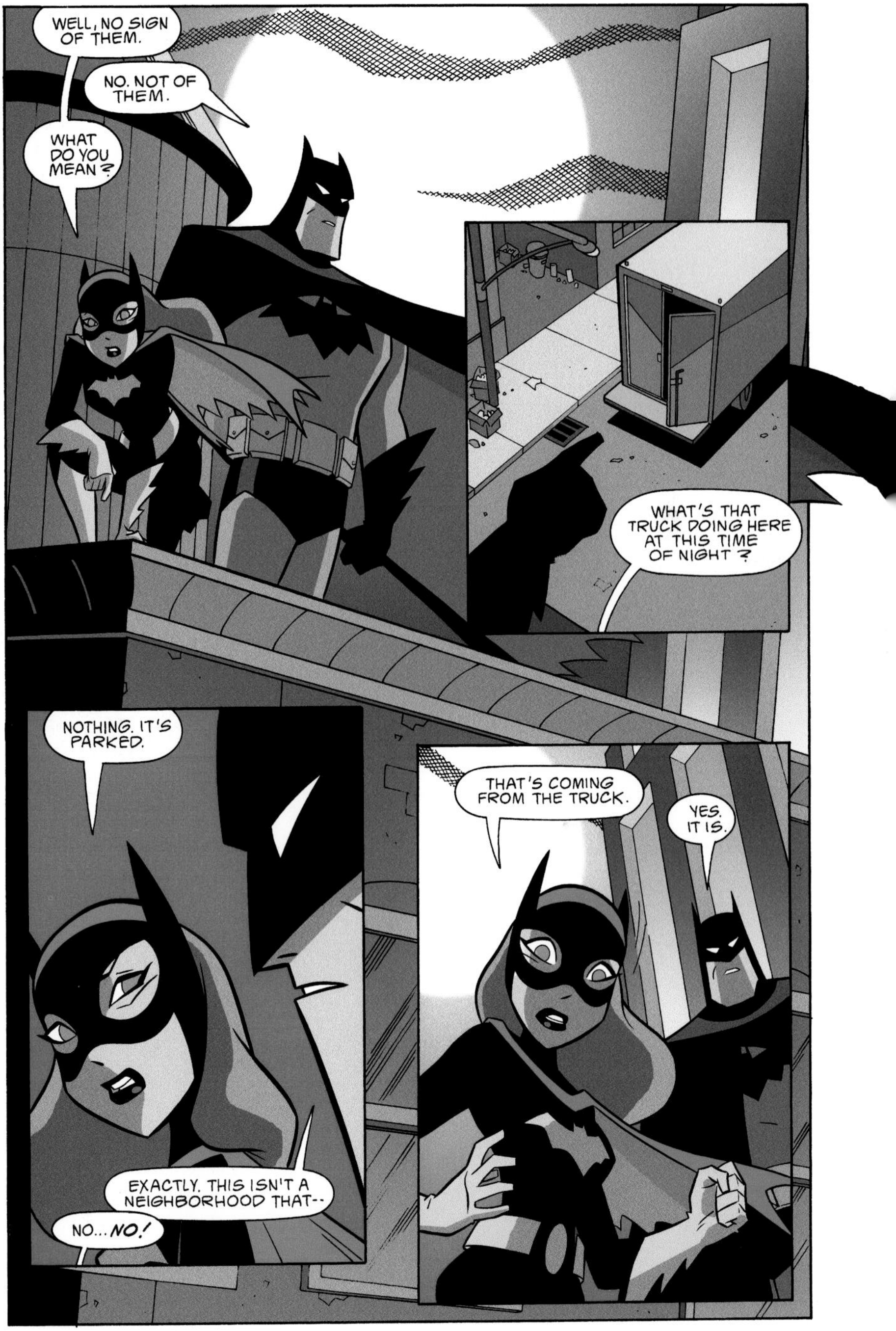

WELL, NO SIGN OF THEM.
NO. NOT OF THEM.
WHAT DO YOU MEAN?
WHAT'S THAT TRUCK DOING HERE AT THIS TIME OF NIGHT?
NOTHING. IT'S PARKED.
EXACTLY. THIS ISN'T A NEIGHBORHOOD THAT--
NO... NO!
THAT'S COMING FROM THE TRUCK.
YES. IT IS.

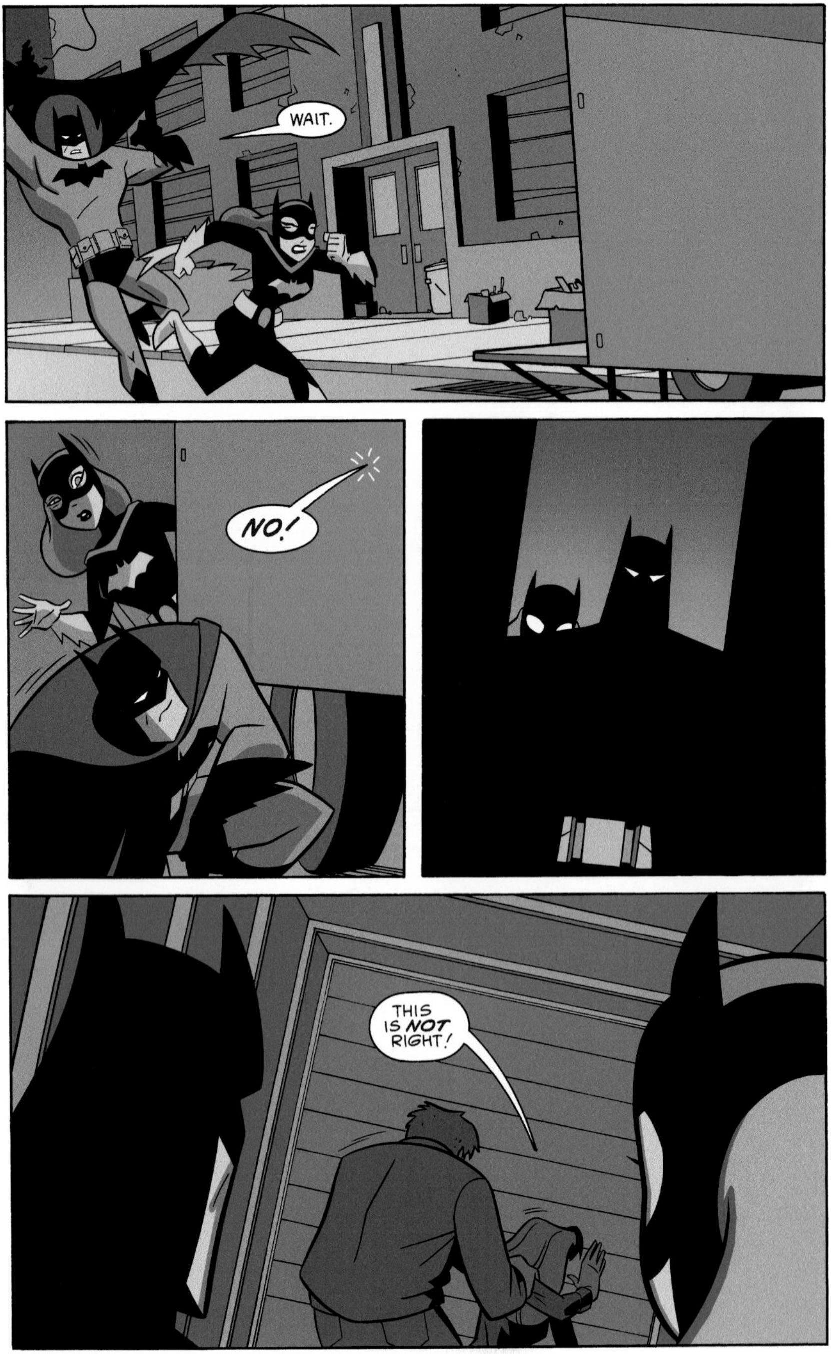
WAIT.
NO!
THIS IS NOT RIGHT!

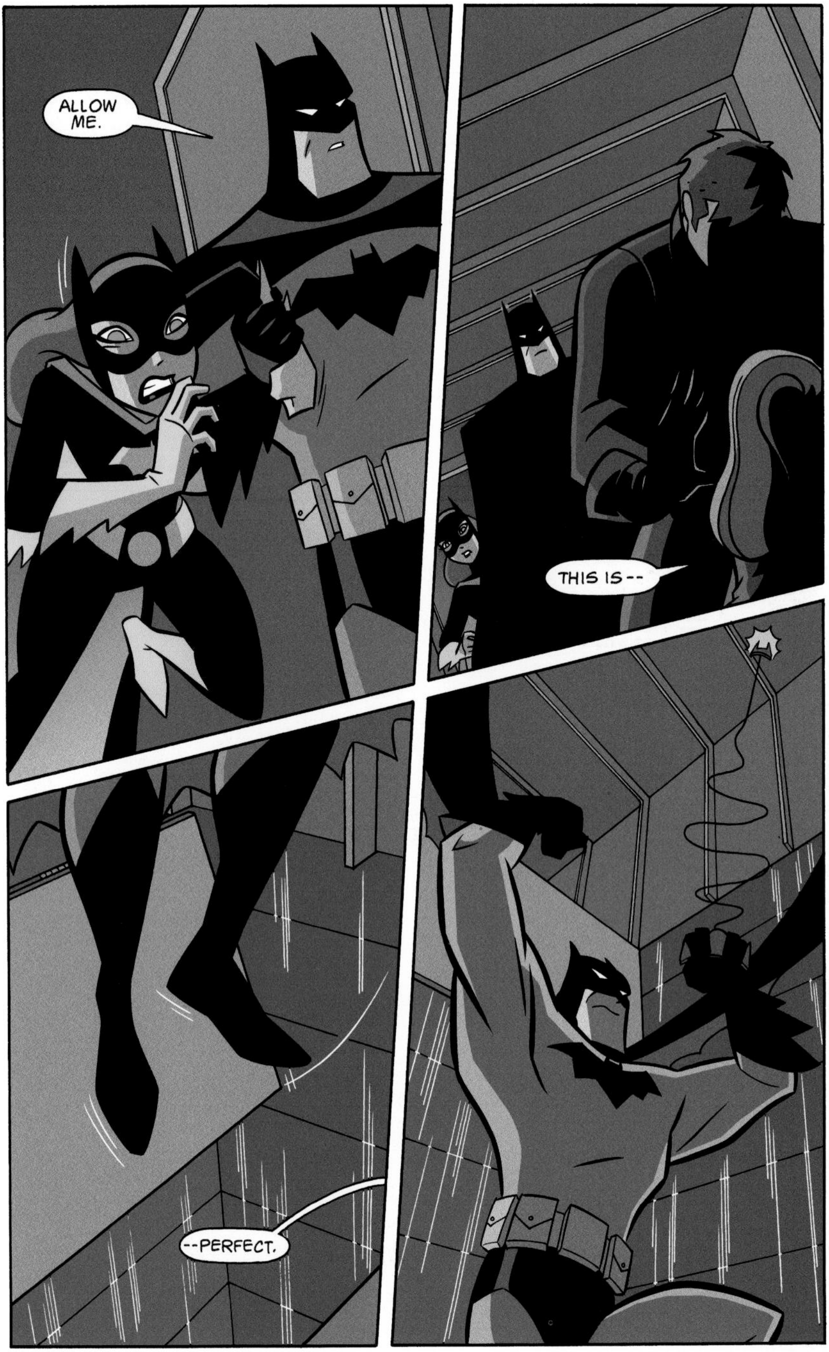
ALLOW ME.
THIS IS--
--PERFECT.

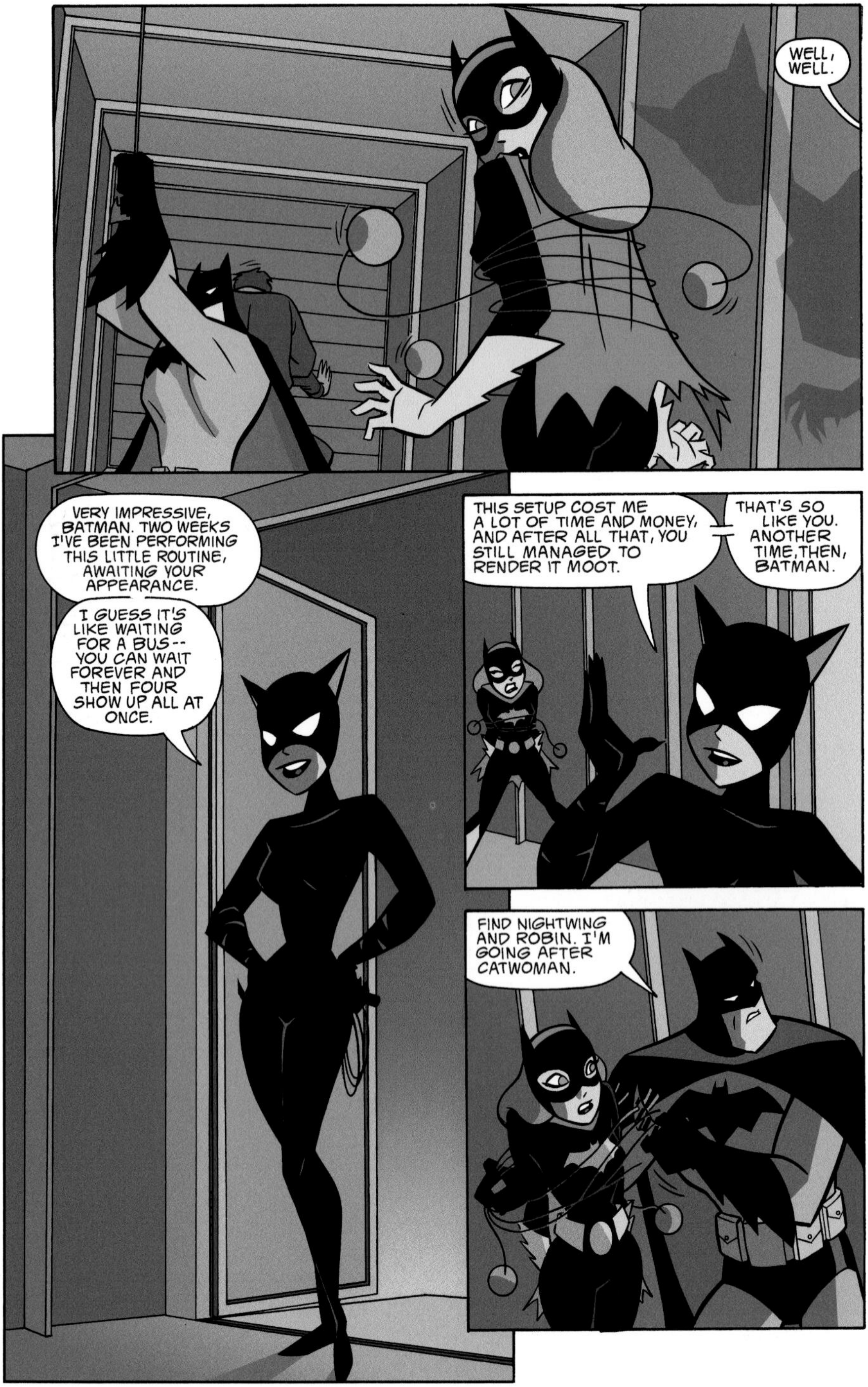
WELL, WELL.
VERY IMPRESSIVE, BATMAN. TWO WEEKS I'VE BEEN PERFORMING THIS LITTLE ROUTINE, AWAITING YOUR APPEARANCE.
I GUESS IT'S LIKE WAITING FOR A BUS-- YOU CAN WAIT FOREVER AND THEN FOUR SHOW UP ALL AT ONCE.
THIS SETUP COST ME A LOT OF TIME AND MONEY, AND AFTER ALL THAT, YOU STILL MANAGED TO RENDER IT MOOT.
THAT'S SO LIKE YOU. ANOTHER TIME, THEN, BATMAN.
FIND NIGHTWING AND ROBIN. I'M GOING AFTER CATWOMAN.

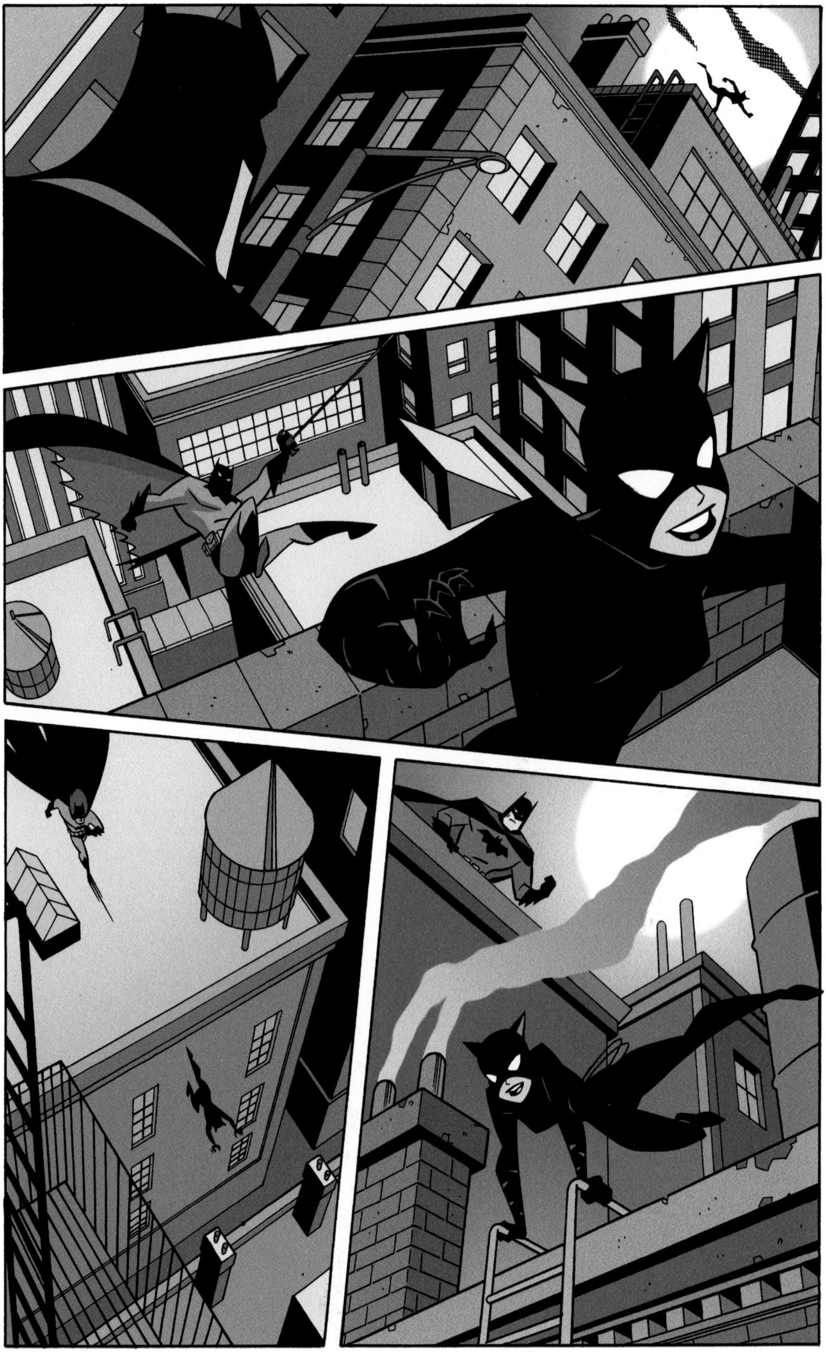

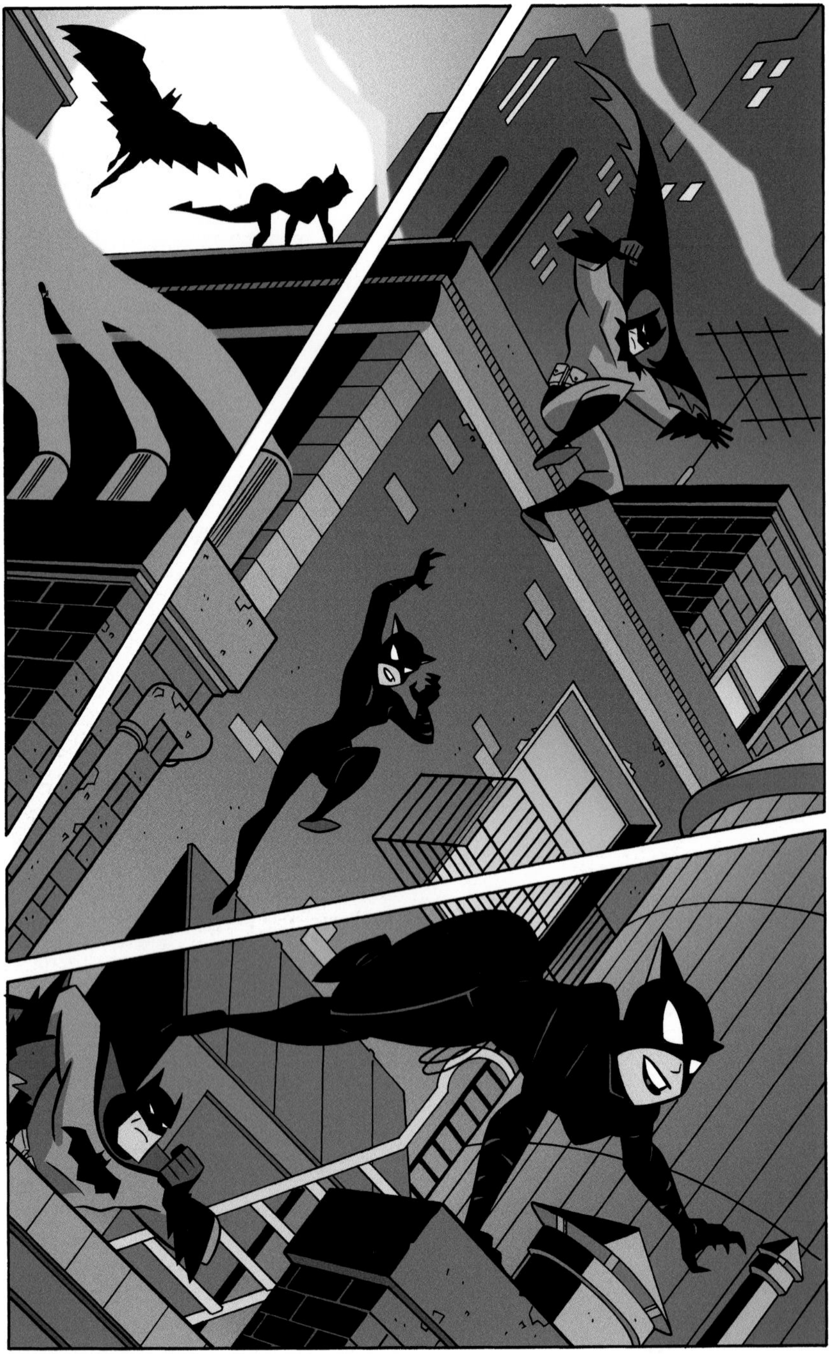

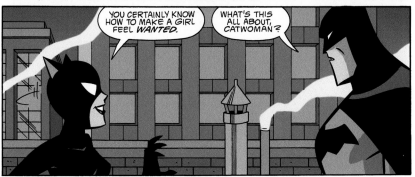

YOU CERTAINLY KNOW HOW TO MAKE A GIRL FEEL *WANTED.*

WHAT'S THIS ALL ABOUT, *CATWOMAN?*

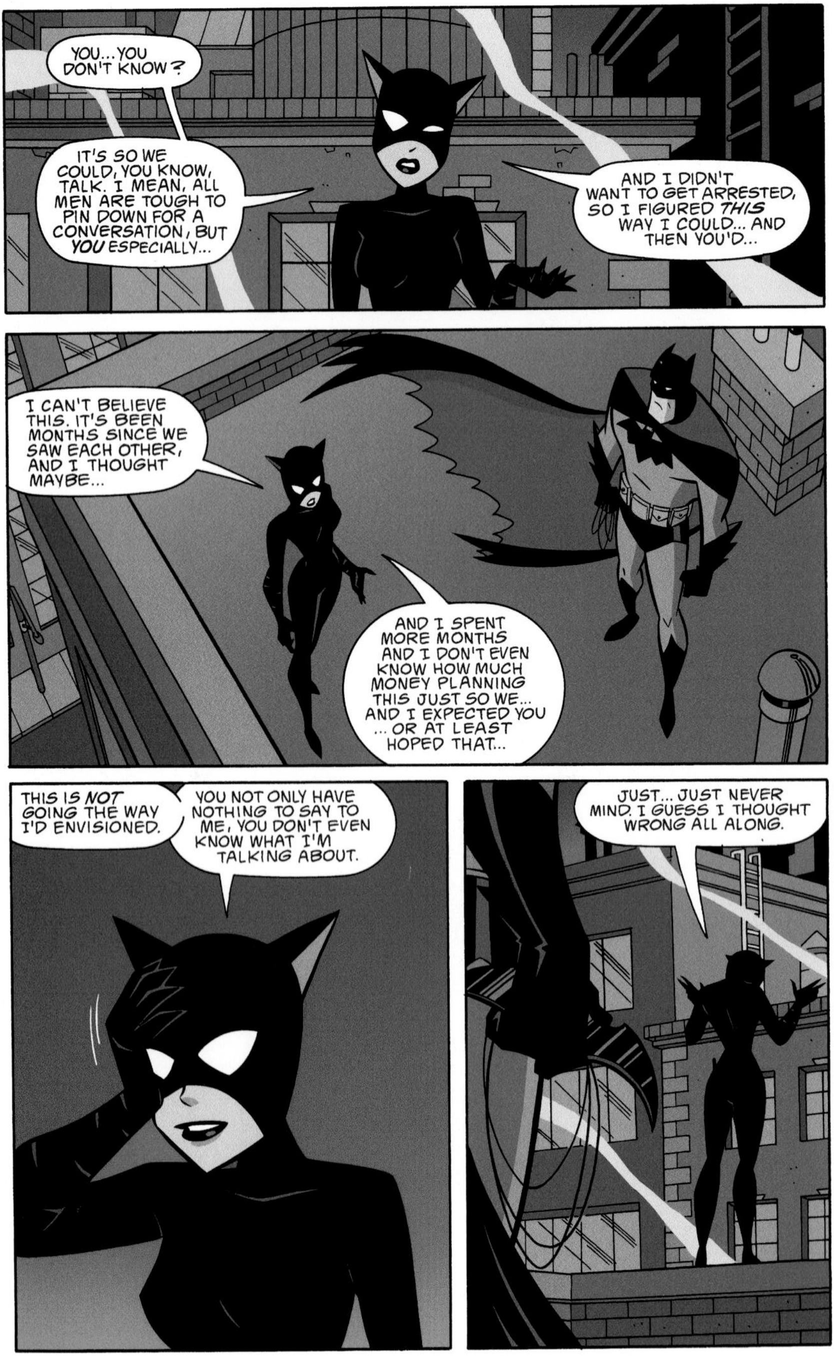
YOU... YOU DON'T KNOW?
IT'S SO WE COULD, YOU KNOW, TALK. I MEAN, ALL MEN ARE TOUGH TO PIN DOWN FOR A CONVERSATION, BUT *YOU* ESPECIALLY...
AND I DIDN'T WANT TO GET ARRESTED, SO I FIGURED *THIS* WAY I COULD... AND THEN YOU'D...
I CAN'T BELIEVE THIS. IT'S BEEN MONTHS SINCE WE SAW EACH OTHER, AND I THOUGHT MAYBE...
AND I SPENT MORE MONTHS AND I DON'T EVEN KNOW HOW MUCH MONEY PLANNING THIS JUST SO WE... AND I EXPECTED YOU ... OR AT LEAST HOPED THAT...
THIS IS *NOT* GOING THE WAY I'D ENVISIONED.
YOU NOT ONLY HAVE NOTHING TO SAY TO ME, YOU DON'T EVEN KNOW WHAT I'M TALKING ABOUT.
JUST... JUST NEVER MIND. I GUESS I THOUGHT WRONG ALL ALONG.

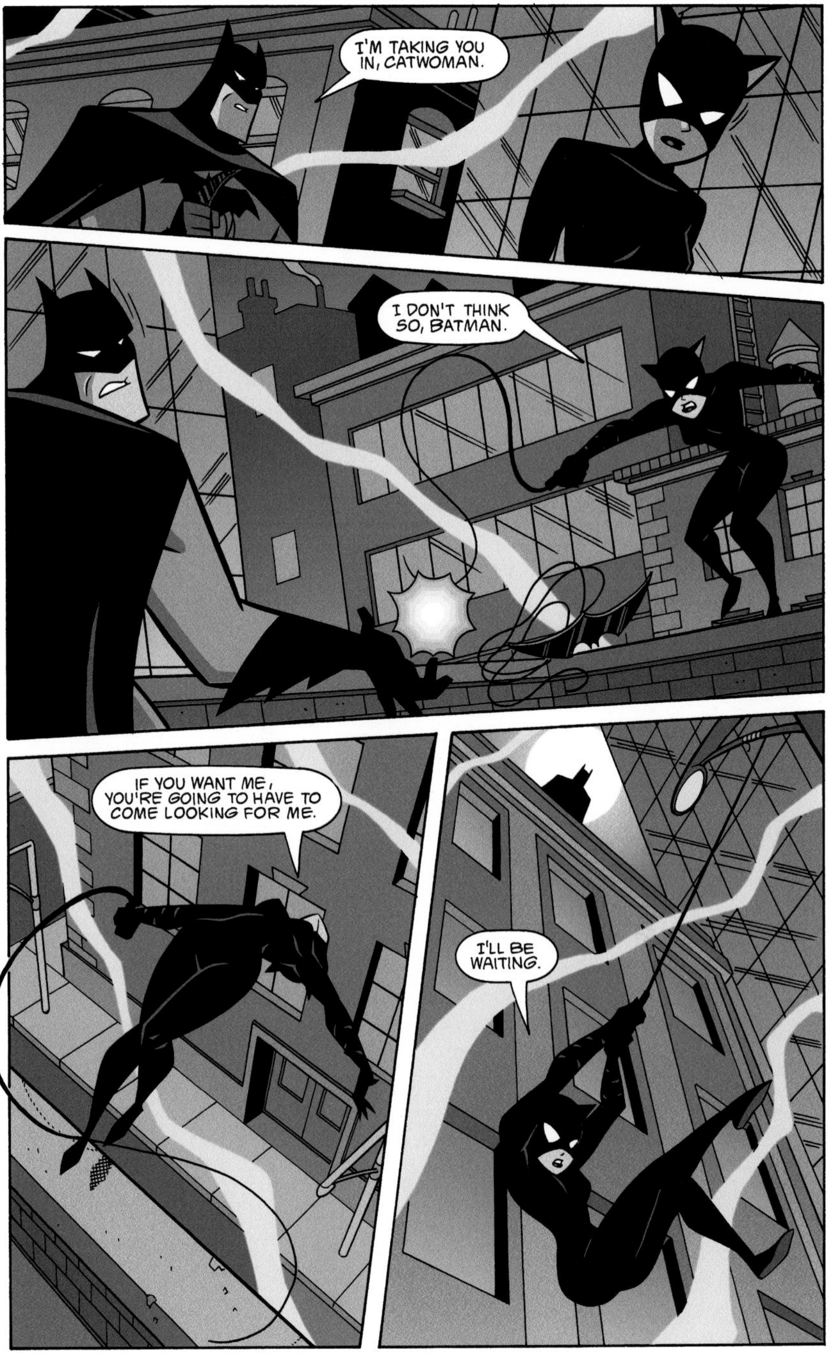
I'M TAKING YOU IN, CATWOMAN.
I DON'T THINK SO, BATMAN.
IF YOU WANT ME, YOU'RE GOING TO HAVE TO COME LOOKING FOR ME.
I'LL BE WAITING.

NO PROBLEMS?

PIECE OF CAKE. CAN'T BELIEVE THEY FELL FOR THAT TRAP IN THE FIRST PLACE.

EASY TO SAY WHEN YOU'VE GOT *HIM* AS YOUR POINT MAN.

SO... DID YOU GUYS FINALLY TALK?

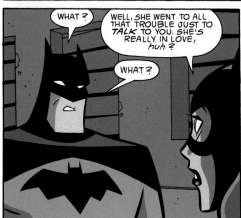

WHAT?

WELL, SHE WENT TO ALL THAT TROUBLE JUST TO *TALK* TO YOU. SHE'S REALLY IN LOVE, *huh?*

WHAT?

THAT *IS* WHAT THIS WAS ALL ABOUT, RIGHT? SHE WAS HOPING YOU GUYS COULD AT LEAST GO BACK TO THE WAY YOU WERE? MAYBE EVEN MORE *SO*?

THAT *WAS* THE POINT, RIGHT, BATMAN?

BATMAN?

THE END

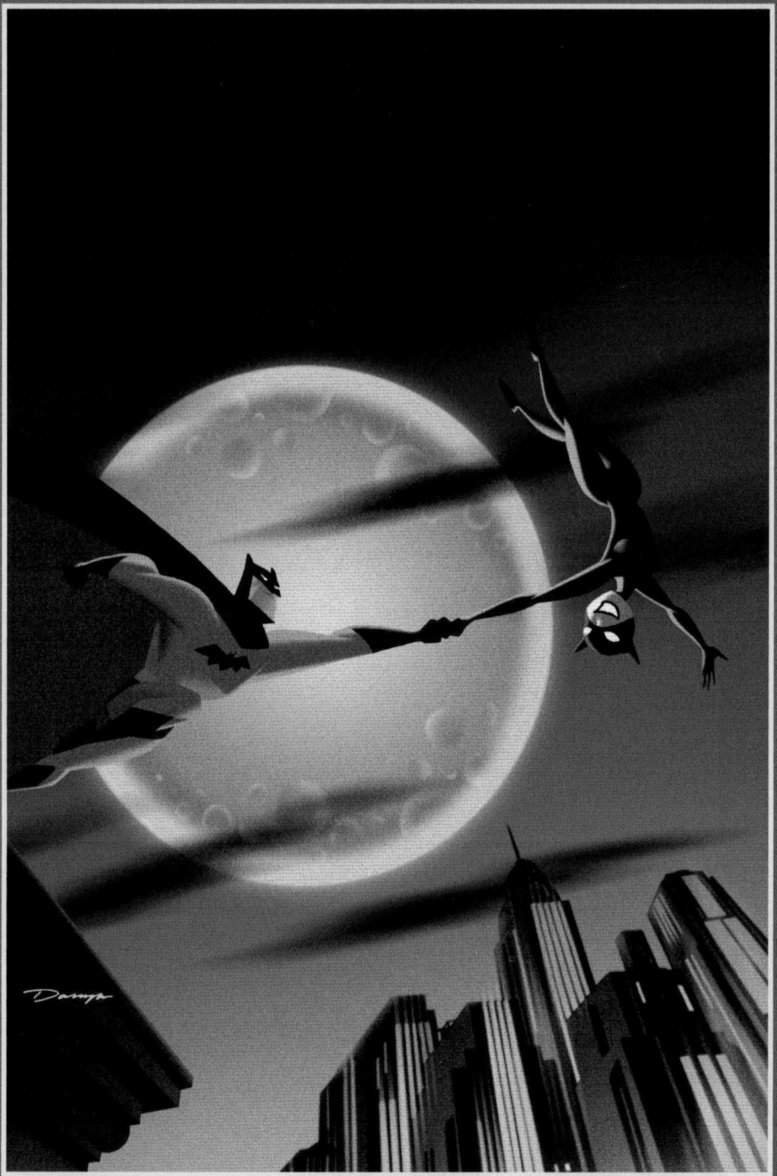

CHAPTER 5: SECOND TIMERS

CATWOMAN

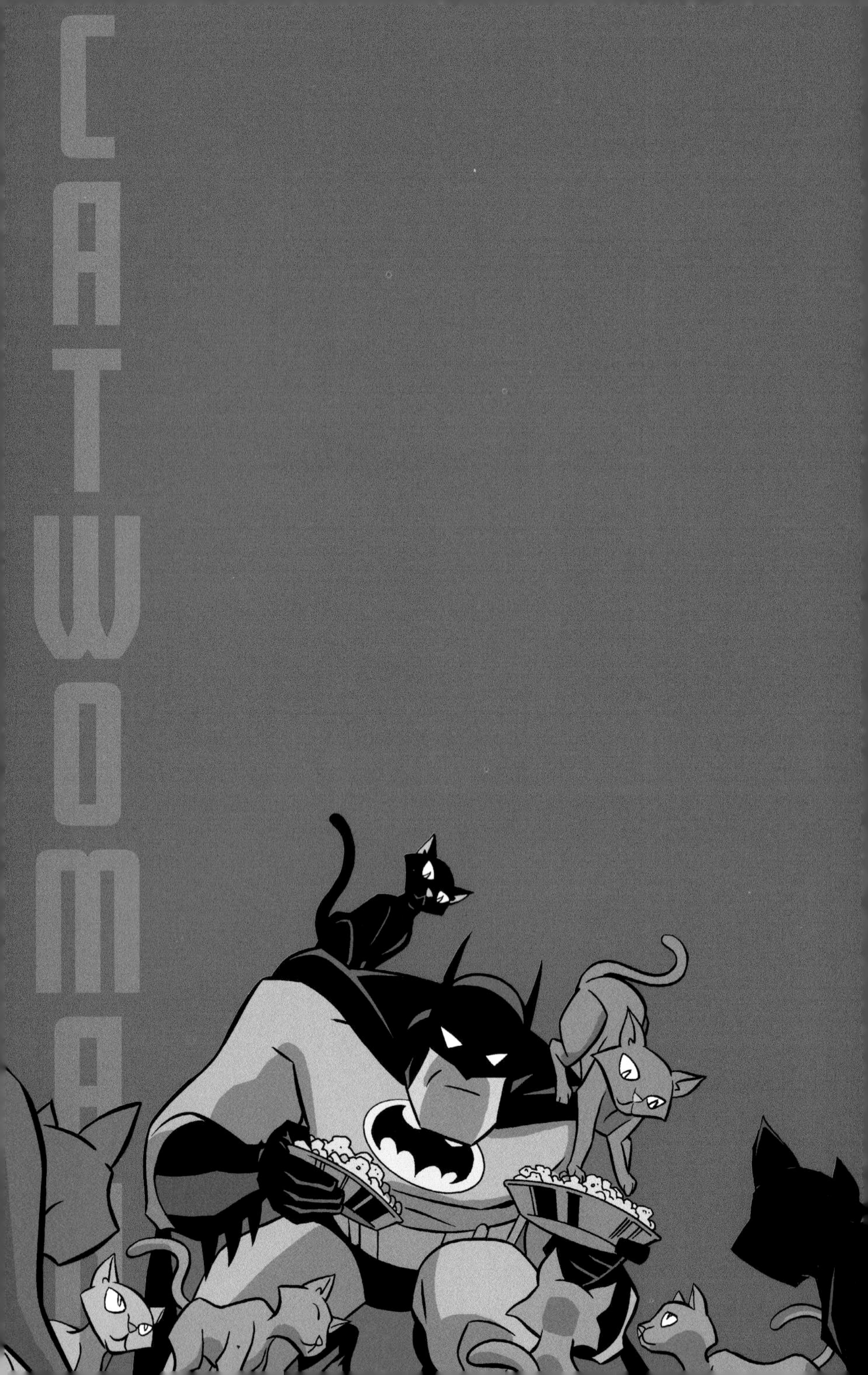
CATWOMA

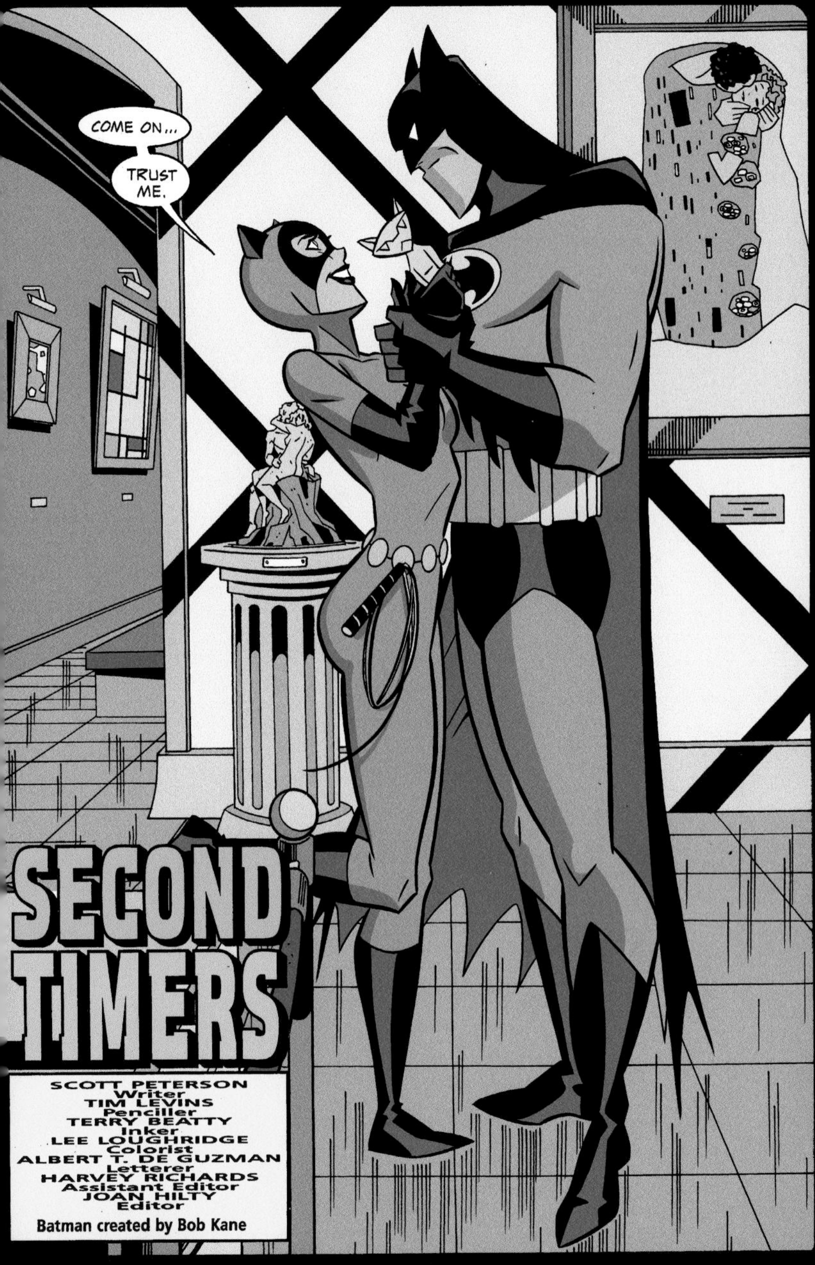
COME ON...
TRUST ME.
SECOND TIMERS
SCOTT PETERSON
Writer
TIM LEVINS
Penciller
TERRY BEATTY
Inker
LEE LOUGHRIDGE
Colorist
ALBERT T. DE GUZMAN
Letterer
HARVEY RICHARDS
Assistant Editor
JOAN HILTY
Editor
Batman created by Bob Kane

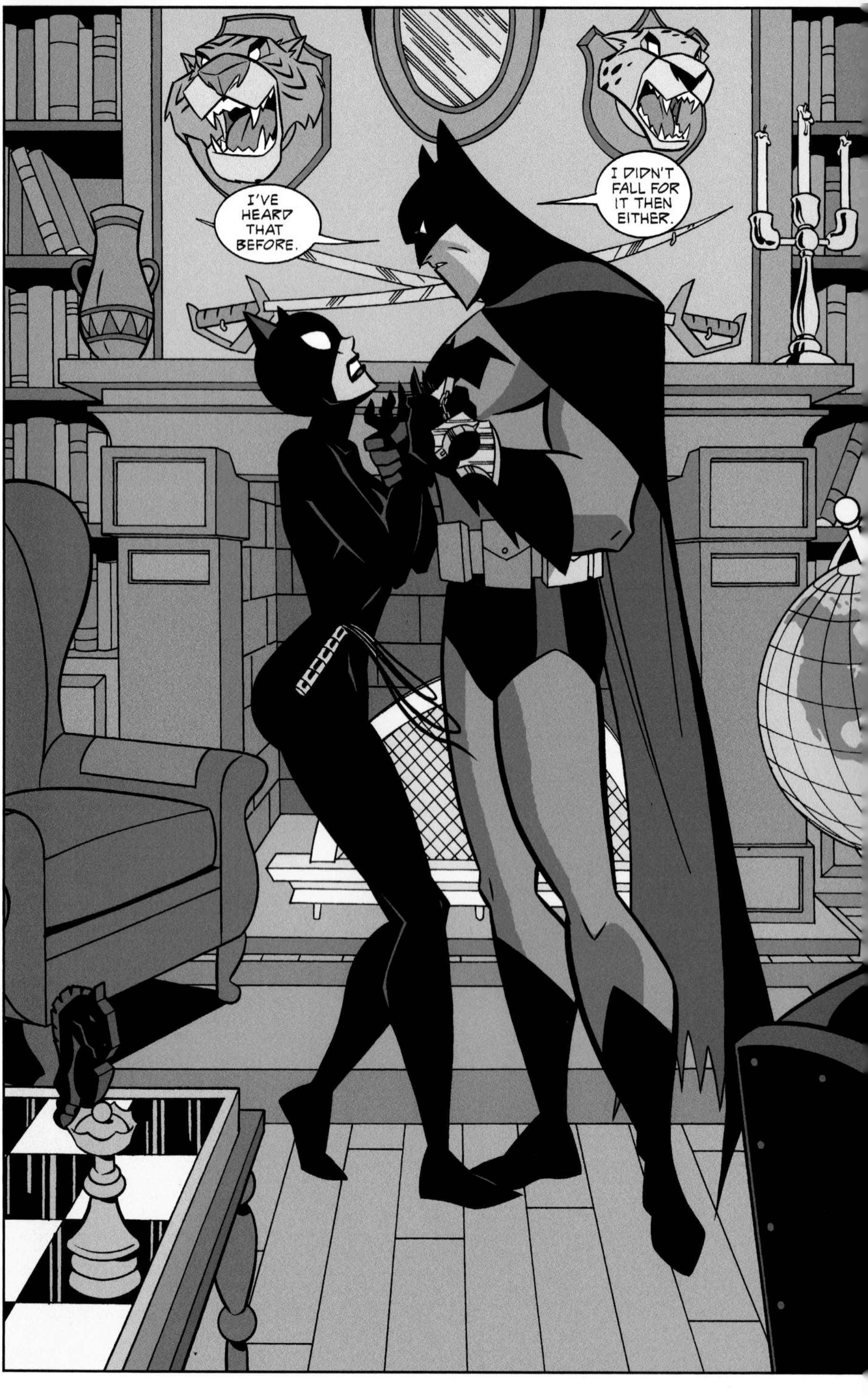
I'VE HEARD THAT BEFORE.
I DIDN'T FALL FOR IT THEN EITHER.

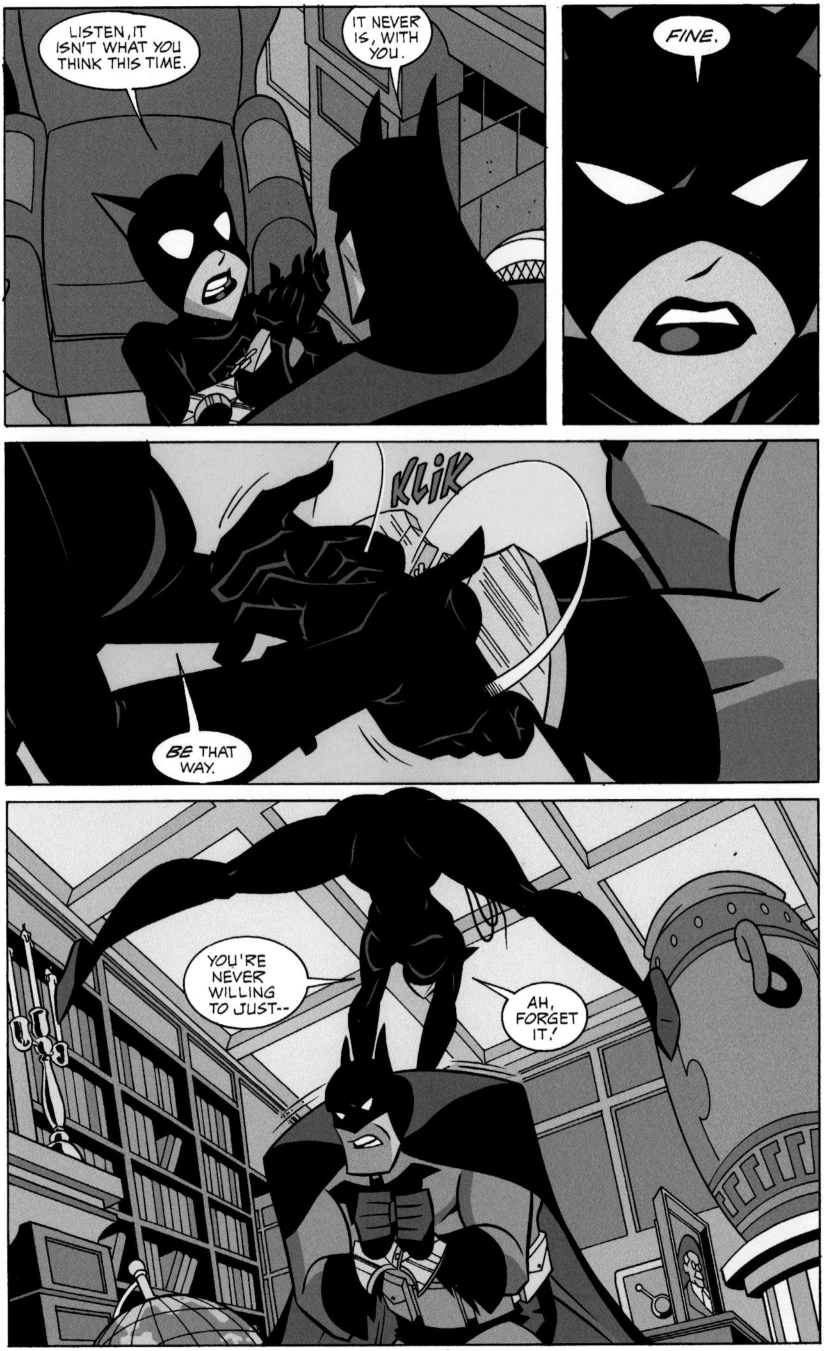
LISTEN, IT ISN'T WHAT YOU THINK THIS TIME.
IT NEVER IS, WITH YOU.
FINE.
KLIK
BE THAT WAY.
YOU'RE NEVER WILLING TO JUST--
AH, FORGET IT!

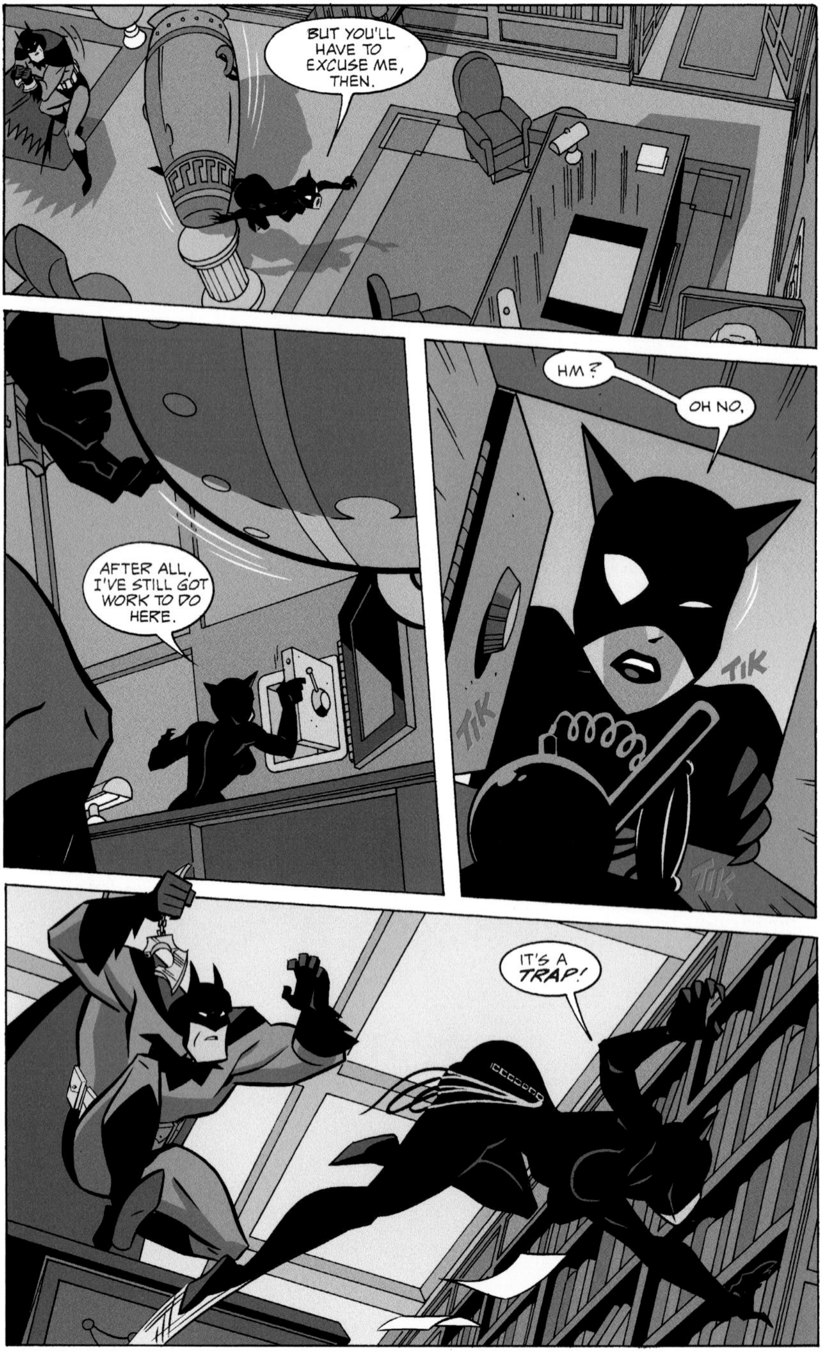
BUT YOU'LL HAVE TO EXCUSE ME, THEN.
AFTER ALL, I'VE STILL GOT WORK TO DO HERE.
HM?
OH NO.
TIK
TIK
TIK
IT'S A TRAP!

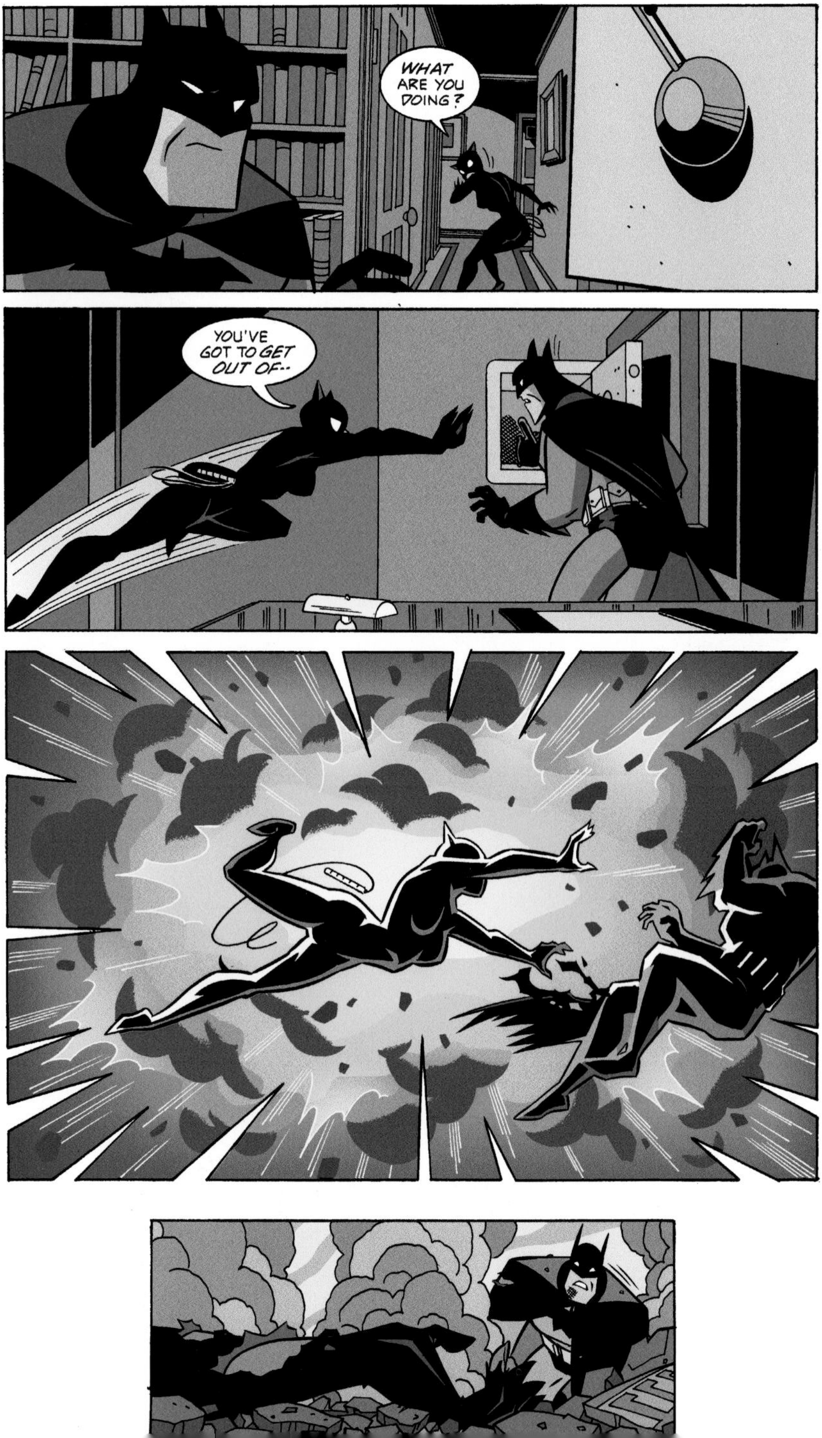
WHAT ARE YOU DOING?
YOU'VE GOT TO GET OUT OF--

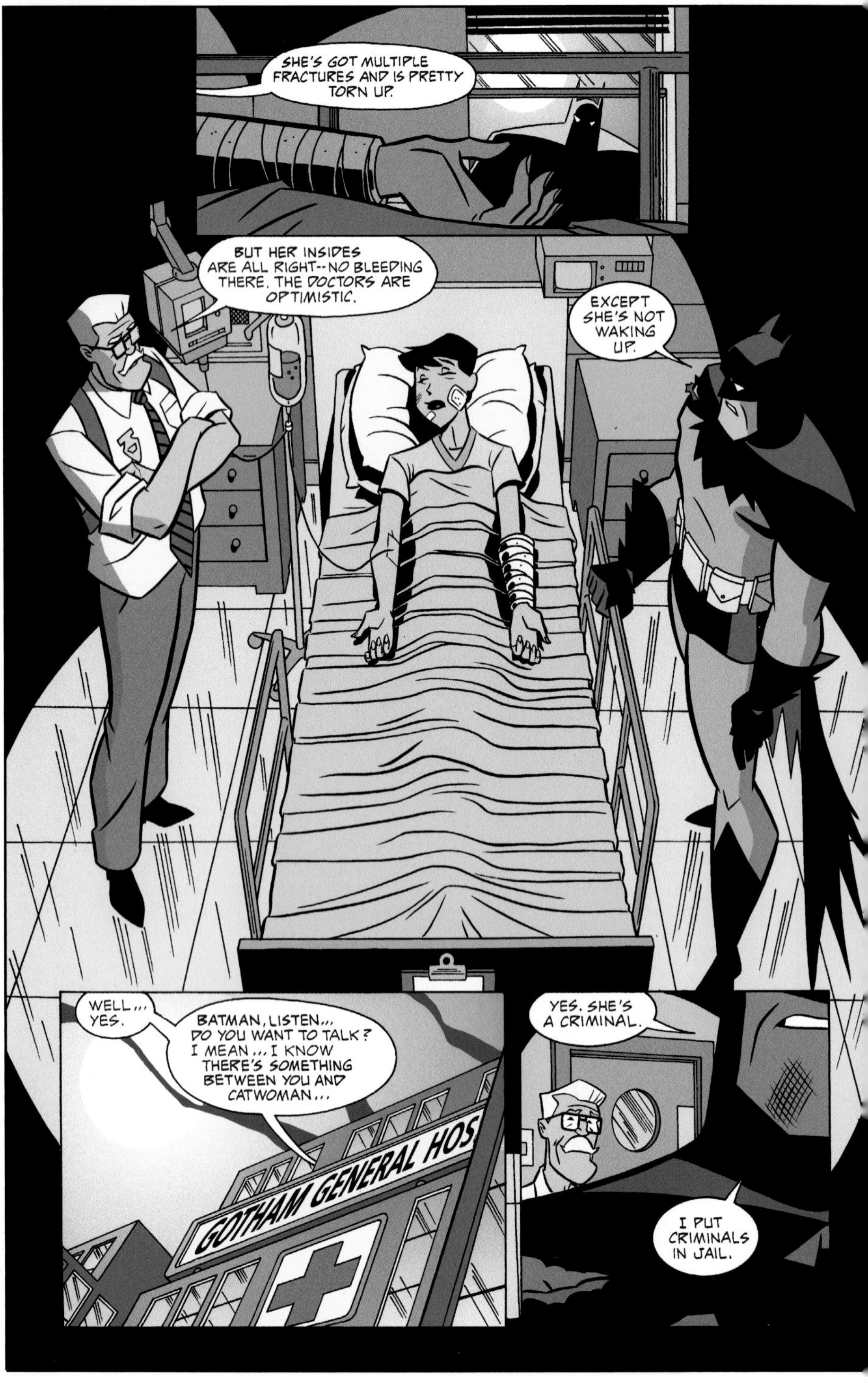
SHE'S GOT MULTIPLE FRACTURES AND IS PRETTY TORN UP.
BUT HER INSIDES ARE ALL RIGHT--NO BLEEDING THERE. THE DOCTORS ARE OPTIMISTIC.
EXCEPT SHE'S NOT WAKING UP.
WELL... YES.
BATMAN, LISTEN... DO YOU WANT TO TALK? I MEAN... I KNOW THERE'S SOMETHING BETWEEN YOU AND CATWOMAN...
GOTHAM GENERAL HOS
YES. SHE'S A CRIMINAL.
I PUT CRIMINALS IN JAIL.

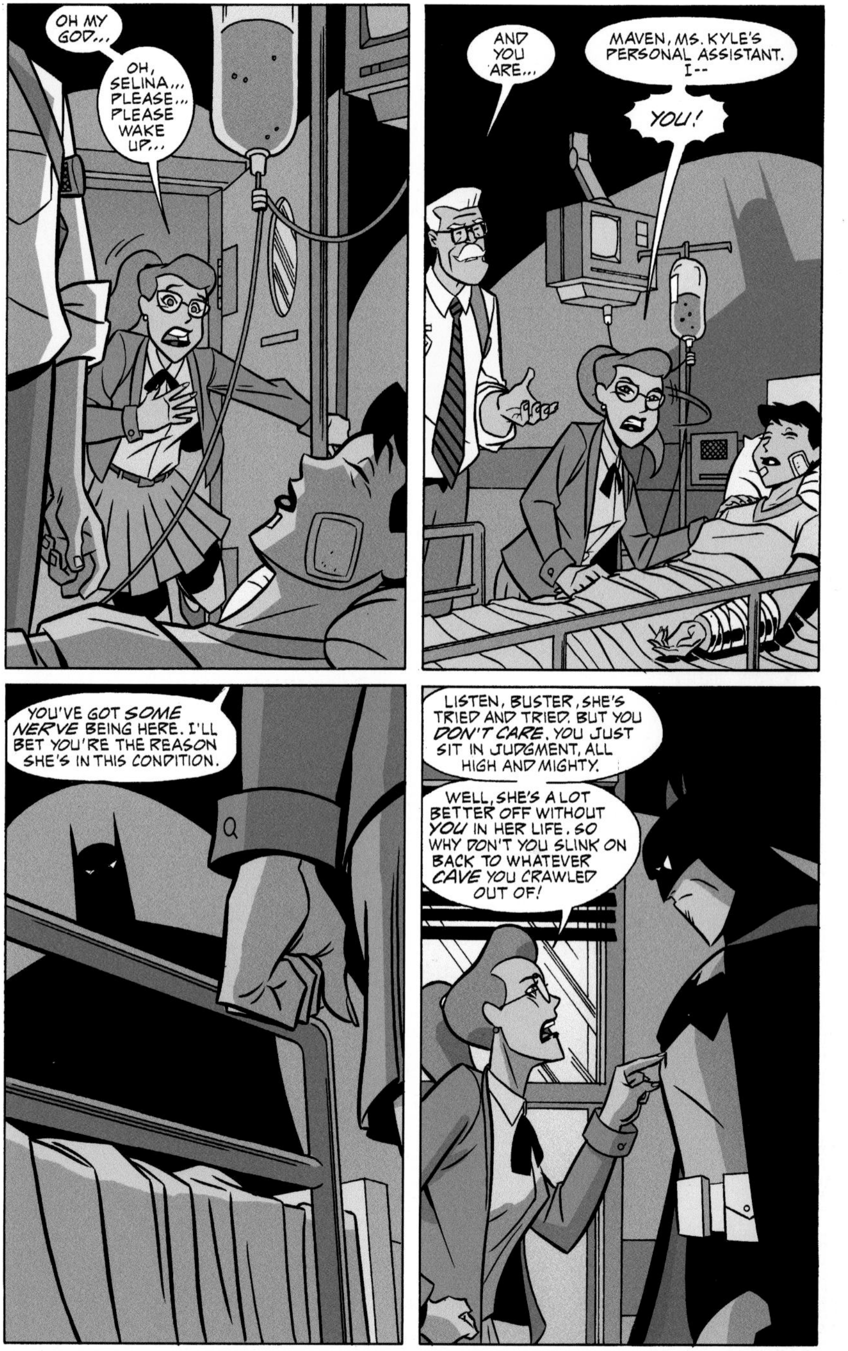
OH MY GOD...
OH, SELINA... PLEASE... PLEASE WAKE UP...
AND YOU ARE...
MAVEN, MS. KYLE'S PERSONAL ASSISTANT. I--
YOU!
YOU'VE GOT SOME NERVE BEING HERE. I'LL BET YOU'RE THE REASON SHE'S IN THIS CONDITION.
LISTEN, BUSTER, SHE'S TRIED AND TRIED. BUT YOU DON'T CARE. YOU JUST SIT IN JUDGMENT, ALL HIGH AND MIGHTY.
WELL, SHE'S A LOT BETTER OFF WITHOUT YOU IN HER LIFE. SO WHY DON'T YOU SLINK ON BACK TO WHATEVER CAVE YOU CRAWLED OUT OF!

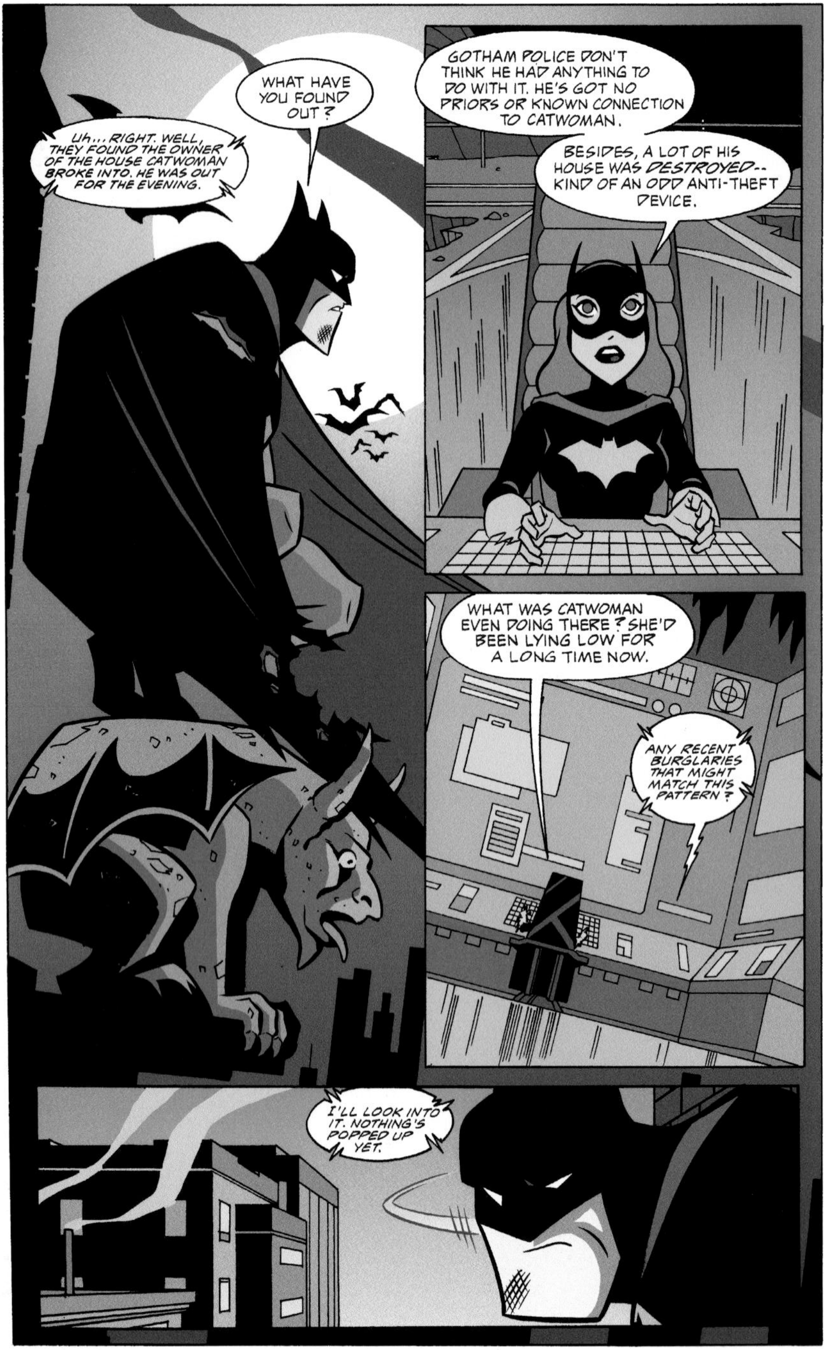
WHAT HAVE YOU FOUND OUT?
Uh... RIGHT. WELL, THEY FOUND THE OWNER OF THE HOUSE CATWOMAN BROKE INTO. HE WAS OUT FOR THE EVENING.
GOTHAM POLICE DON'T THINK HE HAD ANYTHING TO DO WITH IT. HE'S GOT NO PRIORS OR KNOWN CONNECTION TO CATWOMAN.
BESIDES, A LOT OF HIS HOUSE WAS DESTROYED-- KIND OF AN ODD ANTI-THEFT DEVICE.
WHAT WAS CATWOMAN EVEN DOING THERE? SHE'D BEEN LYING LOW FOR A LONG TIME NOW.
ANY RECENT BURGLARIES THAT MIGHT MATCH THIS PATTERN?
I'LL LOOK INTO IT. NOTHING'S POPPED UP YET.

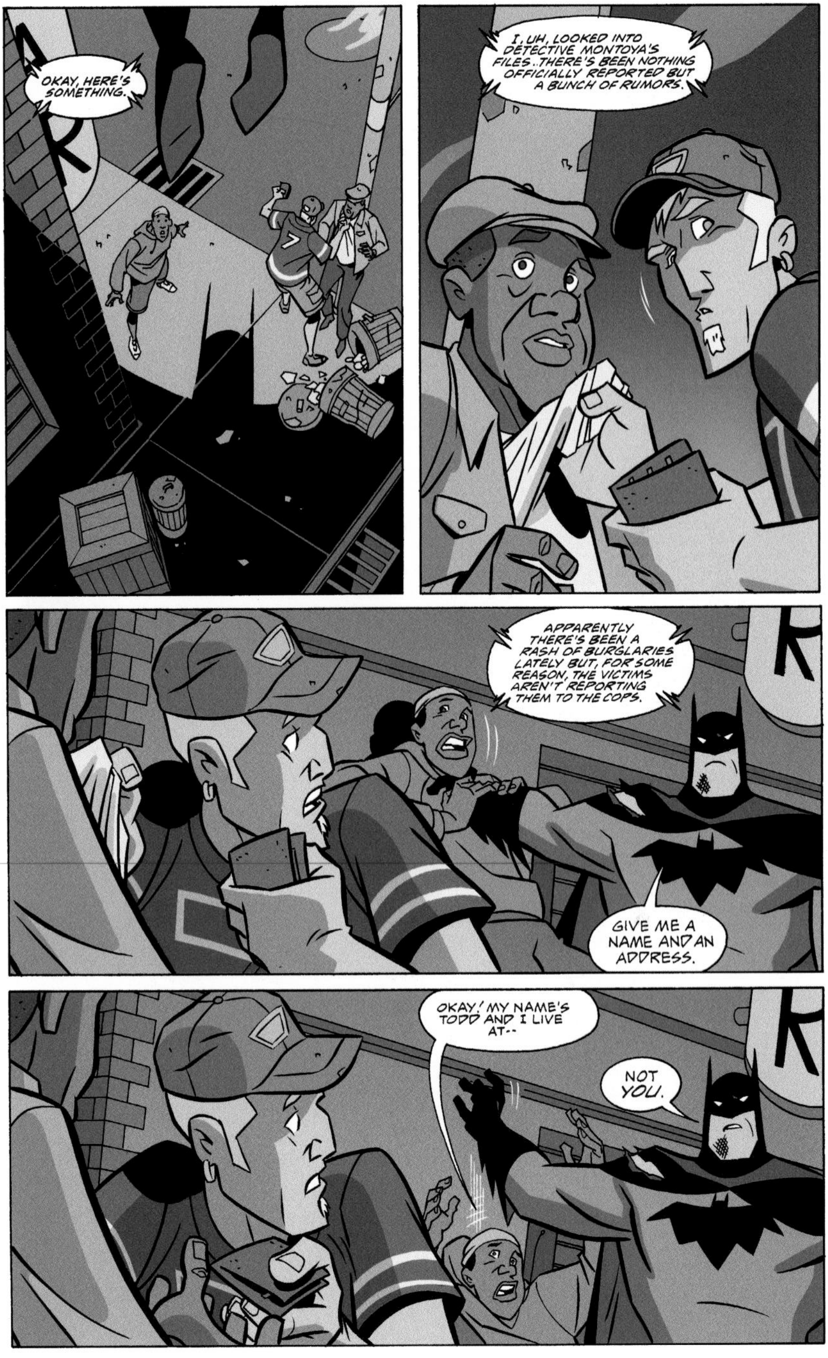
OKAY, HERE'S SOMETHING.
I, UH, LOOKED INTO DETECTIVE MONTOYA'S FILES..THERE'S BEEN NOTHING OFFICIALLY REPORTED BUT A BUNCH OF RUMORS.
APPARENTLY THERE'S BEEN A RASH OF BURGLARIES LATELY BUT, FOR SOME REASON, THE VICTIMS AREN'T REPORTING THEM TO THE COPS.
GIVE ME A NAME AND AN ADDRESS.
OKAY! MY NAME'S TODD AND I LIVE AT--
NOT YOU.

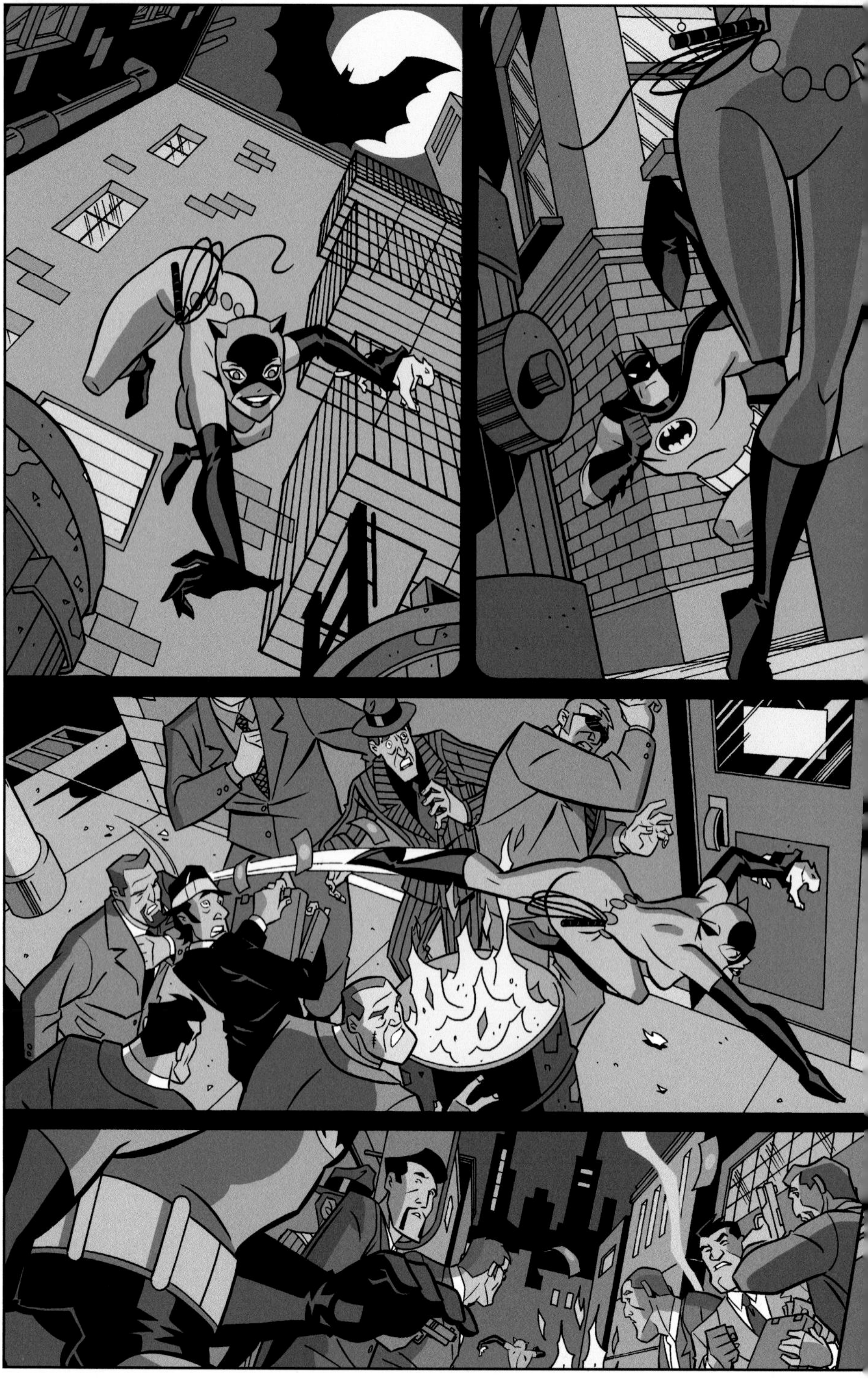

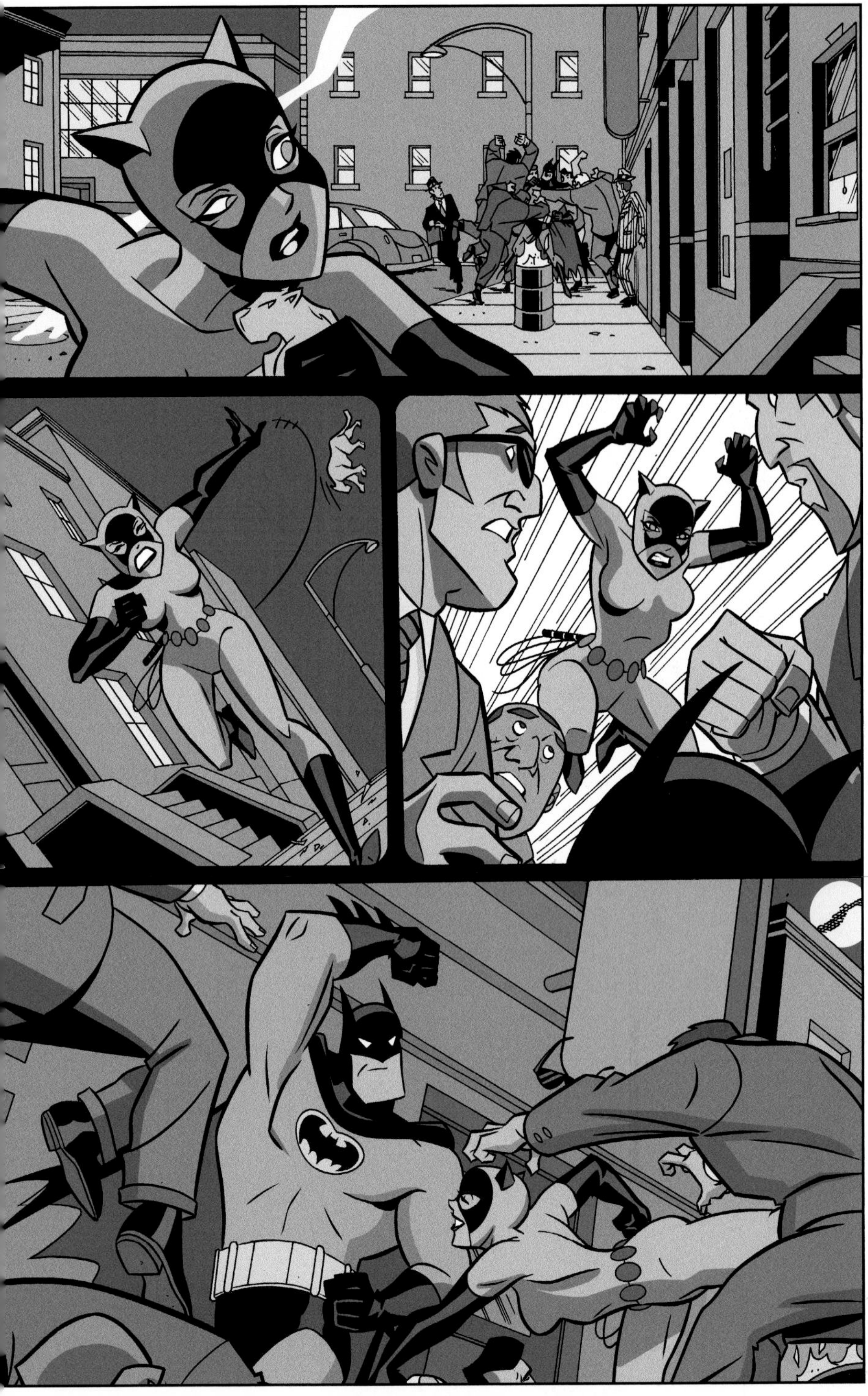

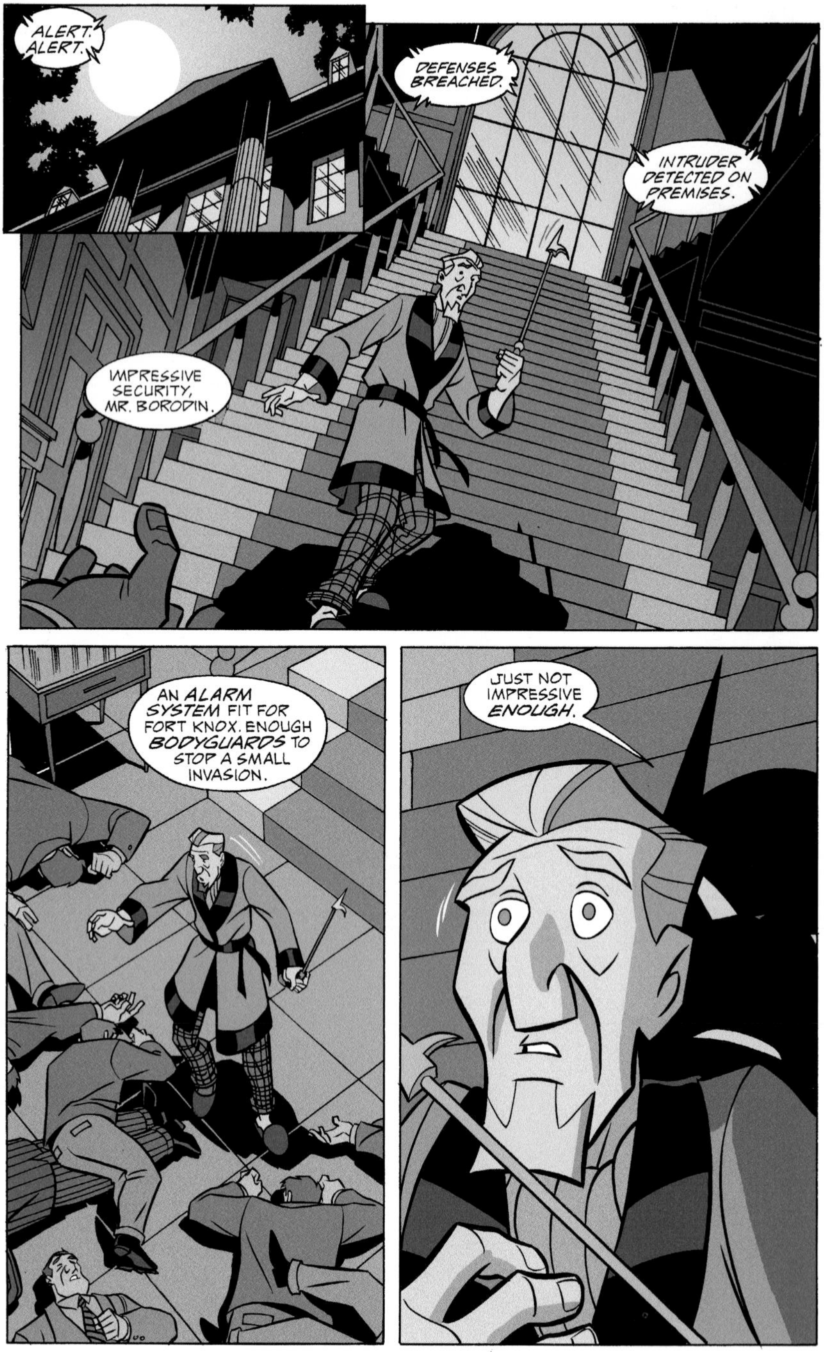
ALERT. ALERT.
DEFENSES BREACHED.
INTRUDER DETECTED ON PREMISES.
IMPRESSIVE SECURITY, MR. BORODIN.
AN ALARM SYSTEM FIT FOR FORT KNOX. ENOUGH BODYGUARDS TO STOP A SMALL INVASION.
JUST NOT IMPRESSIVE ENOUGH.

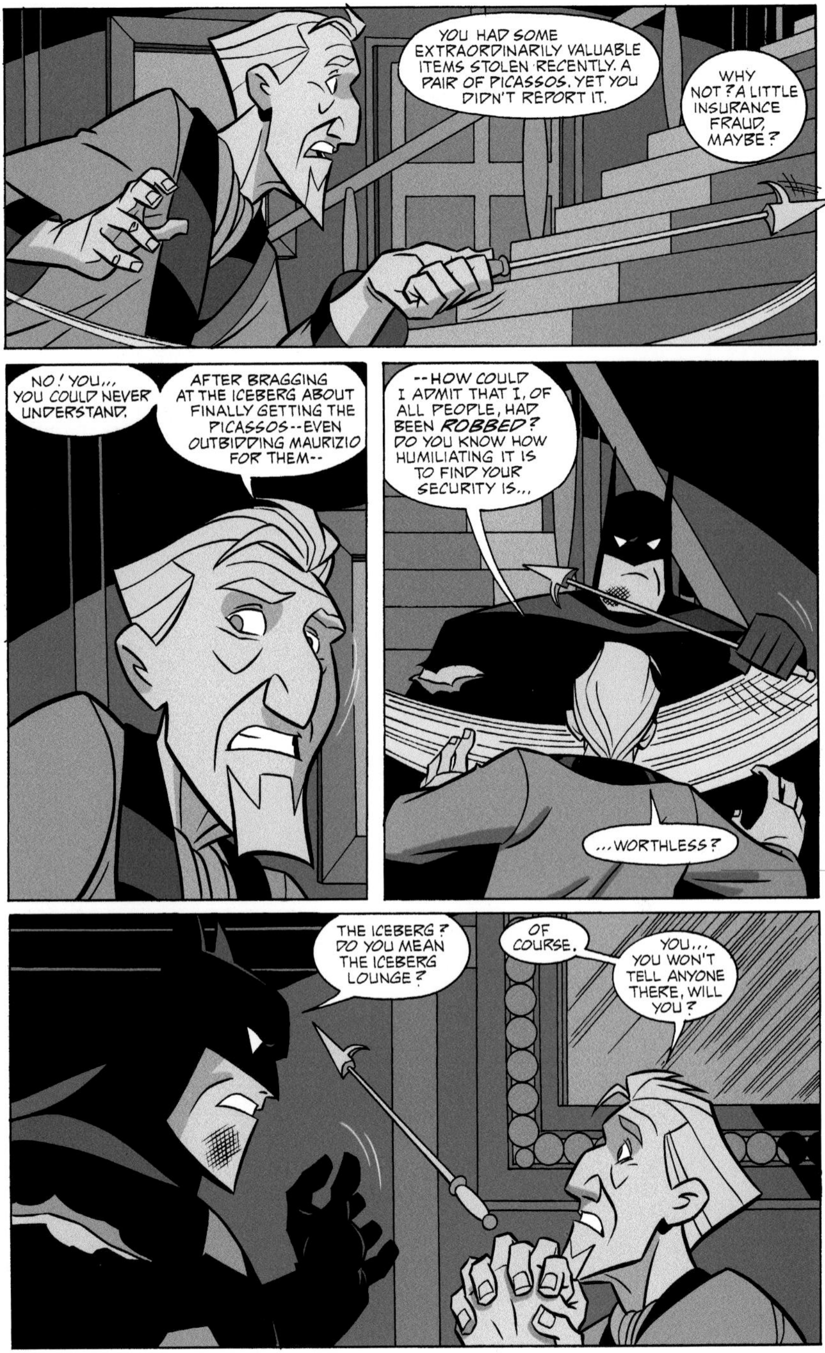
YOU HAD SOME EXTRAORDINARILY VALUABLE ITEMS STOLEN RECENTLY. A PAIR OF PICASSOS. YET YOU DIDN'T REPORT IT.
WHY NOT? A LITTLE INSURANCE FRAUD, MAYBE?
NO! YOU... YOU COULD NEVER UNDERSTAND.
AFTER BRAGGING AT THE ICEBERG ABOUT FINALLY GETTING THE PICASSOS--EVEN OUTBIDDING MAURIZIO FOR THEM--
--HOW COULD I ADMIT THAT I, OF ALL PEOPLE, HAD BEEN ROBBED? DO YOU KNOW HOW HUMILIATING IT IS TO FIND YOUR SECURITY IS...
...WORTHLESS?
THE ICEBERG? DO YOU MEAN THE ICEBERG LOUNGE?
OF COURSE.
YOU... YOU WON'T TELL ANYONE THERE, WILL YOU?

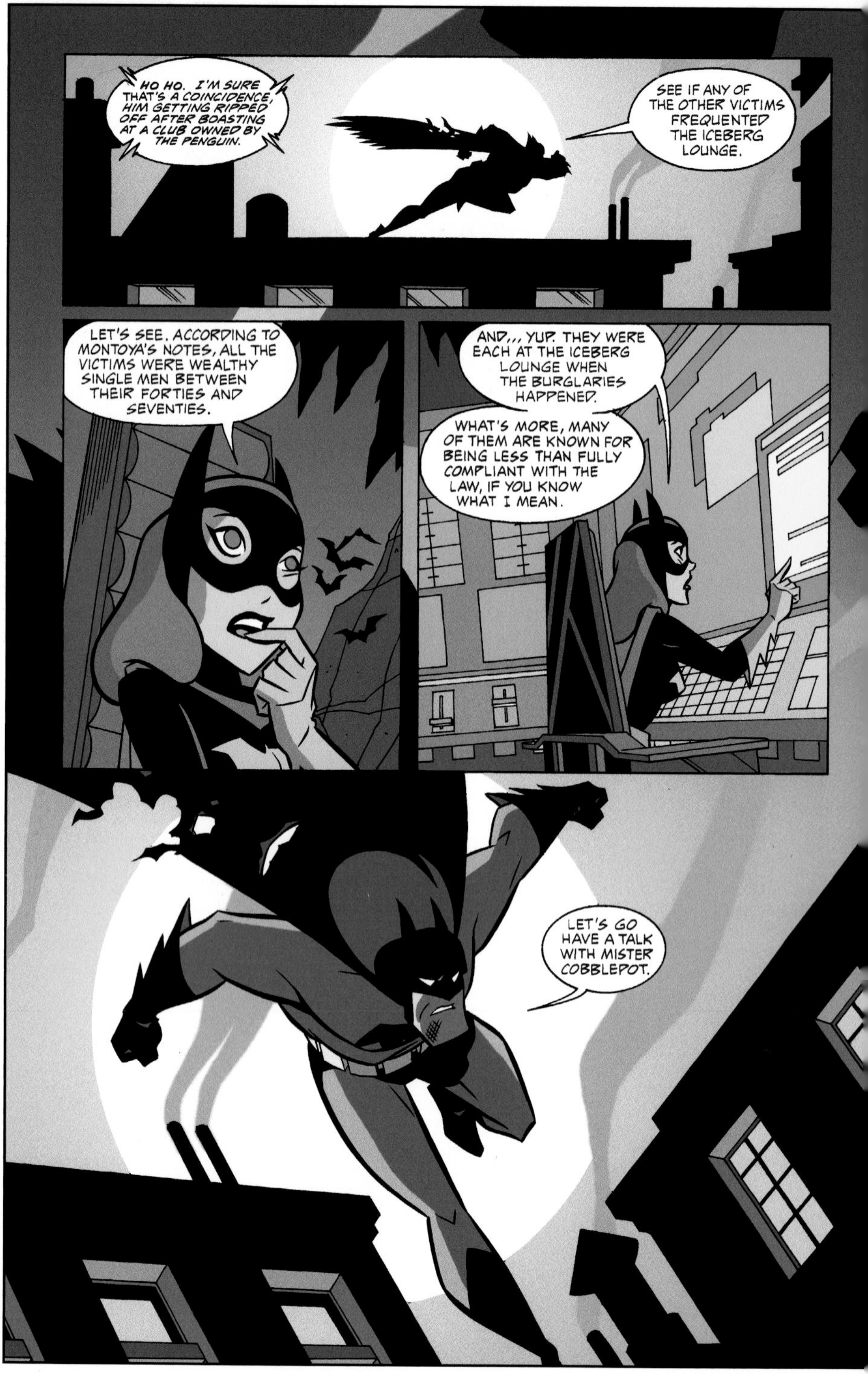
HO HO. I'M SURE THAT'S A COINCIDENCE, HIM GETTING RIPPED OFF AFTER BOASTING AT A CLUB OWNED BY THE PENGUIN.
SEE IF ANY OF THE OTHER VICTIMS FREQUENTED THE ICEBERG LOUNGE.
LET'S SEE. ACCORDING TO MONTOYA'S NOTES, ALL THE VICTIMS WERE WEALTHY SINGLE MEN BETWEEN THEIR FORTIES AND SEVENTIES.
AND,,, YUP. THEY WERE EACH AT THE ICEBERG LOUNGE WHEN THE BURGLARIES HAPPENED.
WHAT'S MORE, MANY OF THEM ARE KNOWN FOR BEING LESS THAN FULLY COMPLIANT WITH THE LAW, IF YOU KNOW WHAT I MEAN.
LET'S GO HAVE A TALK WITH MISTER COBBLEPOT.

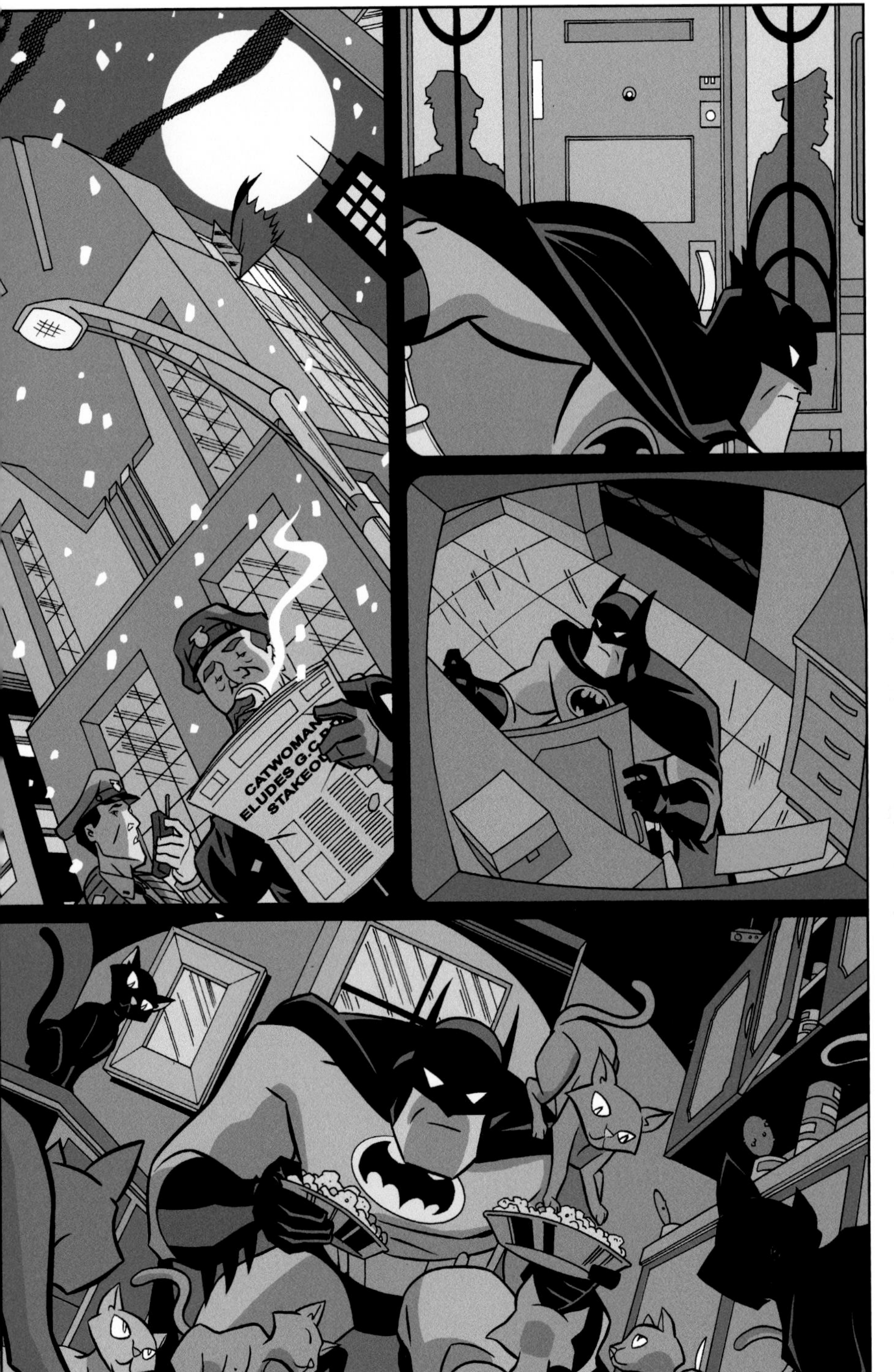
CATWOMAN
ELUDES G.C.P
STAKEOU

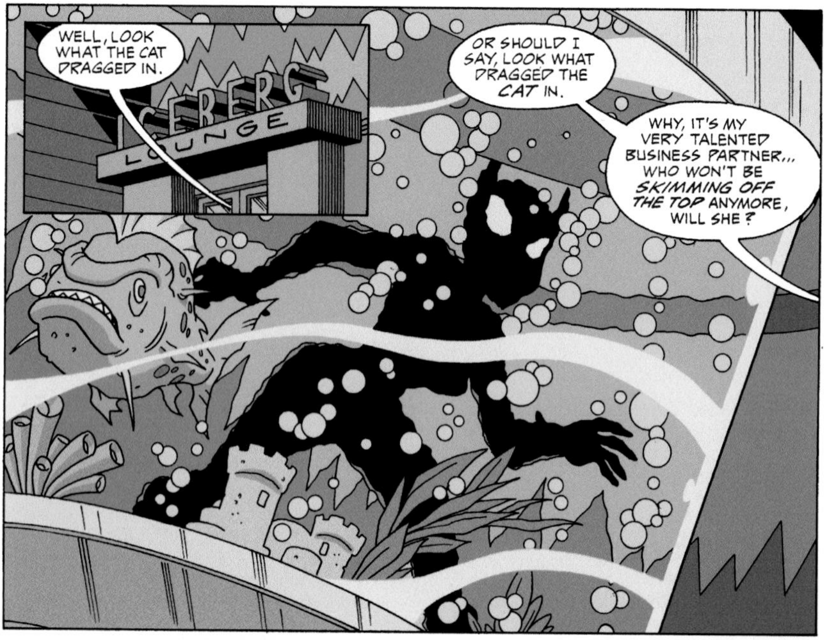
ICEBERG
LOUNGE
WELL, LOOK WHAT THE CAT DRAGGED IN.
OR SHOULD I SAY, LOOK WHAT DRAGGED THE CAT IN.
WHY, IT'S MY VERY TALENTED BUSINESS PARTNER... WHO WON'T BE SKIMMING OFF THE TOP ANYMORE, WILL SHE?

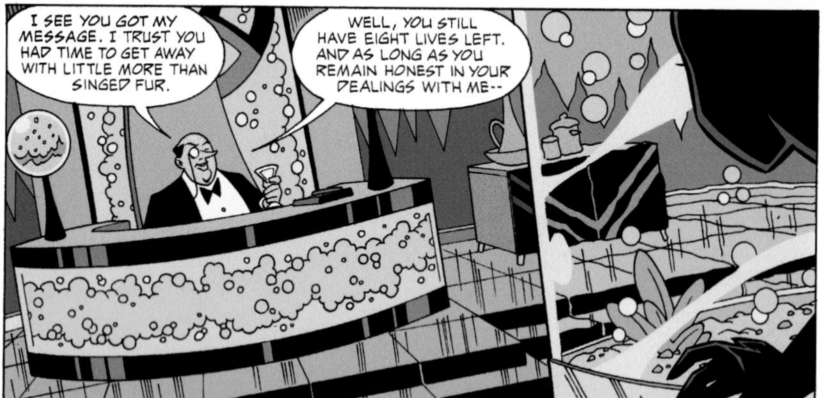
I SEE YOU GOT MY MESSAGE. I TRUST YOU HAD TIME TO GET AWAY WITH LITTLE MORE THAN SINGED FUR.
WELL, YOU STILL HAVE EIGHT LIVES LEFT. AND AS LONG AS YOU REMAIN HONEST IN YOUR DEALINGS WITH ME--

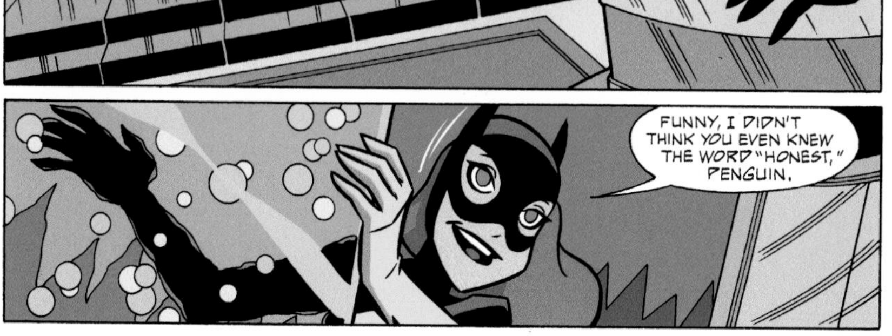
FUNNY, I DIDN'T THINK YOU EVEN KNEW THE WORD "HONEST," PENGUIN.

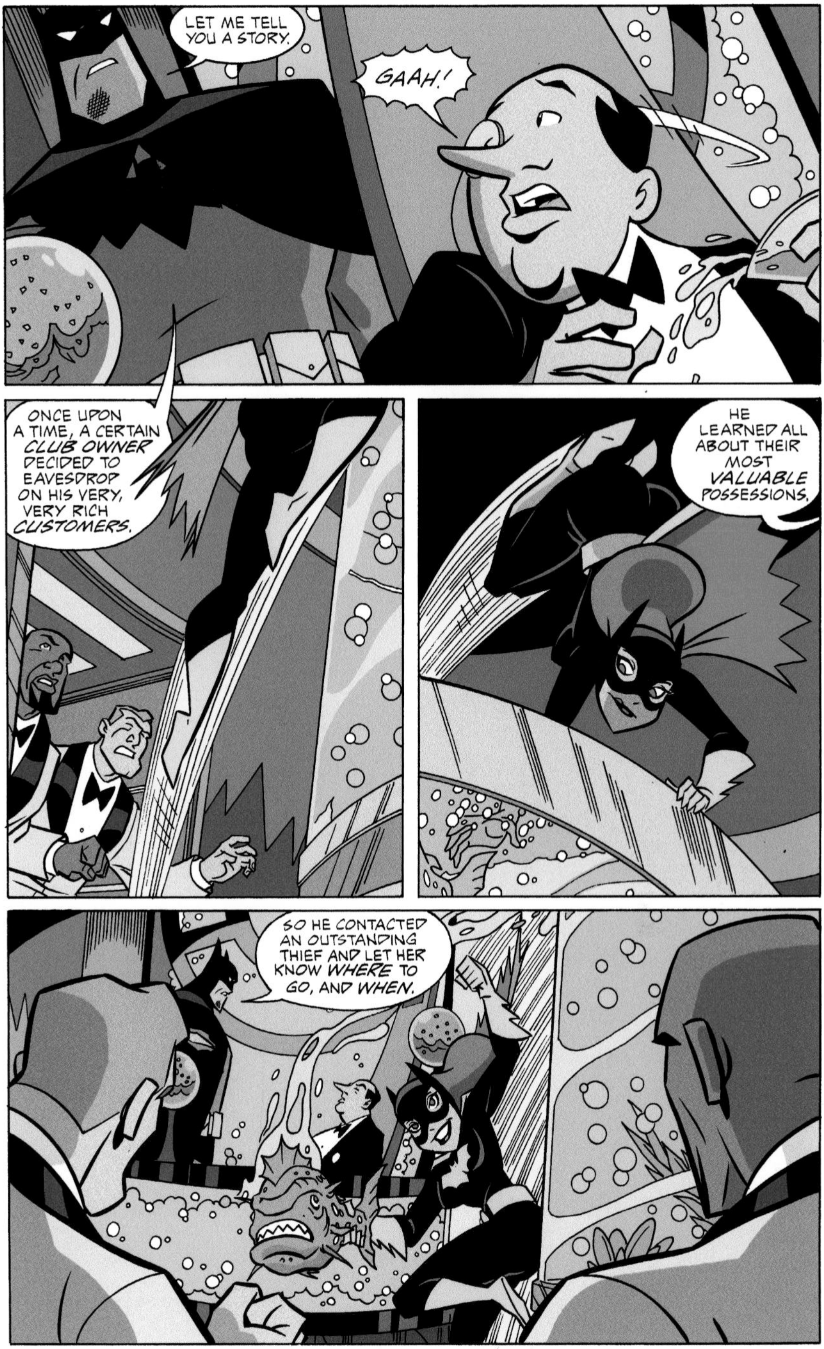
LET ME TELL YOU A STORY.
GAAH!
ONCE UPON A TIME, A CERTAIN CLUB OWNER DECIDED TO EAVESDROP ON HIS VERY, VERY RICH CUSTOMERS.
HE LEARNED ALL ABOUT THEIR MOST VALUABLE POSSESSIONS,
SO HE CONTACTED AN OUTSTANDING THIEF AND LET HER KNOW WHERE TO GO, AND WHEN.

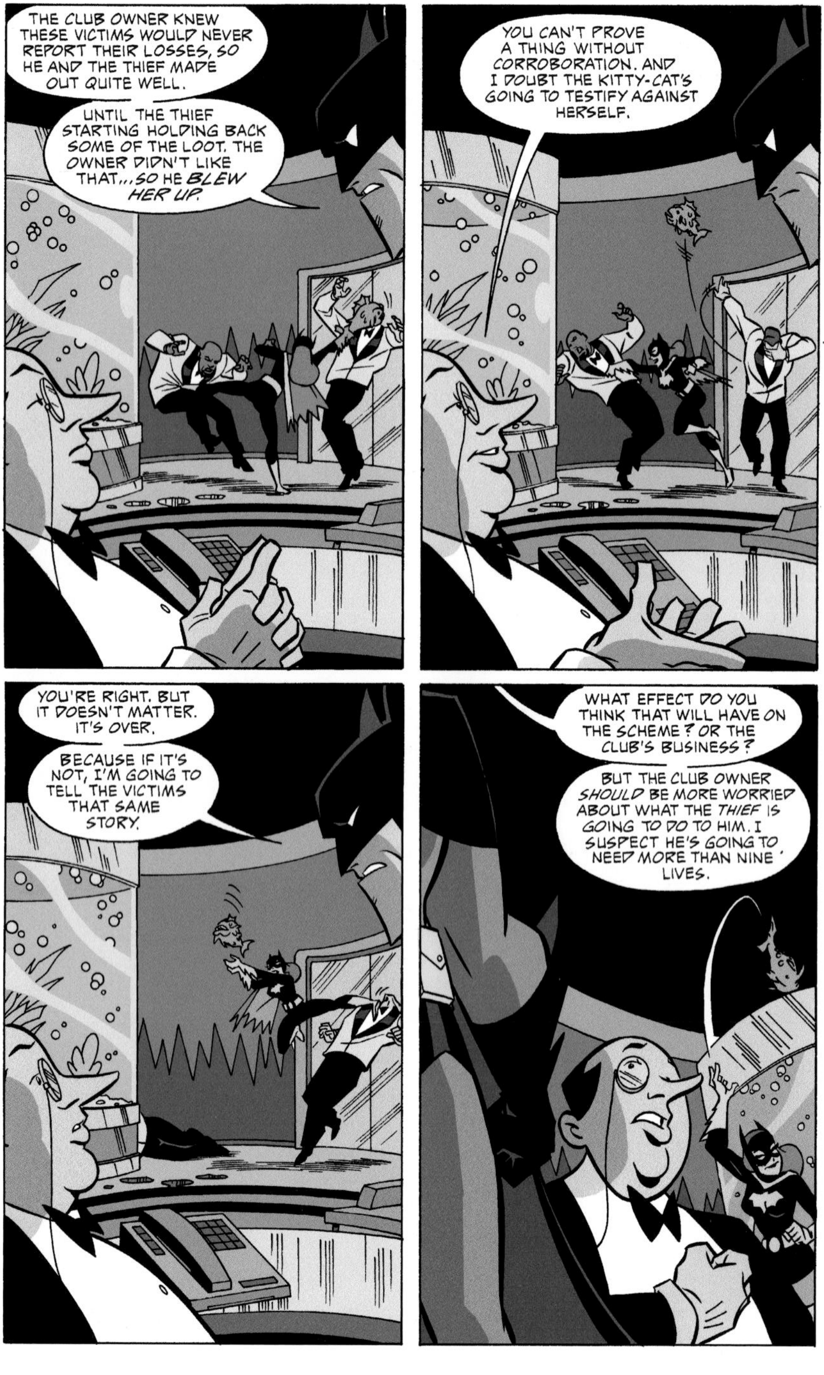
THE CLUB OWNER KNEW THESE VICTIMS WOULD NEVER REPORT THEIR LOSSES, SO HE AND THE THIEF MADE OUT QUITE WELL.
UNTIL THE THIEF STARTING HOLDING BACK SOME OF THE LOOT. THE OWNER DIDN'T LIKE THAT... SO HE *BLEW HER UP.*
YOU CAN'T PROVE A THING WITHOUT CORROBORATION. AND I DOUBT THE KITTY-CAT'S GOING TO TESTIFY AGAINST HERSELF.
YOU'RE RIGHT. BUT IT DOESN'T MATTER. IT'S OVER.
BECAUSE IF IT'S NOT, I'M GOING TO TELL THE VICTIMS THAT SAME STORY.
WHAT EFFECT DO YOU THINK THAT WILL HAVE ON THE SCHEME? OR THE CLUB'S BUSINESS?
BUT THE CLUB OWNER *SHOULD* BE MORE WORRIED ABOUT WHAT THE *THIEF* IS GOING TO DO TO HIM. I SUSPECT HE'S GOING TO NEED MORE THAN NINE LIVES.

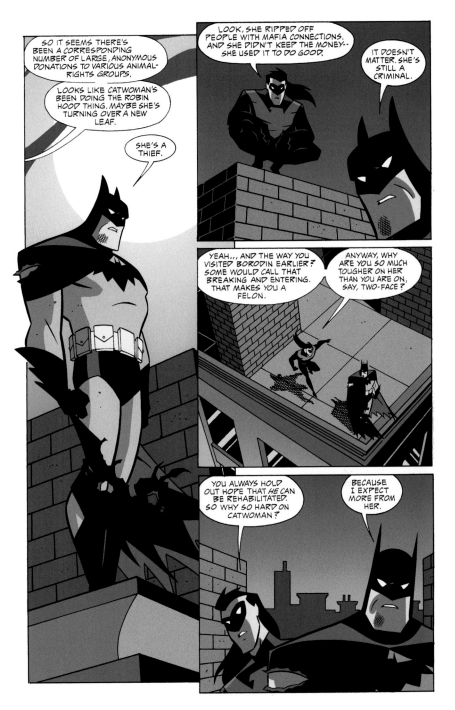

SO IT SEEMS THERE'S BEEN A *CORRESPONDING* NUMBER OF LARGE, ANONYMOUS DONATIONS TO VARIOUS ANIMAL-RIGHTS GROUPS.

LOOKS LIKE CATWOMAN'S BEEN DOING THE *ROBIN HOOD* THING. MAYBE SHE'S TURNING OVER A NEW LEAF.

SHE'S A THIEF.

LOOK, SHE RIPPED OFF PEOPLE WITH MAFIA CONNECTIONS. AND SHE DIDN'T KEEP THE MONEY-- SHE USED IT TO DO *GOOD*.

IT DOESN'T MATTER. SHE'S STILL A CRIMINAL.

YEAH,,, AND THE WAY YOU VISITED BORODIN EARLIER? SOME WOULD CALL THAT BREAKING AND ENTERING. THAT MAKES YOU A FELON.

ANYWAY, WHY ARE YOU SO MUCH TOUGHER ON HER THAN YOU ARE ON, SAY, TWO-FACE?

YOU ALWAYS HOLD OUT HOPE THAT *HE* CAN BE REHABILITATED. SO WHY SO HARD ON CATWOMAN?

BECAUSE I EXPECT MORE FROM HER.

107

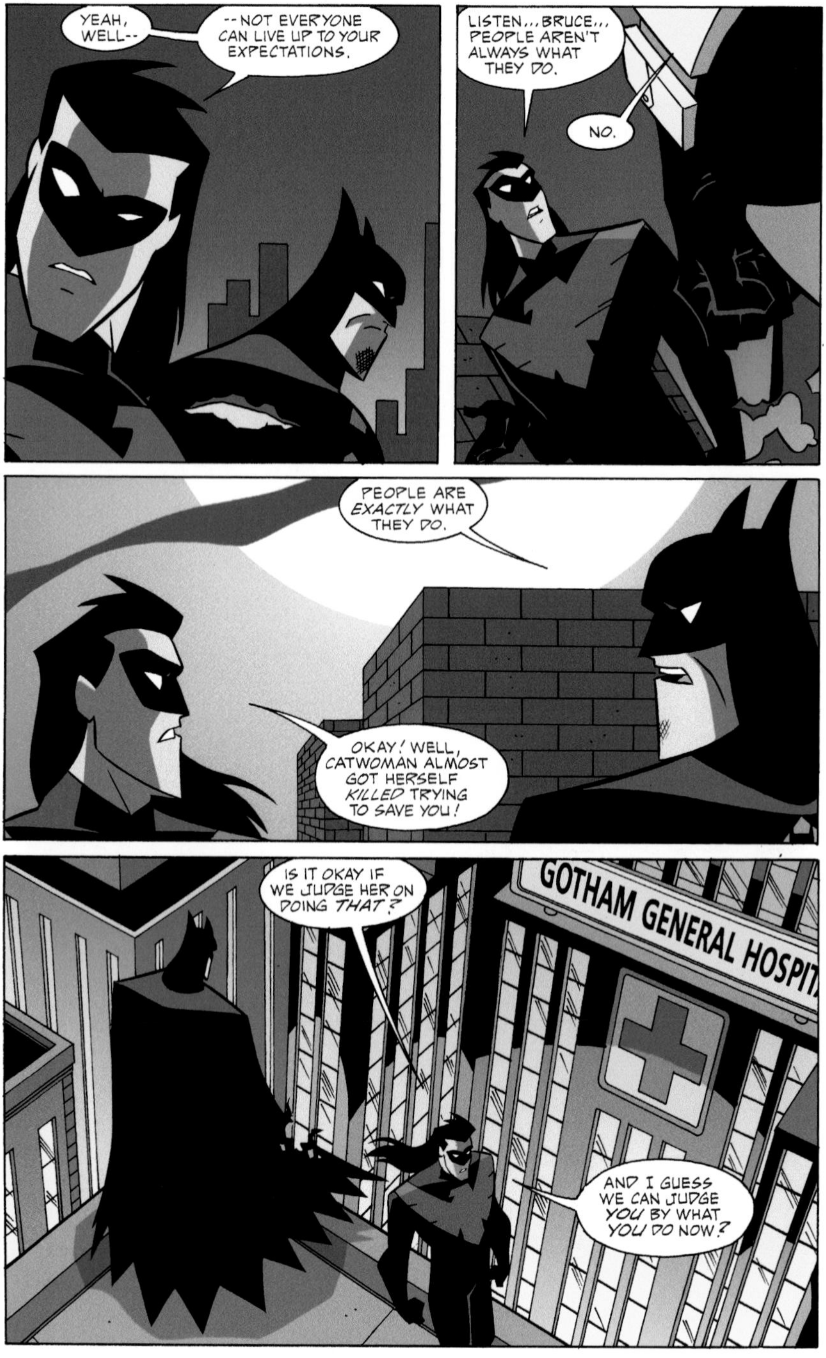
YEAH, WELL--
--NOT EVERYONE CAN LIVE UP TO YOUR EXPECTATIONS.
LISTEN... BRUCE... PEOPLE AREN'T ALWAYS WHAT THEY DO.
NO.
PEOPLE ARE EXACTLY WHAT THEY DO.
OKAY! WELL, CATWOMAN ALMOST GOT HERSELF KILLED TRYING TO SAVE YOU!
IS IT OKAY IF WE JUDGE HER ON DOING THAT?
GOTHAM GENERAL HOSPIT
AND I GUESS WE CAN JUDGE YOU BY WHAT YOU DO NOW?

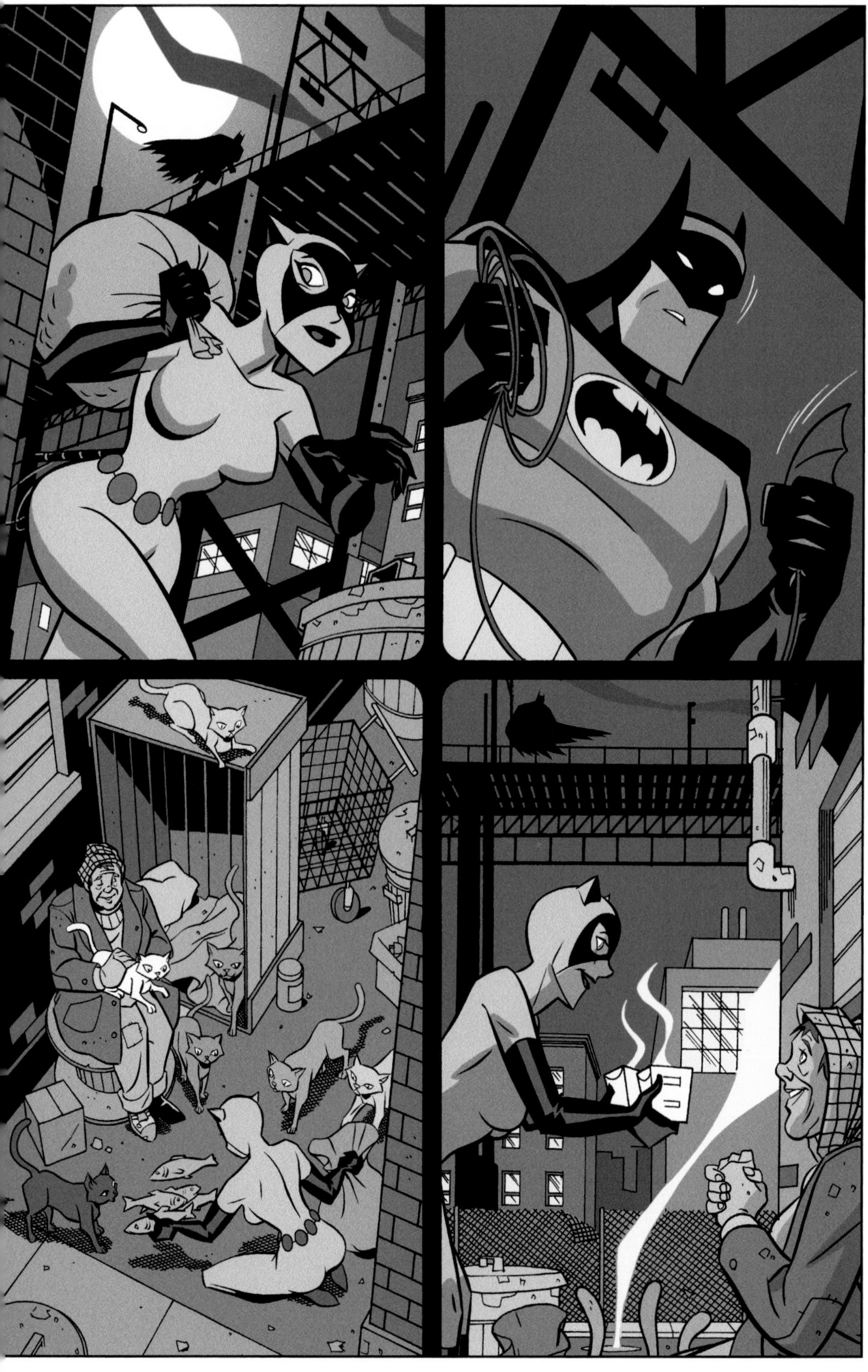

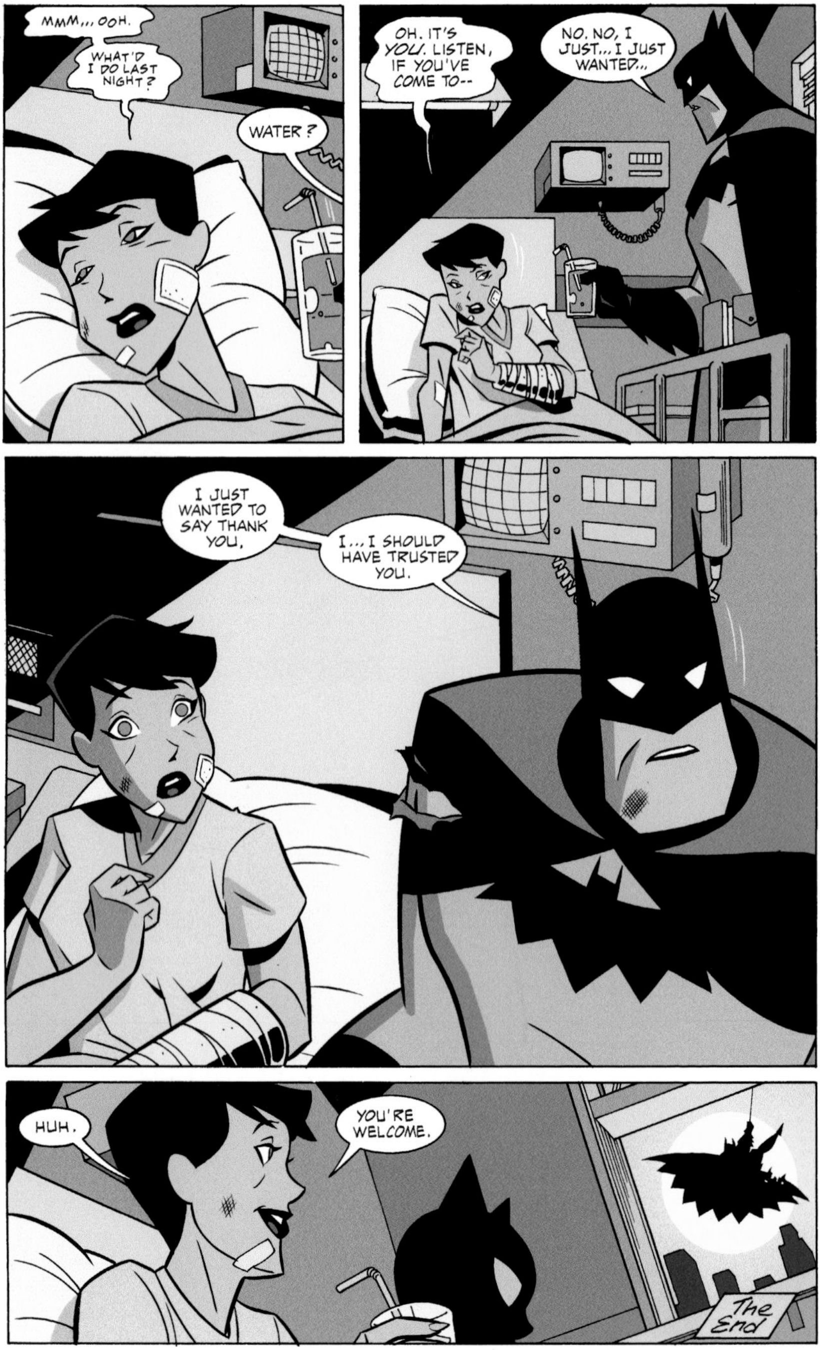
MMM,,, OOH.
WHAT'D I DO LAST NIGHT?
WATER?
OH. IT'S YOU. LISTEN, IF YOU'VE COME TO--
NO. NO, I JUST... I JUST WANTED...
I JUST WANTED TO SAY THANK YOU.
I... I SHOULD HAVE TRUSTED YOU.
HUH.
YOU'RE WELCOME.
The End

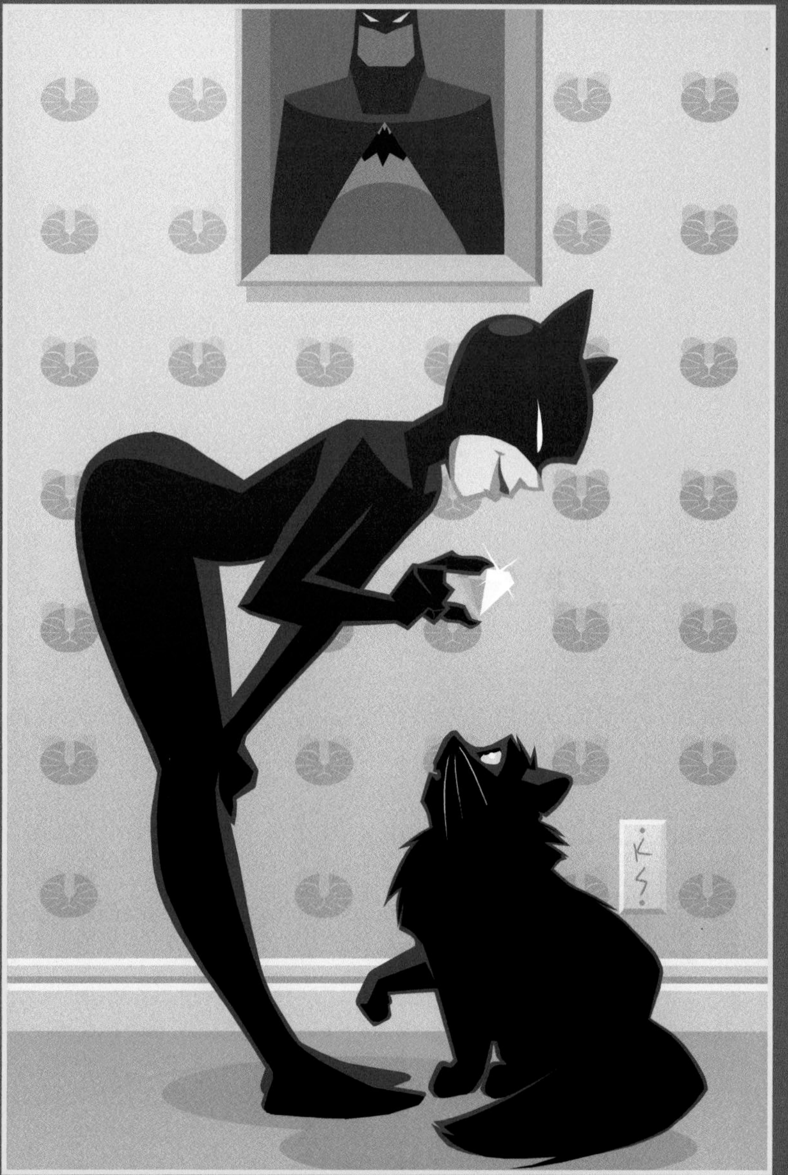

CHAPTER 6: ONE STEP AHEAD

CATWOMAN

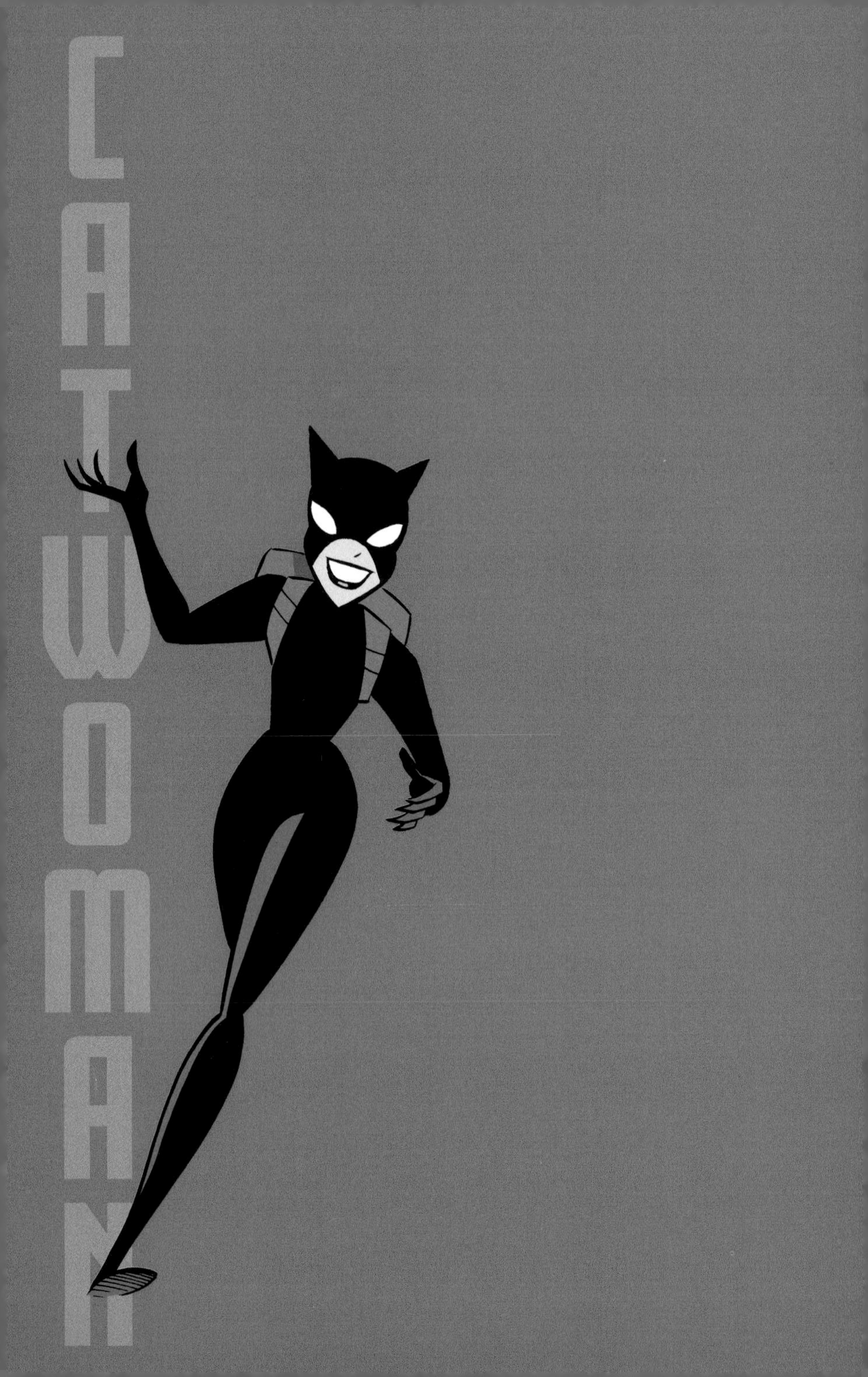
CATWOMAN

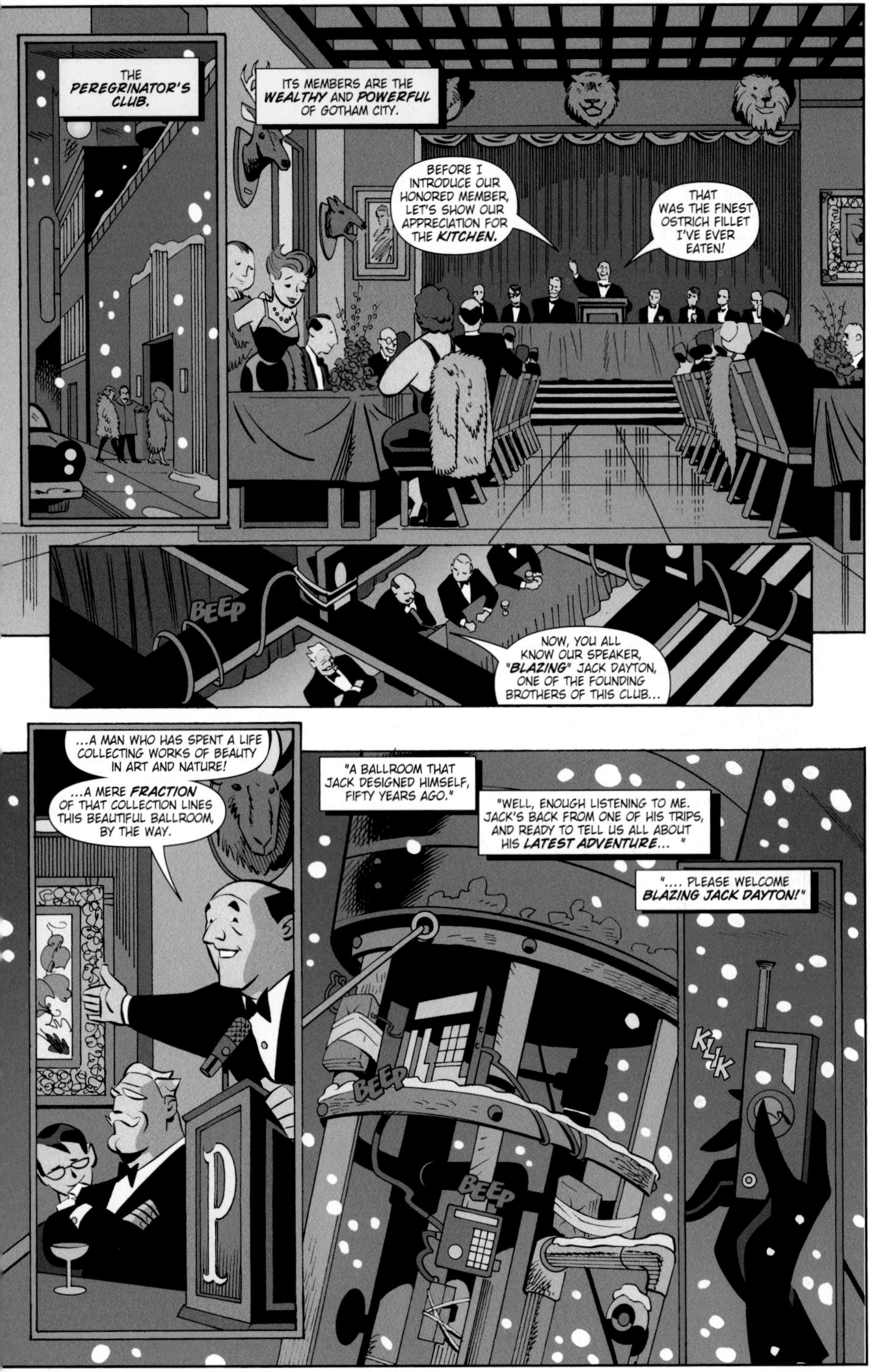
THE PEREGRINATOR'S CLUB.
ITS MEMBERS ARE THE WEALTHY AND POWERFUL OF GOTHAM CITY.
BEFORE I INTRODUCE OUR HONORED MEMBER, LET'S SHOW OUR APPRECIATION FOR THE KITCHEN.
THAT WAS THE FINEST OSTRICH FILLET I'VE EVER EATEN!
BEEP
NOW, YOU ALL KNOW OUR SPEAKER, "BLAZING" JACK DAYTON, ONE OF THE FOUNDING BROTHERS OF THIS CLUB...
...A MAN WHO HAS SPENT A LIFE COLLECTING WORKS OF BEAUTY IN ART AND NATURE!
...A MERE FRACTION OF THAT COLLECTION LINES THIS BEAUTIFUL BALLROOM, BY THE WAY.
P
"A BALLROOM THAT JACK DESIGNED HIMSELF, FIFTY YEARS AGO."
"WELL, ENOUGH LISTENING TO ME. JACK'S BACK FROM ONE OF HIS TRIPS, AND READY TO TELL US ALL ABOUT HIS LATEST ADVENTURE... "
"…. PLEASE WELCOME BLAZING JACK DAYTON!"
BEEP
BEEP
KLIK

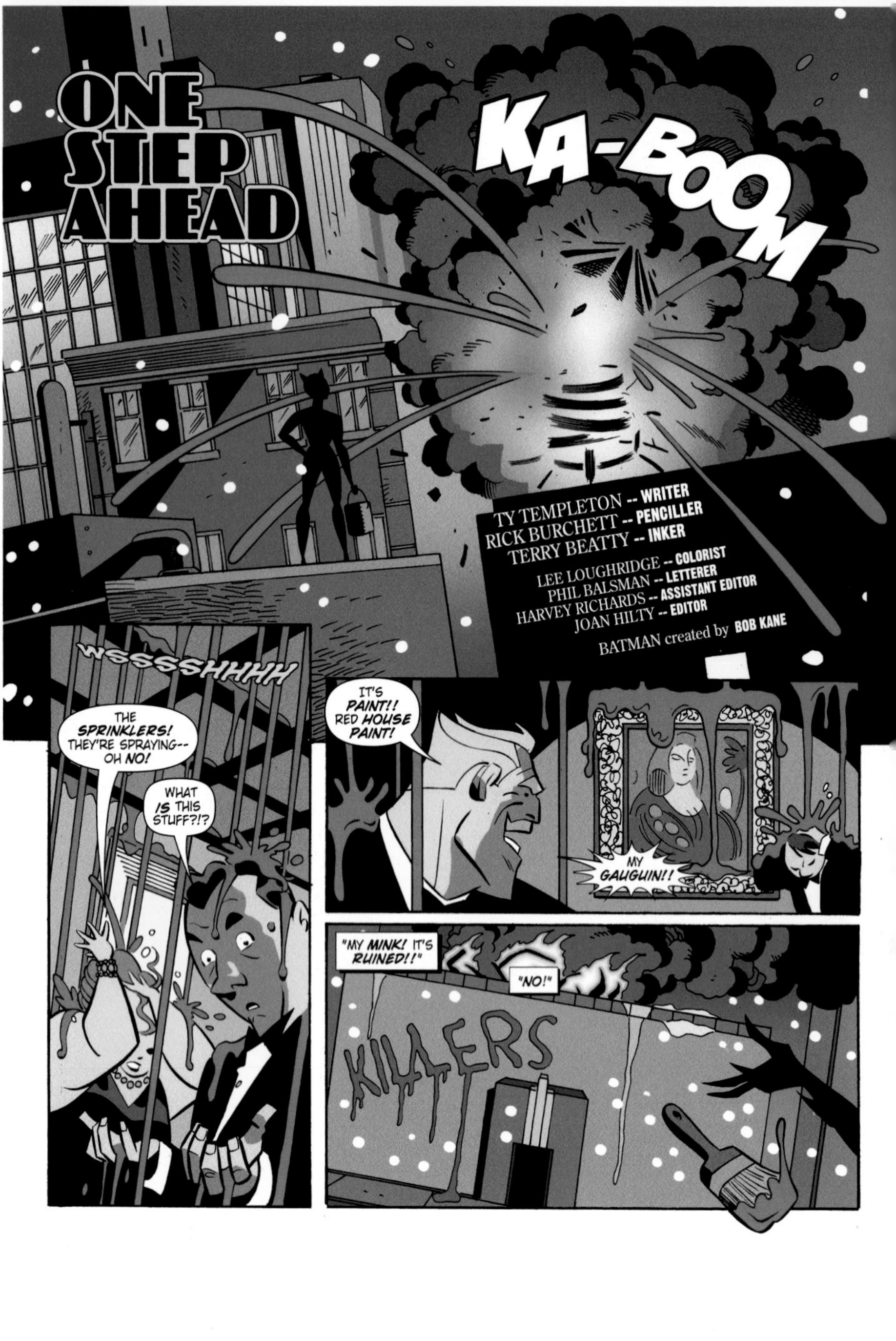

ONE STEP AHEAD
KA-BOOM
TY TEMPLETON -- WRITER
RICK BURCHETT -- PENCILLER
TERRY BEATTY -- INKER
LEE LOUGHRIDGE -- COLORIST
PHIL BALSMAN -- LETTERER
HARVEY RICHARDS -- ASSISTANT EDITOR
JOAN HILTY -- EDITOR
BATMAN created by BOB KANE
WSSSSHHHH
THE SPRINKLERS! THEY'RE SPRAYING-- OH NO!
WHAT IS THIS STUFF?!?
IT'S PAINT!! RED HOUSE PAINT!
MY GAUGUIN!!
"MY MINK! IT'S RUINED!!"
"NO!"
KILLERS

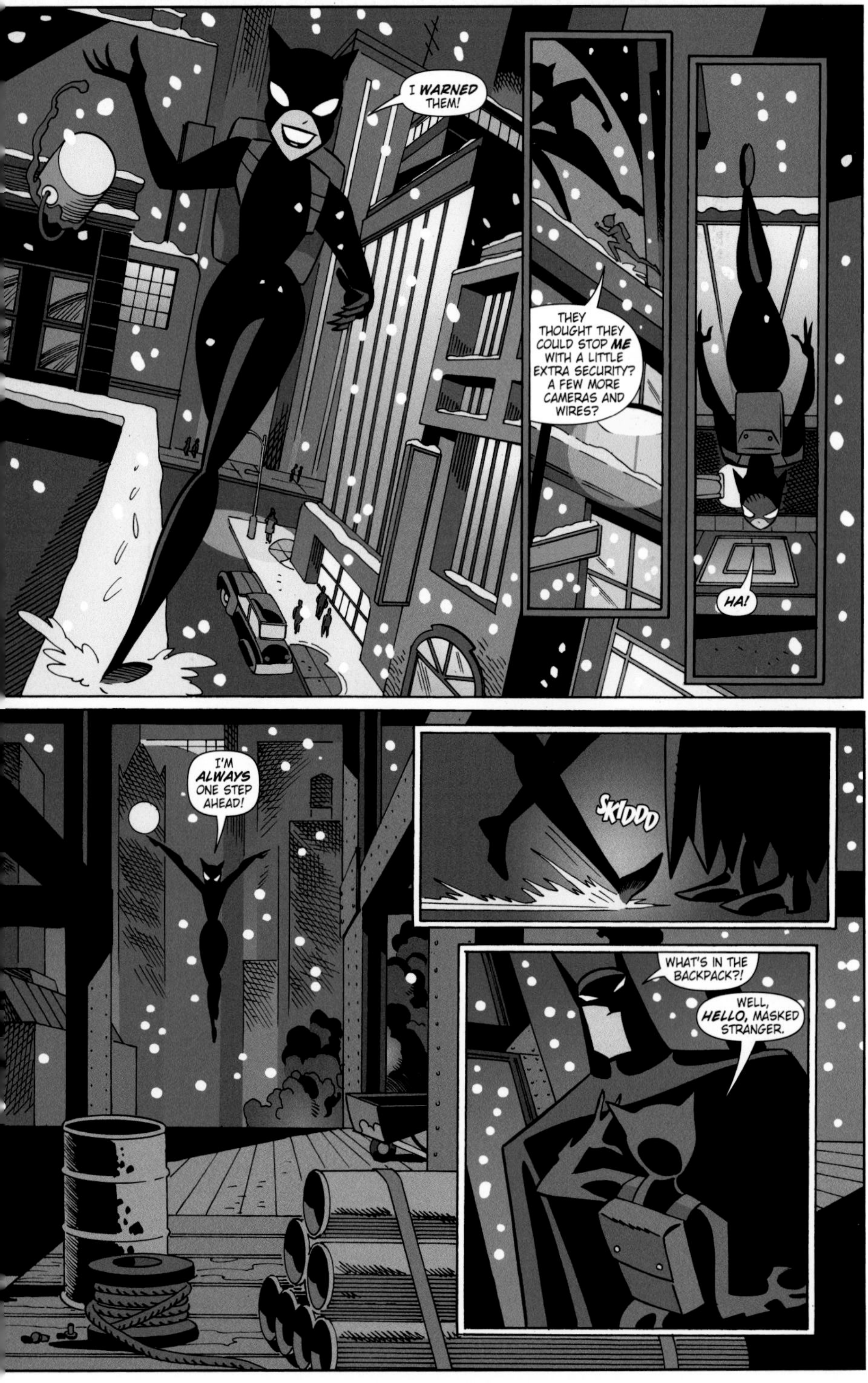
I WARNED THEM!
THEY THOUGHT THEY COULD STOP ME WITH A LITTLE EXTRA SECURITY? A FEW MORE CAMERAS AND WIRES?
HA!
I'M ALWAYS ONE STEP AHEAD!
SKIDDD
WHAT'S IN THE BACKPACK?!
WELL, HELLO, MASKED STRANGER.

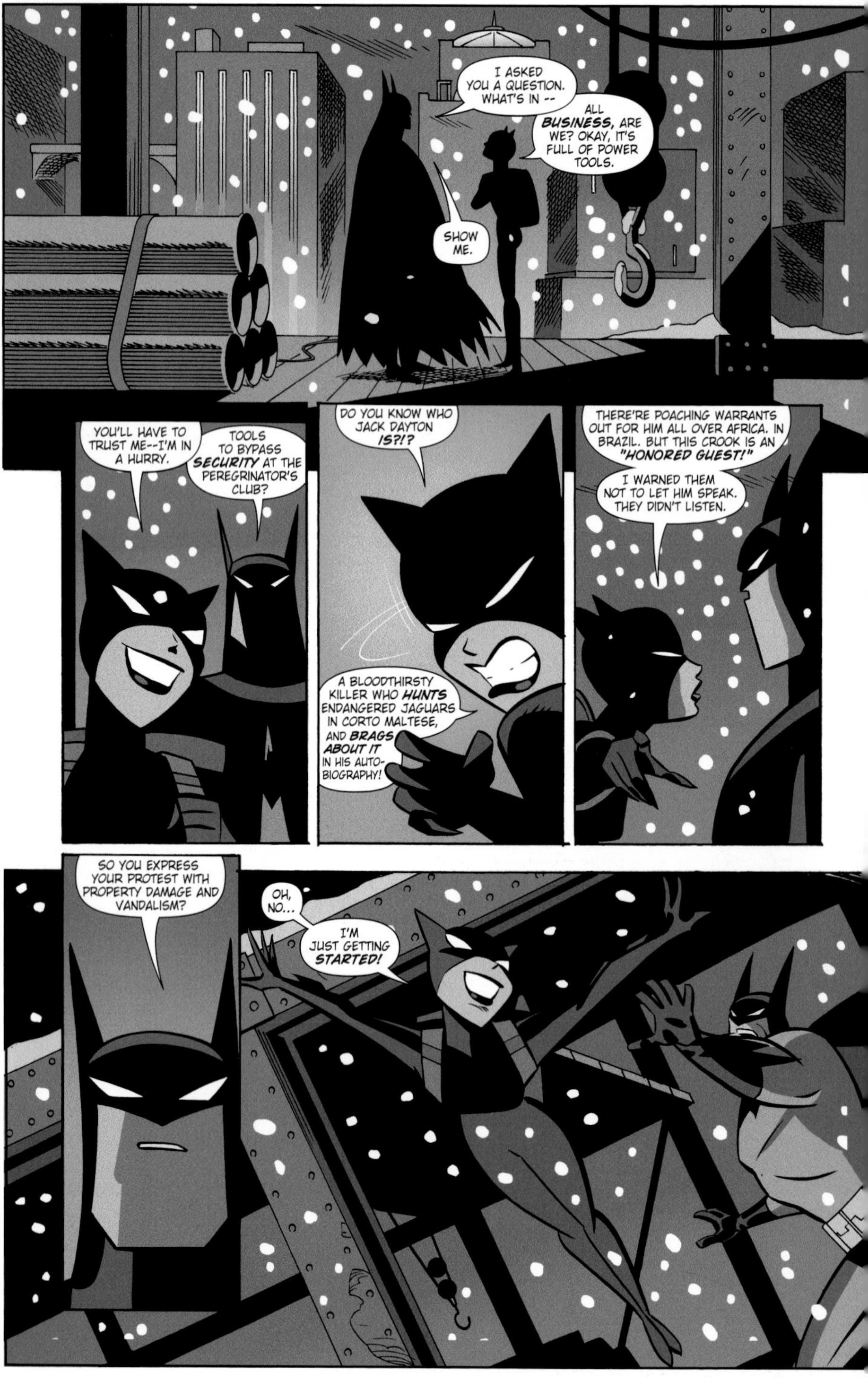
I ASKED YOU A QUESTION. WHAT'S IN --
ALL BUSINESS, ARE WE? OKAY, IT'S FULL OF POWER TOOLS.
SHOW ME.
YOU'LL HAVE TO TRUST ME--I'M IN A HURRY.
TOOLS TO BYPASS SECURITY AT THE PEREGRINATOR'S CLUB?
DO YOU KNOW WHO JACK DAYTON IS?!?
A BLOODTHIRSTY KILLER WHO HUNTS ENDANGERED JAGUARS IN CORTO MALTESE, AND BRAGS ABOUT IT IN HIS AUTO-BIOGRAPHY!
THERE'RE POACHING WARRANTS OUT FOR HIM ALL OVER AFRICA. IN BRAZIL. BUT THIS CROOK IS AN "HONORED GUEST!"
I WARNED THEM NOT TO LET HIM SPEAK. THEY DIDN'T LISTEN.
SO YOU EXPRESS YOUR PROTEST WITH PROPERTY DAMAGE AND VANDALISM?
OH, NO...
I'M JUST GETTING STARTED!

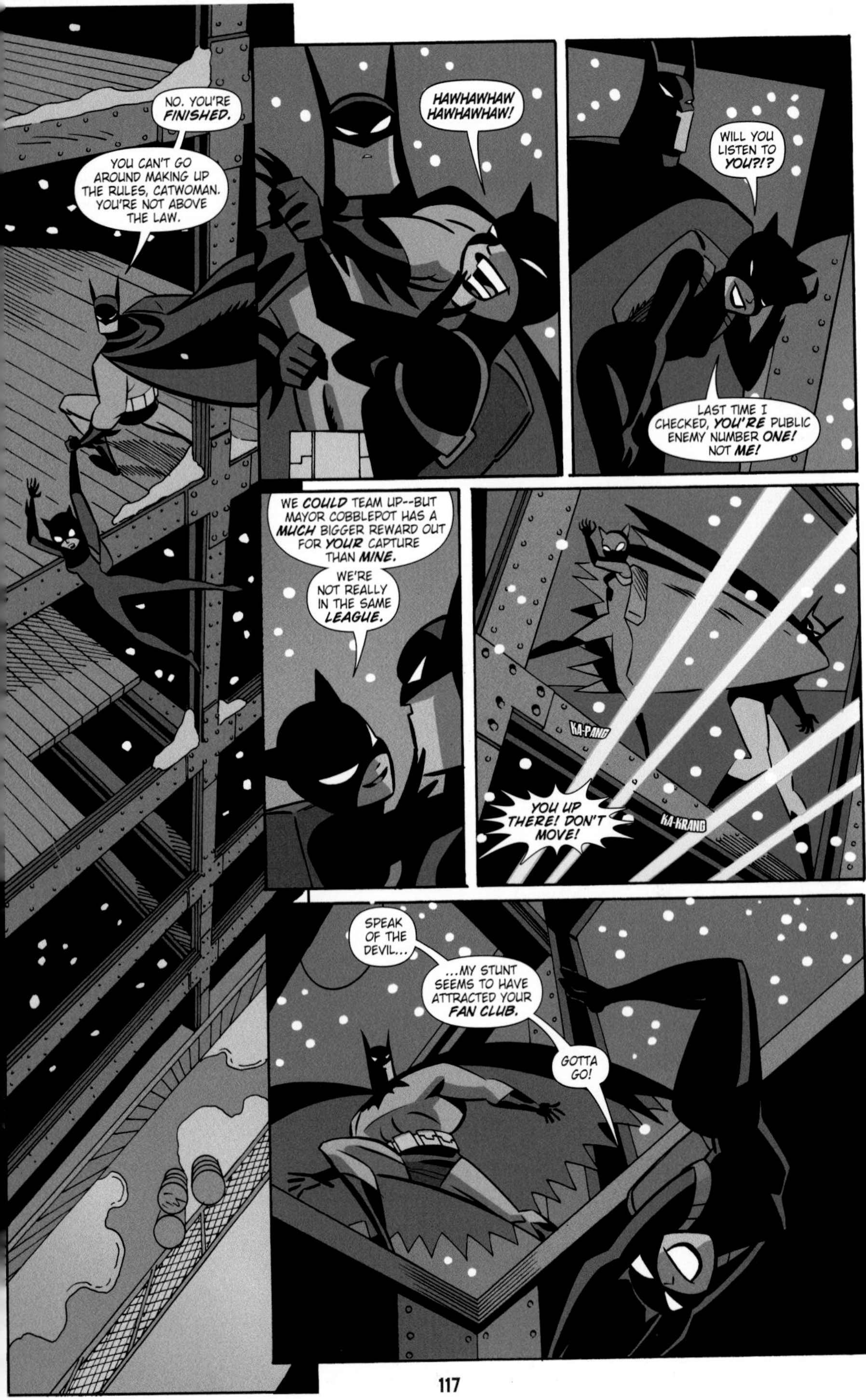
NO. YOU'RE FINISHED.
YOU CAN'T GO AROUND MAKING UP THE RULES, CATWOMAN. YOU'RE NOT ABOVE THE LAW.
HAWHAWHAW HAWHAWHAW!
WILL YOU LISTEN TO YOU?!?
LAST TIME I CHECKED, YOU'RE PUBLIC ENEMY NUMBER ONE! NOT ME!
WE COULD TEAM UP--BUT MAYOR COBBLEPOT HAS A MUCH BIGGER REWARD OUT FOR YOUR CAPTURE THAN MINE.
WE'RE NOT REALLY IN THE SAME LEAGUE.
KA-PANG
YOU UP THERE! DON'T MOVE!
KA-KRANG
SPEAK OF THE DEVIL...
...MY STUNT SEEMS TO HAVE ATTRACTED YOUR FAN CLUB.
GOTTA GO!

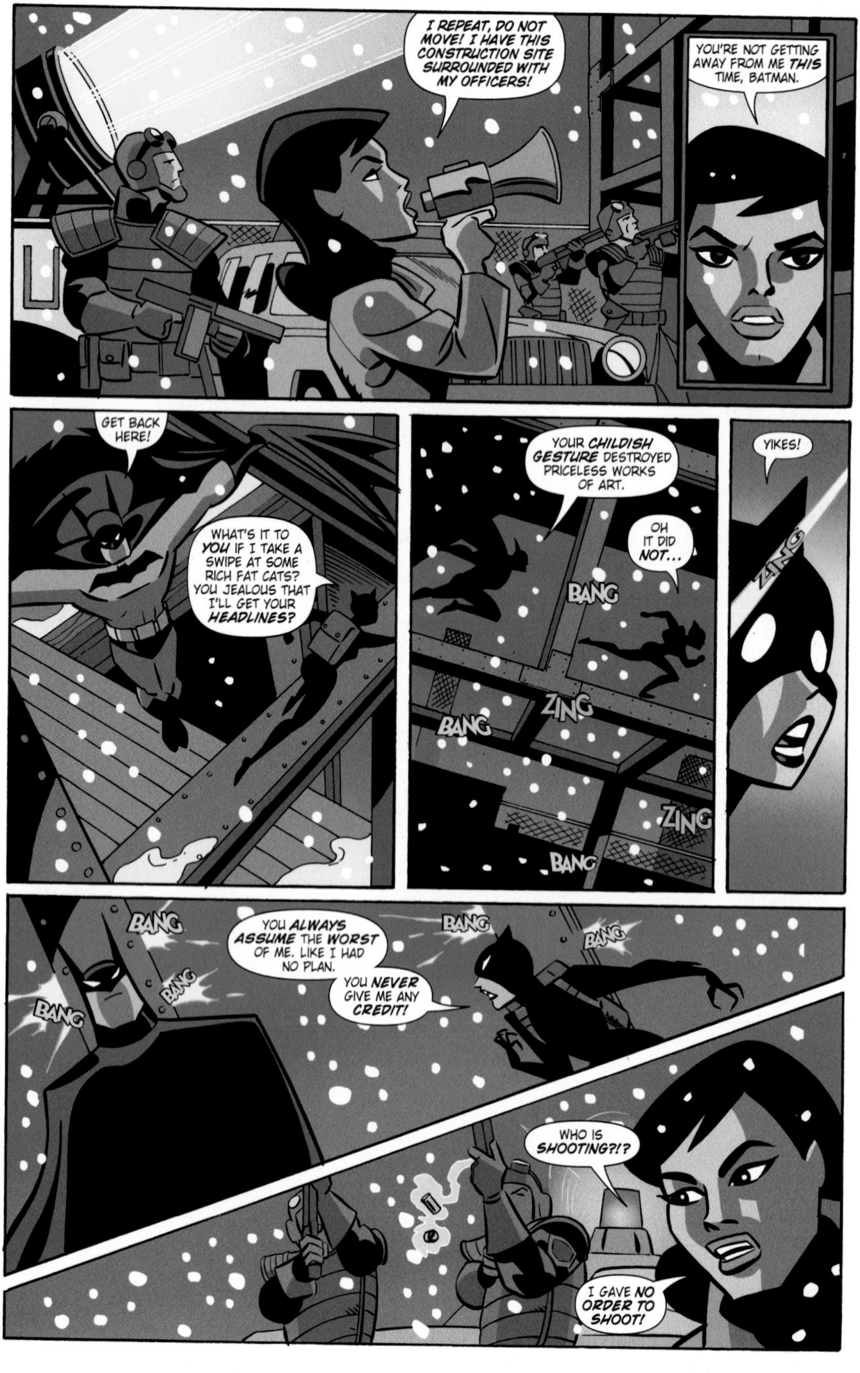
I REPEAT, DO NOT MOVE! I HAVE THIS CONSTRUCTION SITE SURROUNDED WITH MY OFFICERS!
YOU'RE NOT GETTING AWAY FROM ME THIS TIME, BATMAN.
GET BACK HERE!
WHAT'S IT TO YOU IF I TAKE A SWIPE AT SOME RICH FAT CATS? YOU JEALOUS THAT I'LL GET YOUR HEADLINES?
YOUR CHILDISH GESTURE DESTROYED PRICELESS WORKS OF ART.
OH IT DID NOT...
BANG
ZING
BANG
ZING
BANG
YIKES!
ZING
BANG
YOU ALWAYS ASSUME THE WORST OF ME. LIKE I HAD NO PLAN.
BANG
BANG
BANG
BANG
YOU NEVER GIVE ME ANY CREDIT!
WHO IS SHOOTING?!?
I GAVE NO ORDER TO SHOOT!

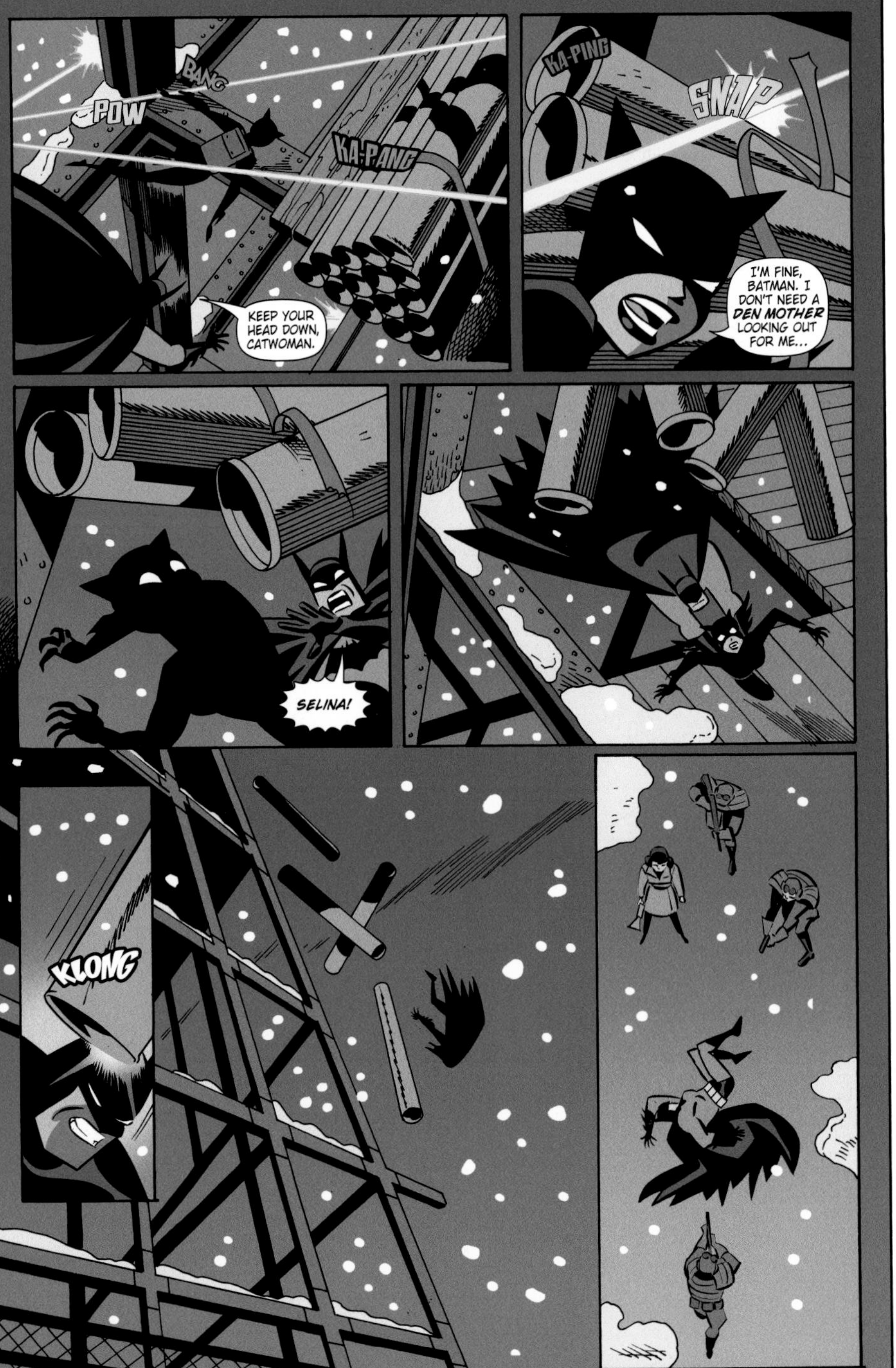

BANG
POW
KA-PANG
KEEP YOUR HEAD DOWN, CATWOMAN.
KA-PING
SNAP
I'M FINE, BATMAN. I DON'T NEED A DEN MOTHER LOOKING OUT FOR ME...
SELINA!
KLONG

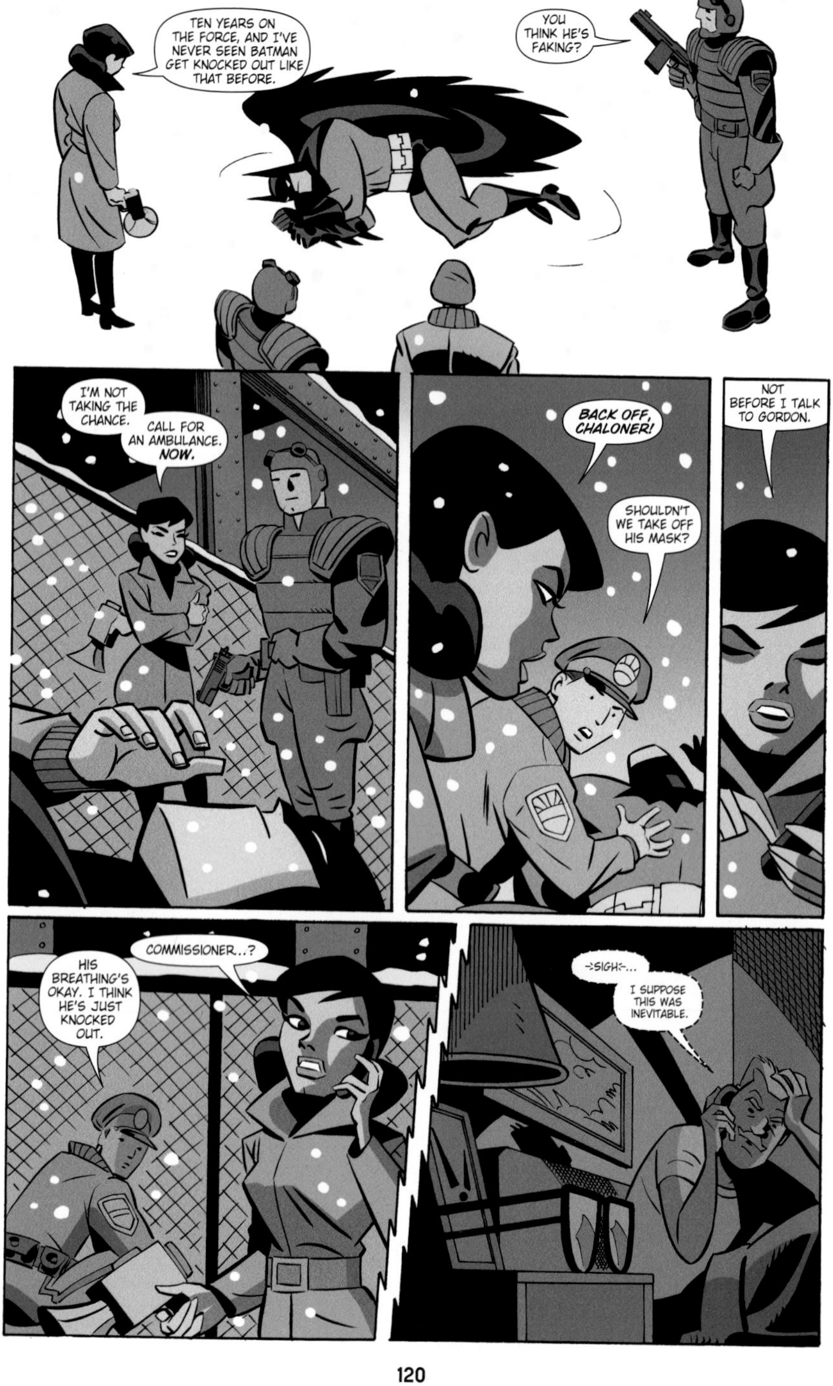
TEN YEARS ON THE FORCE, AND I'VE NEVER SEEN BATMAN GET KNOCKED OUT LIKE THAT BEFORE.
YOU THINK HE'S FAKING?
I'M NOT TAKING THE CHANCE.
CALL FOR AN AMBULANCE. NOW.
BACK OFF, CHALONER!
SHOULDN'T WE TAKE OFF HIS MASK?
NOT BEFORE I TALK TO GORDON.
HIS BREATHING'S OKAY. I THINK HE'S JUST KNOCKED OUT.
COMMISSIONER...?
SIGH...
I SUPPOSE THIS WAS INEVITABLE.

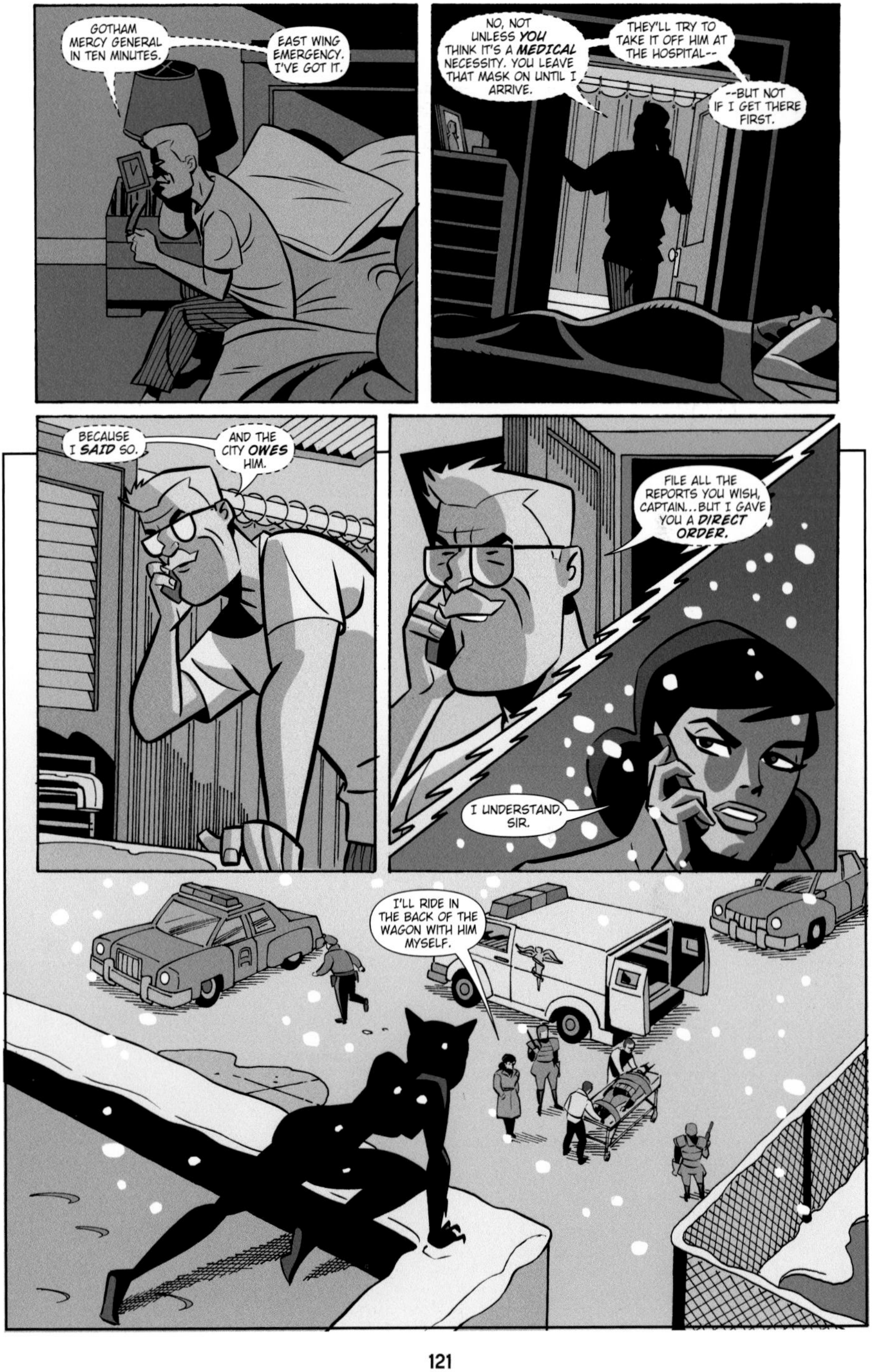

GOTHAM MERCY GENERAL IN TEN MINUTES.
EAST WING EMERGENCY. I'VE GOT IT.
NO, NOT UNLESS **YOU** THINK IT'S A **MEDICAL** NECESSITY. YOU LEAVE THAT MASK ON UNTIL I ARRIVE.
THEY'LL TRY TO TAKE IT OFF HIM AT THE HOSPITAL--
--BUT NOT IF I GET THERE FIRST.
BECAUSE I **SAID** SO.
AND THE CITY **OWES** HIM.
FILE ALL THE REPORTS YOU WISH, CAPTAIN... BUT I GAVE YOU A **DIRECT ORDER.**
I UNDERSTAND, SIR.
I'LL RIDE IN THE BACK OF THE WAGON WITH HIM MYSELF.

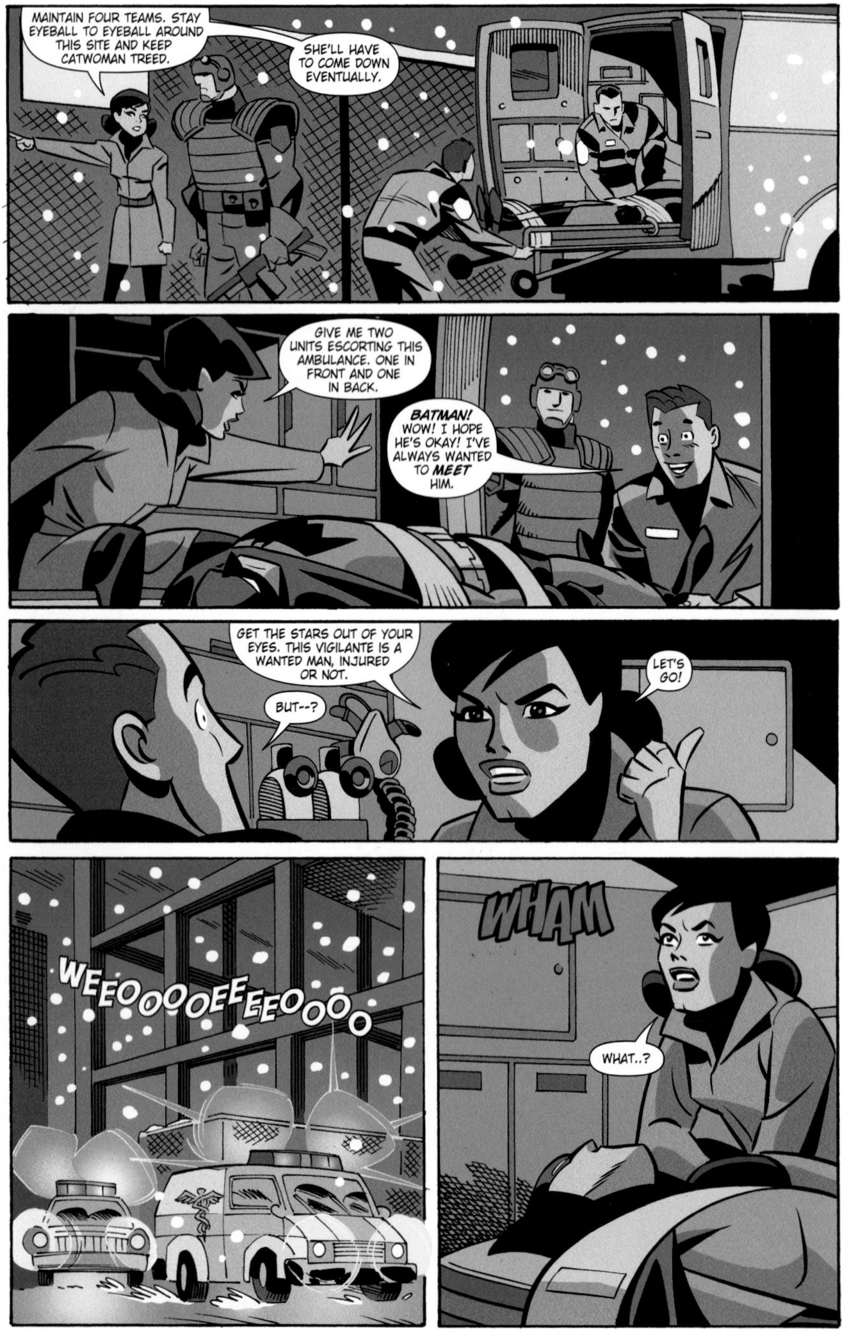
MAINTAIN FOUR TEAMS. STAY EYEBALL TO EYEBALL AROUND THIS SITE AND KEEP CATWOMAN TREED.
SHE'LL HAVE TO COME DOWN EVENTUALLY.
GIVE ME TWO UNITS ESCORTING THIS AMBULANCE. ONE IN FRONT AND ONE IN BACK.
BATMAN! WOW! I HOPE HE'S OKAY! I'VE ALWAYS WANTED TO MEET HIM.
GET THE STARS OUT OF YOUR EYES. THIS VIGILANTE IS A WANTED MAN, INJURED OR NOT.
BUT--?
LET'S GO!
WEEOOOOOEEEEOOOOO
WHAM
WHAT..?

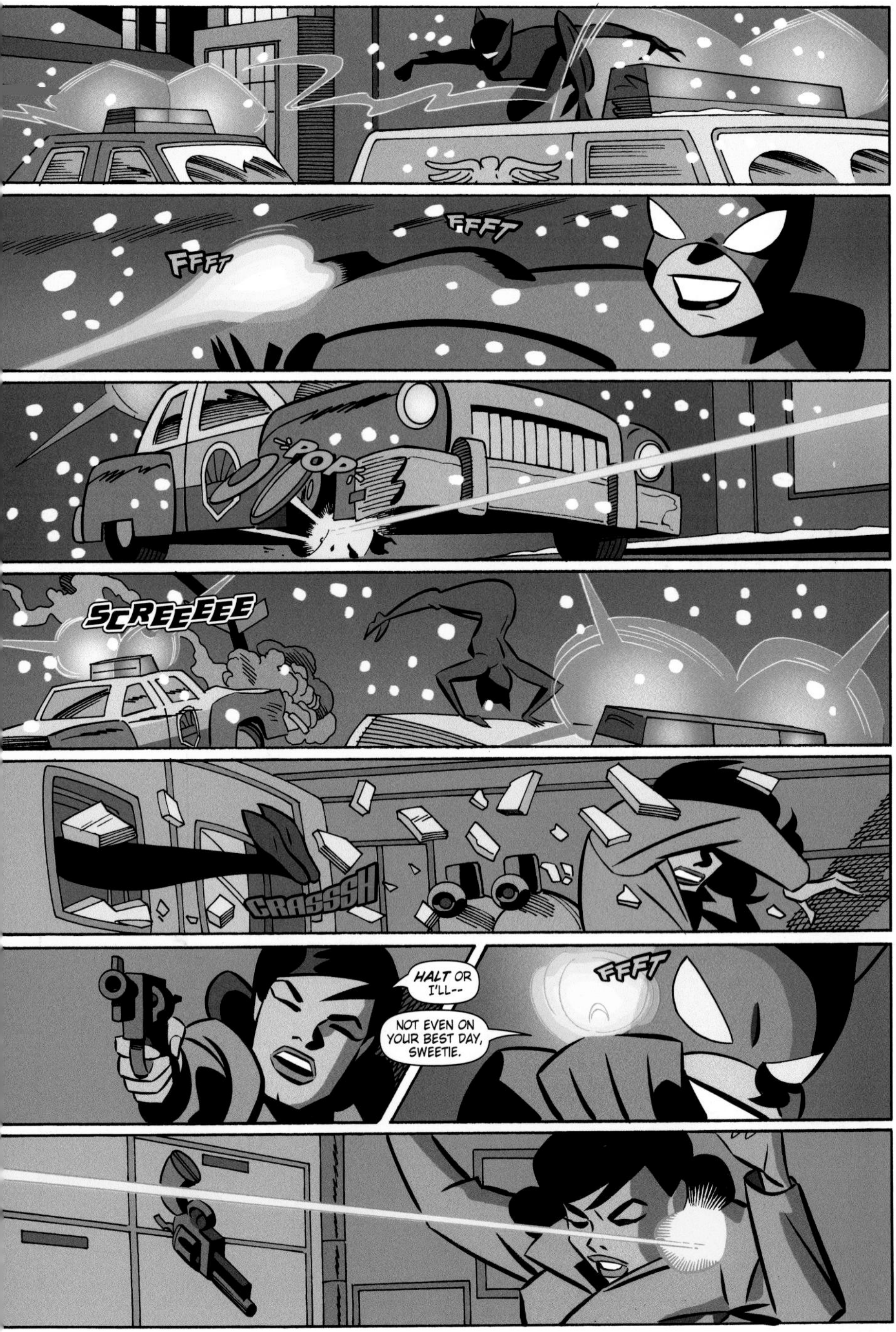
FFFT
FFFT
POP
SCREEEEEE
CRASSSH
HALT OR I'LL--
FFFT
NOT EVEN ON YOUR BEST DAY, SWEETIE.

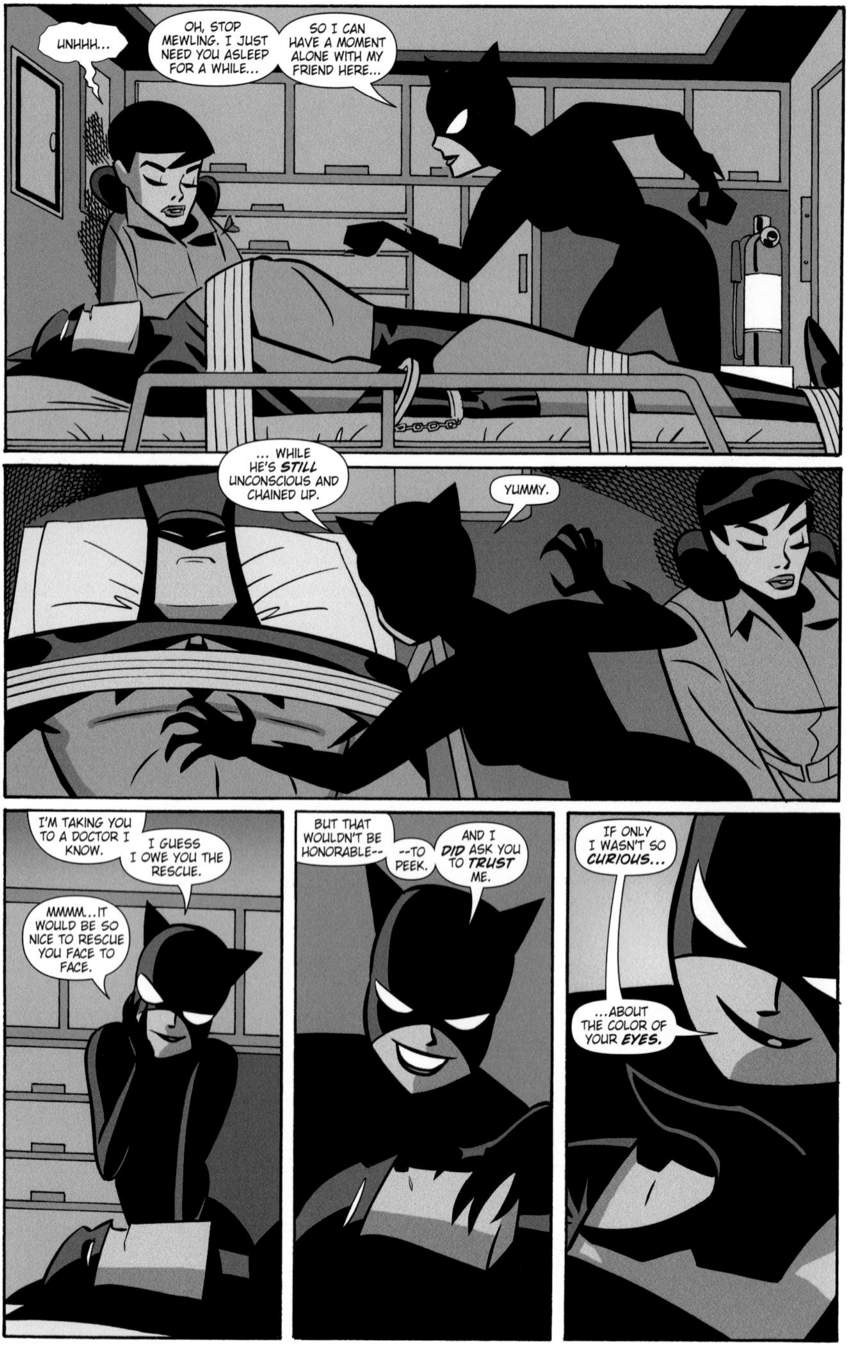
UNHHH...
OH, STOP MEWLING. I JUST NEED YOU ASLEEP FOR A WHILE...
SO I CAN HAVE A MOMENT ALONE WITH MY FRIEND HERE...
... WHILE HE'S STILL UNCONSCIOUS AND CHAINED UP.
YUMMY.
I'M TAKING YOU TO A DOCTOR I KNOW.
I GUESS I OWE YOU THE RESCUE.
MMMM...IT WOULD BE SO NICE TO RESCUE YOU FACE TO FACE.
BUT THAT WOULDN'T BE HONORABLE--
--TO PEEK.
AND I DID ASK YOU TO TRUST ME.
IF ONLY I WASN'T SO CURIOUS...
...ABOUT THE COLOR OF YOUR EYES.

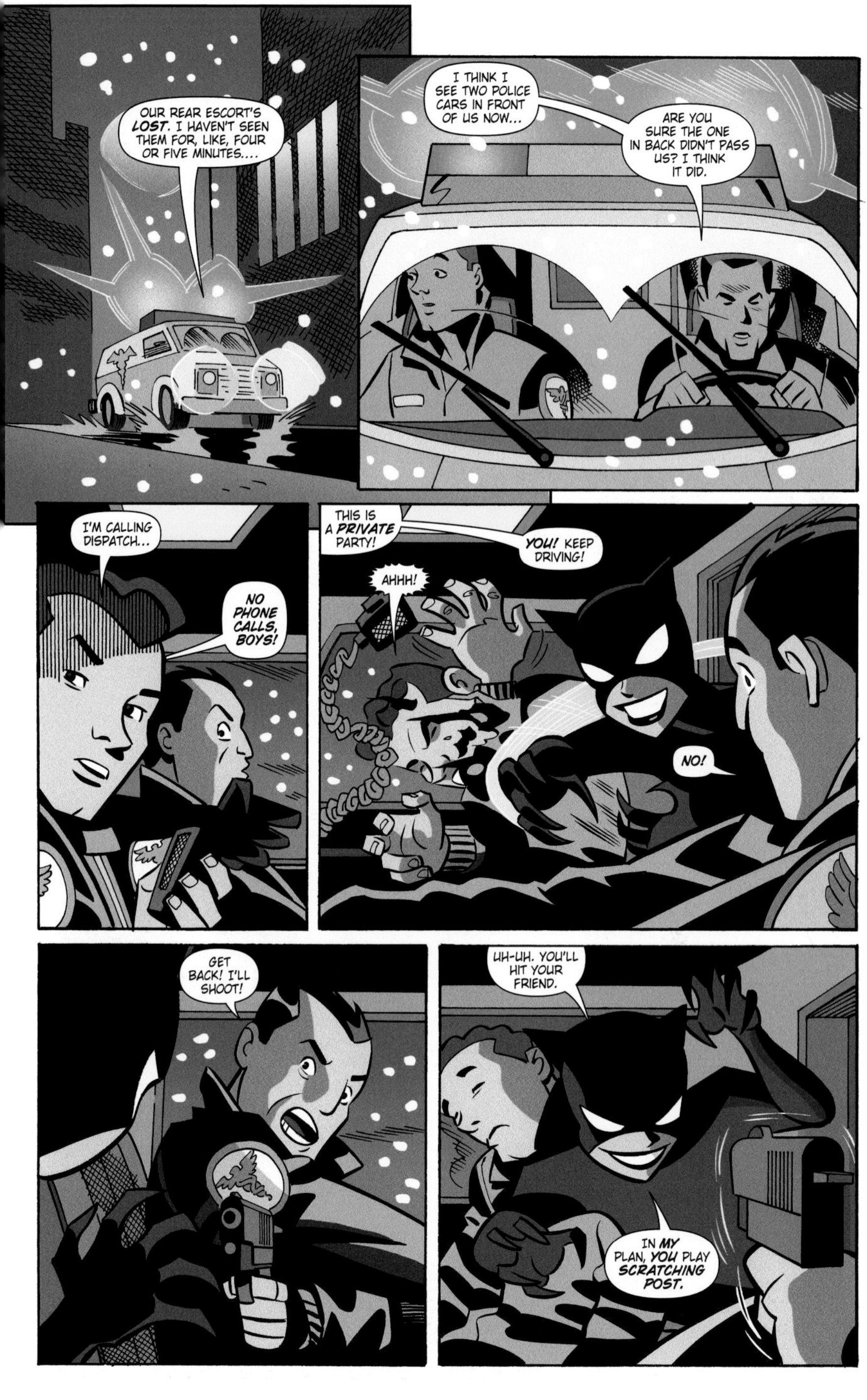
OUR REAR ESCORT'S **LOST**. I HAVEN'T SEEN THEM FOR, LIKE, FOUR OR FIVE MINUTES....
I THINK I SEE TWO POLICE CARS IN FRONT OF US NOW...
ARE YOU SURE THE ONE IN BACK DIDN'T PASS US? I THINK IT DID.
I'M CALLING DISPATCH...
NO PHONE CALLS, BOYS!
THIS IS A **PRIVATE** PARTY!
YOU! KEEP DRIVING!
AHHH!
NO!
GET BACK! I'LL SHOOT!
UH-UH. YOU'LL HIT YOUR FRIEND.
IN **MY** PLAN, **YOU** PLAY **SCRATCHING POST.**

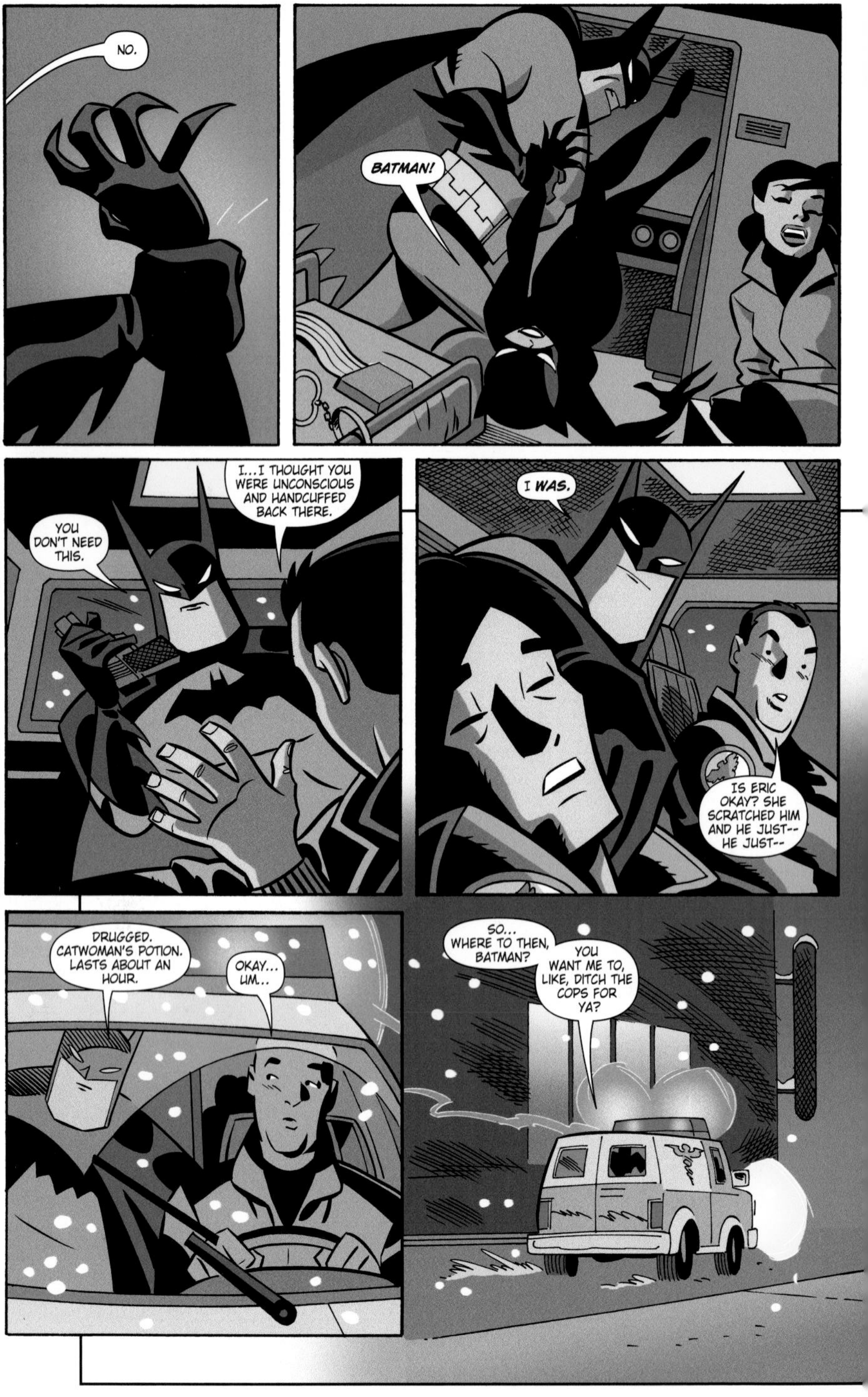

NO.
BATMAN!
YOU DON'T NEED THIS.
I...I THOUGHT YOU WERE UNCONSCIOUS AND HANDCUFFED BACK THERE.
I *WAS.*
IS ERIC OKAY? SHE SCRATCHED HIM AND HE JUST-- HE JUST--
DRUGGED. CATWOMAN'S POTION. LASTS ABOUT AN HOUR.
OKAY... UM...
SO... WHERE TO THEN, BATMAN?
YOU WANT ME TO, LIKE, DITCH THE COPS FOR YA?

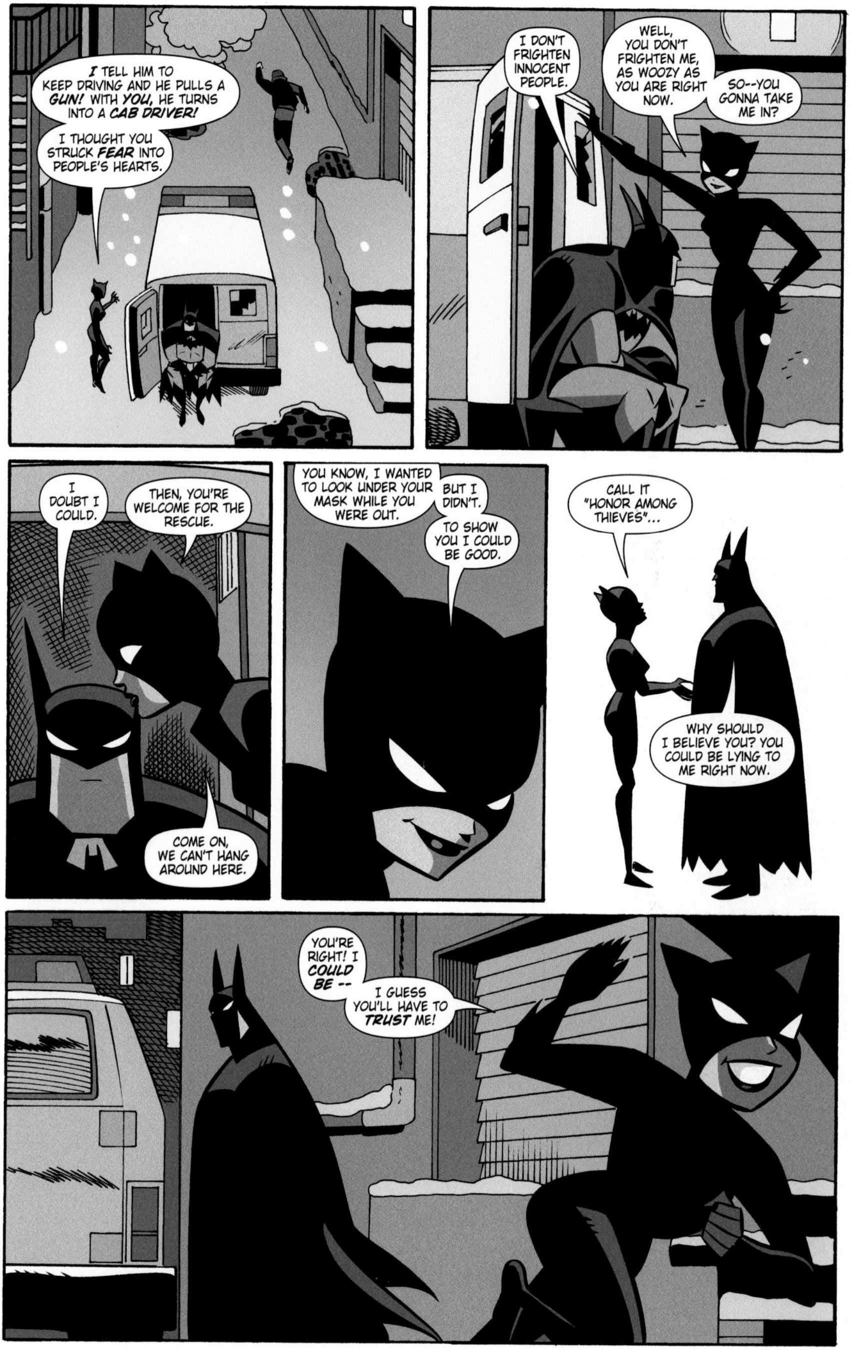
I TELL HIM TO KEEP DRIVING AND HE PULLS A GUN! WITH YOU, HE TURNS INTO A CAB DRIVER!
I THOUGHT YOU STRUCK FEAR INTO PEOPLE'S HEARTS.
I DON'T FRIGHTEN INNOCENT PEOPLE.
WELL, YOU DON'T FRIGHTEN ME, AS WOOZY AS YOU ARE RIGHT NOW.
SO--YOU GONNA TAKE ME IN?
I DOUBT I COULD.
THEN, YOU'RE WELCOME FOR THE RESCUE.
COME ON, WE CAN'T HANG AROUND HERE.
YOU KNOW, I WANTED TO LOOK UNDER YOUR MASK WHILE YOU WERE OUT.
BUT I DIDN'T.
TO SHOW YOU I COULD BE GOOD.
CALL IT "HONOR AMONG THIEVES"...
WHY SHOULD I BELIEVE YOU? YOU COULD BE LYING TO ME RIGHT NOW.
YOU'RE RIGHT! I COULD BE --
I GUESS YOU'LL HAVE TO TRUST ME!

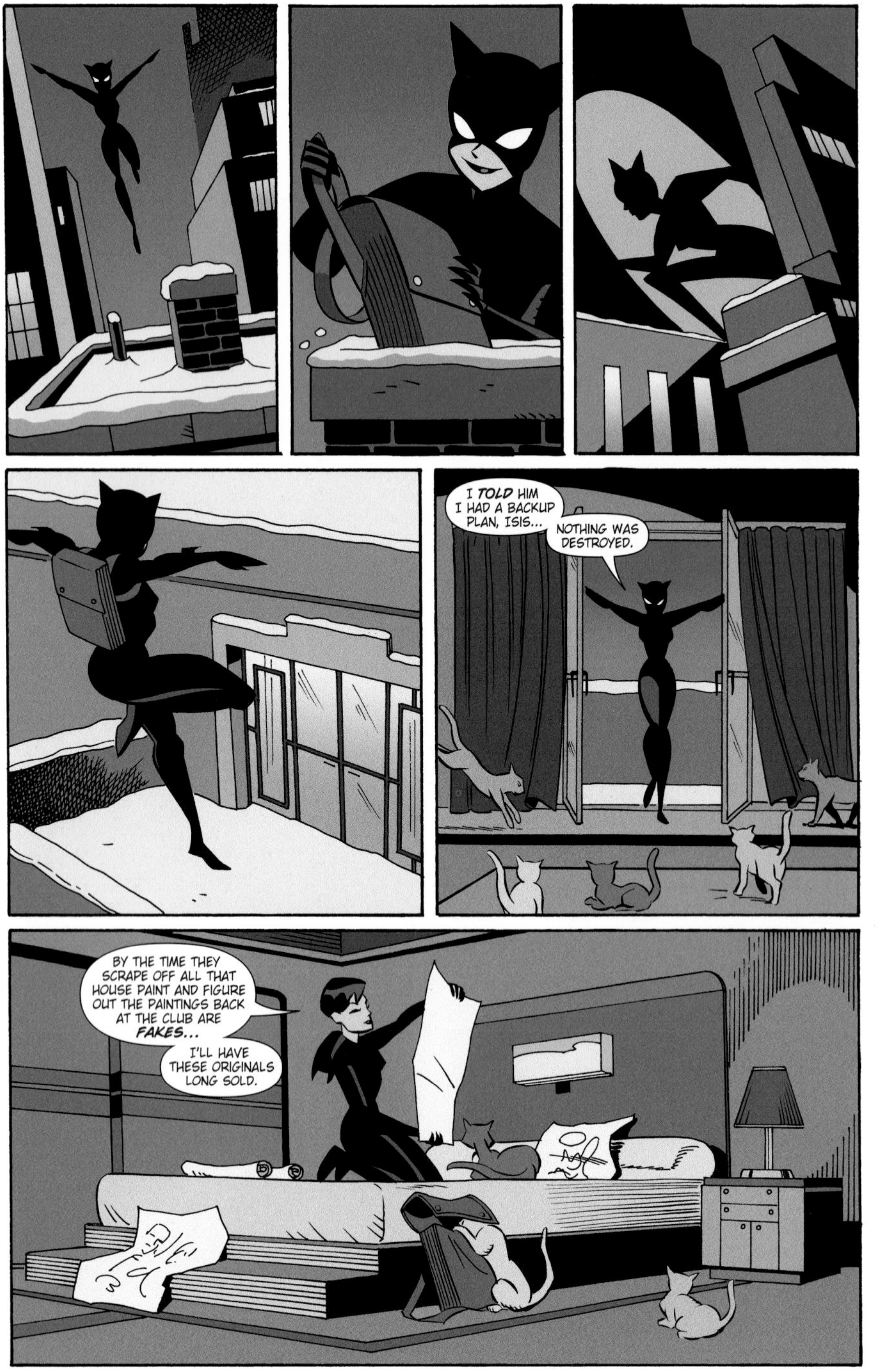
I *TOLD* HIM I HAD A BACKUP PLAN, ISIS...
NOTHING WAS DESTROYED.
BY THE TIME THEY SCRAPE OFF ALL THAT HOUSE PAINT AND FIGURE OUT THE PAINTINGS BACK AT THE CLUB ARE *FAKES...*
I'LL HAVE THESE ORIGINALS LONG SOLD.

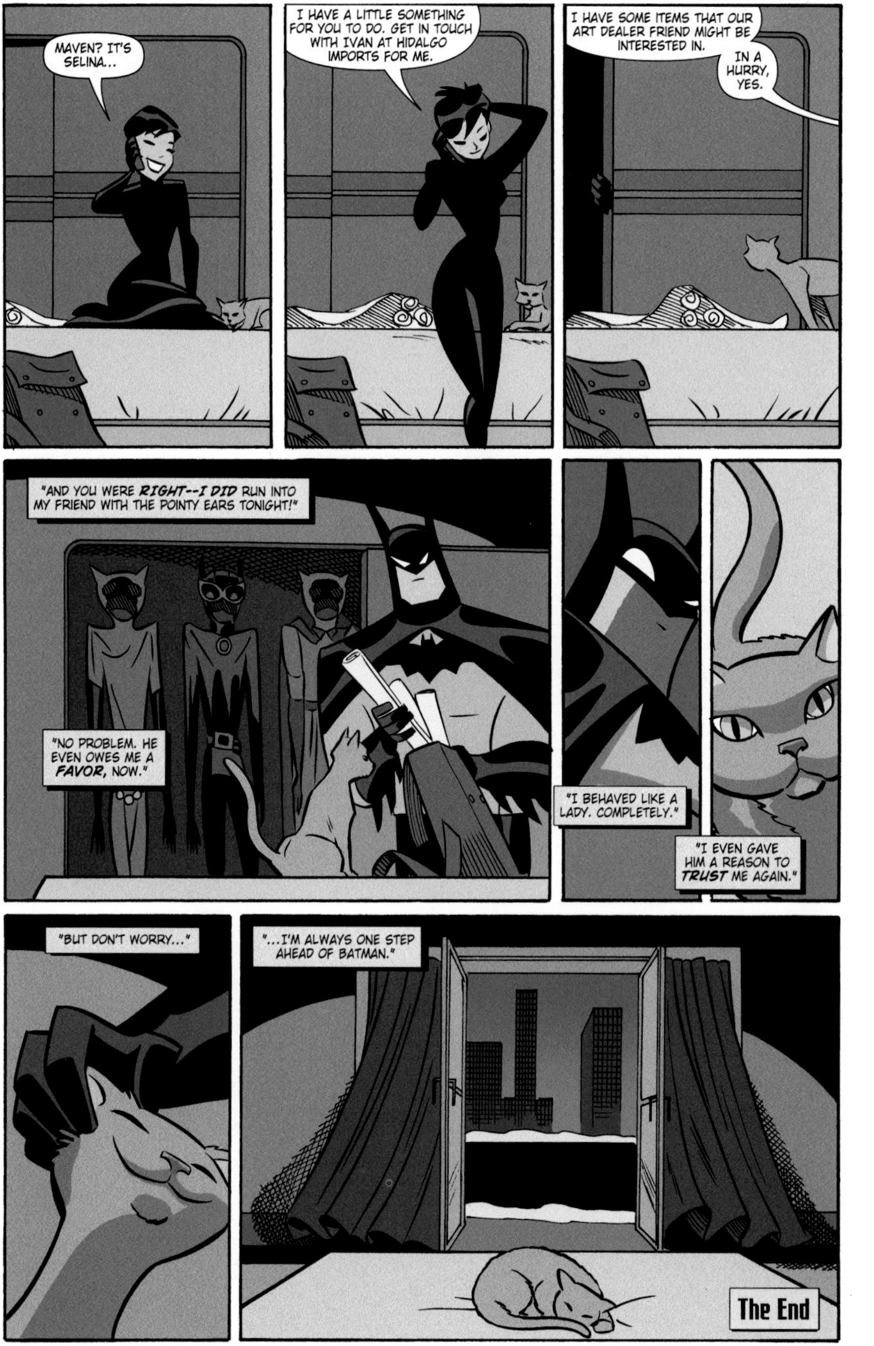
MAVEN? IT'S SELINA...
I HAVE A LITTLE SOMETHING FOR YOU TO DO. GET IN TOUCH WITH IVAN AT HIDALGO IMPORTS FOR ME.
I HAVE SOME ITEMS THAT OUR ART DEALER FRIEND MIGHT BE INTERESTED IN.
IN A HURRY, YES.
"AND YOU WERE RIGHT--I DID RUN INTO MY FRIEND WITH THE POINTY EARS TONIGHT!"
"NO PROBLEM. HE EVEN OWES ME A FAVOR, NOW."
"I BEHAVED LIKE A LADY. COMPLETELY."
"I EVEN GAVE HIM A REASON TO TRUST ME AGAIN."
"BUT DON'T WORRY..."
"...I'M ALWAYS ONE STEP AHEAD OF BATMAN."
The End

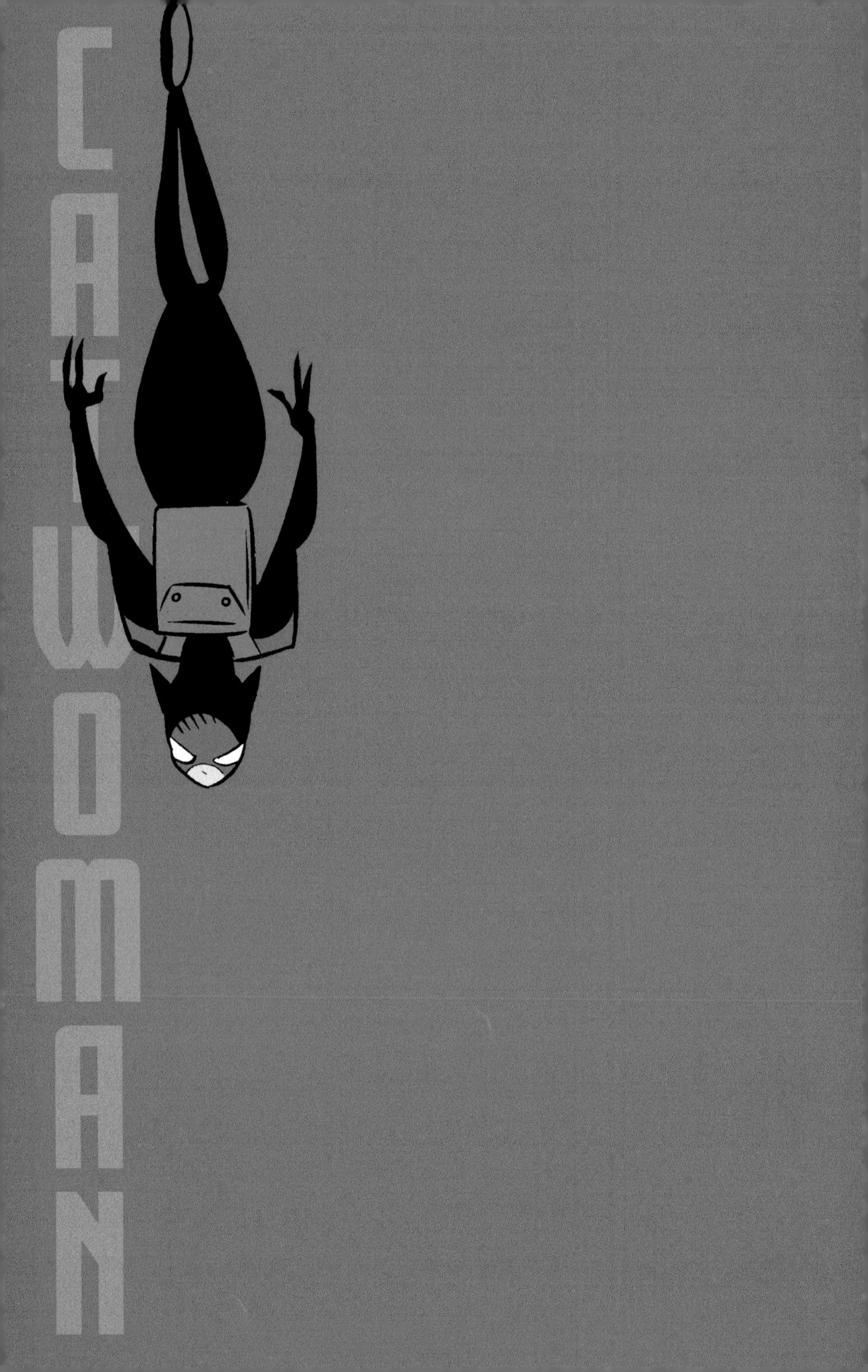
CATWOMAN

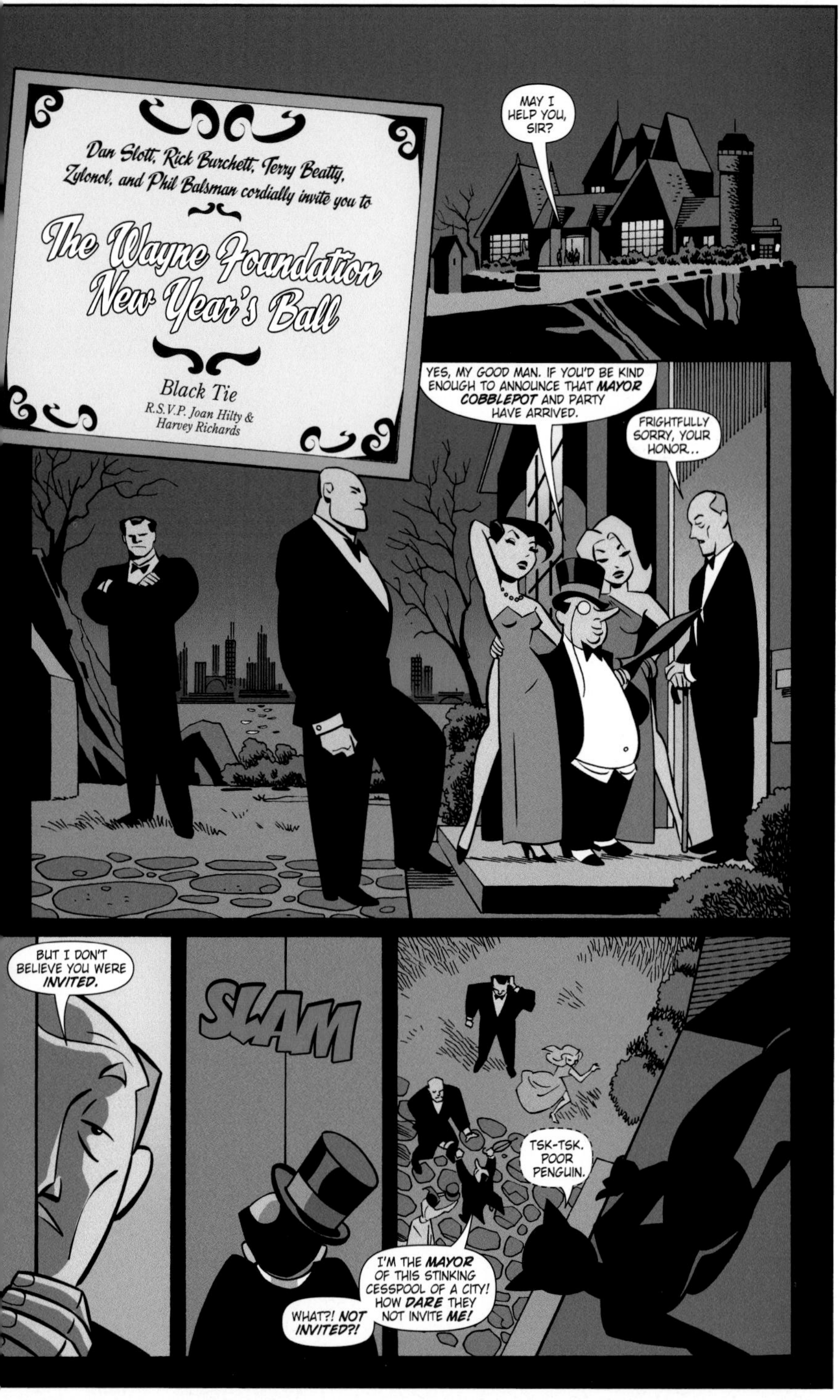

Dan Slott, Rick Burchett, Terry Beatty, Zylonol, and Phil Balsman cordially invite you to
The Wayne Foundation New Year's Ball
Black Tie
R.S.V.P. Joan Hilty & Harvey Richards
MAY I HELP YOU, SIR?
YES, MY GOOD MAN. IF YOU'D BE KIND ENOUGH TO ANNOUNCE THAT MAYOR COBBLEPOT AND PARTY HAVE ARRIVED.
FRIGHTFULLY SORRY, YOUR HONOR...
BUT I DON'T BELIEVE YOU WERE INVITED.
SLAM
WHAT?! NOT INVITED?!
I'M THE MAYOR OF THIS STINKING CESSPOOL OF A CITY! HOW DARE THEY NOT INVITE ME!
TSK-TSK. POOR PENGUIN.

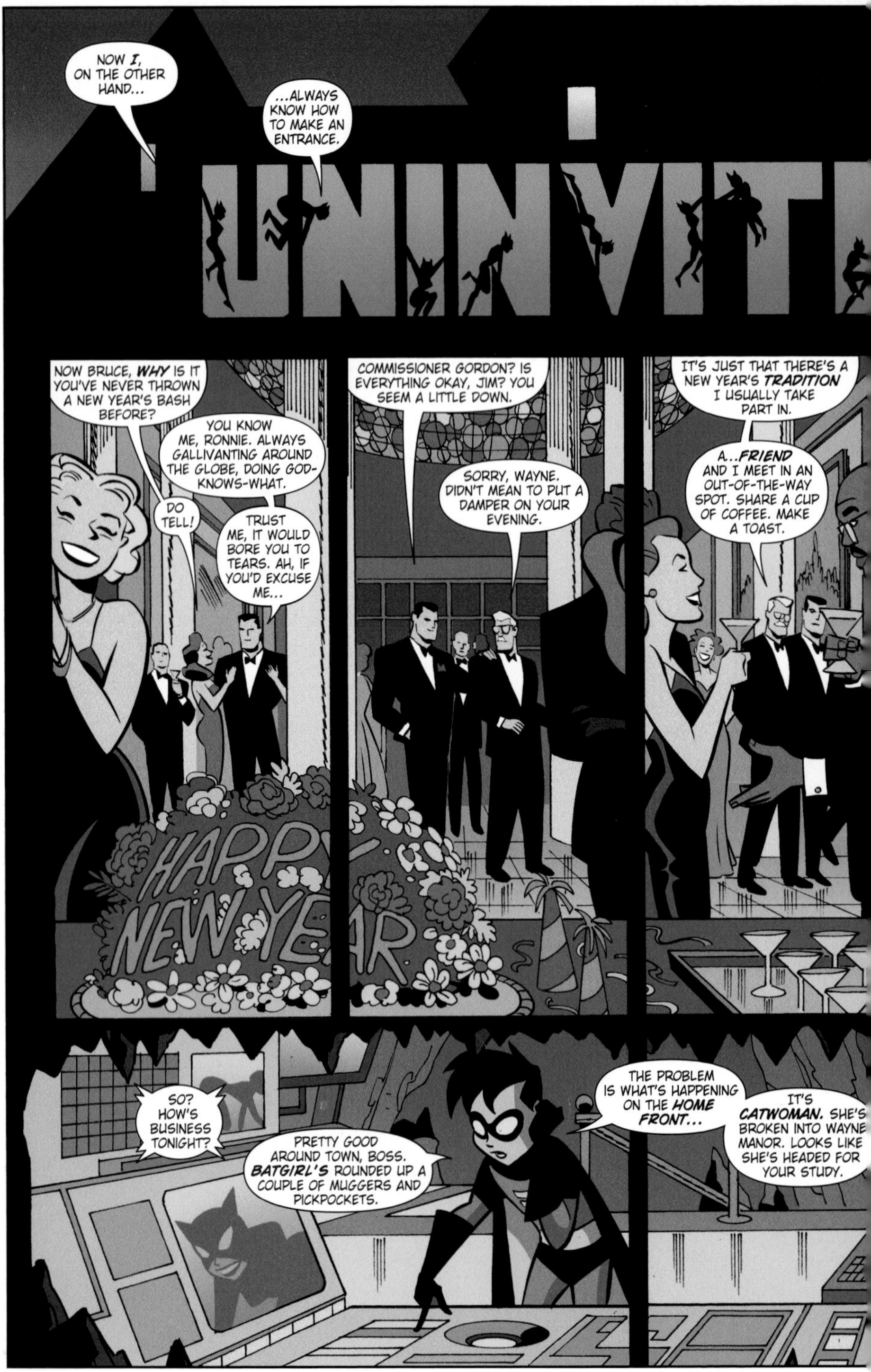

NOW I, ON THE OTHER HAND...
...ALWAYS KNOW HOW TO MAKE AN ENTRANCE.
UNINVIT
NOW BRUCE, WHY IS IT YOU'VE NEVER THROWN A NEW YEAR'S BASH BEFORE?
YOU KNOW ME, RONNIE. ALWAYS GALLIVANTING AROUND THE GLOBE, DOING GOD-KNOWS-WHAT.
DO TELL!
TRUST ME, IT WOULD BORE YOU TO TEARS. AH, IF YOU'D EXCUSE ME...
HAPPY NEW YEAR
COMMISSIONER GORDON? IS EVERYTHING OKAY, JIM? YOU SEEM A LITTLE DOWN.
SORRY, WAYNE. DIDN'T MEAN TO PUT A DAMPER ON YOUR EVENING.
IT'S JUST THAT THERE'S A NEW YEAR'S TRADITION I USUALLY TAKE PART IN.
A...FRIEND AND I MEET IN AN OUT-OF-THE-WAY SPOT. SHARE A CUP OF COFFEE. MAKE A TOAST.
SO? HOW'S BUSINESS TONIGHT?
PRETTY GOOD AROUND TOWN, BOSS. BATGIRL'S ROUNDED UP A COUPLE OF MUGGERS AND PICKPOCKETS.
THE PROBLEM IS WHAT'S HAPPENING ON THE HOME FRONT...
IT'S CATWOMAN. SHE'S BROKEN INTO WAYNE MANOR. LOOKS LIKE SHE'S HEADED FOR YOUR STUDY.

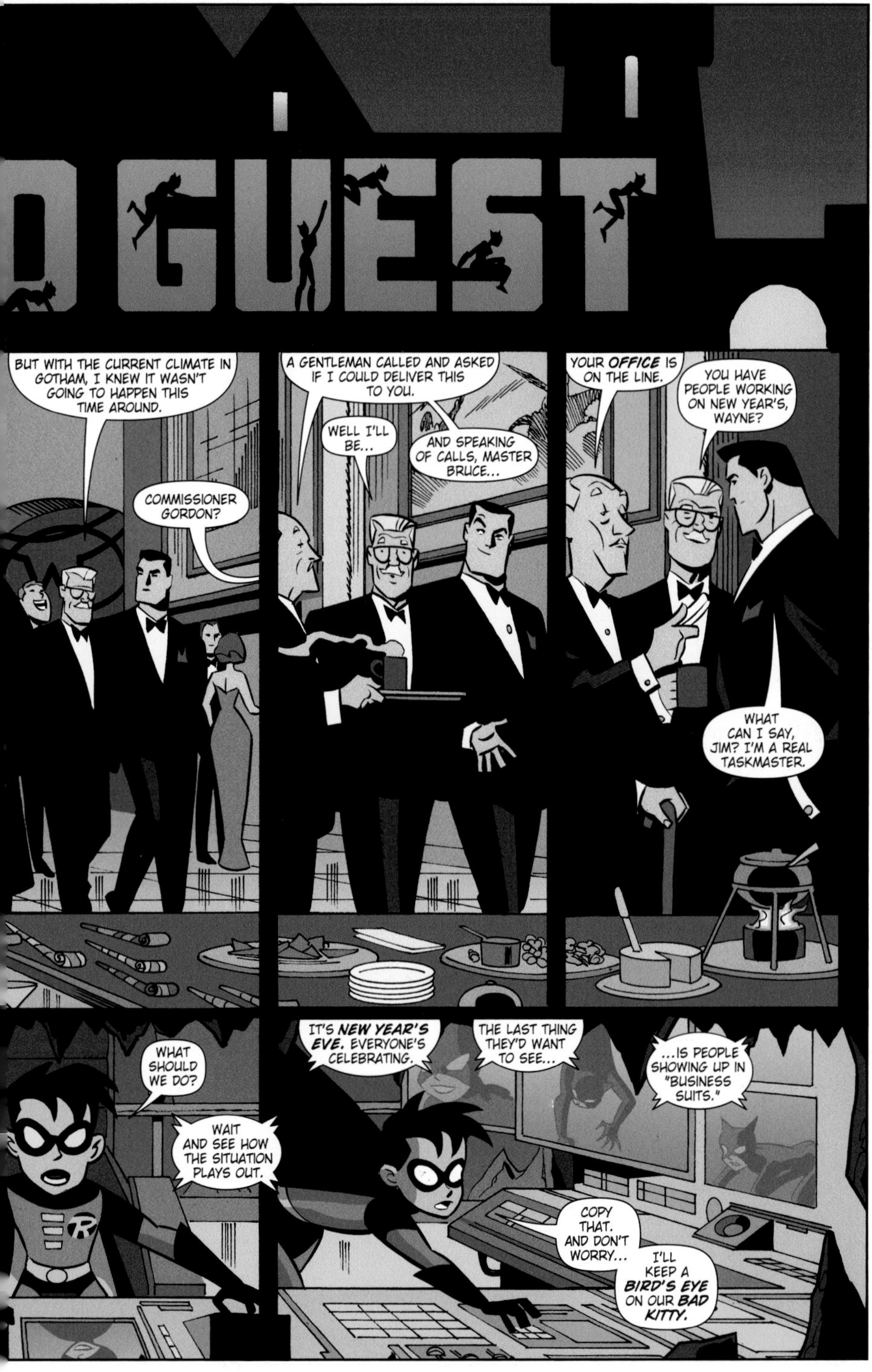

D GUEST
BUT WITH THE CURRENT CLIMATE IN GOTHAM, I KNEW IT WASN'T GOING TO HAPPEN THIS TIME AROUND.
COMMISSIONER GORDON?
A GENTLEMAN CALLED AND ASKED IF I COULD DELIVER THIS TO YOU.
WELL I'LL BE...
AND SPEAKING OF CALLS, MASTER BRUCE...
YOUR OFFICE IS ON THE LINE.
YOU HAVE PEOPLE WORKING ON NEW YEAR'S, WAYNE?
WHAT CAN I SAY, JIM? I'M A REAL TASKMASTER.
WHAT SHOULD WE DO?
WAIT AND SEE HOW THE SITUATION PLAYS OUT.
IT'S NEW YEAR'S EVE. EVERYONE'S CELEBRATING.
THE LAST THING THEY'D WANT TO SEE...
...IS PEOPLE SHOWING UP IN "BUSINESS SUITS."
COPY THAT. AND DON'T WORRY...
I'LL KEEP A BIRD'S EYE ON OUR BAD KITTY.

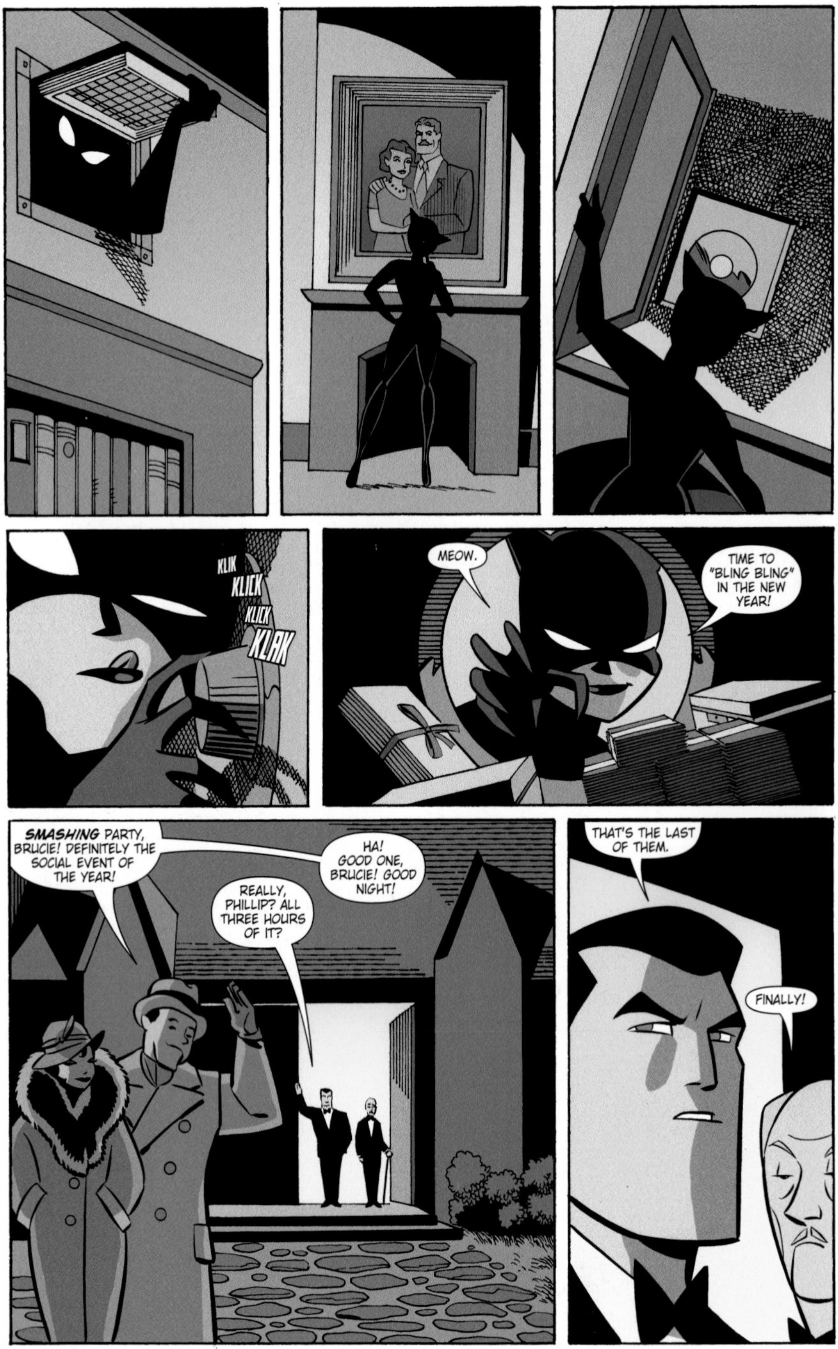
KLIK
KLICK
KLICK
KLAK
MEOW.
TIME TO "BLING BLING" IN THE NEW YEAR!
SMASHING PARTY, BRUCIE! DEFINITELY THE SOCIAL EVENT OF THE YEAR!
REALLY, PHILLIP? ALL THREE HOURS OF IT?
HA! GOOD ONE, BRUCIE! GOOD NIGHT!
THAT'S THE LAST OF THEM.
FINALLY!

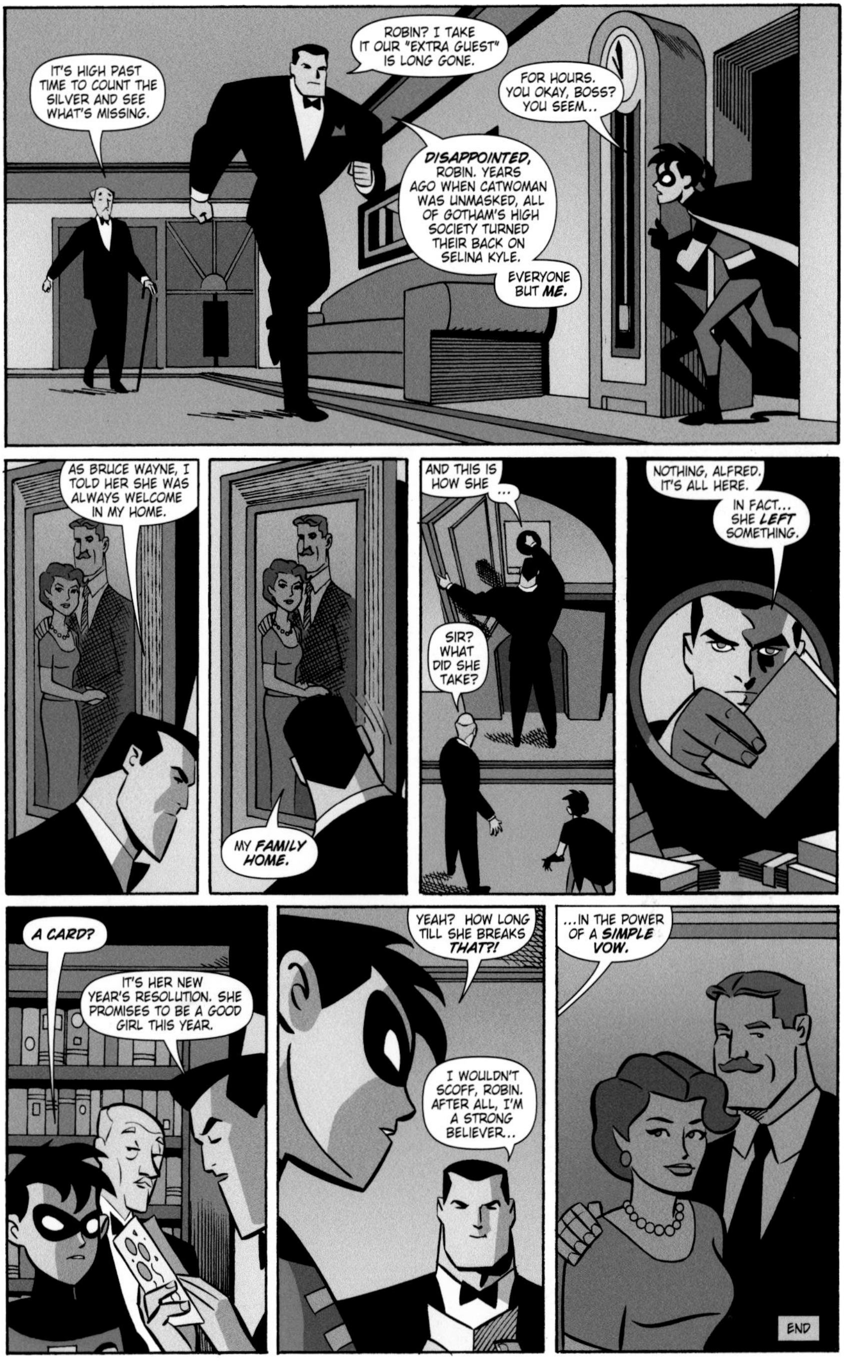
IT'S HIGH PAST TIME TO COUNT THE SILVER AND SEE WHAT'S MISSING.
ROBIN? I TAKE IT OUR "EXTRA GUEST" IS LONG GONE.
FOR HOURS. YOU OKAY, BOSS? YOU SEEM...
DISAPPOINTED, ROBIN. YEARS AGO WHEN CATWOMAN WAS UNMASKED, ALL OF GOTHAM'S HIGH SOCIETY TURNED THEIR BACK ON SELINA KYLE.
EVERYONE BUT ME.
AS BRUCE WAYNE, I TOLD HER SHE WAS ALWAYS WELCOME IN MY HOME.
MY FAMILY HOME.
AND THIS IS HOW SHE
...
SIR? WHAT DID SHE TAKE?
NOTHING, ALFRED. IT'S ALL HERE.
IN FACT... SHE LEFT SOMETHING.
A CARD?
IT'S HER NEW YEAR'S RESOLUTION. SHE PROMISES TO BE A GOOD GIRL THIS YEAR.
YEAH? HOW LONG TILL SHE BREAKS THAT?!
I WOULDN'T SCOFF, ROBIN. AFTER ALL, I'M A STRONG BELIEVER...
...IN THE POWER OF A SIMPLE VOW.
END

Have you ever wondered how heroes like Batman
use technology to come up with creative solutions?
What's at the bottom of the sea? Why does polar ice melt?
Which tools do forensic scientists use to solve a crime?

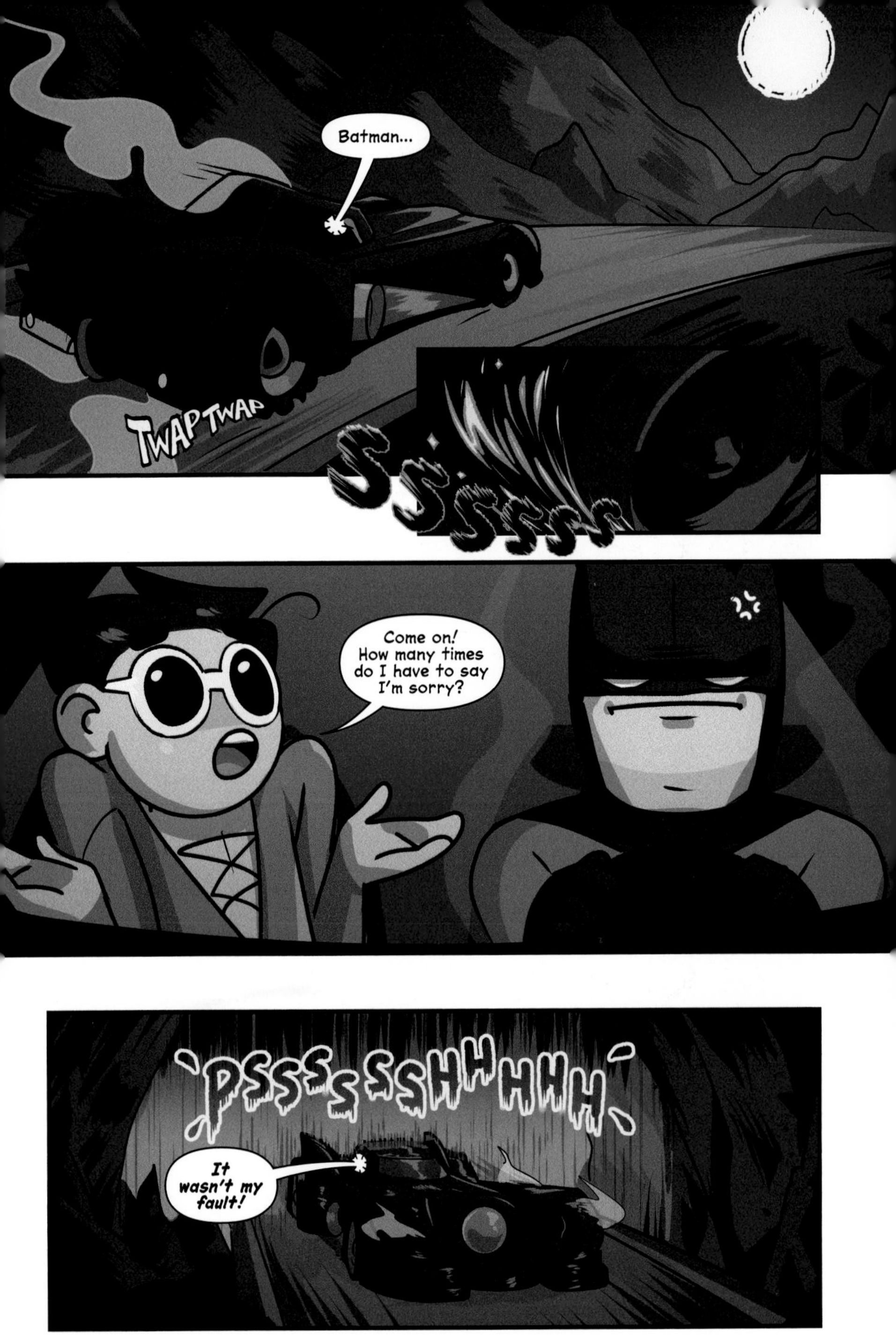
Batman...
TWAP TWAP
SSSSSSS
Come on! How many times do I have to say I'm sorry?
PSSSSSHHHHHH
It wasn't my fault!

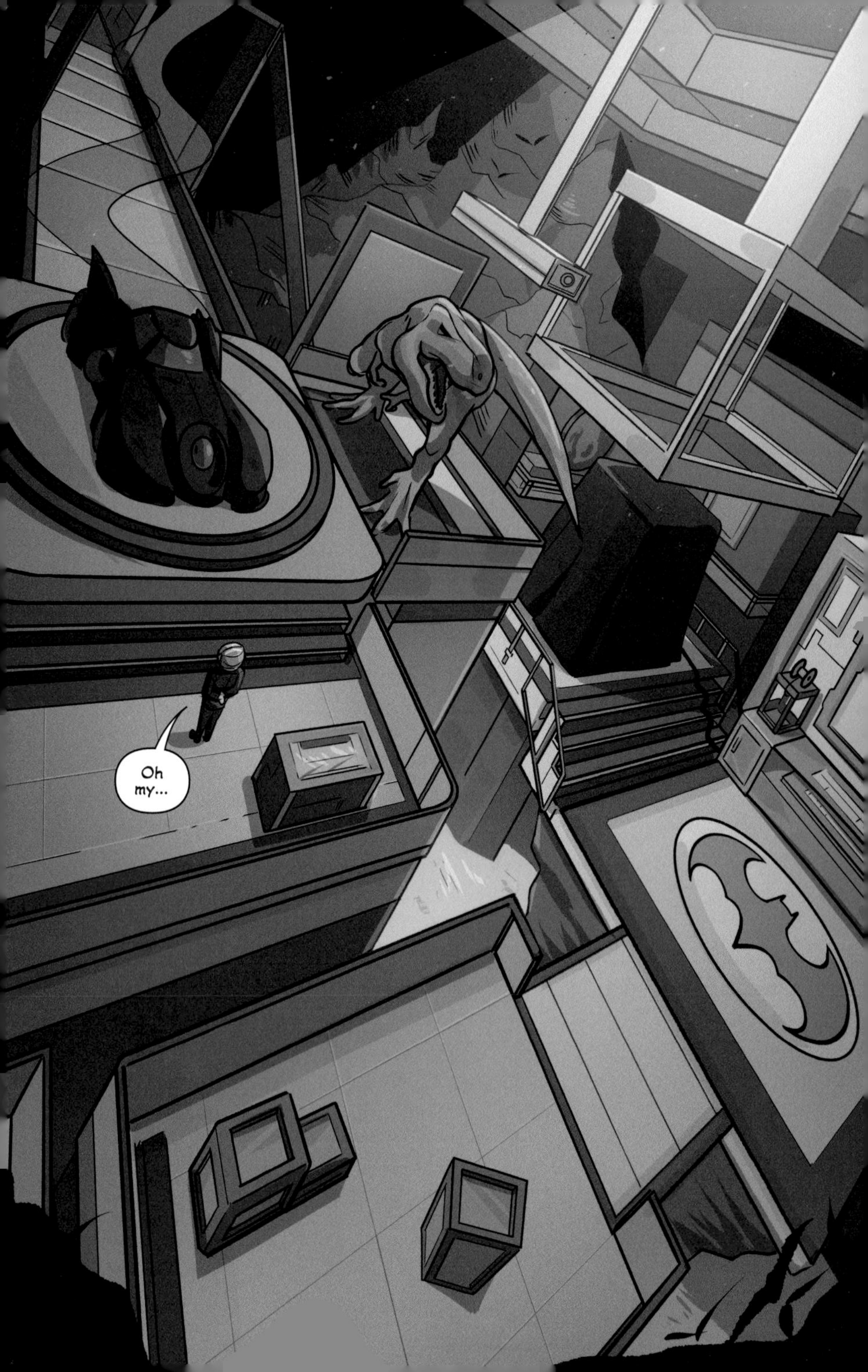
Oh my...

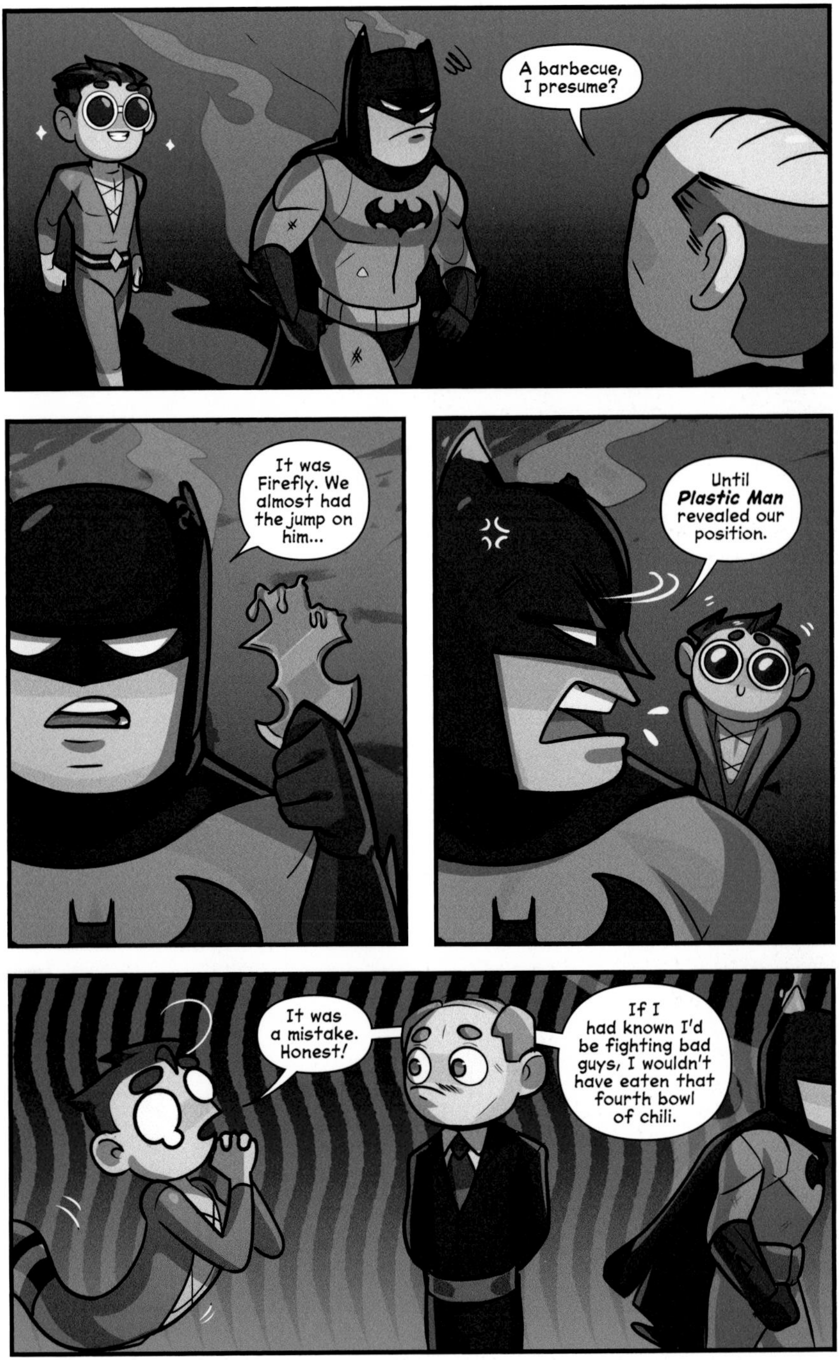
A barbecue, I presume?
It was Firefly. We almost had the jump on him...
Until **Plastic Man** revealed our position.
It was a mistake. Honest!
If I had known I'd be fighting bad guys, I wouldn't have eaten that fourth bowl of chili.

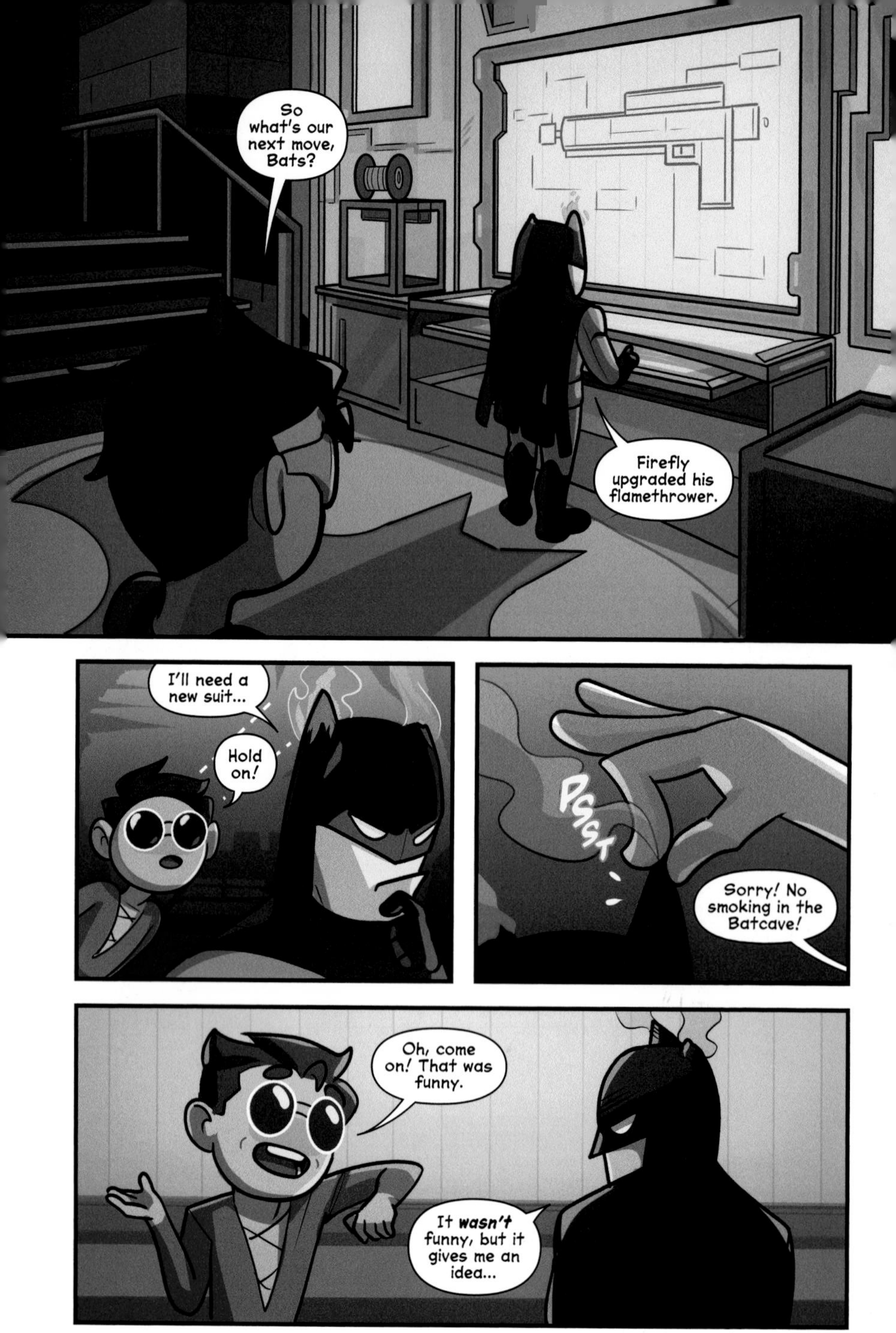
So what's our next move, Bats?
Firefly upgraded his flamethrower.
I'll need a new suit...
Hold on!
PSSSK
Sorry! No smoking in the Batcave!
Oh, come on! That was funny.
It *wasn't* funny, but it gives me an idea...

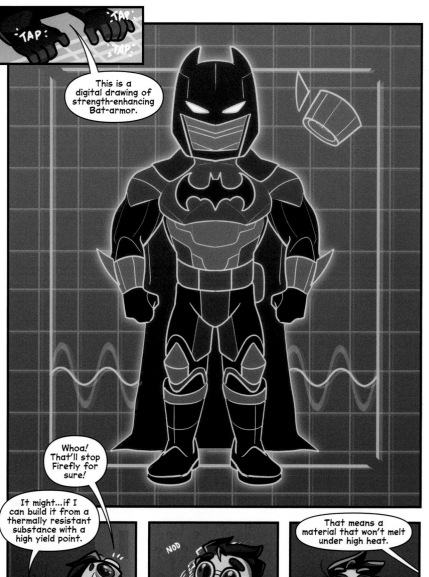

TAP TAP TAP

This is a digital drawing of strength-enhancing Bat-armor.

Whoa! That'll stop Firefly for sure!

It might...if I can build it from a thermally resistant substance with a high yield point.

NOD

Right. Sure. Of course.

That means a material that won't melt under high heat.

Yeah... I knew that.

HMMMMM

I'll make the armor with a 3D printer—a machine that allows you to make almost anything from a computer design.

HMMN

We first use a material—like carbon fiber—in filament form. *Filament* is solid at room temperature and curled into a spool.

Small gears pull the filament into a metal heater called a *hotend*—which is just hot enough to melt the filament. The molten filament is then forced through a nozzle, allowing us to build the object...

HMMMN

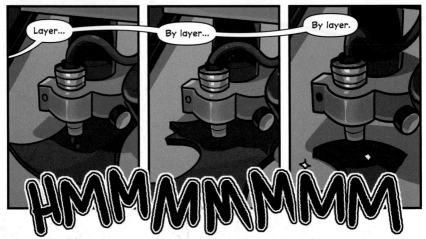

Layer...

By layer...

By layer.

HMMMMMMMM

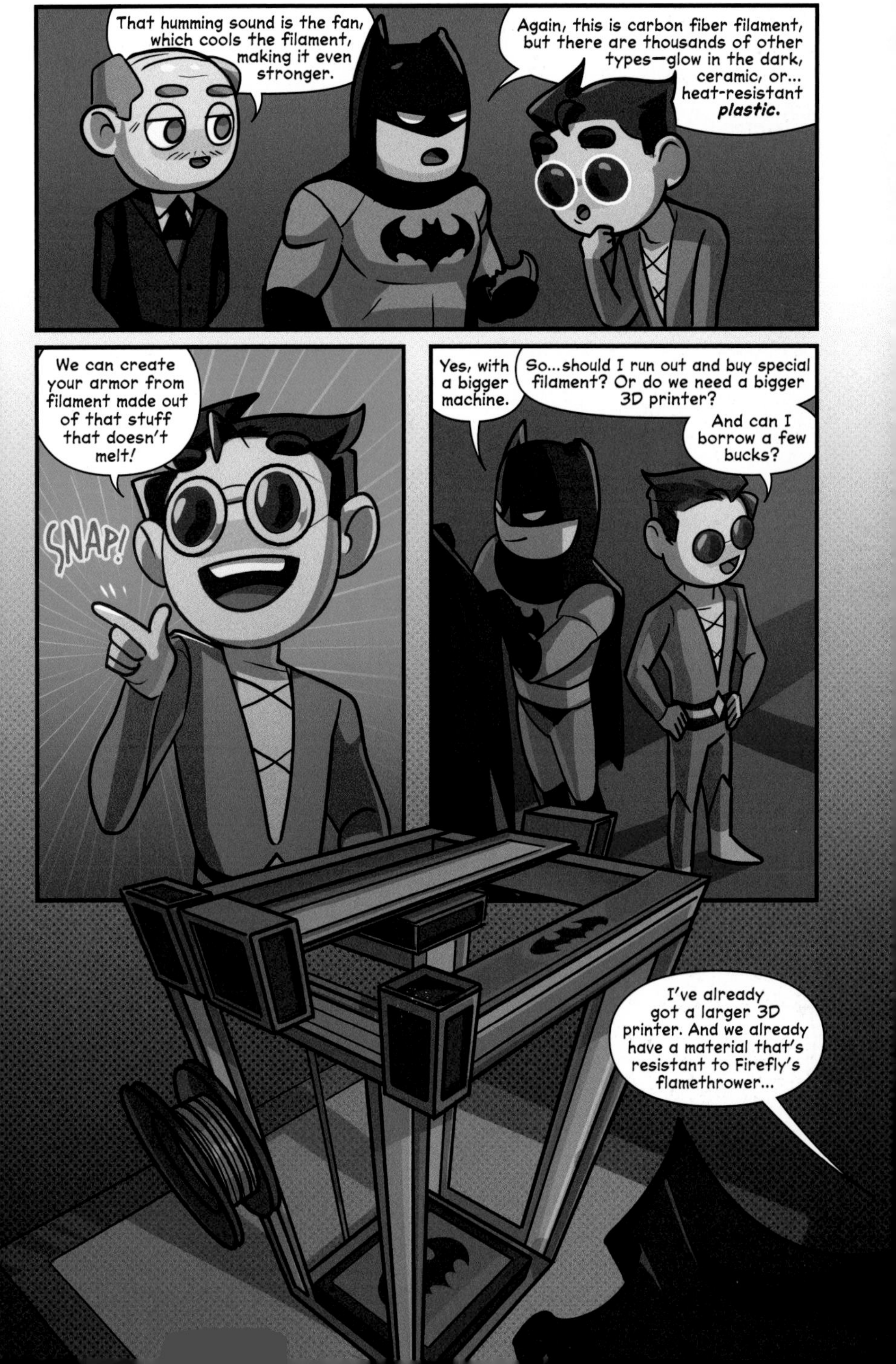
That humming sound is the fan, which cools the filament, making it even stronger.
Again, this is carbon fiber filament, but there are thousands of other types—glow in the dark, ceramic, or... heat-resistant *plastic.*
We can create your armor from filament made out of that stuff that doesn't melt!
SNAP!
So...should I run out and buy special filament? Or do we need a bigger 3D printer?
Yes, with a bigger machine.
And can I borrow a few bucks?
I've already got a larger 3D printer. And we already have a material that's resistant to Firefly's flamethrower...

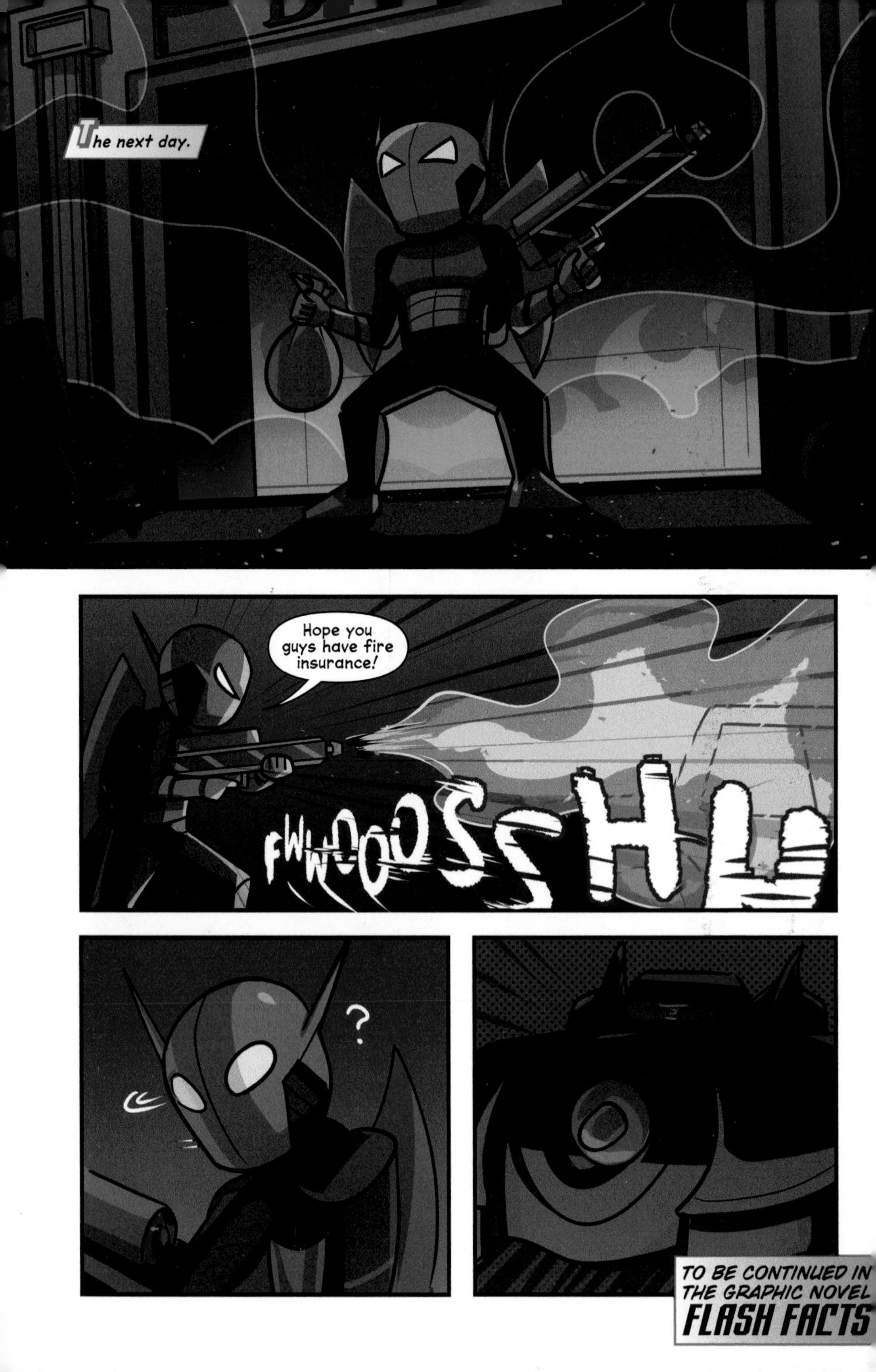
The next day.
Hope you guys have fire insurance!
FWWOOOSSH
?
TO BE CONTINUED IN THE GRAPHIC NOVEL
FLASH FACTS